Rescuing HER Heart

CINDY ERVIN HUFF

Smitten Historical Romance is an imprint of LPCBooks
a division of Iron Stream Media
100 Missionary Ridge, Birmingham, AL 35242
ShopLPC.com

Cover design by Hannah Linder Designs

Library of Congress Control Number: 2021935634.

ISBN-13: 978-1-64526-319-7
Ebook ISBN: 978-1-64526-320-3

PRAISE FOR *RESCUING HER HEART*

I can't remember when I've had such a soul-refreshing read! *Rescuing Her Heart* is a delightful story of redemptive love, gentle healing, and a lost heart finding its home. The characters become friends whom you truly care about and find yourself remembering after you've reluctantly closed the pages. God's love restores brokenness through Jed and Delilah's story in a powerful way that reaches through time and embraces the heart of the reader like a lingering hug. You will cherish this book.

~Debora M. Coty
Speaker, columnist, and award-winning author of over forty books, including the bestselling *Too Blessed to be Stressed* series

This book has it all: tragedy, heartbreak, and misconceptions, as well as family, love, and—my favorite—hope. Cindy Huff holds nothing back, and she delivers a book that's perfect for when you want to feel all the feels.

~Karin Beery
Writer of hopeful fiction with a healthy dose of romance

In this sequel to *Healing Hearts*, Huff's novella in "The Cowboys," *Rescuing Her Heart* draws readers into the story from the beginning. Huff has woven a story of overcoming a past abusive relationship and trust issues that follow. Believable characters tug at the heart in this compelling romance. I highly recommend this novel to readers of historical romance.

~Sandra Merville Hart
Author of Civil War romances *A Musket in My Hands, A Rebel in My House*, and *A Stranger on My Land*

Rescuing Her Heart is Jed and Delilah's tender love story of coping with and recovery from painful events in their pasts. The story also presents the healing power of faith, love, and support of family and friends. As someone familiar with and having written about PTSD, I can attest that Ms. Huff has a clear understanding of a condition that beleaguers so many.

~Janet Grunst
Author of *Setting Two Hearts Free*

Rescuing Her Heart is the perfect blend of inspiration, suspense, and romance. Another hit for Cindy Ervin Huff!

~Kristine Raymond
Author of the Hidden Springs Series

Rescuing Her Heart delves into the power of perseverance, healing, and compassion. Congratulations to Cindy Ervin Huff for another beautiful story, both memorable and inspiring. Jed and Delilah will stay with me for a very long time.

~Rowena Kuo
Editor and speaker

Dedication

My daughter Nicole Huff-Arzola,
you've shown me what true bravery is.

Acknowledgements

I want to thank Word Weavers. Without them, I would not have continued on this writing journey. My Aurora, Illinois, and Page One Word Weaver critique groups and my ACFW critique group, Scribe 242, kept my feet to the flames, constantly tweaking this manuscript. Pegg Thomas for asking me to write *Healing Hearts* for The Cowboys novella collection, which is now the prequel for *Rescuing Her Heart*. Thank you, Denise Weimer, for being so patient to edit this project and believing in the idea. My agent, Cyle Young, for his wise counsel.

My very patient husband, Charles Huff, who read every word over and over again and explained on many occasions my need to fix split infinitives and sentence fragments. Thank you, sweetheart, for keeping me well-fed while I was on a deadline.

I appreciate LPC/Iron Stream Media for continuing to believe in me. Most of all, I thank my Lord Jesus for giving me the gift of words and a mind that can't rest until the story is down on paper.

Chapter 1

Kansas, 1870

The smell of burnt flesh wafted from the blackened shell of a house. Astride his mare, Jed Holt pulled his bandana over his nose in an attempt to blot out memories of the war as he approached the isolated James homestead. Gut tightening, he surveyed the charred remains. *How'd this happen? Ain't been any lightning.*

Lemont James was a cantankerous drunk. The man had purchased the ranch with silver over a year ago, taken a mail-order bride, then seldom came to town. The unpainted barn stood as a silent statue beside the ashen heap of their tiny cabin.

Jed snugged his kerchief tighter over his nose when the breeze blew the smell of death at him again. If anyone had survived, they might be in the barn. Sheba, his collie, sniffed the air, hackles up. A bullet whizzed past Jed's head. Heart pounding, he flattened himself against the mare's neck as she whinnied and jerked away from the sound.

"Calm down, Sally-girl," he whispered, stroking her ear. His pulse hitched up several notches.

Jed reached for his rifle, then stopped. Shooting at his fellow man went against his creed. His father's reminder that taking a life changes a man stayed his hand. Lemont had a breach-loading Maynard. Even a poor shot could hit something with that rifle. Was he drunk? Or just ornery after losing his house? Silence filled the space of two heartbeats.

Jed sat up and raised his hands.

"Hello. You in the barn. It's Jed Holt." A woman appeared at the loft window. "Mrs. James?" He'd not made her acquaintance. When he'd come by, she'd remained in the house while Lemont spoke to him from the porch.

She raised the rifle beside a face streaked with soot. "Go away."

Jed tried an entreating tone with the disheveled woman. "Mrs. James, I'm makin' visitation rounds to the outlying ranches and homesteads for Reverend Logan. The pastor's arthritis keeps him close to home."

Mrs. James stared at him, not lowering the Maynard. Best to hightail it out of there before the next bullet hit him. But deserting someone in need was not the Holt way. Sweat trickled down Jed's back as he checked the area for a hiding place. The water trough seemed a likely spot.

He slid from his horse. "Mrs. James, I'm here to help."

Sheba growled moments before another shot rang out. The bullet hit the dirt several feet from him. Sally balked, and Jed grabbed the reins to steady her. Thankfully, the horse didn't spook easily. "Steady, girl. It's all right." She stood quiet once again, and Jed glanced back at the loft.

He took a cleansing breath as his silent prayer for wisdom and protection went up. "What happened, Mrs. James? Are you all right? Is your husband injured?"

"Get out." Her shoulder slumped, causing the gun barrel to drift away from him.

"Ma'am, let me help." Jed's voice was even. Another bullet slammed into the water trough nearby. *Good thing she ain't much of a shot.* Or maybe she was just trying to scare him away. But he didn't care to get wounded by accident. "Mrs. James, I got some food in my saddlebags."

"What's it going to cost me?" Raven hair fell in her eyes, and she blew it out of her face, not taking her hands off the rifle.

"Nothing." Jed raised his hands to show he was unarmed.

"Always costs something. Men always make women pay."

"Truly, I want nothin' from ya." He removed a brown paper packet from the saddlebag. "I'm a Christian man, here to help."

"Lemont claimed he was a Christian. Your claim brings little comfort."

Jed took the packet of food and held it high. "I'll place this at the barn door and step away." Serving as a chaplain in the Union Army, he'd learned to read people. Mrs. James had more than the charred remains of the house making her anxious.

The sun beat down on Jed as he placed the food on the ground near the barn door. Sweat trickled in his eyes, blurring his vision. He walked backward to his horse's side.

"No chicanery or the next target will be a leg." She disappeared from the loft window and reappeared at the barn door. Snatching the food from the ground, she eyed him.

"Stay there." Mrs. James kept the rifle tucked under her arm as she ate the beef jerky and biscuits. "You can water your horse."

Jed led Sally to the water trough. He whistled for Sheba, and she lapped from the trough too. He noticed a bullet hole above the waterline. *Lucky shot.*

The collie finished drinking and nuzzled close to Jed. "Good girl." While petting Sheba's head, he cast a sideways glance at Mrs. James as she took a large bite of biscuit while glaring his way. The woman's dress was torn and filthy. The mass of curly hair hung to her waist. Taller than most women, her slumped shoulders made her appear small and vulnerable. "Thanks, ma'am."

Jed signaled Sheba, and she walked toward Mrs. James and sat at her feet. The collie's lopsided grin brought a smile to the woman. She lowered the rifle, then patted the dog. "What's its name?"

"Sheba." Jed spoke in a calm voice. The woman reminded him of himself the first few months after the war. Skittish. He'd need to tread carefully to win her trust.

Delilah James relaxed. Papa once told her you could judge a man's character by how he cared for his animals. Lemont had abused his watchdog to the point that it had run off, but Sheba's sweet disposition revealed much about Mr. Holt. The animal nuzzled close, eyeing the biscuit. Delilah chuckled and handed the dog the last of it. "You're a clever one."

She shaded her eyes from the sun, which obscured her vision of Mr. Holt. "I remember you." Few people had come calling, at least of the civilized variety. Lemont preferred it that way. But this man had engaged her husband in conversation. She'd listened through the open window, catching bits of the Scripture quotations. When Mr. Holt had offered to pray, Lemont's swearing had shamed her.

She placed the rifle near the barn door and patted her dress pocket where she hid a small derringer. "I've been here alone since the fire." No sense also telling Mr. Holt her husband had unsavory friends she feared would come calling. Delilah pushed her ash-covered hair back behind her ears. Soap—along with everything else—had been destroyed in the fire. Tears refused to fall as she gazed at the skeletal remains of his house, not her home. Another shiver gripped her. Those came less often than they had yesterday, but still frequent enough to keep her from crossing the burnt threshold.

"Where's Lemont?"

"Dead. Lemont burned the house down during one of his episodes."

"Episodes?"

"My husband woke from a dream thinking he was still in the war. Before I could settle him, the house was on fire." No need to mention she'd fled and hid in the barn. Lemont's screams still haunted her. Was the man at peace? Or burning in hell? Either way, she was free from his cruelty.

"Sorry to hear of your loss."

"He's still under the rubble." *Why did I tell him that?* "I can't lift the rafters."

"Let me handle it." Jed's gentle tone was almost convincing.

"No need." *Just go away.* Delilah winced as Mr. Holt stared at the ruins and shook his head. An implied rebuke for her inability to take care of the body? A quiver overtook her. Lemont expected her to do what needed doing without complaint.

"How you been getting by?" Mr. Holt approached but stopped near the water trough, seeming to sense her need for distance.

"Living in the barn and eating the apples set aside for the horse. Soldier—my horse—ate the last of the feed today."

"Let me take you home with me."

As a bolt of fear shot down her spine, she grabbed the rifle. "I knew the food came with a price."

"No, you misunderstood." Mr. Holt held up his hand, and a blush covered his face. "My sister-in-law would take real good care of ya. Everything'd be right and proper. My brother Lonnie and I own the Single Cross Ranch. Genny'd be glad for the female company."

Delilah looked at her filthy hands gripping the rifle. No woman would be glad for her company. Even soap couldn't cleanse away the last eight months of her life. Mr. Holt waited, every bit as handsome as her husband when she'd stepped off the stage.

Lemont's words had been kind at first. But his promises had melted in a sea of deception. Warning bells clanged in her head. "No, I'll manage."

"Please, let me help." Mr. Holt started toward her.

"I'm not going anywhere with a man." Delilah leveled the rifle at his chest.

"Tell you what." He backed toward his horse. "I'll go fetch Genny, my sister-in-law. I'll bring help to bury Lemont proper-like."

More men. A violent quiver overtook her while loneliness shadowed her heart. A woman's company, though …

Delilah sized him up. Maybe Mr. Holt was telling the truth. *No. I'd rather die of starvation than take such a risk again.* She stepped back inside the barn and closed the heavy doors. Hoofbeats faded into the distance. Sobs choked her. *Wait. Don't go.* She opened the door a crack to find the yard empty, like her soul. Empty of love, peace, joy, anything resembling life.

Delilah went to Soldier and stroked his nose. The horse nuzzled close. "Sorry, boy. There's no more food." A tear traveled her face. "I should have said yes. At least you'd have a better home. So sorry." Soldier wouldn't let anyone ride him and barely tolerated plowing. Yet the two had bonded, living in the barn together, looking after each other. "What a terrible caregiver I am, sending away an opportunity for a better home for you." Soldier made no response, but the truth of it made Delilah's hands shake.

The hopes of a better life she'd held before arriving in Kansas were shattered. She'd been foolish to choose to be a mail-order bride. *I'm here alone with a horse and a head full of nightmares.*

Chapter 2

Jed jumped on Sally and gave her full rein. The mare, sensing his urgency, galloped toward the Single Cross Ranch. The rough road passed through farm fields, open range, and a rambling stream. The sun rested high in the sky as he arrived home and handed the reins to Brody, one of the ranch hands. Recently injured by a bull, the man now worked close to the house.

As he burst into the one-story, three-room cabin, Genny looked up from doing dishes. Tendrils of brown hair fell about her face. Heavy with child, she waddled toward him. "Why are you home a day early? What's wrong?"

"Where's Lonnie?"

"In the bedroom, putting the girls down for a nap." Genny stared at him.

Lonnie came into the kitchen. "Quiet down, the children are napping." The *C*-shaped scar on Lonnie's face was the only thing distinguishing the twin brothers in appearance.

"What you doin' home so soon?" Lonnie strode to the large cast-iron stove and poured himself a cup of coffee from the tin pot.

"Plans changed." Jed stepped to the washstand and rinsed sweat from his face, taking time to figure the best way to ask his favor. "Lonnie, I need Genny to go somewhere with me."

Lonnie scowled. "Does she look fit to go anywhere?"

Genny maneuvered her round form into a chair. She motioned

for the men to sit as she rubbed her belly. They took seats across from one another at the kitchen table.

Jed glanced between the two. "The James' homestead burned to the ground a few days ago."

"Oh, Lord." Genny's hand went to her mouth.

"The homestead is hidden back in a hollow. If you didn't know it was there, you'd pass on by. Lemont liked his solitude, I reckon." Jed shook his head.

"Musta burned in the night afore the rainstorm came through, 'cause I didn't see no smoke." Lonnie sipped his coffee.

"Didn't look like a drop of rain touched the place." Jed made eye contact with Lonnie. "Lemont died in the fire, and Mrs. James is hiding in the barn."

Lonnie's jaw flexed at the news. Often, Jed had awakened to his brother crying out in sleep, reliving the fire which claimed their mother's life. Pa had died when they were teens, leaving his widow with four boys. Jed had left to serve as a chaplain during the war, while Lonnie refused to take a side. The fire had been meant for him, as there were those who considered him a coward. Lonnie never said much afterward, but the wound ran deep. Helping this widow might ease a bit of his pain.

"Mrs. James won't go nowhere with a man. The minute I suggested she come home with me, she all but panicked." The memory of that flash of fear in the widow's face made Jed more determined to enlist Genny's aid. "Lemont wasn't much of a husband for her to feel that way."

"Hear tell the man spent more time making moonshine than ranchin'," Lonnie added. "Drunk, more than sober. No wonder she's afraid."

"I'll come." Genny rose, her hand on the small of her back. "Let me gather a few things."

Jed sat forward, calling after her as she waddled into the next room. "She ain't got but the clothes on her back."

Genny's voice drifted back to him. "Clean clothes are always welcome. I'll bring along soap and food. Surely, we can persuade her to come." When his sister-in-law set her mind to something, it generally happened. He sure hoped so. That widow needed help before it was too late. Trauma made people do crazy things.

While Lonnie sipped his brew in silence, Jed tapped the table and cleared his throat. "Lemont's body is under the rubble. Need a few men to help bury him."

"How awful." Genny returned and set a basket on the table, then went to the cupboard for a container. She filled it with soup from a pot on the stove, then glanced Lonnie's way. "Best go now so we can get home before dark."

"I'll mind the children. Take Carter and Gonzalez with ya." Rising, Lonnie pulled her close and kissed her soundly, pinning Jed with his protector look. "Take care of Genny." He released her with a smile, then frowned at his brother. "If I hear ya drove over any potholes, we'll be havin' a conversation with fists." He chuckled, then pointed at Jed. "I trust ya to keep her safe."

Jed loved Genny like a sister. No way would she come to any harm on his watch.

Wagon wheels and horse hooves sounded in the yard. Delilah peeked out the loft window. *He kept his word.* Quickly, she wiped moisture from her face with the cuff of her sleeve.

Mr. Holt assisted a very pregnant woman from the wagon. She gave a friendly smile to Delilah in the loft. "Mrs. James, I'm Genny Holt. Brought a few things for you." Genny held up a basket, then strolled toward the barn door.

Delilah scurried down the ladder. She paused near Soldier and patted his nose. "We've been rescued." She kissed his muzzle, then walked to the barn door. Drawing in a deep breath, she counted to ten. A small measure of calm descended.

She pushed the doors open and stepped outside.

Genny Holt's gentle smile drove Delilah's fears behind her. She'd missed female companionship. Genny set the basket on a tree stump near the barn and waited with her hands stroking her middle. Delilah stared at the expectant mother, then ran and fell into her arms. Deep sobs wrenched her as the smaller woman cooed like her mother had done when she was a child. The hollow place in her heart closed a little and hope revived. Simple human kindness after the months of cruelty washed over her inner wounds. Genny ran her hand up and down her back, then in circles, each stroke pushing away more of her pain. Several minutes later, she pulled away. "I …" Delilah sniffled.

"No need to explain." Genny patted her shoulder. "You've been through a fright—cry as much as you need."

Delilah hiccupped and Genny handed her a handkerchief. She wiped her eyes and blew her nose. Soot blotted the embroidered cloth. Shame washed through her. "I'm sorry. I've ruined it."

"It'll wash." Genny smiled. "I've brought soap, a change of clothes, and food."

Delilah trembled. "Too kind. I …"

"Now, now. I'm doing what any neighbor would do. Let's go back in the barn and get you cleaned up."

Delilah stared toward the burned-out homestead where Mr. Holt and two other men were sifting through the ruins. She shivered again at the prospect of seeing Lemont's body.

Genny led the way into the barn. "I've brought vegetable soup and bread. Eat while I fetch water from the pump so you can wash."

Soldier eyed them. Delilah patted the horse. "I promise to make sure you're better cared for."

"Here." Genny pulled a carrot from her pocket. "I always have them handy so my girls can feed the horses." Soldier ate the carrot in two bites and nosed Genny for more. She laughed. "When you're in our stables, there'll be something else." Genny patted his massive head, then walked to the door. "Will you be all right while I see what can be found to heat water in?"

Delilah nodded. She followed her to the door and peeked out. Genny went to Mr. Holt, who gathered wood for a fire while his sister-in-law picked through the rubble. Delilah hadn't been brave enough to see if there was anything salvageable. Genny found a pot. The other men moved the rafters, but before they could find Lemont's body, Delilah whirled and fled deeper into the barn. Would she even be able to go outside after her husband was buried?

Her appetite stirred as the aroma of vegetable soup teased her senses. Inside the basket on the bench just inside the door, she found the container along with some fresh bread wrapped in towels, still warm. She took the bread, ripped off a large piece, and chewed.

She was finishing off the delicious meal as Genny entered with a pot of steaming water. "This pot was lying in the wreckage. It's still serviceable. The well was covered, so there was no ash in the water. Jed started a fire for me."

Delilah dipped a clean cloth into the water. Washing her face and hands was heavenly. "If only I could wash my hair."

"Come home with me, and I'll make sure you get a lovely bath." Genny plucked a dress from the basket and held it out. "It may be a bit short, but it's clean. I've also brought undergarments."

"I can't take your things." Delilah's face heated. She turned away before she burst into tears again. Fisting her hands, she fought for composure.

"You're borrowing them." Genny smoothed the green floral dress. "I'm much too big to wear this right now."

"I've no money to repay your kindness." Delilah sagged further on the bench. "And no way to support myself at all."

"Come work for me. I've got three lively girls at home—the older two are twins—and with another child on the way, your help would be welcome."

"I don't know." Delilah looked away. *A ranch is full of men. Men like Lemont.*

"Say yes." Genny took her hand.

The offer of friendship was like water in the desert. But how could she explain her fear? She straightened her spine while her jaw tightened. "I can't live in a house with men. I won't." Her chest pounded as her breath became shallow. Sweat trickled down her back. She wanted to leave this place, but …

"If I promise no men will be living in my home, will you come?"

She stared at the woman for several seconds. "You'd ask your husband to leave for me?" Delilah crossed her arms, sizing up this stranger.

"Until we build a little cabin for you." Genny smiled. "If you ever decide you've had enough of the Holt family, I'll have a nice place for a new housekeeper."

"I'm sure your husband will object." Delilah's brittle tone tasted of ash on her lips.

"Don't worry." Genny's reassurance melted a bit more of her reserve. "Like Jed, Lonnie has a caring heart."

"Men with caring hearts are a myth." Delilah's face warmed as she considered biting off her bitter tongue.

"I've found those mythical beasts, and there're more out there." Genny winked and pushed the garments into her hands. "Now, change clothes. As soon as the men have Mr. James buried, we'll head home."

Home. Could there be such a place in this wild territory? With strangers?

Jed opened his Bible as the group stood around Lemont James' grave. Mrs. James wore Genny's favorite green dress. It was a few inches too short and fit loosely over her slender frame. Her black curls were tamed into a severe bun. Red colored her nose and cheeks and rimmed her eyes. A visible shiver went through her as she stared at the grave for a moment, then at her shoes.

"'I am the resurrection and the life.'" Jed read the words over the grave. It seemed wrong to speak words of peace and assurance over a man who'd clearly hated God. Had the same hatred manifested itself toward his wife? Jed had been in town the day Lemont boarded the stage to go fetch his mail-order bride from Abilene. He'd bragged around town that he'd have a woman for more than keeping house. It was the first time Jed had seen the man clean-shaven. Lemont wore new clothes and said inappropriate things about his future bride, which had gotten him more than a few disgusted looks from the other men.

Jed finished the short service, and his men added a wooden cross to the mound of dirt. Mrs. James turned away, glanced around the homestead, then hurried toward the barn. A few moments later, with a graceful stride, she led a large brown horse out to the wagon. She held her rifle in her right hand, pointed toward the ground.

Placing the weapon in the wagon bed, she tied the horse to the back. Jed knew horses, but this stallion's breeding was a mystery. When the horse jerked, trying to free himself, Mrs. James ran her hand over his neck and whispered in his ear. The horse calmed.

As Jed approached, the widow offered not so much as a nod in his direction. "Please drive slowly until Soldier gets used to following the wagon."

"Yes ma'am." Jed tipped his hat her way.

Mrs. James stroked the horse without looking at him.

He waited a moment, then helped Genny onto the wagon bench. She slid to the center. Jed extended his hand to Mrs. James.

She stepped away with a scowl. "I can manage." Mrs. James climbed into the back of the wagon. "Mrs. Holt need not be squeezed between us in her condition." She pulled her rifle into her lap and settled midpoint of the wagon bed.

The trauma was still too raw if she felt the need to keep her rifle close. Again, she looked at her horse while speaking. "I'll keep an eye on Soldier."

Jed climbed on the bench next to Genny. Gonzalez and Carter rode ahead. The trip home was silent. What had Lemont done to taint this beautiful woman? Jed longed to know her story. Maybe he could help her find joy again. He prayed for wisdom and for the lovely widow as the miles shortened to their destination.

"We're almost home." Genny turned to Mrs. James. "The ranch

is up ahead. I can't wait to get out of this wagon."

Mrs. James remained silent. Genny glanced Jed's way, then swiveled to face the widow again. "I'm sure a bath sounds wonderful."

"I don't want to be a bother." Delilah's voice trembled. "In your condition, it's too much to ask."

Genny laughed, the familiar sound putting everyone at ease. "There're plenty of strong men at the ranch to haul water. It's no trouble."

A gasp came from behind them. Jed glanced back as Mrs. James' fear-filled eyes rested on Genny. "I'd rather do it myself."

Before Genny could object, he shook his head. No need stirring up more fear. Jed had seen plenty of irrational behavior from battle-weary men. Took them a while to find peace. Some never did. Would Mrs. James?

"We'll worry about that after we get home." Genny smiled at the woman, then looked at Jed, her lips forming a firm line. It was the same determined look she'd had when she nursed him back to health when they'd first met.

The single cross on the roof of the barn appeared as they rounded the corner. Jed recalled this same journey from five years ago when he and Lonnie had come to claim their inheritance, to recover from the war and build a fine cattle ranch. Lonnie had fallen for Genny that winter. Jed had recovered his health—thanks to Genny's nursing skills.

Yes, God was in control of their lives. Mrs. James', too, if she would allow Him. She could start a new life. Maybe find a new husband who knew how to treat a woman.

He'd pray on it.

Chapter 3

"Is the woman crazy, booting me out of my own place? A man's house is his castle." Lonnie's aggravation echoed the fury of the bull in the north pasture.

Jed placed a hand on his brother's shoulder. "It's only temporary." He signaled for Lonnie to step farther from the house. "Stop yer fussing."

Jed nudged him toward the bench outside the barn where they often discussed the future of the Single Cross. The improvements Lonnie had made to the place proved rancher blood ran through his veins. He plotted out every detail. Unexpected changes made Lonnie's feisty side surface. Surprises meant delays in his plans, and he hated delays. They settled on the bench.

Lonnie frowned. "Better be temporary. I don't take kindly to being told I gotta sleep in the bunkhouse. 'Sides, Genny's baby is due anytime."

"Things will work out." Jed could only pray so. Terror rested in their guest's eyes when she was introduced to the crew. A single nod was the only recognition she gave them before bolting for the house. "Once the cabin is built, you can move back. Appears Mrs. James is terrified of men. Lemont musta broke her spirit. Ain't good in horses and worse in people. It took a bit of convincing to get her to leave the barn." How long would it take for her to trust? Storms triggered his memories of his abuse in the prison camp. What triggered her fears?

Lonnie shook his head. "Over time, she'll see we ain't mean."

"I hope she didn't hear your complaining, 'cause it sure sounded mean." Jed smacked his brother on the back, receiving a scowl for his trouble.

"I'll mind myself." Lonnie took off his Stetson and fiddled with the brim. "But why are ya using the wood for her place that we'd set aside to build *your* cabin?"

"It's the right thing to do."

Lonnie's family was filling the house. Jed's move into the bunkhouse had given them more space, but Jed lost the quiet time after a hard day's work. He'd already put off building his own home twice to invest in more cattle and land. The spot he'd picked out for his cabin would have to stay vacant a mite longer. He'd have the men cut more wood before winter, then next year, he'd have his cabin built.

"You always choose the right thing, brother." Lonnie put his hat back on. "One of these days, your right thing's gonna be the wrong thing."

"So you say. You're still mad about not having Genny all to yourself in the evenings. At least we can take our meals at the kitchen table. Then there's time for you to play with the girls before Genny kicks you out."

"True. I'll put up with it for Genny. She's a wise woman and wants to help the widow. The two of you can handle her while I tend to the ranch."

"Handle her?" Jed cringed and stared at Lonnie.

"That did sound kinda bad." Lonnie stroked his beard. "I meant, Genny being a woman who once had to deal with an unsavory man understands. And you being a preacher will know the right thing to say. Me? I'll stay outta the way."

Jed nudged his brother's shoulder. "I think you're gonna play a part whether you want to or not. Mrs. James needs to feel safe to heal, and we'll see she is."

"Your preacher heart's speaking."

"It's being a Holt. We do what needs doing." Jed had started to question the call to preach. Life was good on the Single Cross, ranching with his brother. The years serving as an army chaplain were a distant memory. "I'll be busy as you, tendin' the ranch. Most of the helping will fall to Genny."

"Hard work heals, and there will be plenty for Mrs. James to do around the house." Lonnie rose. "I hope her bath don't take too much longer. I'd like vittles sometime soon." Lonnie wandered into the barn, leaving Jed alone with his thoughts. They were full of questions about Mrs. James.

The cabin door opened, and Genny set two buckets on the porch. Jed headed over, but before he reached the house, she brought two more.

"Gonzalez, Chase." He called to the two men who stood near the corral as he relieved his sister-in-law of her load. "I'll take those."

Jed glimpsed Mrs. James' damp hair hanging down the back of her dress as she fled to the bedroom and shut the door. His face warmed. Never had a woman run from him before. He yanked up the full buckets, sloshing ashen water on his boot. "I didn't mean to scare her."

"She'll be fine. Give her time." Genny stretched her back. "Thanks for hauling the buckets."

"Let me come back and empty the tub. The men got other things to do." And the widow didn't need more men making her fearful.

"I'd help, but Lonnie would scold me about doing too much in my condition." Genny rubbed her growing belly.

"And he'd have my hide if I let you." Jed laughed. "Don't worry none, everything will be fine." The ashy water would be good for the vegetable garden. The bit of soap in the water would keep the bugs from eating the plants. "Mrs. James coming is a blessing. She can help with the garden, the young'uns, and give you a chance to nap."

"A true blessing."

Jed made a few more trips to the garden with the bath water, then took the empty tub outside and leaned it against the supply shed. As he turned back toward the house, a movement caught his notice—Mrs. James pulling a comb through her long tresses. His fingers flexed, and he could almost imagine that comb in his own hand. His pa used to comb his mother's wet hair. The ritual had reminded Jed a woman needed to be cared for, even in the little ways.

With nimble fingers, she braided and pinned her hair in a ring around her head. Mrs. James faced the window and stared at him before pulling the curtains closed. Jed's neck warmed. Embarrassment covered him like the time he got caught cheating on a spelling test. The disappointed look from the teacher was worse than the switching he'd received. Now Mrs. James would think he was a peeping Tom. He'd acted like her image of men. Jed kicked a rock as he moved away from the house.

Delilah's pulse stuttered and skin crawled as she pulled the curtains to block Mr. Holt's gaze. Lemont had liked to stare. Neither had he stopped his nefarious friends from staring while they played cards. Yet Mr. Holt's staring eyes held no lust. They seemed reflective, as though he was considering her. Not craving her. Her heart fluttered in response. No. No. No. *These curtains will stay closed at all times with all the men here.*

The bedroom door opened behind her, tangling her nerves further. As she turned, the knot in her stomach relaxed. The Holts' twin girls presented a delightful distraction. "Which one are you?" Delilah smiled at one of the blonde cherubs, who stuck two fingers in her mouth and looked at the floor.

Her sister came to her aid. "I'm Jilly and she's Molly. We're twins."

Delilah laughed at the four-year-old's declaration.

"Our baby sister is Birdie." Jilly came up to her and whispered. "She won't be the baby no more. Mommy's having a new one."

"So I noticed." Delilah stroked the girl's blonde curls.

"Where are your children?" Jilly's innocent question pricked Delilah's heart.

"In heaven." Raw memories of the miscarriage came flooding back like a river overflowing its banks, taking away the innocent along with the evil.

The twins nodded.

"Mommy says heaven is a wonderful place." Jilly smiled. The child's simple declaration eased her pain.

"Mommy wants you," Molly said, then replaced her fingers in her mouth, and the two girls left the room.

Delilah took a deep breath. Her empty arms ached as the girls' giggles echoed back into the room.

Genny was beginning meal preparation.

"How can I help?" Delilah stood with her hands in front of her, waiting for instructions. She admired the well-stocked kitchen cabinets lining the left wall. The four-burner stove had a warming oven, a hot water reserve tank, and two ovens. Perfect for baking. A long table with a blue-checked tablecloth and matching curtains made the room inviting. The dry sink on the other wall had an indoor water pump. Such luxury in comparison to her sparse house.

Genny smiled. "No need to start today. Rest. Tomorrow is soon enough after your tragedy."

"Work is the best remedy." Delilah found an apron hanging on a hook and tied it on. "Let me take over here. Put your feet up and rest."

Genny laughed. "With this bunch, it's a luxury. I'll sit and prepare the potatoes and carrots if you can sear the stew meat and start the biscuits."

Delilah began cutting the meat into chunks.

Genny turned to the girls. "Can one of you check to see if Beatrice is awake?"

"I wondered what Birdie's real name was." Delilah managed a smile, and the pleasure of wearing it, if only for a moment, took her one step farther from the edge of her former abyss.

"Lonnie calls her his little bird. Jilly's name is Jillian Joy after my mother. Lonnie loves nicknames."

"Does Molly have a nickname?" Delilah asked. Her mind didn't have to work too hard to find conversation. Since leaving Baltimore, she hadn't had female company. Oh, how she'd missed it.

"Her name is Molly after Lonnie's mother. Sometimes he calls her Mo."

"How did you ever manage when the twins were babies?"

"I had adult twins to help. Lonnie and Jed doted on them. The men are still a big help. They were disappointed when Beatrice wasn't twins. They had to share her." Genny chuckled. "I'm blessed to be part of such a caring family."

A green-eyed monster raised its ugly head. Delilah remained silent for several minutes. Her husband never lifted a hand to help, only to hurt. Though she was now free from abuse, her throat tightened with the knowledge she'd willingly accepted her lot. Wrapping her arms around herself, she squeezed tight, holding in the urge to cry. No more tears.

Genny looked up from chopping but said nothing. Instead, she pulled a chair out to rest her legs on. "Jed'll be a wonderful father someday, like my husband."

The thought of Lemont raising children had painted a grim picture. But why mention Jed's potential as a parent? *It makes no difference to me how perfect he might appear. He's a man.*

Delilah wiped her sweaty hands on her apron one at a time to still her anxious thoughts. Then she seared the meat in a bit of lard and placed it in the stew pot to brown. The delicious smell of the beef restored her appetite. "Are the vegetables ready?"

"Yes." Genny passed her the bowl of cut vegetables. "But I feel bad. Wouldn't you rather rest?"

"This *is* restful." Delilah stirred the pot, each stroke an attempt to whisk away memories of the fire. She focused on the task of adding in the vegetables. "I've missed female company."

"If you need to talk, I'm here to listen." Genny's gentle eyes settled on her with the same patience she used on her children.

Could she ever tell anyone the truth of her marriage? How could happy Genny Holt have any idea what she'd endured? If she told her, judgment would come. "Where are your spices? If you don't mind, I'd like to flavor this stew with more than salt and pepper."

"Sounds grand. The spices are on the upper shelf of the cabinet. I'd love to try somethin' new." Genny's appreciation was like a cool breeze on a hot day.

A gasp of pleasure escaped her at the assortment of dried herbs on the shelf. "I'll add rosemary and … oh, you have thyme."

"I planted a large area of my garden in herbs. Some are for medicinal purposes."

Delilah relaxed with the change of subject. Gardening was a safer topic than her late husband.

"Do you like working in a garden?" Genny straightened in her chair as Delilah turned to give her a taste from her spoon. Eyes sliding closed for a moment, she chewed her bite. "Hmm, I can see you enjoy cooking."

Delilah stirred the pot, then set the spoon aside, turning the handle away from the flames as she'd been taught. "My mother was head cook for the Hollingsworth family back in Baltimore. My father was head gardener. Papa gave me a love of gardening."

"Your parents were servants?" Genny squirmed in her chair as she found a more comfortable position. "Tell me about your life in Baltimore."

Delilah stirred the stew again, hoping her silence would warrant a subject change. Homesickness nipped at her. The smiling faces of her parents disintegrated into disappointment. Her adventure west was like the leavings in the waste bin of the manor kitchen. She released a sigh and wiped the perspiration from her brow.

"How thoughtless of me to pry. The joy of having another woman around has stolen my manners. Talking about livestock and the weather gets old." Genny sighed and rose to clean her work area.

Delilah pushed a stray hair off her forehead and stared at the pot. Her mother's words rebuked her. *Women were born to need each other. We learn and help and share together.* What could it hurt to answer

Genny's question? "The Hollingsworths were not old money. Mrs. Hollingsworth struggled to fit into high society. When they visited England, they hired my parents and Momma's cousin as their butler. The Hollingsworths hoped European servants would impress their peers. Papa was so excited at the prospect of coming to America." Delilah sighed. Would they be ashamed of her now, reduced to nothing? "They immigrated before I was born."

Genny grabbed a crock from the lower shelf. "What was your childhood like?"

Delilah smiled. "I helped my mother in the kitchen. I weeded the garden with Papa until I was promoted to chambermaid."

"What does a chambermaid do?" Genny took the cheesecloth off the top of the crock.

"Keeps all the upstairs in order." Delilah had found the work boring. Probably why she found Tobias Hollingsworth's attention so exciting. Lies and deceit had fallen on her ears like honey on dry toast. The foolishness of youth had aided her rash decision, forever changing her.

"Are you familiar with sourdough biscuits?" Genny's question brought her back to the present.

"No, my mother used yeast. She baked what she called pastry fancies. Sourdough is a mystery to me." Delilah watched as Genny scooped dough into a bowl from the crock.

"You take a cup of starter and put it in a bowl. Then you add a fresh cup of flour to the starter." Genny stirred the mixture. "The flour feeds it. I brought this starter with me when I moved here. And the lady who shared with me had it for years." She covered the starter with cheesecloth and put it back on the shelf before mixing the biscuit dough. She shaped it into rolls, then covered it with another cheesecloth. "When the stew is almost done, I'll pop these biscuits in the oven." Genny sat again, resting her legs on the other chair. "If I weren't so tired, I'd make a pie."

"I can do it." Delilah needed to prove her worth. And she loved to bake. Lemont had never brought home enough provisions for her to bake often. She shook the thought away.

"Mommy. Mommy, Birdie's awake." The twins shouted in unison.

"Please make a few pies, then. We'll want to share with the crew. I'll see to the baby."

Genny smiled. "You've made my burden lighter already. There're apples in a barrel in the storage closet, along with canned peaches and dried apricots."

"Which would you prefer?"

"Surprise me."

She'd surprised Lemont with scones, and he'd slapped her, accusing her of being uppity. He'd been drunk. He was gone, and she was free to do as she pleased.

Delilah went to the pantry to find the needed ingredients. Her mind filled with the various recipes she'd learned from her mother. Perhaps Genny would allow her to do all the baking. Her shoulders relaxed as she laid the ingredients from the larder on the table.

Chapter 4

Jed followed the delicious smells of baking into the house. Lonnie was washing up and Genny set the table. Mrs. James wasn't in the kitchen. Not surprising, considering all she'd been through.

"Uncle Jed, hurry. We're hungry." Jilly pulled him to the washstand. Jed walked extra slow, teasing the girls. Jilly offered him a frown. Laughing, he picked up his pace.

Lonnie scooped up Jilly and tickled her thoroughly. The girl's bright smile beamed at her pa. Maybe someday, he'd have a sweet little girl of his own.

"You look good enough to eat." Lonnie gave a playful growl, bringing belly laughs from his daughter. He set her down and grabbed Molly and repeated the game. Birdie laughed from the highchair, and Lonnie kissed the baby's cheek and sat beside her.

Genny and his nieces had brought out the best in his grumpy twin. The war had stolen his brother, but his wife and family had brought back his joy for living. The loss of their parents and siblings lessened each day he had with his nieces. He was grateful every day that Genny had come into their lives. God had provided the perfect match for Lonnie. Did God have a wife and children in his future? The thought turned his gaze to the closed bedroom door.

Jed let the girls guide him to the table.

"Hurry and eat." Molly pulled out her chair and scrambled to sit.

Jilly did the same. "Eat quick so we can have dessert."

Genny laughed. "Mrs. James offered to make dessert. Baking seems to make her very happy." She pointed to the sideboard. Jed's mouth watered from the delicious smells of pies, tarts, and cookies. "No one gets dessert unless they clean their plate."

"Are we waiting for Mrs. James?" Jed glanced toward the bedroom again.

Genny shook her head. "She's resting and will eat later." In a whisper, she added, "I think she feels a bit timid around us yet. Give her time—she'll come around."

"I wonder how bad it was living with Lemont." Jed's pa never laid a hand on his ma. Never expected her to do any heavy lifting. Took every opportunity to hold her close. Pa loved to compare her to the woman in Proverbs 31. And never did he consider her property. A stone formed in his chest at the thought of Lemont's abuse. "If we're on our best behavior, we might change her low opinion."

Genny signaled to the girls to bow their heads, then nodded at her husband. "Say the blessing, Lonnie."

Lonnie grabbed Jilly's and Genny's hands, and the circle of prayer formed.

Following the blessing, the men ate heartily, and the girls cleaned their plates without complaining. Genny let them choose two things from the array of baked goods.

The smells took Jed back to Ma's kitchen. "Do we only get two?"

He and Lonnie playfully elbowed each other as they looked at the desserts. Their younger brothers, Willy and Leroy, had always snuck extra cookies. Jed and Lonnie had coated a few with salt and laughed as their siblings spit the cookies on Ma's clean floor. If smell brought such bittersweet memories, what would tasting Delilah's baking do?

"There is no way you men would be satisfied with only two." Genny chuckled. "I know I won't." She helped herself to an apricot tart and two sugar cookies.

As the apple pie melted on his tongue, Jed groaned. "Better'n the dessert at the Astoria Hotel in New York. Maybe she could open her own bakery."

"Don't go puttin' ideas in her mind anytime soon." Lonnie grinned, licking a crumb off his beard. "A fella could get used to fine eats like this."

"Got that right, brother." Jed sampled a tart.

Lonnie filled a plate with tarts and cookies, then wrapped a towel over the treats. "I'll take this to the bunkhouse. The boys are goin' to think they died and went to heaven when they taste these."

As Lonnie headed outside, Jed stepped to the bedroom door and knocked. "Mrs. James."

"Yes?" Her voice wary.

"Wanted to say thank you for the mighty fine baking."

He waited for a few heartbeats, but she didn't respond.

Jed left the house, not bothering to play with the girls this evening. Mrs. James needed time to eat and relax without strangers hovering. *She musta been hurt real bad to be so afraid.* A rock of guilt rested in his stomach. He'd thought Lemont's always wanting to meet outside merely inhospitable. How did he miss the clue something was wrong? Every visit, Lemont had offered his opinion of preachers and church in general. Jed had been occupied with giving answers. He'd no idea Mrs. James was being abused. *God, show me how I can help her now.*

Lonnie sat on the bench outside the barn, whittling. When Jed approached, he looked toward the house, then lowered his voice. "Pies 'n' all are nice, but how long you think I gotta stay away from my own home?"

"I'll go over to Barlow's place and hire his boys to build my … the cabin."

"That'll work." Lonnie's knife peeled off another layer of wood. "This time of year, we're too busy getting ready for the cattle drive to build. Don't wanna miss my wife any longer than it takes to build the cabin."

"I figure the extra privacy should help Mrs. James be more comfortable here. Give her time to sort things out." Jed intended to give her a place of refuge to do it.

Delilah came out of the bedroom and filled an empty plate with stew and a biscuit. Jilly joined her at the table.

"Did you know Bessie's having a calf?" Jilly leaned in, her eyes shining. "We got lots of chickens." The child gave a secretive smile. "There're kittens in the barn."

Delilah smiled at the girl between bites of food. Jilly continued to chatter about the things she and Molly had done that day.

"Mommy, me and Molly's goin' to play with the kittens."

"There's a new horse in the barn. Please stay away from him." Genny stacked dishes in the sink. "Soldier needs time to get used to the place."

Delilah pushed her unfinished plate aside. How long would their kindness last?

"Yes, ma'am." Jilly answered while Molly nodded.

Genny poured some coffee, sat at the table, and put sugar and cream in her brew. "Soldier might adjust easier if he's in the barn a while before slowly being introduced to the stable and the other horses."

"I'm sorry to put you out." Delilah rose and collected her dirty plate and utensils. "I'll get these washed and put away." If she decided to take a different job, she'd leave Soldier with the Holts. She needed to see what other positions might be available. Preferably with no men about.

Genny smiled and sipped her coffee. "Then I'll settle in the rocker and rest while the girls are occupied." Delilah glanced at Birdie sitting on a blanket, playing with blocks. The toddler's joyful giggles as she clapped the blocks together echoed in the cabin.

The young mother struggled to rise from her chair. She tried planting her feet wide apart. Delilah rushed to assist her. Once Genny was up, she waddled to the rocker.

"Are you settled?" Delilah tugged at the pillow at her back. "More comfortable?"

"You spoil me." Genny gave a contented sigh.

The kind compliment touched a wounded place in Delilah's soul. Warmth spread through her chest, loosening tension, and the rock in her stomach transformed to happy butterflies. She'd spent her adult life in service, and words of praise were hard earned. Lemont's had been nonexistent.

Birdie reached up for her mother and found a perch between the rocker and her mother's growing middle. Gingerly, Genny cradled both her daughter and her coffee. "Your pastries made me feel like a princess at a queen's tea party. When I'm not so exhausted, you must teach me how to make them."

"Happy to." The butterflies seemed to have journeyed to her feet, and she resisted the urge to dance. "The larder is full of everything a cook needs to create lovely meals. It would impress my mother."

"Your mother is still living?"

"Yes, and my father." Her pulse quickened. Delilah hadn't written them since she married. Telling the Holts about her life without lying was impossible.

"Why did you become a mail-order bride? A few wives I've met came because they were destitute."

"I came because I was a fool." Delilah reached for the kettle of water on the stove, its heat matching her shame. She poured it into the dishpan and added soap flakes before she felt calm enough to explain. "Back in Baltimore … I told you I was a chambermaid." She scrubbed a plate extra hard. "Mr. Hollingsworth's son, Tobias, hinted at marriage. My parents warned me we were of different stations. Marrying me would endanger his inheritance. I refused to believe them. I was so smitten with Tobias I didn't see the truth." She scrubbed a few more plates, then turned toward Genny.

Birdie leaned in and patted her momma's face. Delilah lost herself in the vision. The babe's unconditional love brought a wave of homesickness. *Oh, how I miss your sweet embrace, Mother.* Delilah cleared her throat, dislodging a lump of sadness.

"Tobias married a rich heiress. Before they left for their European honeymoon, he confessed his love to me. I was flattered but confused. Why marry an heiress if he loved me?"

"I was thinking the same thing." Genny moved Birdie to the other side of her belly.

"Tobias offered to make me his mistress when he returned, setting me up in an apartment." Heat rose on Delilah's face as she willed the confession back in its secret cocoon. She leaned over the dish pan.

"How awful." Genny clicked her tongue. "I see why you left."

A few times, when her face was bruised and her ribs hurt, she'd wished she'd stayed. Which of the two circumstances would have been worse became a blur in her mind.

Genny set Birdie on the floor, and she toddled back to the pile of blocks.

"When I told my parents, Papa said we'd give notice and find new positions." Delilah rinsed the plates. "My parents had me late in life. They're too old to start over. I found a copy of the *Matrimonial News* and answered an ad. My plan was to bring them to live with me. Let them retire and enjoy grandchildren. Instead, they continue to work from dawn to dusk." *What a wretched daughter I am.* Her chin trembled and more heat filled her face.

"You had a loving plan. Don't torment yourself for your mistake. How could you know the measure of the man by letters?"

"Lemont didn't write them. He was illiterate. Someone else wrote those lovely words."

"Oh my." Genny rocked, and Delilah worked in silence for a few moments. "Your plan was to avoid Mr. Hollingsworth and his desire to compromise you."

"It worked." Delilah grabbed the stew pan, clanging it on the side of the dry sink. Lemont didn't compromise her. He'd crushed her soul.

She'd brought a library of books that he'd reduced to kindling in one of his fits of rage. Weeping over the bonfire, she begged him to stop as each of her precious tomes dissolved in the flames. *Don't be all uppity with me. Layin' about readin's a waste of time.* He slapped her hard and sneered. *Now you got more time to finish your chores.* Delilah touched her cheek, recalling the sting. That was the beginning of the physical abuse.

Genny appeared beside her with a dishtowel. She appreciated the silent support as they worked together.

At length, Genny broke the silence. "Jed thinks you should open a bakery."

"I think working for you is enough for me right now." Delilah smiled at her new employer. But she tucked the suggestion away to add to her escape plan.

She'd heard the dinner conversation. She'd left the bedroom door ajar. The high praise for her treats had made her weep. Cleansing tears washed her self-doubt away. It had been too long since anyone valued her. Small stalks of confidence peaked through the hard surface of her scarred heart.

"I'll call the girls and once they're settled, I'll head to bed." Genny stepped to the front porch.

Delilah's thoughts kept replaying her foolish choice. Opening the back door, she threw the dirty water from the dishpan outside and right onto Jed's shoes. She gasped. "I'm so sorry. I didn't see you there." A cringe held her fast as she waited for Mr. Holt's response.

A chuckle. The man was laughing. She stared into his sparkling blue eyes.

"Don't you worry, these are my work boots. The water washed off some of the muck." Mr. Holt touched the brim of his hat and turned toward the barn.

Delilah almost giggled before she found her professional manners. Then she closed the door and wiped the table and swept the floor. Could her past be wiped clean as easily as she'd cleaned the kitchen?

She heard male voices on the porch and scurried to the room she would share with Genny. On the other side of the closed door, the warmth of safety settled around her heart. The colors of the sunset through the bedroom window resembled the bruises she'd endured. Another day without being beaten was a good day, indeed.

Chapter 5

Jed leaned against the open bunkhouse door, listening to the birds greet the morning. *Father, thank You for another day.* Since his time as a prisoner of war where the conditions brought the strongest man to his knees, he'd started his day with the same prayer on his lips.

Dreams haunted his sleep last night for the first time in months. He was back at the camp, and his abusing guard took the form of Lemont James. Rather than submit to the abuse, he punched him. Jed woke in the dusk of morning light in a foul mood.

Lonnie joined him at the door. "I miss my bed. Genny's snores are soft." He chewed on the edge of his mustache. "Sharing a room with a passel of men ain't something I'm used to." He nudged Jed. "Remember how our little brother Leroy used ta talk in his sleep?"

"Yeah." Mostly, Jed recalled prisoners crying out in fear as they slept. His late brother's sleep habits were a pleasant memory.

"Ya talked in your sleep last night." Lonnie touched his shoulder.

"What'd I say?" Did he mention Mrs. James? Jed's single bed was on the far wall away from the other three sets of bunks. A table separated them. Did the ranch hands hear him too? The teasing from the men would never stop.

"Somethin' like, 'I ain't taking no more.'" He spoke in a low tone unlikely to be heard by the men who assembled in the bunkhouse after finishing early morning chores and the cook, who announced that a fresh pot of coffee was ready.

"I was at the camp again." Jed didn't elaborate. Lonnie wouldn't ask. His brother sensed when to listen and when to leave it be.

"Well, I can smell some good cookin' coming from the house. The womenfolk must be up. Genny's coffee is way better than this swill." Lonnie emptied his cup on the ground beside the door, then turned to rest it on the table. "You gents will excuse us while we go get some real vittles."

"When you goin' have us up to the house for dinner again?" Carter scrubbed his three-day growth of beard and yawned.

"We miss your wife's cooking. And the new *señora* makes *mucho* delicious food." Gonzalez raised his eyebrows.

"Boys, don't go turning your charms on the lady." Jed glared at each man. "She's a fresh widow and don't need none of you hanging around her."

The men fell silent, looking anywhere but at Jed. The foreman, Granger, nodded. "They'll show respect." His words brought the men's heads up, and they mumbled ascent.

"Now I gotta know." Granger grinned at Lonnie. "How long are you banished to our bunkhouse?"

"Jed's hiring the Barlow brothers to build her a cabin today. I'd imagine I'll be free of your loud snoring by the week's end." Lonnie pounded Granger's back. "The ruckus in here wakes the dead. Grandma's ghost is likely to show up tonight."

Gonzalez pointed at one of the newest cowhands, Dan. "This *hombre*'s snores conjure the ghosts."

The others joined in the teasing, Dan laughing as heartily as the rest.

Jed waited for Lonnie to stop bantering with the men before heading to the house. Their guest might be nervous if a single man entered alone. Lonnie being married might put her mind at ease. They wiped their feet at the door. In the kitchen, Lonnie grabbed his wife and kissed her like a newlywed, then greeted each of his girls with a hug. "Morning, my little sunflowers."

Jed placed his hat on the hook and took his place at the table.

"Good morning, Genny. Sure smells good."

Genny turned from the stove. "Having a good night's sleep makes it easy to prepare a fine meal."

"You sayin' you prefer sleeping without me?" Lonnie went up behind her and kissed her neck as she fried the eggs.

"Yes, indeed." Her teasing tone made Jed smile. He'd gotten used to their open affection.

Mrs. James' face flamed as she entered the room. Would she bolt for the bedroom?

"Good morning." Jed smiled at her, but she ignored him. "Did you sleep well?"

She took her place near Birdie, across from him. "Yes, thank you for asking." Her tone was formal as she looked over his head at the wall behind him.

Mrs. James took a biscuit and broke off a piece for Birdie. The toddler grinned her approval and took a slobbery bite.

"It looks like Birdie's teething." Jed played peek-a-boo with his niece, loving her wholehearted giggles.

"Delilah walked the floor with her last night so I could rest." Genny set the eggs and a plate of hot cakes on the table. "I imagine you'll need a nap today."

"I require little sleep. I'll be fine." Mrs. James gave the baby another bite of biscuit. "We had a delightful time, didn't we?" Her face lit up for a moment as she talked to Birdie, who jabbered and nodded, offering an infectious smile.

"That was right nice of you to do for Genny." Lonnie nodded his approval before focusing his attention on his meal.

Mrs. James' face paled when Jed smiled at her. Yet she didn't scurry away.

When he'd cleaned his plate, he inquired, "Anyone else want more coffee?"

Jed rose, but Mrs. James was out of her chair in a flash. "I'll get it."

Delilah trembled as she poured his coffee, dripping the hot liquid on Jed's hand. He dropped the cup, and the contents spread in a wide pool. Lonnie jumped from his chair to avoid the liquid flowing his way. The girls scampered back as Genny rolled the tablecloth toward the spill and started removing the dishes. Jed bit back a groan while smearing butter on the burn.

Mrs. James' eyes remained wide with terror as she rushed to help clean up the mess. Jed resisted the urge to pat her arm in comfort. Instead, he offered a smile. "It's all right. Accidents happen."

Her shoulders relaxed. "Are you badly burned, Mr. Holt?"

"No, ma'am. I'll be fine. And you can call me Jed. There are two Mr. Holts, and that's confusing."

She held the damp tablecloth to her chest. "I'd rather not call you by your Christian name. May I suggest Rev. Holt for clarity?"

"No, ma'am. I ain't a preacher anymore. How about Brother Holt? Church members gave me the title 'cause I help out the pastor."

Mrs. James held his gaze. The green in her eyes appeared to brighten, warming him to his toes.

"Would that suit ya?"

"Very much, Brother Holt." Coffee dripped from the bundle of fabric she clutched onto the blue cotton of her bodice.

"You might want to do something with the tablecloth afore it ruins your dress." Jed's remark brought a blush to her cheeks.

Genny exchanged Birdie for the tablecloth. "Looks like we'll be needing to find you another dress."

"I'm so sorry." Her eyes grew wide. "I'm sure I can get the stain out." Mrs. James grabbed a towel and began dabbing the offending spot.

"For now, let's find you a fresh dress." Genny hugged her new friend. "You need new clothes. We'll go to town tomorrow."

The widow hung her head.

"It'll come out of your pay. It's not charity."

She squeezed her close, and Mrs. James nodded as she focused on the floor.

Jed recalled the first dress Lonnie had bought for Genny. It'd been his tongue-tied brother's way of declaring his love. Would Mrs. James think building a house suggested … Warmth filled his collar, and he caught a stutter before it formed. "I'll be on my way to get the carpenters hired."

While Genny changed Birdie on the bed, Delilah opened the wardrobe. "My, you have a lot of dresses."

"My husband loves to buy me new frocks. I have one for every birthday and anniversary since we got married. It's been five years now. Plus, I made a few myself for when I'm with child. Seems like I wear them more than the ones Lonnie gave me." Genny moved to the wardrobe and chose a green poplin frock from a hook. "Take off that dress so we can soak it." She sat Birdie up and changed her out of her nightgown while Delilah slipped out of the soiled dress. She pulled the fresh gown over her head and buttoned the front. A daisy pattern embroidered the collar of the sturdy cotton material.

"Where did he buy such nice, ready-made garments?" Delilah liked the idea of not sewing her own clothes. She wasn't a very good seamstress.

"Polly Clemens and her husband own the mercantile in town. She has a corner of the store for ready-made clothes." Genny pulled the baby's fresh gown over her head.

"I doubt she'll have anything for me. My late husband told me I was built like a man."

"I think you're tall and willowy." Genny pulled two matching dresses from the small trunk near the bed for the twins. "My mother would have appreciated your poise."

Delilah squirmed under the compliments. *Ugly* was a hard brand to remove. "Good posture was drilled into house servants."

"Once my mother passed away, I didn't abide her instructions concerning posture." Genny laid fresh pinafores and undergarments on the bed.

"How old were you when she passed?"

Genny held up her finger, then stepped to the door. "Girls, come. Let's change your clothes." She handed a set of the girls' clothing to Delilah. "We'll talk after we get them dressed for the day. They'll be clean for ten minutes, at least, before they explore outside." Genny laughed. "They're their father's daughters. These girls are not interested in being ladylike."

"I want Mrs. James to help me." Jilly wrapped her arms around Delilah's skirt. A layer of anxiety melted from her with the hug. "I can mostly dress myself." The pride in the child's voice made her chuckle.

"How does one mostly dress?" she teased Jilly, who responded with a bewildered look.

"She can't button, or tie, and you must brush her hair," Genny offered.

"I can put on my own socks and shoes. And pull up my . . ." Jilly's chatter muffled when she tugged her dress over her head. Delilah buttoned the back and tied her pinafore in place.

"My mommy is having twins," Jilly whispered. "That way, Molly and me don't got to share holding the baby."

"You help with babies?" Delilah took up the brush and worked out the tangles in the child's golden locks.

"They took turns holding Birdie when I was finishing up supper. And I have no idea where she got the notion I am having twins." Genny made a part in Molly's hair and began braiding it. "It doesn't feel like twins. Perhaps a baby elephant. Mrs. Kelly, who has ten children, says she got larger with each pregnancy."

"My mother served as midwife to the servants under the stairs. And she would probably disagree with Mrs. Kelly."

"Under the stairs?" Genny started on Molly's second braid.

"It refers to the laundress, cook's helpers, maids. Those servants rarely seen by the family or their guests. They lived in the lower level. We had a separate staircase where we could move unseen by houseguests and visitors. Mrs. Hollingsworth allowed those women with child to work until it was time for their confinement. She claimed to save a fortune with my mother caring for her ladies." Delilah sighed. "There's another reason I wanted them to retire. Momma is in her sixties now."

"You still can bring them here." Genny shooed the girls out to play. "Stay clean." She stretched, placing her hand on her back. "Don't know why I bother to remind them." Genny shook her head. "As I was saying, invite them."

"No." Her neck warmed. "Your offer is too much. I need to be able to support them." She stared at the floor.

"Forgive me. I didn't mean to barrel in with my own solutions." Genny touched her shoulder. "Still, you can have them come for a visit anytime."

"Why? Why would you offer?" Did her employer need more help than she was led to believe? Never would she send for her parents under these circumstances. They would have no choice but to work for their keep.

"I lost my mother to pneumonia when I was ten. My grandparents had disowned her years earlier because of my father's gambling habits. Soon we went from riches to rags. I had a lonely childhood. If your parents are living, you need them nearby."

"Thank you for the offer." So Genny came from means. She certainly didn't act like it. How refreshing. But it was too soon to discern her true motives. "This evening, I need to write my parents and tell them everything."

"You can post it tomorrow." Genny waddled out of the room.

Surely, Genny's attitude would change. Juliet Hollingsworth had been Delilah's friend growing up. Once she had her debutant ball, she pretended they'd never been friends. Like Juliet, Genny would likely adapt the same attitude as the ranch grew. Delilah had best remember her place. Still, it'd be nice to enjoy the friendly camaraderie while it lasted.

Chapter 6

"I'm fine right here." Delilah crossed her arms after settling herself in the wagon bed. "As I said before, Genny needs room in her condition."

Jed climbed onto the wagon bench. "Suit yourself."

Delilah relaxed against the side of the wagon. The idea of a settlement being so close pleased her. If things got unpleasant at the Single Cross, she could always walk to town and seek employment. Lemont had never taken her there. Would the townspeople look at her oddly? After all, she was the mystery bride of the recluse. She lifted her face to the sun, enjoying the feeling of freedom. Even the jarring from potholes couldn't dislodge the peace of a lovely day.

The road smoothed as they entered town. Delilah took in the view. The stage depot sent a chill through her. Could she ever board a stagecoach without thinking of Lemont?

"Delilah, there's the mercantile." Genny pointed at a blue building. "Polly insists the bright color attracts more customers."

"It certainly caught my eye." She let a chuckle slip from her lips.

Jed pulled the wagon in front of the store. "I got business at the blacksmith shop, and the supplies I ordered a while back are waiting in the livery." He gave the women a bright smile.

"We'll join you later." Genny took Jed's hand as he assisted her down.

Delilah scrambled from the wagon bed on her own. Jed tipped his hat before taking the wagon down the street. Her stomach fluttered in response to his dimpled smile. *Stop it. He's just another man.* She joined Genny on the mercantile porch.

Genny sighed. "This is my last visit to the store before my confinement." She took Delilah's arm. "We're going to have a good visit with Polly before we leave."

"My mother encouraged women in the family way to stay close to home once they were showing." Delilah recalled the anxiety those under the stairs had experienced over lost wages and the corsets they wore to hide their growing middles.

"Fiddle-de-de." Genny giggled. "We Kansas women are hardier stock. If I followed that rule, I'd never get to leave the ranch. Polly is with child herself. Half the town is expecting little ones. Winter gets mighty cold here."

Delilah blushed at her friend's declaration. Winter had been a nightmare—confined in a cabin with a drunk. Did the Holt men drink? A shiver coursed through her.

The smell of cinnamon and freshly washed wood floors and the organized clutter of generous amounts of merchandise welcomed them into the store.

"Polly, how are you?" Genny greeted the very pregnant proprietress. The woman waddled around the counter and gave her friend a sidearm hug. Genny was huge compared to Polly. Delilah frowned. When was Polly due?

"Ahh, I can't wait for this little one to make its appearance. But my mother told me to wait until she gets here. She'll arrive on the stage any day now. The doctor says I have another month." Polly smiled at Delilah.

"Where are my manners?" Genny touched Delilah's shoulder. "This is Delilah James. Delilah, my good friend, Polly Clemens."

"I'm pleased to meet you." Delilah offered her hand. "Genny's closet is full of your ready-made dresses. I'm in need of a few."

"Please, come with me." Polly led her to the ready-made clothes corner of the store. "I don't have any black ready-made. Would dark purple or gray suit?" She gave Delilah a once-over and added, "I'll let out a hem and make a few tucks free of charge."

Delilah looked through the dresses. Polly brought a bolt of black crepe. "If you sew, this is wonderful material for a mourning gown."

"I do sew." *After a fashion.* "But I won't be wearing black." Delilah refused to lie to the world. "This purple will do."

The others made no comment about her bold declaration. Instead, Genny touched her shoulder. "Try it on."

"Follow me. I let the ladies try on clothes in my bedroom." Polly led her to their well-appointed rooms in the back of the store. The Clemens' décor reminded her of the east. Lots of doilies and pillows on the chairs and an emerald-green lantern on the table. The light fragrance of rosewater wafted through the sitting room. Polly opened another door. The bedroom had pink rose wallpaper and a beautiful quilt sewn to match the wallpaper on the bed. "Take your time."

Polly left, and Delilah admired the oak headboard as she picked up the new frock. Genny's home was more rustic, and she couldn't imagine Lonnie Holt putting up with rose wallpaper in his bedroom. Mr. Clemens must love his wife a lot to let her decorate as she pleased. Lemont didn't—it didn't matter. His opinion could no longer influence her.

Delilah changed and stepped out of the room. "How I wish this was lavender. Dark colors are not very flattering." She covered her mouth as heat rushed up her neck.

Polly knelt at her feet and measured the hem. "I love lavender. Dark purple suits you, though. The length is perfect. I always make them long so they can be hemmed accordingly."

She struggled to rise, and Delilah helped her. "I'm sorry to inconvenience you in your condition."

Polly signaled for Delilah to raise her arms, ignoring her apology. "I'll take in the sides, and it will fit perfectly."

Delilah nodded and started for the bedroom.

Polly stepped closer and whispered. "I apologize in advance for asking … but was he as horrible in private as he was in public?"

"Worse." Delilah spoke to the floor. Her throat tightened, and she rested her hand on her chest before looking Polly's way. "Far worse."

She changed quickly and returned the dress to Polly.

"My dear, I have some lavender prints I can make up for you." Polly's sympathy embarrassed her. "After what you must have been through, you deserve beauty."

Delilah blinked back moisture. Polly hugged her close. "My uncle beat my aunt so bad, my father took a bullwhip to him. The man left town and never returned. She lived with us for five years until she got word her worthless husband had died. Aunt Agnes then married the blacksmith and had three children."

Delilah assumed the story was meant to cheer her. Oh, how she wished someone had taken a bullwhip to Lemont. Jed's smile came to mind, and she shook her head to loosen the image. "I can't see myself ever marrying again."

"Give yourself time. Your wounds are too fresh." Polly accompanied her to the front, where she introduced Delilah to her reserved, smiling husband before she continued. "I've got your measurements. I'll alter the dress, and you can take it with you. If you pick out some other material, I'll make another dress."

"I can sew." It was a drudgery she hated, but she'd accepted enough charity. "Thank you, Polly, for your kindness."

She chose a plain gray material. Not everyone in town would be quite as understanding as Polly Clemens. A pile of material and notions formed on the counter as Delilah checked off her list. She chose ready-made stockings, a nightgown, and undergarments. A lacy corset drew her. At least underneath the drab, she'd have something lovely. One of the first things Lemont had destroyed was her corset, along with her best dress. He'd grabbed her body as harshly as he had her clothes. She erased the image of her wedding night from her mind. Never again. This was a new beginning. The past needed to be buried under the same tree with her late husband.

Genny added material to the pile as well. "Didn't you notice the sewing machine in my bedroom? Lonnie stubs his toe on it every time he gets out of bed."

"I wanted to take a closer look at it." Delilah had heard that even the worst seamstress could sew a straight seam with the machine. "Can you teach me how to use it?"

"But of course. It will be fun sewing together." Genny took up a pattern book from a rack near the material.

"What are you making?" Delilah leaned over to see the page.

"New shirts for the men. And new frocks for the girls. They are growing like weeds."

"You make shirts for *all* the men?"

"I make each wrangler one new shirt a year." Genny smiled. "I also do their laundry and darn their socks. Having a woman's touch keeps them mindful of the world outside the bunkhouse. Besides, I love to sew with my new machine."

"I look forward to learning how to use it." Although Delilah's joy diminished at the thought that she might be called upon to sew for the men.

Genny touched her arm. "I don't expect you to sew those shirts. It's my gift to them. But if you could help with the girls' frocks and pinafores, I'd appreciate it."

She covered her mouth as a deep sigh escaped. "I'm happy to, but you'll need to guide me. Mother said I couldn't sew a straight seam to save my life."

"The machine makes it easy." Genny laid the book on her pile of material. "Mr. Clemens, here's the rest of my list."

Delilah explored the store while Genny waited at the counter. She didn't care to engage in conversation with Polly's husband—pleasant as he seemed—while waiting for the new frock to be altered.

When she spied shelves of books in the far corner, she bounced from foot to foot. She ran her finger over the spine of *Pride and Prejudice*. Romance was a fantasy. *Godey's Lady's Book* caught her attention, along with the *Farmer's Almanac*. Her father relied on it. She clutched the *Almanac* to her for a moment, imagining her father discussing the content over morning coffee. Snatching up the magazines, she placed them on the counter. "Add these too."

Genny flipped through the periodical. "I've been meaning to buy the newest edition."

"Buying a lady magazine again?" Jed's voice close behind her startled Delilah. She jumped to the side. "Sorry. Shouldna come upon ya like that." He looked over Genny's shoulder. "With Mrs. James here, you might actually have time to read."

"Yes, what a blessing being a lady of leisure." She laughed, and Delilah was reminded of her place once more.

❦

Jed kept his voice firm but gentle as he addressed the stubborn widow standing outside the mercantile with her arms crossed. "Mrs. James, I promise not to touch you, but you have to sit on the bench. There's no room in the wagon."

Delilah scowled at him. "I could sit right there on the crate."

"No, you can't. It's fragile." Jed pointed to the bench.

She sighed and crawled up on the far side of the buckboard seat.

"Delilah, I don't need the whole seat, and Jed won't bite." Genny coming to his defense made the whole scene more embarrassing. "Scoot over a little more, or you'll fly off when Jed hits a pothole." She glared at him. "He always hits a pothole."

"Thanks for your vote of confidence." Jed smiled at his sister-in-law, purposely ignoring the widow. "I've got window glass, so I'll be driving very carefully."

"How many windows do you have planned for the cabin?" Genny altered her position on the bench.

"Four." Jed whistled to the blacks to head home.

"I can make do without window glass." Mrs. James glanced his way, her eyes wide. "Shutters will be fine."

"We have beautiful sunsets and sunrises you won't want to miss. Besides, the cabin will get mighty dark in the winter without windows to let in the light." Jed's practical words broached no argument.

"Why are you being so kind?" Delilah asked.

"I reckon if it was my cabin, it's what I'd want. Light coming in the windows is welcoming."

"Forgive my forwardness." Mrs. James' voice hitched. "How rude of me."

Jed glanced at Genny before leaning over to check on Mrs. James. "Nothing to be sorry about. If I have somethin' built, it needs to be done proper. It's the Holt way. We don't do anything half-a step."

"I fear I've taken the cabin you were building for yourself."

Delilah seemed to read his thoughts. What to say without lying? "I have a site all picked out for a house of my own someday. And it ain't ten feet from my brother's home."

Her shoulders relaxed, and she nodded before staring at the passing scenery.

Silence followed for the rest of the ride, until Sheba ran toward the wagon barking. Jed slowed the horses as she ran beside them home. Once the wagon pulled in front of the house, Sheba flopped on the porch, tongue hanging out of her smiling muzzle.

The women took their purchases inside. The ranch hands were heading into the bunkhouse for supper while sneaking furtive glances at Delilah. Jed glared, and they went about their business. She looked even more beautiful in Genny's red dress. Her work boots covered her ankles under the short hemline.

"Gonzalez, Carter, come help me take this to the work site." Jed grabbed the crate full of nails, hinges, and other sundry things while the other two carried the window glass crate between them. "If there's even a little crack on the glass, it comes out of your pay."

"Looks like a fancy house for a housekeeper," Carter said.

"How do you figure it's fancy?"

"Señor, you have whitewash and yellow paint." Gonzalez chuckled.

"Yeah, well. She had a terrible life with that no-account, Lemont James. Something pretty might help her forget." Jed hadn't thought of a reason until now.

"*Sí*, it is like you, Señor. You always see others' needs." Gonzalez pointed his chin at Jed and smiled.

"Yeah, we'll help you paint when it's ready." Carter winked at Jed.

"I'd appreciate the help." Jed ignored the teasing. "You gents can finish unloading those last two cans of paint, then head for chow."

Jed stepped on the porch of the main cabin and found Lonnie setting the table. "Uh-oh, you cooked." Jed groaned and held his stomach.

"Lucky for you, Genny put together a stew before y'all left. I'm getting us moving along by setting the table. The women are in the bedroom gawking at the latest fashions in that magazine they brung home."

"We were not gawking." Genny waddled to the table. "We were putting away the material, and I was showing Delilah a new pattern in the book." She embraced Lonnie, then he stroked her belly. "Son, we cain't wait to meet ya."

Jed cleared his throat as Delilah entered the room. "My stomach's complaining, so can you two quit being all lovey-dovey so we can eat?" He held out a chair for Mrs. James. She stared at him for a moment, her eyes narrowed. Then she took the seat, and he pushed it closer to the table. "Where are the girls?"

"They already ate and are napping." Lonnie smiled at Genny. "Birdie fell asleep while the girls read to her."

"The girls know how to read?" Delilah's question came across as more conversational than she had at yesterday's mealtime. Maybe she was getting more comfortable with the family.

"Nah, they look at the pictures and make up stories." Lonnie set the stew pot on the table next to a loaf of bread.

"If they don't remember, then they tell it their way." Genny sliced the bread while Lonnie filled the bowls.

"I love to read." Her faraway look and deep sigh caused a tingle to shoot through Jed. Maybe he'd buy some new books next time he was in town.

Lonnie said grace and everyone dug in.

"I have a few books you could read." Genny's offer brought a wonderful smile to the sad woman. "I read more in the winter while the men are underfoot."

"We're not underfoot." Jed didn't want the widow to think they laid about in the winter.

"Right. Besides keeping a watch on the cattle, we repair things we didn't have time to fix in the warmer weather," Lonnie added.

Jed glanced between Lonnie and Delilah. "A lot of those repairs are done in the barn." She looked his way as she reached for the butter. Distracted by her attention, he swallowed a spoonful of stew the wrong way. He gasped for air as horror filled Mrs. James' face.

"Water," Jed croaked, his throat feeling like a too-tight neckerchief.

Soon Lonnie was pounding his back, and Delilah handed him a glass of water. She smelled of fresh-baked bread and cinnamon. Taking a few gulps, the food cleared, and he found his breath. The concern in her eyes stirred a place deep inside. "I'm fine. Y'all can stop fussing over me now." The last time he'd been made over to such a degree, he was fighting pneumonia, and Genny was the one holding the glass of water.

Delilah took a step away and averted her gaze.

Jed finished his meal in silence, warmth creeping up his neck. He stared at his plate until the telltale sign went away. What was it about this woman that made him careless? Maybe he should start eating with the crew.

Chapter 7

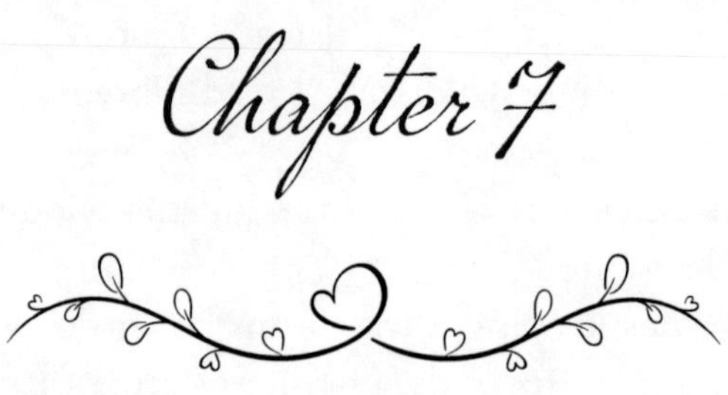

A week later

Delilah gazed at the beautiful cabin the men had finished painting as Brother Holt and a few of the men carried furniture from the shed. She'd overheard the crew say the wood had been meant for Brother Holt's cabin. A knot formed in her stomach. Never could she repay them.

"This is too much." Tears graced her cheeks. She wiped them with a handkerchief she kept up her sleeve. Since coming to the Single Cross, she'd fought the urge to cry at every act of kindness. No one had been so kind since she'd left her mother's side.

"Is the yellow too bright?" Brother Holt's worried expression took her by surprise.

"It's perfect." Her whisper embarrassed her. She cleared her throat and offered a smile. "I can't wait to move in."

Inside, Lonnie and Jed arranged a few pieces of furniture. "There's a carpenter who's got a spread a half a day's ride from here." Lonnie placed the rocker near the stove. "Jed traded a steer for the rocking chair, dresser, and bed frame, and Genny sewed the quilt."

Panic crept near Delilah. *What does Brother Holt expect in return?* She sat in the rocker before she swooned, then shoved her shaking hands under her legs and focused on her words. "Thank you, Brother Holt, for your kindness." She didn't dare glance at him, fearing the look in his eyes. The one Lemont had when his lust was ignited. The few gifts her late husband offered came with the same expected payment.

"Genny suggested we needed to furnish this room for your comfort." Brother Holt's voice remained calm.

Her body relaxed, knowing it was Genny's idea. She took a few deep breaths and counted to ten before she spoke again. "I'll make up some curtains and a matching tablecloth for the lovely table you provided." It had two chairs. She doubted she'd be having visitors.

Genny came in with a vase of wildflowers, the twins trailing behind her ample skirts. "The girls and I went hunting for these."

Molly pulled her fingers from her mouth. "Pretty for you." She smiled before popping her fingers back between her lips.

Jilly sat in a chair at the table. "I'm going to draw at this table every day."

Genny lowered herself onto the other chair. "How do you plan to decorate?"

"Polly slipped some green calico in my order when we were clothes shopping." The shopkeeper's unexpected kindness had brought tears to Delilah's eyes. "I thought it too deep a green for a dress. I prefer lighter colors. But—"

"Perfect for curtains and such." As Delilah agreed, Genny clasped her hands together. "God knew what you needed before you did. I rejoice when that happens."

Delilah pasted on a smile. Her bruised body had been proof of unanswered prayer. Not wanting to spoil the day for Genny, she pushed her opinion of God's provisions away. "I need to gather the ripe produce from the garden. Then I can start supper."

Genny nodded. "I'll take the girls to check on the baby bird nests so they're tired enough to nap after they eat." She lowered her voice on this last.

"I'll take them to the outhouse first, before I get back to the chores," Lonnie offered, and he and the girls followed Jed outside.

Genny leaned closer and grinned. "Since you've been here, I've resumed walking again. It's how Lonnie gets the girls to take a nap so easily."

Delilah chuckled with her.

Genny gazed about the room. "Could I bring the sewing machine in here? There's more room for us to work."

"And it'll save your poor husband's toes. That would be wonderful." Genny's company was becoming a welcome balm to her soul.

Meals had become a pleasant time of conversation. Her hands didn't shake anymore when she served the family. Exhorting herself each day that she was the housekeeper kept her mind on work. Having her own place to retreat to after they put the kitchen in order each night would be a treat. This bustling household rarely had a quiet moment.

Over breakfast, Lonnie had worn a happy smile—no doubt due to being allowed back in his own bed. Delilah's stubborn refusal to sleep in the same house with men had been met with grace. When would she stop being frightened? Maybe a few extra pies to show her appreciation for the inconvenience were in order.

Since her arrival, the men on the Single Cross had been perfect gentlemen. But that could change like the shifting winds. They were still strangers. She'd be locking her cabin door each night.

"Thank you, Genny, for helping me improve my sewing skills. I learned so much as we made the pinafores. You've done more than …" Here came more tears. She wiped them with the hankie still wadded in her hand from her last bout and gave a wry chuckle. "I suppose I'll spend my free time making handkerchiefs."

"It was my pleasure, and you helped me as well. Once winter comes, you'll have time to get lots of sewing done." Genny patted her hand and rose.

Delilah saw her to the door. Could she ever trust a man enough to create this sort of life for herself? Jed's dimpled smile crossed her mind. She slammed the door on the thought quicker than quick.

Jed hadn't missed Delilah's eyes darkening and worry lines framing her mouth when Lonnie had let slip that Jed had bought the furniture. He hefted new straw into Sally's stall. "I ordered the furniture for my cabin months ago. Byron Dodge is a master craftsman." The mare leaned in, and Jed produced a chunk of carrot. "Had I known she'd misunderstand my intention, I'd never have brought it to her cabin." He began brushing Sally. "I didn't lie when I said it was Genny's idea to put the furniture in there."

"You talking to your horse again?" Lonnie brought his black stallion into the stall at the far end of the stable. "You might want to tell Sally to be friendlier to Drake while you're discussing your lot in life."

"She'll be ready for Drake in about a week." They'd produce a fine foal. Drake had sired a filly with Prissy, Jed's other black mare, last spring. Star was champion bloodline.

"If Drake covers all the mares, we'll have a fine herd to sell in a few years." Lonnie fed a chunk of carrot to him.

"Sometimes I don't know why we run cattle when horses are your passion."

"Don't you recall? You was the one tellin' me the East was hankerin' for beef."

"True enough. You needed inspiring when we came out here." Soldier whinnied from the stall across from Drake. Jed frowned. He hoped Soldier hadn't gotten inspired to mate with Sally.

Lonnie came to stand beside Jed. "Sally'll be a fine ma."

"Excuse me." Delilah appeared in the stable door. "I've brought apples for Soldier." She walked past them to his stall. "There's my fine boy." She extended a chuck of apple on an open palm. The horse took the treat and Delilah stroked his face. "Do you think we could train him to ride?"

Lonnie removed his hat and held it in front of him. "Do you ride, Mrs. James?"

"No." She gave Soldier the rest of the apple. "In Baltimore, we either walked or took a lorry wherever we needed to go. Most servants didn't have personal mounts. But I'd like to learn."

Jed sized up the beast. "You want to ride him—a plow horse?"

"Well, he *is* my horse." She patted him again. "Soldier might be persuaded to plow your fields as well." Delilah stroked his ears and kissed his muzzle. "Lemont called him lazy, among other things. I find him comforting." Soldier pressed his head against hers. The two appeared content.

She needs this. "I'd be happy to teach ya." Jed offered what he hoped was a friendly smile. "The saddle-maker will need to create a saddle for his larger girth."

"I don't want to put you out." She stepped to the other side of Soldier's head, away from the men. The barrier strengthened her voice. "It can wait until I can purchase it myself. For now, you may need to gentle him for farm work. Lemont declared Soldier unbreakable." Her tone became a bit shrill when she spoke her late husband's name.

"Ain't no horse that can't be broke if you treat 'em right." Jed smiled her way. "Lonnie's the best horse trainer around."

"If you'll excuse me, I need to finish washing the garden vegetables." She nodded their direction.

The gentle sway of Delilah's hips as she departed from the barn sent moths darting around in Jed's belly. He took a deep breath.

Lonnie grinned at him. "I think you ought to marry her."

"Are you l-loco?" Jed stuttered.

Lonnie's hearty laugh softened the urge to pummel him. "No more than you five years ago when you said the same thing to me." His brother chuckled again. "You wait and see if that scared filly don't come around to admiring you over time."

"She needs friends, not suitors." Jed checked the latch on Sally's stall. She nickered, and Soldier responded. Hmm. Jed marched over to Soldier's stall and double-checked the bolt. "We better keep an eye on this one."

Lonnie removed his hat and wiped the band inside with his neckerchief, then put the hat back on. The summer heat warmed the stables to stifling—like Jed felt around Mrs. James.

"When it's time to breed the blacks, you should teach Mrs. James to ride Soldier. I think we got a saddle we can change up a mite to suit our purpose." Lonnie winked at him.

"Sounds wise. I don't want Soldier taking Drake's place."

As much as Jed liked the idea of spending time with the widow, he doubted she'd cotton to the notion. "But I don't know how that's supposed to happen when she won't linger more than five minutes in my presence."

Chapter 8

Delilah hummed an Irish melody as she reached for a bowl in the cupboard. Her new purple dress gave her confidence—something she'd not experienced for an eternity.

"Got any coffee?" The baritone voice startled her.

The bowl teetered and slipped from Delilah's fingers, smashing on the floor. She covered her face with her hands, gasping for breath as she fought for composure.

Jed grabbed the broom. "I'm terrible sorry, ma'am. I didn't mean to frighten you."

She glared at him as she wiped her clammy hands on her apron. "You scared the dickens out of me." She hurried to snatch the broom from Jed. "I can take care of it."

He jerked it back and kept sweeping. "I caused ya to drop it. I'll sweep it up. Grab the dustpan."

Delilah brought the dustpan and held it out to Jed as Genny came out of the bedroom. "What's going on?"

"I broke …" Delilah bit her lower lip.

"I startled her."

"It was my fault." Delilah dumped the dustpan of pottery shards into the trash bin.

"Which one?" Genny looked inside the trash bin. "The blue floral pattern." She sighed.

Delilah cringed. She'd broken something precious. "I'm sorry,

Genny. If I hadn't been so clumsy—"

"You're not clumsy. I scared ya." Brother Holt's insistence was downright irritating.

Her stomach knotted. Was the bowl a family heirloom? "Please, take the cost out of my pay."

"Ain't necessary, Genny." Brother Holt glared at his sister-in-law. "It was an accident."

"My, oh my, you two are each a little too determined to take the blame." Genny chuckled. "I have an excuse to buy new bowls. Lonnie broke the other two." She pointed her finger toward the front door as her husband entered. "Now, that man is clumsy in the kitchen."

"You tellin' tales on me, woman?" Lonnie hung his hat on a hook and winked at his wife.

"The third serving bowl has met its demise. The next time you're in town, pick me up three more like it."

"Next time means tomorrow." Lonnie poured himself a cup of coffee. "Want some, Jed?"

When his brother nodded, he gave his cup to Jed and poured another. Delilah chided herself for not getting the coffee.

"The meal is ready, so please take your seats." Delilah dished out the chicken and dumplings and peas from the pans on the stove, filling each plate and passing it to Genny. The girls had eaten earlier and were napping. Feeding them first made mealtime less hectic. She suspected Genny enjoyed uninterrupted adult conversation. The men chatted about the afternoon chores as they finished two helpings of food and peach cobbler.

"Darlin', I want to show you somethin' when you have the time." Lonnie put down his fork and squeezed his wife's hand.

"I have time now." Genny turned to Delilah. "You don't mind clearing away the table by yourself?"

"It's my job." She smiled at her friend, jealousy itching its way up her neck. She refrained from scratching. Envy hadn't taken the form of an itchy neck since she was a child. Why did the itch choose to return now? Watching the couple walk out the door hand in hand made her wonder if she'd break out in hives.

"May I help you?" Brother Holt placed his dishes on the sideboard. She'd forgotten he was still in the room.

"No need." She stacked the plates, then made a shooing motion. "I'll get the kitchen in order."

Brother Holt kept clearing.

"I am perfectly capable—" She grabbed for the plates. Their fingers touched, and something flicked in his eyes as warmth ran up her arm. They stood staring. Delilah found her voice. "I'm perfectly capable of doing the dishes by myself."

"I know you are." He released the plate to her and grabbed a rag. "You'll find me handy with a dish towel."

"You don't understand the meaning of no, do you, Brother Holt?" Delilah placed her hands on her hips and shook her head.

The dimples that appeared with his endearing smile made her heart flutter. Delilah forced an almost-smile into a frown.

"Fine." She pumped cold water into the dishpan, then added hot water from the kettle. The soap flakes dissolved as she stirred the water to make suds. "Plates, please." Without looking at him, she took the stack of plates and placed them in the water. Keeping her eyes on her work, she held up the first clean plate.

Jed dried it thoroughly and placed it on the cupboard shelf. "I used to dry dishes for my ma. She enjoyed having her boys take turns. It gave us time to talk about whatever was on our minds."

"Do you have something on your mind?" What possessed her to ask? If she could kick her own shin, this was the perfect time.

"No … maybe … yes." Jed took another wet plate and dried it. "You look plum tuckered. Are ya sleepin' at all?"

"Not really." Lying to a pastor was a mortal sin. Wasn't it?

"Is it the fire?" His gentle prodding held no judgment, but rather put her at ease.

"Every time I close my eyes, I'm burning." Delilah stopped washing and leaned forward; her chest hurt with the confession. "I often dream Lemont did set me on fire." The pungent smell of burning flesh always accompanied the flames in her nightmare. "He grabbed a piece of lit kindling and set the curtains on fire, then the rug."

"What did you do?" Jed's voice was soft.

"I yelled his name over and over, but he didn't respond. When his mind got trapped in the war, it was near impossible to get him back."

"That I understand." Jed sighed. "Then what?"

"His face was fearsome." Delilah's voice caught at the memory. "I dared not touch him. I did that once, and he almost choked me to death before he came back to reality." Perspiration dotted her brow and began to roll into her eyes. She wiped the moisture with her sleeve.

"The rocker I'd just been sitting in caught fire as he gave his wretched Rebel yell." Delilah placed her hand on her chest, leaving a soapy, wet spot. "It was …" Tears clogged her throat. She gulped for air as the sound echoed through her mind. "Terrifying."

Jed took her hand and guided her to a kitchen chair. His eyes, filled with compassion, gave her courage to continue.

"I fled out the door. The house burned fast."

"Was he drunk?"

"Yes. But I thought he'd get out. I didn't expect …" She still couldn't say it … could only speak her justification. "I barely escaped."

His mouth opened and closed, then finally, he spoke. "The horrors of war do things to a man's mind. I know that first hand. Not sure there was anything you could have done. Most importantly, God promises to heal the brokenhearted and set the captive free."

Delilah blinked at him. Maybe it was God who set her free.

"Ma'am, let me finish the dishes, and you go to your cabin and get some rest."

"I can't …"

He helped her up. "No arguments, now. You're no good to Genny wore out." His gentle touch and kind, compassionate eyes removed the rock that had settled in her stomach while reliving her traumatic memories.

Jed turned to the sink and set to work.

She chewed on her lip. "Thank you."

Relief settled over her while she strolled to her cabin. Sharing her story with no judgment had given her a measure of peace.

Chapter 9

Delilah had been observing Genny's movements since first light. Gentle moans escaped her lips as they dressed the girls. She'd managed to stay cheerful during breakfast, but she'd leaned against the counter, then a kitchen chair, to steady herself.

Genny had started labor. Lonnie had left early for town. Why had she kept it from her husband? The man would never have gone to town today.

A slight flicker of pain passed across Genny's face, and she took a deep breath before tying Molly's pinafore. "Girls, do try to stay clean," she called after them as they ran to the door.

"You remind them every time." Delilah chuckled.

"I'm hoping, if I say it enough, they might remember. Ah!" Genny grabbed her belly.

"I knew it." Delilah took her arm. "Shall I help you into bed?"

"Not yet." Genny rubbed her middle. "It's not near time. The pains started after breakfast. I've hours to go before I must take to my bed."

"Are you sure? You look ready to me."

Genny laughed, then moaned and took measured breaths. "And you know this how?"

Delilah kept back tears at the memory of her miscarriage. "My mother left me in charge of watching the expecting women when they began labor. I was to run and fetch her when it was time. You act much more uncomfortable than someone who's just started labor."

"I forgot your mother was a midwife." Genny made Molly's bed while Delilah made Jilly's and changed Birdie.

Holding Birdie on her hip, Delilah kissed the toddler's downy hair. "Who's your midwife?"

"I'm the midwife, so when the time comes, I'll send someone for the doctor."

"My mother refused to allow a doctor near the women unless things were dire. She felt no man should view a woman in such a state. Delivering babies was a woman's calling." How she wished her mother were here now. "In case you wonder, I'm not called to be a midwife."

Genny reached for Birdie but stopped as another contraction took her.

"I think you should call for the doctor now." Delilah placed Birdie on the floor, and she toddled toward her sisters' bed. She reached for a rag doll perched there, then plopped on the floor and jabbered to it.

"Looks like Birdie is preparing for the new baby too." Delilah chuckled as she observed Genny. Her friend went pale. Delilah grabbed her before she swooned. "Genny, come back to me." She patted her face. "Genny." Her limp body sent alarm through Delilah.

Color returned to Genny's face, and her eyes flickered open. "Best fetch the doctor."

Delilah helped her change into her nightgown and settled her in bed. Dread nagged her. *Did my worry over her pains cause this? Mother always said to keep your concerns to yourself lest you put fear in the hearts of the laboring woman.*

Delilah strode to the front door. The yard was empty, so she ran to the stable. "Hello?"

"I'm here," Brother Holt called from Sally's stall.

"Genny's in labor. You need to go for the doctor and Mr. Holt."

"Tarnation, the baby would decide to come when Lonnie's gone. Told that fool I'd go in his place." His gruff tone brought the hair up on her neck. "I'll saddle Prissy."

She scurried toward the door.

"Ma'am, sorry for my rudeness. Ain't no excuse." Concern settled on his handsome face. "I'll be back as quick as I can."

Delilah stood transfixed as he galloped away. It had been a long time since anyone had apologized to her. She shook her head to focus her thoughts on the present. *One thing I know I can do—care for Genny until the doctor comes.*

Jed reached town as Lonnie hefted the last bag of flour into the wagon. "What you doin' here? Genny send you for something I forgot?"

Jed leapt from his horse. "The doc."

Lonnie's face paled. "Now?" Looking skyward, he groused. "I had a feeling … but she looked normal. I should have—"

"Stop fretting and get." Jed handed Prissy's reins to Lonnie, then ran for the doctor.

Dr. Murdoch's office was full of patients. Jed paced, waiting for him to emerge from his examination room. Once again, Genny'd kept her labor to herself until the last minute.

"Take care now, Mrs. Henderson." Dr. Murdoch escorted his patient to the front door.

Jed strode across the room, bumping into the nurse. "My apologies, ma'am." Not looking her way, he continued toward the doctor.

"It's Genny. It's her time." Jed waited as the doctor stared at a file. The temptation to push him out the door almost overwhelmed him.

"I have to set little Sammy Broden's arm. My nurse can handle things from there. I'll be there shortly, Mr. Holt."

There's no time. He'd sensed the urgency in Mrs. James' voice.

He glanced over at the tow-headed boy with tears on his cheeks. Poor young'un. Jed found his manners and nodded, holding his tongue rather than hollering about the delay. "We'll see ya at the house, then."

He rushed toward the wagon and climbed on the bench. No need to hurry and risk toppling the load. Lonnie didn't need something else to worry over. He prayed the entire ride home. *Father, help the doc get there quick. Keep Genny and deliver the baby safely.*

Prissy stood saddled in the yard. Jed set the brake on the wagon in front of the house.

"Prissy-girl, I'll be right with ya." Jed ran to the cabin and burst through the door. The front area of the house was vacant. He stepped toward the bedroom, raising his voice without looking inside. "Doc has to set a boy's arm. Then he'll be here directly."

Lonnie came from the bedroom and glared at him. "Directly! You didn't make him come with you?"

"I couldn't ask after seeing the boy."

Lonnie's glare turned to panic. "Something ain't right." He strode away, brushing past Delilah in the bedroom door.

She scowled at him, then addressed Jed. "Can you make your brother leave? It's not proper for the husband to be in the birthing room." Her ramrod-straight posture and look of disgust almost made him laugh.

"Lonnie was there for the birthing of all his girls. I reckon it ain't gonna change now." Jed pulled off his hat and ran his fingers through his hair. "What do you expect me to do about it?"

"Makes me nervous with his pacing and declaring things are amiss." Sweeping into the living area, Delilah peeked out the window. "Carter took the girls to the barn to play with the kittens. Is the doctor on his way?" Dropping the curtain, she twisted her hands in her skirt.

"Doc promised to come once he set a boy's broken arm. Dr. Murdoch has a nurse now, so it makes things easier. He offered Genny the job when she first come. But she declined." Why was he jabbering like an old woman?

Delilah drew in a long breath and pushed a stray hair behind her ear. She stared at the bedroom door and chewed on her lower lip. "I'll go back in there once Genny calms her husband. Ridiculous, her doing the calming. This is exactly why husbands shouldn't be in the birthing room."

"You know, it was Genny's idea. Lonnie frets so much, it's easier on him to be in the room and holding her hand. With the twins, she dug her nails into his palm something fierce."

"Interesting. Often, men pass out in the birthing room." Her mischievous smile made him chuckle.

Genny's scream sent Delilah running to the bedroom. Jed stood helpless. What if something truly was wrong? His pulse raced. *Father, we can't lose 'em.*

The doctor arrived at the same moment as a second scream. Jed grabbed a basket Genny had prepared in advance for the girls and a few cookies, then led his horse to the barn, where all three girls rushed to him with tear-stained faces.

"It's goin' be fine." Pasting on a brave face, he hugged them. "Show me the newest kittens."

Jilly wiped her eyes with her sleeve and led the way. Molly remained silent, clinging to Jed while Jilly cuddled an orange tabby and Birdie petted the momma cat.

Hours after Jed brought lunch to the barn, he sat on a bench while Birdie slept on a blanket on a pile of hay nearby. The hired men took turns keeping the girls entertained. Gonzalez was doing card tricks—to the twins' delight.

"Uncle Jed, when are the babies coming?" Jilly sighed and pulled handfuls of hay from the pile where Birdie slept.

Jed drew her close as darkness crept into the barn. Pushing his worry aside, he stroked her face. "Who told you there were twins?"

"I just know." Jilly's solemn declaration brought laughter from the men. Jilly stuck out her chin. "You'll see."

Molly nodded. "You see."

Birdie chose that moment to awaken. Her cries filled the barn. The smell of soiled diapers emptied the area of everyone but Jed.

"Cowards." Jed chuckled as he gathered up his niece. "Birdie, let Uncle Jed change you, then I'll see if Cook has any of his fried pies."

He reached into the basket and found a fresh diaper and a clean gown. Holding his breath, he managed to make the child presentable. He walked toward the bunkhouse with Birdie cuddled on his shoulder as the wail of a baby split the air.

"You got a new baby, Birdie." He tickled her. She grabbed his hair and giggled, spraying slobber on his head. Jed repositioned the toddler onto his hip and removed his neckerchief to wipe his head. As he did, his gaze fell on the pasture, and bile rose in his throat. Sally pranced around with Soldier by her side. *Oh Lord, no.*

The men stood on the bunkhouse porch with the girls, everyone's eyes fixed on the house.

"Carter, get Sally and lock her in her stall. Gonzalez, put the plow horse in the barn."

The ranch hands ran to do his bidding. With all the excitement of a new baby, no one had thought to keep Soldier away from the mare.

Irritation fled when Lonnie came out onto the porch with a bundle in his arms. Jed and the girls gathered around him, but Lonnie had eyes only for the new infant.

"I got a son." His lip quivered before he looked Jed's way. "This is Peter John, after our pa." He sat on the bench so the girls could get a good look at the boy. "Your ma wanted you to see him right quick."

"Where's the other brother?" Jilly looked toward the door.

"He's not come yet."

The ranch hands had regathered on the porch. Cook smiled down at the girls. "Why don't you all come and get some fried pies?" He took Birdie from Jed, and the twins followed him, each taking a hand offered by Dan.

Once they were out of ear shot, Jed stared at his brother. "How are things? Really?"

"The other one might not make it." Lonnie's voice broke as he kissed his son.

Oh, God, no! Numbness overtook Jed. He squeezed his brother's shoulder. "Let's pray."

Jed prayed for God's mercy toward the unborn child while Lonnie wept.

Delilah ached for the big man as she stood near the front door. Jed's prayer seemed to comfort his brother. At the sight of Lonnie's tears, her mind shot back across the years to her own father weeping as he cradled the lifeless forms of Momma's many stillborn children.

Genny cried out just as the men entered the house. Delilah took Peter from his father. Mr. Holt dashed to the bedroom, followed by his brother. They stared at the babe in the doctor's arms.

Lonnie's face paled. "Why's he blue?" he asked as Delilah placed Peter in the cradle near the bed.

The doctor worked on the too-small babe until the infant let out a mewing cry. Delilah took the child, gently cleaned him, then wrapped him in a blanket. "You're a strong one, sweet boy." She kissed his cheek before laying the tiny bundle in Genny's outstretched arms.

Catching her eye, Jed nodded her way, then stepped into the other room.

"Keep him warm and nurse him often." The doctor turned to Delilah. "Mrs. Holt told me you have experience caring for new mothers and their babes. Watch them closely tonight. I'll come by tomorrow and every day this week to check on them." Dr. Murdoch picked up his bag and put on his hat. "If something happens in the night, come get me."

"Doc, I'll see you out." Jed's familiar footfalls followed the doctor's outside.

Delilah passed the babe to Mr. Holt. "Keep him warm while I clean up Genny."

Once Genny was settled again, she nursed her boys. "We need to name him, Lonnie." She gazed at the babies nestled in her arms.

"I'm afraid he won't make it," Mr. Holt whispered as he stroked the boy's cheek. "He ain't no bigger than my hand."

"Dr. Murdoch said he must have been hiding behind Peter,

because he only heard one heartbeat. They aren't identical twins either." Genny smiled at her husband. "See? Peter looks like you. Robert Jonas looks like me. We'll name him after my father because he was a determined soul."

"Robert it is." Mr. Holt stroked the downy hair with his pinkie finger.

Delilah stood transfixed, watching the loving parents.

"My father never gave up, and Robert won't either." Genny kissed her husband. "He'll grow into a fine man like his pa."

Delilah found her voice. "Now, Mr. Holt, please take your leave. Genny and the babies need to rest from their ordeal."

Mr. Holt kissed his wife once more. "If we keep having twins, we'll reach a dozen in no time."

Genny snorted. "Definitely time for you to go."

Delilah crossed her arms as he shuffled out, winking over his shoulder. "Just like men to take credit for the birth, as if they endured the pain."

"So true." Genny gave a weary smile. "Now we need to sleep. But I'm afraid I'll smother little Robert."

"Let me take him. I'll keep him warm while you sleep." Delilah tucked the blanket around the babe.

"Wake me if he cries out." Genny's eyes fluttered closed as she cuddled Peter close.

Robert rested in Delilah's arms while she rocked him.

Lonnie peeked in the bedroom door. "I'll take the girls to the neighbors. Mrs. Laughlin offered to watch them for a few days so Genny can rest."

After much crying and protests, the sound of the wagon wheels filled the yard. Delilah rocked, humming a lullaby as the evening light faded. Peter cried out and Robert followed. Delilah relinquished Robert to his mother, then changed Peter and held him until he slumbered. She laid him in the crib near Genny's bed, soon joined by Robert.

An emptiness came over Delilah. What if her child had lived

and had been a son? If Lemont had survived, the boy's life would have been unbearable. Pushing the horrid thought aside, she went to start supper.

Chapter 10

Delilah stood to the side as Dr. Murdoch examined the week-old newborns on the kitchen table. Peter was pink and thriving. Robert's constant cries were weak mews. *Should I have done more?* She'd kept him wrapped in an apron tied across her chest to keep him warm. Her mother had done this with a tiny babe, and it had survived. But there had also been the laundress' sweet baby girl. The agony on the mother's face as she held her lifeless child was something she never wanted to see again. Delilah wrung her hands as she waited for the doctor's prognosis.

Mr. Holt had his arm around his wife while she focused on the doctor. "Do you think I don't have enough milk for them both?"

"You managed with Molly and Jillian." Dr. Murdoch cradled Robert. "Has he been keeping his milk down?"

"It comes up as fast as it goes down." Genny's face flushed with the admission.

"I think your milk isn't agreeing with him." The doctor placed him in the second cradle near the fireplace next to Peter. "It's not your fault, Mrs. Holt. Robert was born too early. I want you to buy a goat."

"You think the boy needs goat's milk?" Mr. Holt frowned. "We got cows."

"According to medical journals, and to quote my grandma Murdoch, 'goat's milk fattens up little cherubs' like Robert." He closed his black bag. "You get the goat, and my nurse will stop by with the bottles and instructions for sterilizing them."

Genny burst into tears the moment the doctor left.

"It'll be fine, darlin'." Mr. Holt held his wife and patted her back.

"Sorry, I'm just tired. Let me rest and I'll be right as rain." Genny headed to the bedroom.

Delilah attempted to encourage Mr. Holt. "She'll be all right. My mother said new mothers get weepy."

"Yeah. She's done the same with the others. I shoulda remembered." Mr. Holt pulled on his hat. "The Laughlins have a few goats. I'll see if they'll part with one. Besides, I miss the girls."

Delilah missed them too. She sat in one of the rockers and pulled a sock from the darning basket. The simple task gave her time to think. Adjusting her darning egg underneath the hole, she closed the opening with her thread. She could still feel the imprint of Robert's tiny body on her chest. Would he survive? A tremor went through her as she repaired another sock. Her fear had shifted from the men on the ranch to Robert's well-being.

She'd taken over the laundry duties since Genny's confinement. Washing and mending strange men's clothes hadn't bothered her like she thought it would. Her friend had a way of making every drudgery pleasant—an attitude she was trying to emulate. Genny made her laugh when she'd frown at washing the men's unmentionables. "It makes them more pleasant to be around." She'd do anything for Genny, for this family.

Brother Holt entered. "Hello. I wanted to check the wood supply in here. What'd the doctor say?"

"Robert needs goat's milk."

"Goat's milk?" Jed removed his hat and ran his fingers through his hair. A blond lock dropped on his forehead, giving him a boyish air. "I reckon my brother's gone to buy a goat."

"The doctor said his nurse will bring bottles by later."

Jed rocked from one foot to the other, his arms folded, a trait both the brothers shared when they were anxious. "Do you think it'll work?"

"My mother encouraged Mrs. Hollingsworth's daughter to try it. Laura is five years old now."

"You lessened my worry." He smiled her way, sending a tingle to her toes.

She held his gaze. "I'm happy to lighten your load." She placed the darning basket on the floor lest she stab her finger in his presence. "I often helped sterilize bottles. It's extra work, but Robert will thrive on the goat's milk." Delilah hadn't mentioned her skills, afraid of the doctor's response, a ridiculous fear. He relied on her to care for Genny and the babes. She used to speak her mind. Would she ever find her old self?

"Something smells mighty good." Brother Holt grabbed a towel and started toward the oven.

"Stop." Delilah dashed for the stove, placing her hand on top of his to make sure he shut the door softly. His eyes widened with her touch, and warmth shot up her neck. "A chocolate soufflé will fall flat if you open the door before it is done."

"Sorry." His sweet smile made her face flame more. "I never heard of a chocolate whatever-you-said."

"We have extra eggs, and I didn't want them to go to waste. Mrs. Clemens brought Baker's chocolate when she came to bring the babies' gifts. So … we are having a soufflé."

"I look forward to tasting it." He pulled off his hat, pushed the stray hair back in place, and replaced the Stetson on his head. "I'll bring more wood at suppertime. Got lots of chores to finish yet."

She returned to her darning, pretending the sock was Brother Holt's. Warmth covered her face.

With the girls back home, the table was full at suppertime. "I hope I didn't add to your load, Mrs. James, but we missed our girls." Lonnie placed a kiss on Birdie's head as he spooned beans into her mouth.

"So did I." Delilah passed around sliced bread. "I'm sorry dinner isn't something more interesting. Beans and salt pork are—"

"Our favorite." Brother Holt smiled between bites. "It's the only thing Lonnie can make. Yours is tastier."

"Sure is, ma'am." Mr. Holt smiled, then grabbed a few bites before feeding Birdie another spoonful.

How sweet to be content with simple fare. She hoped the soufflé would make up for it.

Genny came out from the bedroom, her robe at last tied around her middle. "My darlings are back." Jilly and Molly ran to greet her. They'd not been allowed in the bedroom while she slept. "I've missed you terribly." She kissed the girls and hugged them. Birdie cried from her place in the highchair. Genny whisked her out of her chair and held her close. "Momma didn't forget you."

Delilah watched the reunion as if she were in the audience at a theater. Perhaps one day, she would get her own happy ending. She rose from her place and busied herself serving the soufflé.

Brother Holt grabbed his fork. "I been waiting to taste this since you put it in the oven."

Was that a wink? Her skin crawled with memories of Lemont's winks and their prelude to a slap or something worse. Slowly, she backed away. Her breath caught as the room closed in on her. She bolted from the house and scurried to her cabin, barring the door. Bitter memories came flooding back.

A shiver went through her. He'd winked at her while his friends sat around the table drinking his moonshine. She'd only wanted fresh air. The cigarette smoke and body odors were overwhelming. After gathering her thoughts, she'd returned inside and served them the stew she'd prepared. Hours later, when his guests had left, he'd pounced. *You are more trouble than you're worth.* Slap. *You need a lesson in obedience.* Slap. *I'll teach you to leave this house without permission.* The punch had left her unconscious. No matter what she did, she couldn't avoid his violent reactions.

Tears moistened her cheeks as she silently wept. Brother Holt's wink couldn't mean the same thing. Surely, he wasn't lying in wait to teach her a lesson. Didn't preachers have higher moral standards? She wiped her tears with her sleeve and sniffed. The thought of preachers reminded her of the day she'd walked down the aisle at a revival. She'd been so full of hope. Perhaps she could find hope again. Could she put the past behind her?

Filling her lungs with air, she exhaled her worry, then rose from her bed. She poured water in her washbasin and splashed her face as a knock sounded.

"Delilah."

She opened the door to Genny's worried expression. "Are you well? You ran out the door. I checked the outhouse first."

"It was just … I'm fine now." She squeezed Genny's hand, attempting to convey confidence as she surveyed her face. Were her recent thoughts written in her eyes?

"All right, then." Genny let out a sigh. "Jed said you know how to sterilize bottles. The nurse is here, and my mind is too full of worry to remember anything."

"Yes, I do." Delilah hugged Genny. "I'll take care of it. You concentrate on getting enough rest."

The men were off doing evening chores when Nurse Dune explained how to feed Robert. Goat's milk sat in a bucket on the counter. "The goat should produce more than enough milk each day to feed your son. If you have extra, throw it out unless you have a root cellar cold enough to keep it from spoiling."

Delilah jotted down the instructions while Genny listened to the nurse. She positioned Robert in her arms as instructed, and he drank his fill with gusto. Then they waited. The milk seemed to be staying down. Genny placed him on her shoulder and patted his back. *Burp*!

The nurse nodded approval. "Very good." She peered into Robert's face. "I think we've found milk that agrees with you."

Delilah placed Robert in the crib with his sleeping brother. They'd been separated because Robert was always crying. Peter's arm stretched across his brother.

After a few more instructions, Delilah escorted Nurse Dune to the door, then went back to the kitchen. Genny had organized the bottles on a shelf. "Would you mind taking the goat's milk to the root cellar? It will stay fresh there."

Delilah poured the rest of the goat's milk in a small jar. A breeze blew across her face, cooling her skin from the heat in the kitchen as she strolled across the yard toward the root cellar. It had been dug several feet from the garden. She smiled at the prospect of seeing what treasures it held. Never before had she been asked to retrieve anything from the cellar, and it wasn't proper for her to nose about without permission.

Double doors set in the ground opened to a narrow stairway. The middle stair made a cracking sound as she descended. She placed the milk on a shelf. The root cellar's dark interior was several degrees cooler than the breeze. Lighting a candle, she took stock. Several jars of canned peaches filled a shelf. The candlelight flickered over two barrels, both full of apples. Three burlap bags lined the other wall. She peeked inside the open one to find potatoes. The Holts' pantry inside the house was filled to overflowing too. Mr. Holt had been bringing in whatever Genny wanted from the cellar. There was no reason she couldn't take on the task. Especially if she needed to store the remains of the goat's milk there.

Genny had a good provider, and she'd had … *God forgive my envy. Thank You for bringing me to this safe place.* Her faith had dissolved to a tiny speck over the past year. She could thank God for the present but doubted she'd ever forgive Him for the nightmare she'd endured.

Delilah blew out the candle and placed it on the shelf near the door. By the dim light of the fading day, she started up the stairs. The middle stair snapped, tossing her down into the darkened cellar. She landed with a hard bump, and her ankle twisted beneath her, shooting pain up her leg.

Jed sprinted toward the scream with Sheba at his side. He peered down the cellar stairs. Mrs. James sat on the floor moaning, her hand on her leg. His throat constricted. "I'm here." He started descending the stairs.

"Stop." Mrs. James gasped as she moved her leg. "The fourth step is broken."

Jed counted the steps as he descended into the semi-darkness and lengthened his stride to avoid the broken step. At the bottom, he paused. "Ma'am. You all right?" Her mew of pain as she straightened her leg tore through him. "Mrs. James, I'll get you out of here, but I need to carry you in case something is broken."

He waited until she nodded to scoop her up and bear her out of the cellar. The warmth of her body in his arms awakened a longing he'd never experienced. He cleared the huskiness from his voice before venturing to speak again. "I'll take you into the house."

"No, I can walk now." She attempted to break his hold.

"No, ma'am, we're almost there." Jed pulled her closer.

She stilled in his arms and rested her head on his shoulder. He slowed his pace to enjoy her closeness longer. "Genny will look at your ankle."

When he called out, Genny opened the back door, eyes widening. Jed set Delilah on a kitchen chair. She winced.

"I'll tend her. It's not proper for you to view her ankle." Genny frowned his way.

He stood there gazing at the damsel he'd rescued from the cellar, the memory of her in his arms playing through his mind. "Right. I'll be outside if ya need anything."

Genny shooed him out and closed the door in his face.

The space separating him from the woman who attracted him seemed like miles rather than feet. Jed repositioned his hat. Then went to find something to distract his mind from the beautiful Mrs. James.

Chapter 11

Delilah limped to her cabin with Genny's help, the pain in her ankle a reminder of Brother Holt's gentle care. What must he think of her? She'd rested her head on his shoulder. His heart had pounded against her ear. His muscular arms holding her close had brought a warm peace that battled with memories of being thrown against a wall. *I mustn't let him touch me again, ever.*

"Are you cold?" Genny helped her to her bed.

Jilly and Molly had followed them. "Do you hurt?" Jilly's concerned expression calmed her dark thoughts.

"Yes. But your mother has done a fine job of wrapping my ankle. I'll be fine tomorrow."

"No, you won't." Genny crossed her arms and scolded. "You will stay off your foot for the rest of the week."

"I can't inconvenience you. I'm here to make your life easier, not become your patient."

Genny helped her lie on the bed and propped pillows under her foot. "Girls, go find your pa and ask him to find those crutches."

They raced from the room.

"Tomorrow, you stay in bed. The crutches will help you get around." Genny pointed at Delilah. "Only to the necessary and the table."

"All the work will fall on you." She stared at her friend. Fatigue rested in the dark rings under Genny's eyes. Her carelessness added to the burden. "I insist on fulfilling our agreement." Delilah pushed the covers aside and rose. Her ankle throbbed, and she plopped back on the bed and cried out.

Genny resettled her. "Delilah, I can manage without you for a while. I need to get used to feeding Robert with a bottle." She stroked her arm and smiled. "Day after tomorrow, I'll prop you at my kitchen table and bring you things to do."

"Fine." Delilah crossed her arms with a sigh. "Only one day in bed. Then it's back to work."

"Unless you aren't up to it."

"I'll be." Even if she wasn't, Delilah would be there to help Genny.

"You need some willow bark tea for the pain."

The tea Genny brought not only dulled the pain but also supplied much-needed rest. She awoke when the sunlight touched her face. Delilah rose with a start. What time was it? Judging by the view through the windows, the morning was well underway.

Several knocks echoed through her cabin. "Mrs. James." Jilly yelled through the door. "It's Jilly and Molly."

"Come in."

The girls rushed to her side and climbed on the bed. Jilly touched her forehead, then Molly did. "No fever." Jilly smiled and Molly nodded. "Good, now it's time for breakfast."

Another knock drew her attention. Genny entered. "Mornin'."

Before Delilah could return the greeting, Genny set the breakfast tray on the table, then helped her into her robe and to a sitting position on the end of the bed.

"Y'all can come in now. She's decent." Genny opened the door for the Holt men. Delilah fought the urge to scream, feeling less than decent in her nightgown and robe. Her breath caught while her hands became clammy. Before she could protest the male invasion, Genny smiled her way. "I hope you had a lovely rest."

Mr. Holt carried the coffeepot, and Brother Holt had a pair of crutches. His ears flamed when he glanced her way.

"These were Lonnie's when he broke his leg. Might be too long.

We'll help you stand, and I can see how much to cut off." Brother Holt retained a remnant of pink on his face.

Good. Maybe next time he'd stay away from her cabin.

She stared at the crutches. Best get this over with. "Give those to me. I can do it myself." No way was he touching her again. Brother Holt obliged. Their fingers brushed, sending warmth up her arm. Her face grew hot. She held onto a crutch and pushed off the bed with the other hand.

Brother Holt caught her as she tottered, the crutches extended wide out to the side. "They need to fit closer to your body. I'll cut off a few inches from the bottom."

Together, the Holt men took her arms, assisting her to the table. She shivered and drew in a sharp inhale. Nothing untoward about their touch, but another shiver overtook her despite her mental lecture. Once she was settled, they tipped their hats and left the cabin. Her heart still raced and beads of sweat rested on her brow. She stared at the breakfast tray and swallowed the knot in her throat. Pressing a smile to her lips, she took up her fork. "This looks delicious."

"The girls insisted flapjacks with honey would make you well." Genny poured coffee. "I need to return to the boys and Birdie before they wake. I'll come back for your dishes."

Delilah smiled at the twins, who remained behind. "I'm sure these flapjacks are indeed the best medicine."

Jilly chattered away while Delilah ate. Molly stood sentry. Delilah muffled a giggle as she caught the girl's serious expression. Molly's hand was at her side, not in her mouth as it usually was if she wasn't speaking or eating. After Delilah finished her meal, Genny entered with a gentle knock.

"The boys are asleep, and Lonnie is feeding Birdie, so I've come for the dishes." She pushed a loose hair behind her ear.

Brother Holt appeared at the door with the shortened crutches.

"Try them. I figured ya for five-feet-nine." His gazed rested on Delilah for longer than necessary, causing her cheeks to warm again.

Sheba streaked into the room and sat at her feet. "You're such a sweet thing to come and see me." She petted the dog, and Brother Holt signaled for Sheba to join him. The dog obeyed, then Delilah raised her eyes to her owner.

"Thank you, Brother Holt, for your kindness. I'm sure they will be fine. I've never measured myself. A tall woman is not considered attractive, so I never bothered to confirm my height." Why did she mention it? Her mother had encouraged her to stand tall and not let what other women said bother her. Until she arrived in Kansas, it hadn't. Another barb her late husband had thrust at her.

"I think your height is perfect, ma'am. You carry yourself with grace." Now Brother Holt's face was red. He turned and walked away without another word.

Genny chuckled, her eyes sparkling. "Someone gets tongue-tied around you. I have never seen Jed at a loss for words."

"Pastors say kind things. It's their job." Delilah put the crutches under her arms and took a few tentative steps. They fit well, even if her balance wasn't the best yet. Walking and holding her foot up behind her while maneuvering these sticks was a challenge. "Please, would you walk with me to the necessary until I master these?"

Genny and the girls followed her to the outhouse, then back. Delilah's stride was better after the short excursion.

After Genny and the girls left, Delilah fluffed the pillow under her leg, then laid back on the bed. The gentle tick of the mantel clock filled the room. She missed holding the babies. After her nightmare marriage, even the thought of the intimacy required to create a child felt unbearable. For now, the Holt children would have to fill the void.

Even though her home was mere feet from the family's cabin, the silence made it feel farther away. What was Genny doing right now? The girls? Brother Holt? Her faced flushed. What was it about the man? Besides his wondrous blue eyes and gentle laughter, he was kind. Thoughtful and too good to be true. Shaking her head, she grabbed the *Almanac* from her bedside table and perused it.

A knock woke her from the nap she'd succumbed to. The *Almanac* content hadn't been as interesting as she remembered when Papa read it aloud.

"Lunchtime." Genny carried a tray, followed by the three girls. "You girls can leave now."

"Can't we stay and watch Mrs. James eat?" Jilly ran to the bed and hugged Delilah. Her sisters followed suit. Then Jilly put on her best pouty face for her mother, and Molly mimicked it. Birdie stood quietly beside them.

Genny shook her head and placed the tray on the table. "That would be very rude. Join your father for lunch, and shut the door on your way out."

The girls hugged Delilah once more, then traipsed outside. Genny chuckled once the door was closed. Then she stood near as Delilah clomped to the table on her crutches. "After you eat, I wonder if you could help me feed Robert."

Her heart squeezed with the joy of being needed. "I'll come."

"No, I'll bring him to you with the bottle. Then I'll put him back in the crib after he's asleep. Peter should be finished nursing by then too." Genny sighed. "I'm hoping their feeding schedules will be different over time" She placed the plate of food and utensils from the tray onto the table. "I forgot a slice of pie."

"Don't bother going back for it. This is plenty."

"I have to come back for the dishes, anyway. Besides, it's an excuse to be sure the men don't eat it all before we get our share." She winked and left Delilah to a solitary meal.

Delilah finished lunch, then waited with anticipation for her visit with Robert. A gentle tap and a crying baby made her smile.

"Come in." Delilah's breath caught at the vision of Brother Holt stepping inside her cabin with an infant in his strong arms.

He gave her the bottle, then cuddled the fussing baby close. "I let Genny finish her lunch." His sheepish smile brought out his adorable dimples. "Could ya teach me how to feed him?"

Delilah stared into his sea-blue eyes that studied her in return.

Was this man genuine?

"I want to help." Jed kissed Robert's downy head.

Delilah stared. Shaking her head, she tried to speak in a neutral tone. "Well, first you need to reattach the nipple. It's crooked. Are your hands clean?"

Jed set the bottle on the table. "May I?" He indicated the washstand.

She nodded and jiggled Robert.

"I already washed, but I want to do this right."

"Take the nipple off carefully and then reattach it by pulling the rubber more securely around the lip of the bottle."

Brother Holt followed her directions, then held the bottle for her to inspect.

"Perfect." She signaled for him to bring it to her. "You need to make sure the baby's head is secure in the crook of your arm. Hold the bottle at a slight angle for the milk to flow. Not too fast or you'll choke him."

Jed wore a determined look, observing as Delilah demonstrated. He reached out and stroked Robert's cheek. His closeness rattled her fragile composure. "Me and him got somethin' in common."

"Really?" She concentrated on feeding the babe as the scent of hay and horses captured her senses.

"Yeah, we're both second born. Lonnie's a whole ten minutes older than me." He kissed Robert's hand, then moved away. Heat perched on her cheeks. "He's got better color, don't ya think?"

She turned her head away, grateful he'd been focused on the babe and not her hue.

"Yes, the goat's milk agrees with him." Robert suckled the last of the milk from the bottle. "Would you like to burp him?"

He took his nephew and gently placed him on his shoulder and patted. A tiny burp escaped. Robert snuggled on his uncle's shoulder and closed his eyes. The sight of the big man caressing the tiny infant set her mind on visions of hearth and home. She mentally shook herself. "You can take him to his crib now."

Jed nodded, grabbed the empty bottle, and carried the babe toward the door. Delilah had so looked forward to cuddling with the wee one while he slept. But waiting for Genny meant Jed would be standing too close. Why was she using his Christian name? Even in her mind, it sounded risky. She was ruined for any man. Lemont had seen to that.

Jed opened Delilah's cabin door to find Genny there with two plates. "I had a time keeping Lonnie from finishing off the apple pie." She entered and placed the pie on the table, then took two clean forks from her apron pocket. "Why don't you give me Robert while you two enjoy your dessert?" Before he could think of a response, she scooped up her son and disappeared out the door.

"Mighty nice, don't you think?" Jed stood in awkward silence. "I should leave the door open so no one thinks … or I can take my pie and leave."

"No, it's fine. Eating alone is … well, lonely." She offered a half smile.

Jed took the chair across from Delilah before she changed her mind. He noticed a bit of spittle on his shirt. Wiping it away reminded him of growing up.

"The boys look like Leroy and Willie. Lonnie and I were six when Leroy was born. He had brown hair like Robert, and Willie was a year younger and blond like us."

"Where are they now?" She took a bite, then looked his way.

"Buried in Texas." He focused on his dessert.

"I'm so sorry." She started to reach his way, then withdrew. Concern etched her face.

"I wish I'd been home to talk 'em out of enlisting. They was fifteen and fourteen, too young to serve." The bitter edge to his words hurt to hear.

"People aren't always easy to sway. I had this noble notion I could help my family by answering an ad. My parents couldn't talk me out of it. I was convinced it was the right thing to do."

"I'm talking about war." Brother Holt pushed his half-eaten slice away. Addressing him as *brother* in her mind created a needed barrier.

"As my mother always says, 'Once the advice is given, the results of the action are no longer in your hands.'"

"You're sayin' I done what I could." All the sadness of his loss flashed in his eyes. A deep sigh followed. "Your ma is a smart woman. I'll take those words under consideration." Then she was graced with another gorgeous smile. "Although you didn't take her advice, I hope you see your life getting better now."

"Yes, I do." She sipped her tea and forced the last of the pie through her lips. Better to sit in silence than confess how much he'd made a difference in her present condition. She finished her tea and stacked up her lunch dishes on the tray. Brother Holt added their dessert plates. Their fingers touched, and she pulled back quickly as warmth shot through her. She reached for her crutches. "I need to go …" How embarrassing. She'd almost confessed her destination was the outhouse.

Brother Holt nodded and reached for the tray of dirty dishes. "I'll take these back to the kitchen and get back to work." He left without another word, not even offering to help her with her crutches. Probably a good thing, considering how his touch affected her.

Jed deposited the tray near the dry sink, then stepped toward the cradle in the adjoining room. He stroked Robert's head, picturing Delilah feeding the boy, her raven hair glistening as the sun from the window shone on it. Jed shook his head. *Rein in those thoughts.* Would she run like a doe scared from her hiding place if he suggested anything more than friendship? *Father, keep my heart.* He'd never told anyone other than Lonnie about his guilt over his brothers' death. Mrs. James didn't judge, only offered sensible advice, a lot like Genny.

He gazed at the sleeping newborns, his thoughts lingering on a dark-haired beauty whose heart and soul were crushed. Could he help her heal without losing his heart in the process? It was becoming a losing battle. If he kept telling himself he only offered friendship, perhaps his heart would start to believe it.

Chapter 12

A week later

Black clouds covered the midday sun. Thunder cracked as Jed and Lonnie rode toward home. Rain pelted them. Jed looked behind him as panic rose.

"We're closer to home than the line cabin." Lonnie's words, meant to assure, did the opposite.

Jed gritted his teeth and did his best not to grip the reins too tight. "Are you sure?" Fear laced his voice. Thunderstorms ignited his panic and brought back visions of being lashed to a pole in a storm—his punishment for punching a Confederate prison guard. Another bolt of lightning streaked the sky.

"Jed, don't be thinking' on it." Lonnie angled his horse closer. "Don't do no good."

"I know. I'm trying." Jed's heart pounded, and air was trapped in his lungs.

"Do ya recall the time we caught a barrel of fish during a rainstorm when we was kids?"

Lonnie prattled on, attempting to keep him distracted. Jed focused on the memory of fishing with his brothers. Then a large streak of lightning lit the sky, followed by a loud clap of thunder. Jed jumped and gripped the reins hard, jerking his mare's head to the side. Sally whinnied and reared up, depositing Jed on the ground, then galloped for home. As he struggled to rise, another bolt brought a shiver, then a scream joined the thunder crash as he curled in a ball in the mud.

"Jed, get yourself up." Lonnie's voice sounded distant as the lightning cracked overhead.

Jed laid there trembling, mentally strapped to the pole in the middle of the prison yard, the fierce wind driving rain through his clothes, thunder echoing with every streak of lightning. A piece of debris slammed into the back of his head as he struggled to free himself. "Please, help me, help me." His mind stayed frozen in the day terror.

"Come on, I got ya. It'll be all right soon." Lonnie's voice loosened the memory's grip. Lonnie rubbed Jed's back as his mind came back to earth. His brother led him to his stallion.

The storm lessened as they rode double the rest of the way home. Jed's teeth chattered while tiny trickles of sweat dripped down his face.

"Forgive me."

"Ain't nothing to forgive." Lonnie's matter-of-fact tone didn't make him less ashamed.

The rain turned to drizzle as the Single Cross appeared before them. Jed breathed easier and loosened his grip on the back of Lonnie's saddle. "I hate being a coward." His voice came out barely above a whisper.

Lonnie halted his horse and stared forward, his voice soft. "Don't never want to hear you calling yourself a coward. Ain't true. You're the bravest man I know."

Jed didn't feel brave, only weak. His brother whistled and Drake carried them to the ranch.

Delilah sat at the kitchen table peeling potatoes, watching the storm out the window. The fresh smell of rain always cheered her. Sweet memories of Papa sitting with her and reading when the weather was too wet to garden cloaked and warmed her.

A riderless horse bolted across the yard into the stable. Her pulse quickened. She couldn't tell the matching blacks apart from a distance. Which Holt brother had been unseated in the storm? Was he hurt? "One of the horses came back alone."

Genny stopped basting the roast, shut the oven, and ran to the door. "I'll be right back." She pulled her shawl over her head and stepped into the rainstorm.

Delilah took calming breaths as the girls watched out the window. Birdie kept pushing Molly into Jilly to get a better look.

"Stop!" Jilly pushed Molly, who pushed Birdie. She plopped on her bottom on the floor and wailed.

"Jilly, help Birdie up." Delilah grabbed her crutch and hobbled toward them. "Molly, get away from the window. "Play with Birdie—build something with blocks." Jilly and Molly took Birdie's hands and walked her to her blocks.

Delilah went back to peeling potatoes. Worry settled in her stomach while the thunderstorm lessened.

First, Jilly slipped back to the window, then Molly. The rain had turned to drizzle.

"Here comes Momma," Jilly shouted and ran to the door. Genny's dress and shawl were dripping.

"Don't hug me, girls. I don't want you to get wet. Wait until I change." Genny removed her shoes at the door. "It was Sally, Jed's horse."

Delilah trembled as she set the knife and potatoes aside, retrieved her crutches, and hopped to the window. A horse with two riders came into view. Jed slid off the back of Lonnie's mount and ran to the bunkhouse.

The crew said nothing when Jed entered. They'd seen him embarrass himself during a thunderstorm before. Still, his pride condemned him for his weakness.

"Boss." Carter handed him a towel. "Want to join our card game?"

"Thanks, but no." Jed dried his hair and searched through his trunk for a change of clothes. "I could use coffee."

"It'll be ready when you are." Sam, the crew cook, went to the stove.

Jed changed out of muddy clothes, washed up, and combed his hair.

Sam placed a cup on the table and signaled for Jed to sit. "Your color's back."

"I'm fine."

"I know." Sam sat across from him. "Battle of Vicksburg haunts me when I hear fireworks on the Fourth of July. It's why I don't go into town to celebrate."

Jed's shame decreased at the cook's confession. "Being out in the open during the storm is worse. In shelter, I can handle it."

"War changes a man." Sam shook his head. "When I got home, my wife and children were gone. Took me six months to find out what happened to them. She'd heard I'd died and went home to her parents. By the time I reached her parents' home in Ohio, she'd went west with her new husband."

"What'd you do?" Jed's mind unwound as he focused on his friend's story. Sam never talked about the war.

"I changed my name and came to work here. No need upsetting Edith and letting her grieve over living in sin."

"Didn't you love her enough to fight for her?"

Sam flinched, filling Jed with regret for his careless words.

"Edith is real religious. We fought a lot about it. I promised if I made it back alive, I'd go to church with her. She promised to pray." Sam stared at him over his cup. "Letting her go is the best way I can fight for her, don't you see? What she don't know will save her reputation."

Jed didn't argue. "I see you kept your promise and have been going to church every Sunday."

"Unless we're on the cattle drive." Sam sighed. "Too bad I didn't do it sooner. Edith might have had more faith I was alive and waited for me." He rose from the table. "I need to rustle up some supper. You staying?"

"I'll head to the house. Looks like the rain has stopped." Jed's panic attack had passed.

Father, when will I overcome this childish fear? What grown man's afraid of a thunderstorm? He'd come to believe his confinement in the prison camp had been his penance for not keeping his promise to his late father to watch over his mother. Jed shook off the rain from his hat along with the fainthearted thoughts in his mind.

"How's Jed?" Genny asked her husband the question on Delilah's tongue.

The front door opened, and the focus of her concern entered.

"Supper goin' be ready anytime soon? My stomach's so empty, my bellybutton stuck to my backbone." Jed's pale face belied his attempt at humor.

Delilah chewed her lower lip, searching for something comforting to say.

Genny rose from her place, Peter resting on her shoulder. "It won't be long. Why don't you sit by the fire and warm up?" She placed Peter in his arms.

Jed took the rocker near the fire. Robert fussed in Delilah's arms. He'd finished the bottle while she'd stared at Brother Holt. She placed the empty bottle on the table and the baby on her shoulder. A few gentle pats brought a resounding burp.

"That's my boy." Lonnie laughed. He set Birdie in her highchair with a wooden spoon, then scooped Robert from Delilah's arms.

"How's your ankle?" Jed asked her.

"Better." Delilah pushed a stray hair off her face. "I think I'll put the crutches aside tomorrow."

"Don't be in a hurry. A sprained ankle takes time to heal." Jed rubbed Peter's back. "Be sure yer up to it." His kind words were a soft caress.

"We will see what tomorrow brings." Her voice came out husky. "Thank you for your concern." She looked away, ashamed of her response to simple kindness.

Delilah rose to help Genny set food on the table.

Avoiding Jed while sitting across the table from him proved challenging. Birdie's jabbering helped her focus on the child beside her. Once Birdie was full, Delilah hurried through her meal. "I think I'll go lie down. Leave the dishes—I'll do them later."

Delilah stumbled over her left crutch as she hurried out the back door. She regained her footing, then paced herself. The irregular, muddy ground made the short trek to her cabin more hazardous. Water dripped from her roof down the back of her dress.

A chill accompanied her inside. Fear grabbed her body in a series of shivers, and sweat formed on her skin. Maybe she should consider moving to a convent. Being surrounded by women might take the fear away. She placed a cool washcloth on her face, cleansing the perspiration. What was wrong with her? It had been three months since she'd been rescued from her nightmare. Would the memory ever fade enough to allow her to be happy again?

Count your blessings. Her mother's ever-present exhortation gave her pause. Delilah sat on the bed. *All right, let me count my blessings.*

Being rescued was number one. She lifted her index finger.

Number two, caring for the Holt children made her happy.

Genny's friendship made three. She stared at the three raised fingers.

Then why was she still so sad? Sensitive to every look, word, and action of the men on this ranch?

A memory formed in her mind, blotting out her blessing list. *You're a harlot, Delilah, just like yer name. Dirty, filthy, lying harlot. I'll teach ya obedience. Don't never question me again.* She flinched. Lemont had taunted her often about her name. Another excuse to lay heavy hands on her. Every day, his foul mouth and cruel ways had beaten her into submission. If she'd had a different name, maybe …

Why couldn't Grandma Kildare have had a different Bible name? Why did Papa have to *bless* her with it? One blessing she could do without.

She wrinkled her nose and undid her braid as her mind wandered down another path. The revival her family had attended right after the war ended had been life changing. An Irish preacher explained the need for Jesus clearly, and the three of them had prayed to receive Christ. She brushed her tresses with vigorous strokes, reliving the excitement of new-found faith—now a distant memory.

Delilah redid her braid and frowned at her reflection. "At first, it was grand, then life sure took a turn for the worse since saying that prayer."

She glanced around the cabin. In a few months, she'd gone from destitute to—safe. This refuge was an answer to prayer. Robert thriving was another answered prayer. And deep down, she recognized God had sent Brother Holt after the fire. God had given her a sister in Genny and filled a hole in her soul as she cared for the children. Releasing a deep sigh, she smiled at her reflection. The panic had passed and her mind calmed. Now she needed to get back to the present. Adding a few pins to capture stray hairs, she went back to the Holts' home to do the dishes.

Before Delilah finished preparing the dishwater, Brother Holt grabbed a towel. Once again, they worked in companionable silence while Lonnie and Genny played with their children.

Something had changed when Mrs. James returned to the house. Jed's attempts at conversation while doing the dishes fell flat. They finished their task.

"I'll sweep and everything will be in order." Delilah shooed him toward his family.

"Have I done something to offend ya?' Jed's question brought a scowl from her.

"Why would you think so?"

"You were quiet at dinner, refused to look my way, and fled to your cabin. And you ain't said much while we worked together. If I've offended you, please tell me, so I don't do it again."

Mrs. James' face pinkened, and she turned away, hobbling on one crutch as she focused on sweeping. Her strokes quickened as she moved across the floor. Once there was distance between them, she gave him a smile which didn't reach her eyes. "I have a lot on my mind. You've done nothing to offend me."

"You've set my mind at ease." Jed wasn't convinced, so he ventured another question. "Want to play checkers?"

"What?" Mrs. James set the broom aside. "Checkers?" She removed her apron and hung it on a hook. "My papa and I used to play every Sunday."

"I'll set up the board." Jed grabbed it from a shelf near the fireplace and set up the pieces before she changed her mind. "I ain't played anyone but Lonnie in a coon's age."

She sat across from him at the kitchen table. Were her hands trembling? She placed them in her lap. "I don't believe I know how old a coon is."

He laughed, and she appeared to relax. Delilah was a challenging opponent. She beat him three out of three games. Then her face went ashen.

"I'm sorry." She fidgeted in her chair.

"For what? Winning?" Jed detected a flinch. "I like a challenge."

The smile she gave him reached her eyes this time. "Well, then, I suppose you'll want a rematch."

"For sure. I can't let the crew know I lost to a woman." Jed chuckled.

"Do you know how to play chess?" Her voice held a challenge.

"No ma'am. But I hear it's a thinkin' man's game."

Lonnie chuckled from his chair near the fireplace. "Then you ain't got a chance."

Genny scowled at Lonnie, and Delilah giggled.

"I'm a thinkin' man. I'll have to get me a chess set, and maybe

Mrs. James can teach me how to play."

"Maybe." Delilah went quiet again. "I think I'll retire for the evening." She rose from her chair, leaving her crutches, and limped toward the door.

"Can I escort you to your cabin?" Jed reached the threshold before her.

"No. It's only a few steps away. I'll be fine."

"Do you mind if I watch to be sure ya don't fall?"

Alarm flashed through her eyes. Then she sighed.

"If you must." Delilah made it without incident, not looking back as she closed the door behind her.

"That went well." Genny's remark caught Jed off guard.

"What?"

"You managed to keep Delilah here with us for over an hour. Progress, indeed."

The babies fussed. "I'll feed Peter." She took the babe and headed to the bedroom, then she nodded to her daughters. "Girls, it's time for Pa to put you to bed." Genny smiled at Jed. "And you can feed Robert."

Jed washed his hands and warmed the bottle Genny had already prepared. Then he retrieved the wailing infant and rested him in the crook of his arm. Sitting in a kitchen chair, he held the bottle to Robert's lips. The baby suckled, then choked. Yanking the bottle away, he sat Robert up, holding him against his left hand while he rubbed his back with his right.

"Sorry." Jed glanced toward the bedrooms, then gazed into the infant's eyes. "Give me a minute." He recalled Delilah's instruction and began again. With Jed holding the bottle at a slight angle, Robert drank without further incident. Jed burped him, then paced the floor until Genny came out to retrieve him.

"I need to get to bed. We got a full day tomorrow." Jed headed for the door.

"You just don't want to change a diaper," Genny teased.

"You got that right." Jed grabbed his hat and strode across the yard to the bunkhouse, his thoughts on the lovely woman who'd bested him in checkers. *Remember, your focus is friendship. Your mission is helping her heal.* His heart refused to agree. Why was this so hard? Those sad green eyes drew him in a way none of the single women in town ever had.

Chapter 13

Delilah stepped over Sheba, who was sunning herself on the porch. The dog waited there whenever Jed worked in the stable. Any other time, the faithful pooch stuck to him like flies in a honey pot. She started toward the chicken coop, and Sheba paced beside her, pressing a bit too close. Delilah stepped to the side. The dog moved with her. Even before they reached their destination, the chickens were clucking and scurrying about.

"Shoo, Sheba, you're scaring them." She pointed to the porch.

Sheba refused to leave her side. Nearing the coop, the canine got between her and the gate.

"What is wrong with you?" Delilah tried to sidestep her.

The chickens clucked and ran frantically around the pen.

"Sheba, get away."

The collie rose and placed her paws on Delilah. She pushed the collie down and again tried to pass. The dog stood sentry, refusing to budge. Sheba tugged her skirt.

"Stop." Delilah's pulsed quickened at the collie's strange behavior.

"Mrs. James, don't move."

Delilah froze as a shot rang out. She screamed and shrank to the ground in a ball. Sheba licked her hand. Brother Holt approached, holding his rifle. "It's all right now."

Her eyes widened. "Are you mad?" Her voice quivered in unison with her body. "Why were you shooting at me?"

"I wasn't." Brother Holt extended his hand. She refused the man's help and scrambled to her feet, retrieving the basket she'd dropped.

He petted the canine. "Good girl." Sheba followed him to the coop. He held up a headless snake from the corner of the pen. The dog sniffed the carcass, then ran to Delilah and barked.

Her hand covered her fast-beating heart. Dropping her egg basket, she squatted beside her four-legged savior. "I'm sorry for scolding you."

Sheba's tongue hung out as Delilah gave her a thorough rub. Rising, she nodded toward Jed. "Brother Holt, I'm in your debt."

"Well, then, you could start by calling me Jed."

Refusal loomed in her mind, but how could she say no after he'd killed the vile thing? Using his Christian name didn't imply more than friendship, did it? Before she could change her mind, she faced him.

"All right, Jed." She smiled, then bit her lip. "It's inappropriate to call my employer by his Christian name."

"I'm not your employer—Lonnie is. No, Genny is." Jed gave her a teasing smile. "And second, I'd like to think we've become friends after all these months."

"Perhaps we have." Delilah tried his name again. "Jed."

"My Christian name is Jedidiah. Jed be my nickname."

"My mother doesn't approve of nicknames." How rude. Why did every little thought in her head pop out of her mouth? She glanced at his face. A smile rested there.

"We all got nicknames around here. How about I call you Dee?"

She turned it over in her mind. "I like it."

"Then Dee it is." Jed nodded his head in her direction, his hands full of a rifle and a snake carcass. He carried it behind the barn—she assumed, to bury the nasty thing.

Why had she not insisted on a nickname before? *Dee* didn't hold the same stigma of her given name. Mrs. Hollingsworth wouldn't have liked it. But Mother had been too afraid of being dismissed to disagree. *How did I not realize it before?* Poor mother, the older she got, the more she worried. *I need to start thinking for myself.* Being a servant, then a slave, appeared to have stolen her freedom of speech.

She released a deep sigh as a longing for her parents overwhelmed her. If only she could provide a home for them to take their ease. A new life, like her new name. She'd continue to save her wages, and perhaps next year, she could send for them. A year seemed like an eternity. The plan made her sad. But a happy thought manifested itself, a certain blond rancher with sparkling blue eyes and a dimpled smile framed in a short beard.

Dee. It sounded so nice when Jed said it. Her cheeks warmed. *Control your thoughts—they'll only lead to ruin. This sweet man deserves better.* A rock dropped in her stomach.

She reached for the egg basket and walked to the chicken coop. Her furry savior went back to the porch and stretched out in the sun. Ah, to be a dog. Then she recalled how Lemont had treated his hunting dog. On second thought, maybe not. Poor thing was brave enough to run off. She hoped he'd found a better home. For now, Delilah had, and if she kept her mind on the prospect of moving her parents and not on Jed …

Jed returned the shovel to the toolshed behind the barn. What was he thinking? *I should have pulled her away from the coop. Explained myself first.* The fear in her eyes had rebuked him. Then when she'd refused his assistance to rise, her eyes shone fire, bringing a desire to kiss away her temper. Her eye color had changed to emerald, dark and brooding. Jed wished she'd thrown herself in his arms, rather than make over Sheba. But he was kinda undesirable while holding a disgusting snake. At least the incident had changed her attitude. Agreeing to a nickname was a start. Jed grinned on his way toward the barn. Yep, a start.

Sheba raced to him.

"Good girl." Jed knelt and held her muzzle. "Thanks for protecting her." He stroked her head. "Keep watch over Dee." Sheba woofed.

Jed laughed, and the two continued their trek to the barn.

Dee. He repeated the nickname in his mind a few times while pitching fresh straw into the cow's stall. With every turn of the pitchfork, he hummed. The solitary task gave him time to think. Today his mind filled with the green-eyed beauty. *Maybe she'll feel less skittish using her new name. Then she might feel more comfortable around men.* His gut twisted, envisioning all the flirty glances those fellas would probably give her.

He rubbed the frown from his brow and strode to the stable. Sally's stall door was open. The hasp was broken, making it easy for the mare to let herself out. When did this happen? Dread overtook him as he headed toward the pasture. "No."

Sally stood calming grazing next to Soldier. If Dee became comfortable around men, she might choose someone else over him. Man, he had it bad, if every situation brought her to mind. Jed shook his head to clear it as he marched to the pasture fence and whistled for Sally. Both horses trotted over. "Well, Sally, are you trying to tell me I ain't getting a black foal from you?"

He gave them pieces of carrot. Drake cantered up from the far side of the pasture. Jed stroked the stallion's muzzle and gave him a carrot. Jed had stopped riding Sally after the thunderstorm. She would never have thrown him if she weren't nervous being in heat. The next day, they'd tried mating her to Drake, but she wouldn't have it. Jed had hoped she'd chosen the Morgan Quarter horse Lonnie had purchased recently. That'd be a more valuable match. Well, time would tell.

I should be mad the ornery plow horse is here, but then Dee wouldn't be either. He gave the huge horse another carrot. "Time for you to earn your keep, fella."

Jed jumped the pasture fence and grabbed Soldier's bridle and led him out of the pasture gate. "Gonzalez."

The Mexican trotted toward him. "Sí."

"This horse is only half broke. We need to get him ready to work in the hay fields. Best get a few of the other men to help."

Gonzalez nodded and walked Soldier toward the corral. The horse remained docile. The blacks whinnied and Soldier responded.

"Looks like the big ol' horse has found his herd." Jed chuckled as Lonnie joined him. "He don't let anyone but Gonzalez and Dee near him unless they have food."

Soldier bared his teeth when the men tried to put a blanket on him.

"Dee, is it now?" Lonnie grinned and cuffed his shoulder.

"Yeah." Jed looked away as his neck warmed.

"Maybe she'll consider the Holts her herd." Lonnie widened his smile and added, "And you her stallion."

Jed's face heated more, then he glared at his brother. "I think comparing her to a horse is downright insulting."

"Sorry. Reckon you're right." Lonnie's embarrassed nod settled Jed's urge to punch him. "It's past time you found a wife and started a family too."

"In God's time." Jed leaned against the corral fence, watching Gonzalez and Carter walk the big horse around in a circle.

"I think God brung you His choice." Lonnie turned his attention to the corral before adding, "We need to get some tack made for Soldier. What we got won't fit him."

"Tomorrow I plan to go to town to visit the reverend. I could head over to the livery and see to it then."

"Take Dee with ya." Lonnie winked—and Jed frowned.

Great, now I'm his new project. The fool won't let it go 'til he's finished the task. Enough was enough. "She ain't been to town since she first arrived. I don't think she'd cotton to goin' with me without Genny."

Lonnie pushed his hat toward the back of his head and crossed his arms. "We need supplies, and Genny won't be going to town until the boys are bigger. She's got a long list. I'll ask her to speak to Mrs. James."

The knowing look his brother gave him made Jed laugh. When they'd first arrived to claim their inheritance and discovered Genny living at the ranch, Jed had told Lonnie he should marry her.

Blizzards, Jed's sickness, and Lonnie's broken leg kept her around long enough for them to fall in love. They'd celebrate their fifth anniversary this winter.

Jed had often counseled people not to assume God would answer their prayers in the same way He did for someone else. Yet the first time he'd laid eyes on the soot-covered woman, he'd …

Lord, don't let me make a fool of myself if this ain't Your will. I don't want to hurt or frighten her. Please keep my heart until Ya want me to give it away.

"I'll plan on going tomorrow with or without Dee."

Even after the prayer, he hoped she'd come.

Chapter 14

Jed's chest tightened when Dee appeared on the porch in a new frock and bonnet, carrying a basket. The purple color—no, she'd referred to it as lavender—suited her. Jed set the brake, but before he could do the gentlemanly thing and help her up, she'd climbed aboard, arranged her skirts, and left ample space between them on the buckboard seat.

"Mornin', Dee." Jed offered a smile, which she returned. "Nice dress."

"Thank you."

He noticed the blush before she turned to watch the road.

"Did you bring the list?"

"Yes." She indicated the basket as she set it between them. "Genny needs some more bottles and nipples. The more we have clean, the faster we can tend to Robert. She said his nighttime feedings are problematic, going to the root cellar for the chilled goat's milk. We've been discussing how to make it easier."

Jed loved the lilt in her voice. "Problematic—I ain't heard that word used since my school days."

"I love words." Dee smiled, a faraway look in her eyes. "It's been a while since I've used my vocabulary. Lemont …" She glanced at her hands.

Beat it out of you. The thought angered Jed. "He didn't like your vocabulary?"

"Exactly." Her voice trembled for a moment, then gained strength. "He was illiterate, and it shamed him when I used words he didn't understand."

Silence fell between them as Dee smoothed the front of her skirt, then folded her hands in her lap. The wagon wheel hit a rut, toppling the basket and pushing him into her. He scooted back to his side of the buckboard, her face aflame as she righted the basket.

Jed gripped the reins and focused on the road ahead. "I don't mind how you talk. If you love words, use 'em, I say. Genny's smart. She was studyin' to be a nurse. Her knowledge comes in handy on the ranch."

"She said she's the midwife." The basket knocked against the bench as she repositioned it.

"The doc appreciates her help." Jed held the reins in one hand to resettle his Stetson on his head, then glanced her way.

Dee sighed and turned toward him, her bonnet catching the breeze and slipping away from her face. If they were sitting closer, he'd be tempted to kiss her.

"I appreciate all your family has done for me. You've all been so kind and understanding." She tugged her bonnet back in place and retied the ribbon to secure it against the breeze. "It's hard to explain." She smiled his way, then faced forward. "I'm reacquainting myself with who I was before I came here, before Lemont, before the fire. So many things I need to change."

You look perfect to me. I can't see anything needs changin'. Jed remained quiet, not wanting her openness evidenced by her confession to become guarded because of his compliment.

"I made a foolish decision when I answered the ad in the *Matrimonial News*."

The clip-clop of the horse's hooves almost drowned out her whispered admission.

"I was naïve thinking it was God's will for me. Apparently, I don't know God well enough to discern His will." Delilah's eyes glistened with unshed tears. "How do you know God's will, Brother Holt?"

Her more formal address forced him to put on his chaplain's hat. *Father, I need wisdom.*

"I reckon the best way to know is reading the Bible. I find much wisdom there. A verse in Ecclesiastes is a comfort when I mistake His will. He promises to make all things beautiful in His time. That's chapter three, verse eleven. I've missed the mark many times in my life. I got regrets. But He is a loving God. He promises to work things out for our good. And then Isaiah tells us God gives us 'beauty for ashes, the oil of joy for mourning, the garment of praise for the spirit of heaviness, that we might be the planting of the Lord.'" Jed glanced her way before continuing—her expression one of contemplation. "Knowing God can still use and restore me, no matter what, is comforting." Without a thought, he patted Dee's hand now resting on the basket between them. A trickle of warmth wiggled up his arm, startling him. Jerking away, he rested his hand on his leg. "I came back from the war broken and confused, and I still struggle. But God is there for me every day."

"I appreciate your words of counsel and your honesty." Her genuine smile drew him. Despite his resolve, he squeezed her hand. She didn't pull back. He ran his thumb over her knuckle, then released his hold slowly, savoring the feel of her long, slender fingers. He'd made her blush. *Stop.* She needed his counsel, not his affection.

"Dee, I'll be praying for ya. And if you need to talk, I'm a good listener."

Delilah relished the thought of Jed praying for her. So different from what other men offered to do for her. No. She brushed the comparison away so as not to soil his sincerity. She held her hands in her lap, caressing the one he'd held, still feeling the warmth of his touch. "Thank you, Jed."

She searched for a change of subject before things got awkward. Jed's presence no longer frightened her, but anything beyond friendship was too overwhelming. "I've brought something for Mrs.

Clemens and her baby. Genny's teaching me to sew."

"Last time I was in town, Mr. Clemens was busting his button, he's so proud of his beautiful daughter."

"Good to hear. Some men only want sons."

"Lonnie adores his girls."

"But now he has sons." Surely Lonnie's attitude would change, and his affection too.

"Won't make any difference. My ma only had boys. We wished often we had a sister. Genny's helped us be more genteel. If Lonnie only had girls, he'd not complain."

"What about you?" The question was out of her mouth before she could check it. A question reserved for courting couples, not friends. She turned her focus on the horses, grateful her bonnet hid her blush.

"I'd love daughters every bit as much as sons. I'll take whatever God will give me and be thankful. 'Course, I need a wife first. Waiting for God to provide her too."

Something in the tone of Jed's voice sent a sweet shiver through her. She felt his eyes on her, but she refused to glance his way. There was no way she would lead this man on.

"I love all the Holt children." Their sweet hugs and kisses brought her joy.

"You're good with them and a blessing to Genny."

Jed's encouragement served as a salve to her wounded spirit. Unworthiness whispered and settled like a rotted board in her heart. Her focus stayed on the horses, the rhythm of their gait calming her fluttering stomach.

"I'm grateful for the job. When the boys are older, I'll find another position so I can bring my parents here."

"You'd leave us?"

She drowned the growing attraction with the memory of what can happen if a man controls your life.

"I don't wish to be a housekeeper forever. I'm saving my wages in hopes of buying a house in town and perhaps opening a bakery."

The idea popped into her head and felt right. Was God giving her direction? It was certainly safer than being a mail-order bride. "I was going to ask Mrs. Clemens' thoughts on it. I brought scones I made for breakfast."

"What does Genny say?" Jed's expression was unreadable.

"She isn't ready for me to leave quite yet, but we've discussed various possibilities for my future. I can't impose on you further by bringing my parents to your home."

"You know they'd be welcome." Jed's bright smile sent a quaver through her.

"True, but they'd also feel obligated to work for you."

Jed nodded. Their wagon reached the edge of town, then headed toward the mercantile. "I'll leave you here to fill the list and have your visit with Mrs. Clemens. I got an appointment with the reverend and an order to place at the leather shop. It'll be at least an hour."

"Sounds perfect." She smiled and slid from the wagon without help, then noticed his frown. Did her unwillingness to let Jed assist her from the wagon cause him shame in town? Delilah glanced at those on the street around them to gauge what reaction they might have, then wiped sweaty palms down the side of her skirt and tried to read the man on the wagon.

Jed passed her the basket and tipped his hat. "See ya later."

The wagon headed down the street. Delilah stood there until he pulled in front of a whitewashed house near the church. Coming to her senses, she scurried inside the mercantile before Jed noticed her staring.

Chapter 15

Jed rapped on the parsonage door, then let himself in. "How are you, sir?" Jed placed his hat on the coat rack near the door.

Pain etched the minister's face as he rubbed his knee and offered a smile. "Come, sit." Reverend Logan indicated the chair beside him. "I'm fit as a fiddle with a broken string. It still plays, just a mite off-key."

"Your rheumatism acting up today?" Jed pulled the footstool closer to the reverend's chair.

The minister propped up his foot, then pointed toward the kitchen. "If you please, pour the coffee and slice Mrs. Bradshaw's cinnamon cake."

"She makes fine cakes." Jed placed a tray on the table between them.

They enjoyed their dessert while discussing trivial things. Their time together filled a void left by Jed's father's passing. Once the cake was consumed, Reverend Logan stroked his beard, a sure sign something serious was on his mind.

"Brother Holt, I'm not as young as I used to be. Tending to the growing church here in Cooperville is a challenge. You've been such a help to take on the visitation to the homesteaders and ranchers. I appreciate your faithfulness. I'm sure God is well-pleased."

Jed squirmed in his chair like a schoolboy who didn't know his recitation. The coffee sloshed in his cup. *Please, God. No.*

"I think it's time for you to take up my mantle. Pastor the church. The congregation respects you, and I'd preach occasionally, but mostly be retired." The satisfied look on his face was irritating.

Jed chewed his lip. "Reverend, I gotta respectfully decline. I made a promise to my brother before we came here. I convinced him to come. The Single Cross is our legacy. I won't go back on my word. Lonnie needs my help more'n ever with his growing family."

Silence filled the room, and Reverend Logan's disappointed expression hurt. Despite the guilt whispering in his ears, he wasn't backing down. "Forgive me. Can't you write the church council for a replacement?"

"I can." His resolute sigh made Jed cringe. *Here it comes.*

Reverend Logan swallowed the rest of his coffee, then frowned. "It takes time, months, even years, to find the proper replacement." His eyes had a faraway look. "When I came west from Pennsylvania some thirty years ago as a circuit rider, I never expected to start a church of my own." The minister pinned Jed with a stare, making him feel more like a low-down skunk than he already did. Jed focused on his boots. "I need to know the church is well-cared-for when I retire. I don't want to take the first candidate the council sends because I fear they won't send another. What if he doesn't suit the congregation?" He took a long breath.

Jed set his cold coffee on the table and crossed his legs, hoping to look relaxed.

"Brother Holt, I prayed long and hard. I had a dream you stepped up and took the call." The minister pierced him with a solemn look. Jed hated the man's tenacity when it was focused on him. "Pray about it, son. I'm sure God will confirm it."

"I'll pray." *The answer will still be no. Shoot, his own son's clergy.* If his son took over the church, Reverend Logan could see his grandchildren every day without worrying about train travel. No need mentioning this fact until he could find the courage to say no a second time. Reverend Logan could be a stubborn man.

"I'd expect no less." The minister's knowing smile accompanied by a raised eyebrow was a silent pronouncement of his well-honed wisdom. "Now, let's talk about your visitation route next week."

Jed pulled out a paper to compare notes with the minister. His mind was elsewhere, arguing with God.

Delilah's eyes took a moment to adjust to the dimmer interior of the store. Mr. Clemens stood behind the counter in the back. "Welcome, Mrs. James. Good to see ya."

She approached the cheerful proprietor with her list. "If you don't have everything, Mrs. Holt says to please order it."

"Sure 'nough. How are the twins?" He checked the list.

"Thriving. We're grateful for the doctor's goat milk recommendation for Robert. He was so tiny at birth. He'll be catching up to Peter in no time." She grinned.

"Sounds like you've gotten quite attached to them little ones." He started pulling items from his shelves as he talked.

"Yes, as if they were my own." Her cheeks warmed. How selfish. She clutched the basket. "How is your new daughter? I've a gift for her."

"Analisa is perfect, fat and rosy and the love of my life." Mr. Clemens chuckled. "Go on back while I fill your order."

"There are a few items I need to select first. Then I'll pay my call." Dee hurried to collect additional undergarments and a bolt of heavy cotton to cut into diapers. The twins were going through two dozen or more diapers a day. Gathering a few more notions, she added them to the stack on the counter. "Do you have Bibles?"

"What kind do ya fancy?"

"A big family Bible. Mine burned in the fire." Not the house fire, but the book burning Lemont had two months into their marriage.

"Sorry to hear it. I'll need to order one. It should be here next month. Will that suit?"

"Fine. What others do you have?" Jed's talk of Scripture made her curious.

Mr. Clemens directed her to the Bibles, and she selected a small one to fit in her pocket when she went to church. She hadn't gone since she left Baltimore. Perhaps it was time. "How much is this?"

"A dollar." Mr. Clemens took her money and wrapped the Bible in brown paper and placed it with the Holts' order.

"Call me when Brother Holt arrives, if you'd be so kind." Delilah retrieved her basket and slipped into the Clemens' living quarters to find Polly burping her daughter.

"What a wonderful surprise. Take a seat." Polly Clemens' bright smile belied the dark rings under her eyes. "My mother left last week, and I've been longing for female company."

"I brought a gift for the baby and scones for you." Delilah admired the babe in her mother's arms, then placed the basket on the table.

Polly handed Analisa to her and reached in the basket. The sweet smell of newborn clung to the child. Delilah stroked her silky red hair and kissed her forehead. "Such a pretty thing."

"We are so happy to finally start a family. After five years, I was beginning to think the Almighty had forsaken us. Analisa is His blessing." Polly opened the basket. Unfolding the brown paper wrapping, she stroked the handmade gown. "So beautiful, thank you."

"It's not much." Delilah apologized, focusing on the irregular hem.

"I love the embroidered ducks and flowers along the collar and hem. Such a thoughtful gift." She held the garment to her cheek, seeming to enjoy its softness, then folded it and put it in a drawer. "I'll save it for church."

Delilah smiled. "I'm honored you think my small gift so precious."

"If God blesses us with more babies, they'll have a church gown fit for royalty." Delilah focused on the sweet child in her arms rather than the praise. Any more kind words and she'd embarrass herself with tears.

"Now, let's try these scones. I've strawberry jam my mother made before she left. I'll fix a pot of tea while you rock my baby to sleep."

Delilah happily complied, but the mother returned too soon to retrieve her baby and place her in her crib. "Now, tell me the news from the Holt ranch." She poured tea and took a nibble of a scone. "Oh, these are heavenly."

"You like them?" Pleasure washed over Delilah.

Polly added jam to her scone.

"So wonderful." She took a sip of tea, set her cup on its saucer, and snapped her fingers. "I have an idea. Why not bring baked goods for me to market? The ready-made shirts sell well to the single gents in the area. I bet they'd love your baking. When Lonnie picked up supplies last month, he raved about your tarts and cookies." She took another scone, a satisfied look on her face. "What do you think?"

Joy circled through Delilah. Could she make a success of it? *Yes* was on her lips, but she held it back. "I need to discuss this with Genny. My commitment to her comes first." She calculated what supplies she'd need. "First, I have to save the funds for ingredients." Polly nodded her understanding. "If I decide to do it and Genny is agreeable …"

"You could bring baked goods once a month or send them along with whoever buys supplies. If it goes as well as I believe it will, then bring them in every week."

Polly's encouragement excited her. *Maybe I can be independent and bring Mother and Papa here sooner.* That would be a dream come true. "I'll let you know."

"Your carriage awaits," Mr. Clemens called through the door.

Delilah gave her friend a hug. "When I decide the time is right, I'll send baking along."

Polly smiled. "I look forward to it."

The hour had flown by. In the store, Jed waited at the counter. Delilah smiled and resisted the urge to push back the few locks of blond hair resting on his forehead. Nodding at the pile of goods stacked on the edge of the counter, she found her voice. "I'm ready."

Jed circled his hat in his hands, then paused and pushed the stray hair back. He turned to Mr. Clemens. "I forgot to add ammunition and a new hammer to the list." He glanced her way. "I'm sorry for calling you from your visit to make ya wait."

"I'll take these smaller packages to the wagon." Delilah grabbed the bundles and hurried to the door, away from the awkwardness. His sweet look and contrition sent butterflies flitting in her stomach. The fresh air cooled her emotions and her cheeks as she placed her items in the wagon bed.

Two men passed on the sidewalk. The odor in the air turned her stomach.

"Why, if it ain't delicious Delilah." The lecherous voice sent fear skittering down her spine. George Hawkins spit chaw on the ground near her feet. Bertram Foley, his shadow, stood grinning beside him. Both had been among Lemont's moonshine customers.

She glanced toward the mercantile and stepped closer to the wagon.

"Fancy meetin' ya here." Bertram winked at her.

"Pretty dress. Didn't mourn ol' Lemont very long, did ya?" George grabbed her arm. She tried to jerk away from the tight grip. "I took over his moonshine customers." He sniffed her hair. "We been playing cards at our spread. Sure could use a fine-looking gal like you to pour our drinks."

"Unhand me." She kept her voice low and tried to pull free again. Pain shot through her arm.

"A lonely widow like you gots needs." Bertram leered and leaned in.

A lump formed in her throat. She fought her rising terror and kicked George in the shin, hoping to free herself.

"Ain't very ladylike." Anger flashed in his eyes as his grip tightened. "Looks like ya need to be taught manners." George's vile breath surrounded her. Nausea rose in her throat.

Never would another man teach her a lesson. She struggled to free herself. Would any of the gathering spectators help her?

"Yeah, manners." Bertram took her other arm. She tugged against them despite nails sinking into her flesh.

"Step away from the lady." The menacing voice startled her, and the cock of Jed's gun made the men holding her freeze. Would he blame her for causing a ruckus in the middle of the street?

Jed's blue eyes darkened under hooded lids. "Are y'all deaf or blame fools?"

The men released her, and she bolted toward Jed. He stayed focused on the dolts.

"We was just givin' our condolences to the widow here." George pointed with his chin toward her. "We was real good friends with her late husband."

"Yeah, thought she might need looking after," Bertram said.

Jed wrapped his arm around her shoulder. She leaned into him. His strong, muscular presence melted some of the fear.

"Real neighborly of you gents." Jed spoke through gritted teeth. He signaled with his Colt for them to move along. "But I got it handled, thank you just the same."

"Didn't take ya too long to find a new bed to lie in." George leered at her, then spit, his chaw landing on Jed's boot. He didn't so much as flinch.

The ruffians tipped their hats her way. She stared at the ground as humiliation radiated through her.

"If I ever see you near Mrs. James again, I'll shoot you on sight." Her pulse quickened, and she glanced at Jed. His jawline was tight under his beard. He pulled her closer. His heart seemed to match the rhythm of hers. Was he afraid too?

Bertram rested his palm on his gun, cocking his head toward Jed. "We'll see."

Mr. Clemens stepped out on the porch with his rifle raised. A few of the men standing near drew theirs.

George's eyes widened, then he shook his head at Bertram and smiled at Jed. "We didn't mean no harm. Have a good day." The two left, arguing as they headed to their horses.

Mr. Clemens stepped toward them. "Are ya all right, Mrs. James?"

"Yes." It was all she could say without bursting into tears. The townsfolk turned back to their own business. Her knees wobbled. Did everyone think she had lain with Brother Holt?

Jed holstered his gun and released her. "You don't look all right." He touched her arm, and she winced. "I'm taking you to the doc."

"It's not necessary." How often had Lemont done far worse, and her wounds had mended on their own? Delilah wanted to flee before any rumors spread to ruin Brother Holt's reputation.

"You go along, Mrs. James. I'm sorry I didn't see those two fellas earlier." Mr. Clemens rested his rifle across his arm. "I've banned them from my store because of a remark they made to my wife."

Delilah struggled to find her voice. Not since her father had taken a switch to the stable boy for bothering her had she been defended so nobly. "Thank you both. I'll be fine."

"Nope, I'm taking you to the doc." Jed placed her hand in the crook of his arm. Not to embarrass him, she left it there even though every fiber of her being wanted to put space between them. His tender look made things more awkward. Better to go along than make a scene.

"I'll load your wagon while you're gone," Mr. Clemens called after them.

She glanced at Jed. "I've never seen a pastor pull a gun on someone."

"It ain't loaded."

"Why not?" The thought of George drawing his weapon on Jed sent a shiver through her.

"I don't want to do something I'll regret. Knowin' it ain't loaded keeps me using my words."

"But you shot the snake."

"Yep, we leave loaded rifles handy for such things on the ranch. But I've run into a few fools in town like those fellas." He leaned in. "Don't tell my secret." Jed's whisper tickled her ear, sending an unfamiliar yet pleasant sensation through her. "Just so ya know, the rifle under the wagon seat is loaded."

Jed sat ramrod straight in the waiting room chair while the doctor examined Delilah. *If I'd walked her out of the store, them no-account lowlifes wouldn't dare approach her.*

Nurse Dune scurried out the front door. Jed jumped from his seat as Dee and the doc came out of the examining room. "The bruising will heal." Dr. Murdoch smiled at her, sending jealous alarms through Jed.

"I told Brother Holt I didn't need a doctor." Dee nodded in Jed's direction. He refused to apologize, preferring to be absolutely sure.

The doctor gestured toward the door. "I've sent my nurse to the sheriff to have those miscreants thrown in jail for battery."

"You can do that?" Dee's question surprised Jed.

The physician's brows descended. "Mistreating women is not tolerated here. Mrs. James, I heard your late husband was abusive. If you'd have come to me, I'd have seen him jailed."

"He told me no court convicts a husband for keeping his wife in line." Dee's green eyes appeared olive with her confession.

"He lied." Dr. Murdoch huffed.

"Any man who beats his wife ain't a man. He's a coward." Jed stretched his fingers to keep them from fisting. Punching a wall was out of the question, so he counted to ten. "Mrs. James, I promise, no man will lay a hand on you again." He tipped his hat to the doctor. "Send me the bill."

"No, you can't." Dee's eyes widened.

"No charge." Dr. Murdoch nodded her way.

She stared between them for a moment.

"Thank you for your kindness." Delilah extended her hand. The doc shook it and smiled. "If you need anything, you can call on me."

Jed wanted to jerk the doc's hand off hers. Instead, he tipped his hat. "Much obliged." The doc released her hand to shake his.

"Yes, I'm in your debt." Dee gave the doctor a smile, and Jed led her out the door and to the wagon at a trot. "Are we late?"

Jed slowed his pace. "Sorry. Lot on my mind." He hoped she didn't ask what those things were. 'Cause he couldn't make up a good enough lie to cover his jealous schoolboy thoughts right now.

Chapter 16

"What were you lookin' at him for?" Lemont growled and gripped her shoulder as she trembled. "If I told you once, I've told you a thousand times, a married woman don't look at no other men."

"I had to clean the wound on his head." Delilah had held her breath to complete the task Lemont had requested. The injured man reeked of manure and body odor. "How was I supposed to clean the blood without looking at him?"

He glared at her. She'd dared to challenge him. The smell of moonshine stronger than usual should have been a warning.

"Don't get smart with me, woman." Lemont slapped her hard, her head snapped back, and she grabbed a kitchen chair to keep from stumbling. He reached for his belt.

"Please, I promise to obey."

The belt buckle came down hard on her back. With every vile accusation, another welt formed on her body.

Delilah muffled a scream with her bedsheet as she woke from the nightmare. *God, why can't I be at peace now he's gone?*

He claimed she was damaged goods. Lemont had been the one to damage her. Delilah pushed the quilt aside with trembling hands and sat on the edge of the bed. Then she reached for the new Bible on her bedside table, holding it to her chest while the nightmare was still fresh. Even looking up Jed's Bible references before bed hadn't calmed her mind. How could any beauty come from the ashes of the horror she'd lived through? Maybe for her, those verses didn't apply.

The dawn shadows flitted around her room as the wind rattled the shutters. She made her bed and dressed.

"No need trying to sleep anymore." She spoke to her reflection in the mirror over the washstand. There'd been no mirrors in Lemont's home. The water in the washbasin had offered a primitive reflection to examine her bruises and cuts, the memory raw as she touched her cheek. "No bruises on my face from a nightmare."

The smell of coffee greeted her as she neared the main house. "I didn't think I was late." Delilah paused at the door. "What are you doing here?"

"Stoking the fire." Jed placed the coffeepot on the stove. "Gonzalez and Carter took turns raising the roof with their snoring." He stepped to the cupboard, retrieving two cups. "If I can get to sleep afore they do, I don't notice the snoring. Last night, I had a lot on my mind."

"Me too." She took a chair at the table and allowed Jed to pour her coffee. Tea was her preferred beverage unless her sleep was robbed. "Thank you."

His sweet smile made her uncomfortable after her nightmare. How could one explain the dread those dreams stirred? She focused on adding sugar and cream to her coffee.

"What was on your mind last night?" Delilah asked first, hoping he'd forget she'd mention her poor sleep.

"When we went to town, I visited Reverend Logan. We usually discuss who I should visit on my visitation rounds. Before we got started, he offered me the pastorate of the church. His health isn't the best." Jed sipped his brew, then stared into his cup before continuing. "I declined."

"Why?" The man was surely as gifted a speaker as he was a counselor.

He frowned, then answered in almost a whisper. "I promised my brother we'd build this ranch together. We lost our spread in Texas. We lost our whole family. He's all I got. I won't abandon him."

"Have you discussed it with your brother?" She took a tentative sip of coffee. The hot liquid burned her tongue—a just punishment for nosing in his business.

"A promise is a promise. Holt men don't break their promises." Jed's jaw tightened as he reached for his cup.

Delilah rose and pressed her hand to his shoulder a moment before stepping to the cupboard, forgetting why she stood there. Butterflies beat in her stomach at her brazenness. Why'd she touched the man? She swallowed hard.

"Keeping a promise is fine, but sometimes things change." Her father had promised to send her to finishing school, but the cost was far more than Papa imagined. What her parents had saved wasn't enough. Everything else that made up their life belonged to the Hollingsworths.

"Unless God tells me otherwise, I'm not discussing it with Lonnie. I'd appreciate if you didn't either. It's a closed subject."

She nodded. "I need to gather the eggs before breakfast."

"Let me help." Jed grabbed the egg basket from the pantry.

"That's unnecessary." She tried to take the basket from him.

"I know." He held firm. "But you do so much. Let me help."

She looked away before she read too much in his eyes. "All right." No need causing a fuss.

Jed led the way. The hens squawked at the unaccustomed hand searching for eggs. "Ouch!"

She chuckled as he shook his hand. "Clarabelle needs to be shooed off her nest before you check. The others don't mind."

"You've named the chickens." Jed shook his head.

"Jilly named her. If she ends up in my cooking pot, don't let on." Delilah gathered a few more eggs from the other hens. "My mother forbade me to name the poultry. But I named the bunnies, and when they ended up on the menu, it devastated me."

The sun began to light the sky as Jed carried the basket to the house. Her chest tightened when she noticed the cowhands staring at them from the bunkhouse. Delilah picked up her pace and entered the cabin first. The nightmare replayed in her mind. She pressed her hand on her chest. Her late husband would not haunt her from the grave. Lifting a bowl from the shelf, she took the basket from Jed.

"Something the matter?" Jed stood behind her, his masculine presence unnerving.

"No." She stepped away from him.

"You raced by me like a varmint was after ya." Jed hung up his hat, then stepped close again. "The men always stand near the door drinking coffee, waiting for breakfast."

How did he know what she was thinking?

"They'll probably tease me about doing women's work. They don't mean any harm."

"I'm sorry." Delilah's whispered tone matched her plea in her dream. She sliced bread, trying to ignore the outdoor scent of the man standing too close.

"Their teasing don't bother me." Jed chuckled.

She didn't join in his laughter.

Jed observed Dee from his place at the table. She prepared a plate for Birdie before filling her own. Her countenance was more relaxed than it'd been earlier.

Snores hadn't kept him awake. Rather, a prompting to come to the house early had roused him from a sound sleep. He'd mulled over the conversation with Reverend Logan. And he'd hoped that sharing his burden would prompt her to reveal hers. But even though the rings under her frightened eyes emphasized her need to do just that, she stayed mute on the subject.

Jed had sat with many men terrified by dreams of war. Some shared their troubles and others sat quiet. His fear of thunderstorms seemed trivial compared to their visions of the lifeless eyes of the men they'd killed in the name of war.

Lonnie nudged his shoulder. "Where you at?"

Jed shook his head.

"I said we need to start branding." Lonnie poked him again.

Jed scowled and nudged him back. His face warmed when Dee stared at them. Sometimes Lonnie was downright childish. He took a sip of his cooling coffee before picking up the conversation. "I think we got a few more cows hiding on the far south pasture. I figure four."

"Probably find newborn calves too." Lonnie rose and smiled Dee's way. "Fine grub. Thank you."

"I'm right behind you." Jed rose, not bothering to finish his coffee. "Thanks for cooking for us."

Her smile stopped him in his tracks. *A fella be blessed seeing that smile across the table every day.* He ran to catch up with his brother before he spoke his thoughts out loud.

Carter joined them as they rode after the strays, Sheba keeping pace with Jed's horse.

Jed ruminated over the pastor's question and Dee's comment. Had things changed since he made his promise to Lonnie? He'd been the one to insist they ranch. Lonnie'd been hiding with his scars in the Colorado mountains. Ranching was in his blood, but he'd lost his passion. Jed was broken, too, after his time as a prisoner of war. The brothers had found healing through ranching. And married life had brought back the Lonnie he'd known before the war.

People assumed because he'd been a chaplain, he had a special connection with God. There was no way he could shepherd a flock when fear chased him with every thunderclap.

"Hey, Jed." Lonnie moved his horse alongside Jed's. "When Mrs. Richardson came by yesterday to see the babies, she told Genny the pastor wants to retire."

"Yeah, he told me." Jed looked across the pasture, avoiding eye contact.

"He offer the job to you?" Lonnie kept Drake moving at the same pace with Jed's mount.

"What makes you think that?" Jed wished his twin couldn't read his thoughts.

"'Cause you're ordained, went to seminary, and been a chaplain." Lonnie stared at him. "Makes you the best qualified."

"I ain't interested." Jed's jaw twitched. "He'll write denomination headquarters for a replacement. Did you know his son is a pastor back in Philadelphia? Because he can't travel, he should ask his son to take the pulpit. Then he could see his grandkids every day. I think he feels obligated to ask me."

"You know lyin's a sin." Lonnie whistled and Drake broke into a trot.

If his brother was teasing, it wasn't funny. Jed had wrestled the question of ministry for the last five years and felt a peace walking the line between ranching and assisting the pastor. He signaled his mount to match Drake's stride.

After a few minutes, the men slowed their horses, and Jed adjusted his hat. "I can't see myself ever taking a pulpit. In the army, I counseled men, not preached to 'em. I was fulfilling my calling when I ministered one on one." Speaking it out loud made it feel right. "I ain't breakin' my promise to you."

Lonnie remained silent as they continued searching for the cattle.

Finally, Jed spotted four cows grazing near the north pasture pond. "I found 'em."

They rode toward the cattle. Soon the four new mommas and their babies ran back toward the herd with Sheba barking at their heels. The story of the good shepherd leaving his flock to look for the one lost sheep played in Jed's mind. It reminded him of Dee, the woman who'd lost her way. *Now that's a far more pleasant thought than Reverend Logan's request. Life with her on this ranch, I can envision.* But fairly soon, he'd need to address the pastor's question. *Lord, help him understand.*

Chapter 17

Dee stretched her back after picking rows of green beans. "How do you manage this every year?" She'd never tended a vegetable garden. Her papa's job focused on flowers and shrubs and creating beautiful places to reflect as one walked the grounds.

Genny smiled at Jilly and Molly playing tea party with Birdie in the shade of the only tree in the yard. Their attempts at picking tomatoes had needed a diversion so the women could harvest in peace.

"Dee, it took a lot of trial and error." The family had adopted her new nickname, and the rightness of it refreshed her soul. Maybe she'd change her last name too. Trial and error defined her struggle to find herself again.

"I'm amazed at the amount of food you've grown." Dee gazed at the areas beyond the garden where a hayfield spread toward the prairie. The garden lay about thirty feet from the backdoor of the ranch house and was double the width. "My papa will find this new land a challenge. Lemont tried planting corn, but it barely produced enough for his moonshine."

Genny grew squash at the base of corn. Cucumber vines interlaced with bean plants, and carrots wrestled beets for space.

"True. Farmers have it harder than ranchers in Kansas. My family needs healthy food, so I make the effort. The first couple years, the garden yielded very little. A neighbor taught me how to fertilize and irrigate it. Did you know coffee grounds are good for soil?"

"I had no idea." Dee began picking cucumbers. "This garden might feed more than your family."

"I sell some of my canned produce to the mercantile. Right now, I send fresh items."

"Genny, I want your opinion on something. Polly wants to sell my baked goods in her mercantile." She waited, gauging Genny's expression.

"I think it's a wonderful idea." Her genuine smile encouraged Delilah to continue.

"At first, only once a month. Then if the sales are good, every week. Polly thinks it will do as well as her ready-made clothes."

"You should share your wonderful gift with the world." Genny paused and turned toward the sound of a crying infant. They had left the windows open to let a breeze into the house. "Peter's awake. Can you finish this and keep an eye on the girls?"

"Of course. How do you know it's Peter?"

"His cry is different from Robert's. Listen and you'll see." Genny ran to the house.

Dee finished filling their baskets with produce and set them near the door. Birdie's delightful laughter caught her attention. The child was covered in mud, and her sisters were smearing more on her.

"What on earth?" Dee lifted her skirt and marched toward them. "Stop this instant."

Jilly and Molly froze in place, their hands filled with mud. Jilly stared at her. "Momma lets us make mud pies."

"I doubt she intends for Birdie to be covered in mud pie."

"Birdie's the blackbirds baked in the pie." Molly patted her handful of mud on her little sister.

She squelched a laugh and attempted a scowl. "Wait here and do not put any more mud on your sister." She quickly retrieved a bucket from the shed. "Come along, girls."

They followed her to the nearby stream. Dee filled the bucket and poured it over Birdie's head. She giggled. "Again."

She continued to pour water on the girls until most of the mud was washed away. "Your mother won't be happy you've ruined your frocks."

"What's a flock?" Molly asked, then placed her clean fingers in her mouth.

"A frock is a dress." She inspected each child. A muddy hue stained the garments. *What will Genny think of me when she sees the results of my carelessness?* Shame made her snap, "You've ruined your dresses." When did she start sounding like her mother?

The girls tromped toward the house, wailing.

A sigh escaped as she shook away her irritation. Together they entered the house. Before she could stop them, they ran to their mother, dripping water across the floor. Dee grabbed a towel and began wiping their tracks, waiting for a rebuke from Genny.

"We sorry, Momma." Jilly flung herself at her mother's knees as she sat in the rocker feeding Robert.

"Sorry, Momma," Molly wailed and sat beside Jilly.

Birdie muttered something unintelligible.

Genny glanced Dee's way. "Did they wander off to the river?"

"No, they tried to bake Birdie in a mud pie." Her face warmed as she sopped up the puddles with a towel. "I'm sorry I didn't notice the tea party turned into mud."

"I'm not surprised. These girls love playing in mud." She turned to her daughters and frowned. "Lucky for you, Miss Dee washed you off right away. You should be ashamed of making extra work for her."

The girls' heads drooped.

Genny placed Robert in the crib with his brother. "Let's put on fresh clothes. If I catch you playing in the mud again, you won't be allowed outside for a week."

Once the girls were presentable, the women began cleaning the vegetables. Genny made no comment about her incompetency. Dee let out a breath.

Genny turned to her. "Do you know an interesting way to cook squash so the girls will eat it?"

"Yes, ma'am, squash bread, and I recall a pie recipe, and if you cut it very tiny, they won't notice it prepared in soup." Dee appreciated being asked her thoughts. It'd been too long since she was free to share them.

Genny hugged her shoulder. "Wonderful. After we make tonight's dessert, why don't you get started baking for the mercantile?"

Had she heard right? "But we're so busy."

"We will always be busy. Just do it. I'm not an invalid, and I've got my routine for managing the children." Genny pointed at the pantry. "See what we have for your baking."

"I'll pay you for the ingredients, then I'll buy my own." How long would it be before she could send for her parents?

"Consider today an investment in your future." Genny brought apples to the table.

"You are much too kind." She sniffed and refused to let the stupid tears fall as she perused the pantry. When would she be the strong, confident woman she had been before she made her foolish decision to marry a stranger? Perhaps after her baking endeavor was a success.

They worked together making apple pies. Dee kept one eye on the girls, who sat sedately playing with their dolls in the corner. Would the girls behave for their mother so she could bake? She poured the prepared filling in the bottom of the pie crust, then added a top crust and pinched the edges, creating a fluted pattern.

"I think it's time to talk Lonnie into building a summer kitchen." Genny popped the pies in the oven.

"I'm sorry I keep it so hot in the house when I bake." Another expense because of her. First her cabin and now a summer kitchen. "Perhaps we should wait until cooler weather for me to start this business venture. I don't want to put you out."

"The men's eyes light up every time they eat your baking. I doubt it will be hard to convince my husband. We've done well the last few years, and a summer kitchen would be a welcome addition. Mrs. McLaughlin says canning in her summer kitchen allows the house to stay so much cooler."

"That makes sense, I suppose." If the venture failed, the summer kitchen still benefited the Holts.

"I've been begging him for one the last few years. Now that we have a wonderful baker working for us, Lonnie has no more excuses not to build it." Genny cleared the table and wiped off the remnants of the pie-making. "It's ready for you to get to work."

"Oh, how I wish I still had the recipes Mother copied for me. I've memorized my favorites, though." Dee grabbed a paper and pencil and went back to the pantry. Looking at the ingredients stirred her memory. Pies, tarts, sweet breads, and various cake recipes filled her mental list, making her homesick for her parents.

She spent the afternoon creating delicious things. Sweat covered her as the room filled with wonderful smells and additional heat. When she finished, the effort produced less than she expected. *It'll be years before I can send for my parents.*

"My, my, what are we celebrating today?" Lonnie sauntered toward the table, followed by Jed.

"Stop." Genny blocked the table. "Don't touch. It's not for you."

"Then who's it for?" Lonnie playfully tried to get around Genny.

"The mercantile." Dee waited to see their response. "Polly suggested I bring some to sell." Would Lonnie tell her no?

"I'm jealous. They get this, and we get none." Lonnie pouted and laughed.

"Those pies on the sideboard are for us." Genny hugged her husband.

"I'm proud of you, Miss Dee." Lonnie leaned in to smell the pies.

When was the last time anyone was proud of her? Tears pooled in her eyes, and she quickly dabbed them with the hem of her apron. The Holts' encouragement gave her courage to give this idea a chance. She turned to Jed.

"I'm mighty proud too." Despite the proper words, his tone somehow sounded less sincere.

She twisted her apron in her fingers. "Thank you."

"Would you mind continuing to set some of your baking by for us?" Jed grinned and elbowed his brother. "Otherwise, the temptation will overtake us, and you'll have nothing to sell." His voice was lighter, but his eyes seemed sad. How odd. Did he not like the idea?

Maybe he thought she'd fail—like she'd failed her marriage. Like she'd failed her parents. She stiffened her back and faced Jed. His deep blue eyes never left her face. There was no judgment there. Dee released the breath she'd held. If her plan worked, her parents would soon be taking their ease rather than waiting on others.

Jed forked clean hay into Sally's stall. Sheba watched from a safe distance to avoid horse hooves. "How you doing, Sally?" His mare was due to foal soon. "I hope you're going to give me a thoroughbred and not some large oaf of a colt." Jed glared at Soldier in the farthest stall.

The plow horse brought Dee to mind—and her new venture. "I hope it fails." Jed continued talking to his horse while he brushed her. "Ain't nice, I know."

If she leaves the ranch, Doc or one of the bachelors from the church might come courting. God, she ain't ready. What if she favors someone who turns out like Lemont?

Sally puffed her cheeks and blew out air. "I know you're anxious. Your young'un will be here soon." He stroked her nose and pulled a carrot from his pocket. Sally took it daintily from his palm. "I'm jealous over nothing. She ain't interested in marriage."

Jed took a deep breath, filling his lungs with the familiar scent of horses and hay. *Lord, I gotta let this go and take things day by day.*

The more time spent with Dee, the deeper the attraction. If he could convince Lonnie to let him go on the cattle drive, the few months apart might clear his head, and the distance should quench the attraction.

He went in search of his brother and found him leaning on the corral fence watching Gonzalez work with one of the new, unbroken horses they'd acquired. "Take your time. The mare will be more obedient if you use less force," Lonnie yelled. "Your way makes a horse more prone to bite, and if'n it gets scared and runs off, it won't come back."

Before Lonnie could take over the training, Jed joined him at the fence.

"Lonnie." He nodded for his brother to follow him behind the barn. "I want to go on the cattle drive this year. You can leave one of the newer hires to mind the ranch."

"We've gone over this. I don't trust nobody else to care for the ranch and my family. 'Sides, you know how sensitive your lungs are."

"Not anymore. I'm healthy as that plow horse." Jed crossed his arms. "I'm a good tracker."

"I'm better, and ya know it." Lonnie turned to leave. Jed grabbed his arm.

"We've owned this ranch for five years, and I haven't been on one cattle drive." The sharpness of his tone matched his desperation.

"The day you stop rolling up in a ball during a thunderstorm is the day I'll consider it." Lonnie jerked his arm away.

"You calling me a coward?" Jed stepped closer, his jaw tight.

"That's foolish talk." Lonnie faced him.

"So now I'm a fool." Jed stepped toe-to-toe, fists at his side.

Lonnie glared at Jed. "What in the Sam Hill is wrong with you?" Underneath the hard stare was compassion. "When you're done being loco, we'll talk."

His brother would have fired any of the cowhands for such insolence.

Jed whistled for Sheba, and they walked beside the creek running through their property. Walking gave him time to clear his head. When his pa had made him help with cattle drives, he'd hated every aspect of it. Lying on the ground, wearing the same clothes every day, crossing rivers … and the list went on. He'd bear it all if it helped get Dee off his mind.

Sheba lay beside him on the riverbank. The lapping of the water on the shore soothed his anxious thoughts. The dog barked, interrupting his solace as a horse and rider approached.

Lonnie dismounted. "Well, are you still loco?"

"No. It was stupid." Jed rose and extended his hand. "Forgive me."

Lonnie shook it. "Always."

The two stared at one another for a few heartbeats before Lonnie broke the silence. "Now what's eatin' ya?"

Jed looked toward the river, watching the gentle flow of the current.

"Might it be a dark-haired, green-eyed gal?" There was no jest in his question.

"Maybe." Jed turned to his brother. "I'm tryin' to be a friend and help Dee move forward. But the more time I spend with her, I find I want more than friendship … something she don't want."

"She mentioned the bakery, and you don't cotton to the idea."

"I think too much." Jed sighed and pulled the brim down on his hat. "If she lived in town, all the fellas would be coming around and …"

"You got jealous like I done when you were just friends with Genny." Lonnie chuckled.

"I reckon." A rock formed in his chest. Was it as big as the one Lonnie had when he fought his feelings for Genny? "Dee's not looking for a husband anytime soon, maybe never." The two walked along the river, Lonnie leading his horse and Sheba racing ahead. "She isn't ready to live in town. I think she's having nightmares. The dark circles under her eyes show she's not sleeping."

"Maybe she's losin' sleep over you." Lonnie grinned and Jed harrumphed.

"Now who's being foolish?" Jed picked up a pebble and skipped it across the creek.

"I ain't taking you on the cattle drive. 'Sides, you hate 'em." Lonnie smiled. "I reckon you'll need to take the advice you gave me. When the moment is right, tell her how you feel. You'll have lots of time when I take the cattle to Abilene."

"Oh Lord, deliver me." Jed sighed.

Sheba chased a rabbit before heading back his way. Jed squatted to scratch her head, then stared at his brother.

"And whatever you decide about pastoring, I'll support you." Lonnie mounted his horse and headed toward home.

Jed stared at the river, then scanned the surrounding land. "I reckon I'm likely to get answers while he's gone. If it's a broken heart, not sure I'm up for it."

Lonnie's earlier words, that someday, doing the right thing was goin' be the wrong thing, echoed in his mind. Which of his dilemmas was the wrong thing? He could live without being a parson, couldn't he? If he never got too close to Dee, maybe he could live without her too. And if the pastor's disappointed look stopped haunting him, maybe he could rest in his decision to ranch alongside his brother.

Jed groaned, then started the trek back to the house. Dark clouds were forming to the east. Was there time to make it home before the showers started? He whistled for Sheba. The dog kept pace with him. Suppressed panic caused him to walk faster. *I can't humiliate myself in front of Dee.* He wanted to be her protector, not a coward.

He broke into a run until his chest burned. Gasping for air, he ran faster, hoping to make it home before the clap of thunder. He pushed the thought of curling in a ball from his mind. "Please God, help me get home before the storm starts."

Chapter 18

The calm pitter-patter of rain beat against the windows. The hour or so alone each day while Genny and the children napped was golden. Rainy days had been her favorite times as a child. She and Papa would stand at the window and watch the flowers enjoy the shower. He had regaled her with stories of the fairies who lived beneath the leaves of the plants in the gardens. Her favorite story involved a brave fairy named Lily Rose who overcame her fears of the wiggly worms. Papa always had a new fairy story to tell when she needed to be brave or reassured. Maybe when the girls woke from their nap, she'd tell them a Fairy Lily Rose story.

Pleasant memories vanished when Jed burst through the door, his face pale and lips trembling. Dee stared at him but made no comment. Having one's anxiety pointed out was humiliating. "You're soaked. Don't move or you'll drip water all over the clean floor." She hoped her obvious and trivial remarks gave him time to calm. "I'll bring you a quilt." His fear evoked a far different reaction than Lemont's. Instead of angry outbursts and Rebel yells, this man looked almost childlike.

Dee crept into Genny's room and took a quilt from the trunk. Mother and babies rested peacefully. She tiptoed through the door and stepped toward Jed. He stood shirtless in his stocking feet as he dried his hair with a towel near the washstand. Her face warmed at his half-dressed appearance. Staring at his muscular form a bit longer than was proper quickened her pulse. She cleared her throat.

"Here you go." Dee forced a light tone. "My, my, what a downpour." The urge to wrap her arms around him shook her to her core. The ever-present unruly curl lay across his forehead.

Jed wrapped himself in the quilt. "Sorry for the wet floor." A visible tremor shook him, and his pupils remained wide. This was more than a childhood fear.

"Don't worry, I'll wipe it up. You get warm." Dee observed him as she cleaned up the water with several rags. The summer rain hadn't cooled the house near enough after her baking to put a chill in the air. Jed's trembling continued as he clutched the quilt. "I'll fetch coffee."

Jed nodded, then sat in the rocker, trying to pull the panic back inside. Dee brought him coffee. He willed the shaking in his hands to cease.

"Careful, it's hot." Her gentle tone comforted him. She stepped away and mopped up the remainder of the water. Jed inhaled the familiar aroma, blew on the coffee, and then took a sip. The simple act gave him a different focus than the day terrors in his head.

Dee hummed as she mopped, the melody familiar and calming. "What's that song?"

"An old Irish lullaby my mother used to sing to me. I sing it to the boys."

"Sing it for me." Jed searched his memory for the words.

"I sing it in Gaelic, but I remember the English translation." Dee blushed and cleared her throat. Her mop kept the tempo as her sweet contralto filled the cabin.

On the wings of the wind o'er the dark rolling deep
Angels are coming to watch o'er thy sleep
Angels are coming to watch over thee
So list to the wind coming over the sea.

Hear the wind blow love, hear the wind blow
Lean your head over and hear the wind blow
Hear the wind blow love, hear the wind blow
Hang your head over and hear the wind blow.

Jed let the words flow over him. The melody brought a new memory, replacing the horrors of the prison camp. Ma had sung him to sleep with those very words as a little shaver. A tear escaped, trailing down his cheek. He wiped it away. The stiff grip of fear on his body loosened as the trembling ceased. But a fog of dread encompassed him as he rocked.

Dee seemed to sense his struggle. She took up a different tune. "Amazing Grace, how sweet the sound …" Her sweet voice calmed him more than any other.

He latched onto the tune and found his own voice. Each stanza released more of the dread. Each verse became a prayer. By the end of the hymn, peace rested on him.

"You've a beautiful voice." Her blush warmed Jed inside. "How many more hymns do you know?"

"My voice is average. I know a few hymns by rote. I can read music and play most anything on a piano." Dee set her mop aside and looked out the window. "Appears the rain is past. I wonder what Fairy Lily Rose is up to?"

Jed joined her at the window. "Now I'm curious. My granny used to tell me fairy stories."

"But my fairy is real."

"Oh, is it now?" Jed could appreciate the silly banter now that his body had relaxed and the terror had passed. "Can I meet your fairy?"

"Only if you look really hard. She's hiding out there under the cucumber leaves. She's shy and fearful." Dee smiled his way. "My papa claimed to see her every day, and he entertained me with tales of her exploits. Rainy days remind me of Papa."

Jed turned from the window and gazed at her. "That's when he'd spin his yarns?"

"Indeed." Dee's eyes shone. "When I sing, it makes me miss my parents so much."

"Your voice is a wonderful gift from God." An idea formed in his mind.

"Perhaps." She continued to stare out the window while her cheeks reddened. "I'm glad I feel like singing again." She graced him with a sweet smile.

"I was wondering if you'd go with me next week on my visitation rounds." A glint of fear crossed her face. He should've bit his tongue.

"Whatever for?" Dee stepped away from the window, the moment of camaraderie broken.

"I was thinkin', your fine voice would add so much to the little worship service we have at the Fenwick ranch. They got a few neighbors close by, bringing the number to about twenty. I read the Word, preach a little, and lead a song service. I'm ordained, so I also perform weddings."

The quilt added to the heat in the room and the warmth going up his neck. As sweat trickled down his bare back, Jed considered grabbing one of Lonnie's shirts. "Josie Fenwick brought her ma's piano when she married. She doesn't play, so we got no accompaniment. I'm sure she'd be mighty blessed if someone played her ma's piano again."

Dee twisted a loose tendril of hair. "Why would she bring a piano way out here if she doesn't play?"

"She's hoping someone will teach her young'uns."

"Do they want to play?"

"She got all boys, so I don't know."

Dee pursed her lips in the cute way she did before answering, as if she were forming the words in her mouth before letting them loose on her lovely lips. "It sounds as though you think women are the only ones who play the piano." Her endearing harrumph almost made him laugh. "I'll have you know, my grandfather and uncle played—which is why my mother wanted lessons for me."

"Why didn't she learn?" Jed mentally shook himself. It wasn't the pastor in him asking the question. No, it was the nervous schoolboy still living in his subconscious.

"She claims a tin ear." Dee grinned. "Do I need to define tin ear?"

"No, ma'am, my little brother Willy had one of them."

Before Jed had a chance to restate his request, Lonnie came in carrying two chickens.

"Fool things decided the worms were better outside the coop. Sheba started to chase them back. When they resisted, she grabbed them by the neck and provided us with dinner."

"Bet she was right proud of herself." Jed chuckled.

Dee took the wet chickens and dried them with a towel.

Lonnie went to the bedroom and returned with one of his shirts for Jed. "Looks like my gals are wakin' up, but the boys are still asleep." He nodded Dee's way. "I appreciate you being here. Genny gets plum wore out."

"I'm happy to lighten the burden." Dee turned her gaze to the chickens as Jed pulled on the shirt.

"Wait. I'll pluck those for ya." Jed wasn't ready to venture away from the ranch until the sky was cloudless again.

"I dislike dressing fowls, so thank you very kindly." Dee's smile made him happy he'd volunteered.

The bedroom door opened, and Genny emerged, carrying Birdie on her hip, the toddler leaning on her shoulder. She glared at him and Lonnie. "I hope someone plans on telling me how my best layers were selected for dinner."

Jed grabbed the birds and made himself scarce. Plucking chickens delayed the lecture she'd give him once she learned Sheba's part. Jed made a mental note to purchase a few new laying hens from Josie Fenwick. Later, he'd again ask Dee to come with him on visitation. A trip in the opposite direction of her old home might be good for her. *Maybe, Lord, she'll like playing the piano for the service so much, she'll make it a regular thing.*

He hummed the lullaby as he prepared the birds for cooking.

Chapter 19

The next day, after Jed returned from his pastoral visits to some local homesteads, he strolled toward Dee. She leaned over a wooden tub and scrubbed a diaper on the washboard. He slowed his pace, not wanting her to notice him quite yet. She pushed damp hair out of her face with her wrist, fingers dripping. He cleared his throat.

She looked his way and smiled. "Jed, you're back earlier than we expected."

Was she pleased? Had she counted the minutes like Genny did when his brother was gone? *Jed Holt, get them foolish thoughts outta yer head.* "I didn't visit Morton Jennings today. That ol' man can talk both yer ears off." Jed laughed and then stood there.

"What is it?" Dee tossed the diaper into the rinse tub and straightened, stretching the kinks from her back. "You've got that look. Tell me what's on your mind."

She crossed her arms and pursed her lips, bringing a familiar, contented warmth to his chest. She understood his look. Was it a friend thing or something more? When Genny said it to Lonnie, it didn't always end well. He gathered his gumption and gave her a smile.

"I never got an answer yesterday."

"About what?" Dee's confused expression might mean she hadn't fretted over his request.

"Accompanying me tomorrow on my visitation."

"It would be very inappropriate for me to travel with you

unchaperoned."

Ah, but her response wasn't an outright no.

He brightened. "Nurse Dune is coming along. The town of Last Chance doesn't have a doc." Jed waited for her to uncross her arms. "Each of you being widows, traveling together is proper. I didn't want gossip to ruin either of your reputations."

Dee relaxed her arms. "I see you have worked out the details." She chewed her lower lip before answering. "I suppose one has to start living life again. How long will we be gone?"

Jed remained calm on the outside while his mind shouted with satisfaction. "Nurse Dune will meet us here shortly after sunrise, then we'll travel all day and camp for the night. Reach the Fenwick ranch about noon the next day. We'll stay a few days, then be back in time for Sunday service."

"I'm not sure Genny can spare me so long." Dee wiped her hands on her apron.

"Lonnie thought it was a dandy idea." He signaled to his brother, who was leaving the stable.

Lonnie sauntered up and smiled at Dee. "Are you talkin' about playin' for your service?"

"Yep." Jed's confidence rose with Lonnie by his side.

"A right good idea."

"But Genny ..." Dee's gaze wandered to the woman in question, bent over in her garden.

"Ask her yourself." He called for his sister-in-law to come over. She approached, wiping her hands on her apron, flashing them a questioning smile. "Genny, Dee here is debating whether she should leave you to go to the Fenwicks'."

"I think it's a wonderful idea." Genny reached over and took Dee's hands. "Don't look at me like I'll faint away from overwork. I can manage for a few days without you."

"Very well, I will." Dee's smile brightened her eyes, causing heat to radiate through Jed's chest.

"Dee, I got something for you." Lonnie reached into his pocket and pulled out an envelope. "Carter gave me this when he came back from town a few minutes ago. Mrs. Clemens told him to give this to you. It's payment for your baked goods."

Opening the envelope, she gasped. "Oh my, this is much too much." Dee shoved the cash back inside and hugged it to herself. "I never imagine simple baked goods could be so profitable."

Dee stared at the group, her eyes moist, then fled to her cabin. Jed started to follow.

"Leave her be, Jed." Genny smiled. "Let her have her happy cry in private."

"Happy cry?" Jed shook his head. "When she's done, can you help her pack what's needed for the trip?" His pulsed raced at the prospect of her accompanying him. But did it mean she wanted to spend time with him? The envelope full of cash spoke of a future bakery, in town, away from him. *Reckon I got to make this trip count for somethin', or …* He didn't want to mull over the alternative.

Jed had the wagon hitched and Nurse Dune had her things loaded when Dee joined them. The damp, early morning air brought a respite from the heat. The mist that covered the sunrise didn't dull the excitement in Dee's voice. "Genny told me what to bring. I hope I'm not forgetting anything." She perused the contents in the wagon bed.

"I have something for you, Mrs. James." Nurse Dune handed her a brown-paper-wrapped package. "Jed mentioned you would be playing piano, so I thought …"

Dee untied the string and pulled back the paper. "Sheet music and a hymn book, how wonderful." Her nervousness over playing faded knowing she had musical notes to guide her. "Thank you, Nurse Dune."

"Please call me Edna." She offered her hand.

"Call me Dee." She shook it and smiled at her new friend. "I've never played for strangers."

"I haven't traveled to the sick since the war." Edna allowed Jed to help her onto the back bench of the wagon.

Rather than make things awkward for him in Edna's presence, Dee allowed him to help her too. His hand in hers sent warmth up her arm. Thankfully, her bonnet shielded her smile. Once aboard, she turned so she could see Edna. "Tell me how you got started as a nurse." The idea of a woman having a career appealed to her.

"I never wanted to be a nurse." Edna sighed. "I went to medical school to be a doctor, graduated top of my class. I met my husband there. We married, and I was his nurse until he died."

"I'm sorry to hear of your loss." Trying to face Edna while the wagon rumbled down the road was awkward. "Jed, stop the wagon, please."

"What's wrong?" Jed's furrowed brow nearly made her change her mind.

"Please." She gave him her best smile. He pulled the wagon to a stop. "I'd like to sit with Edna."

"Of course." A frown furrowed Jed's brow before he smiled and helped her to the back bench. "All settled?"

She nodded and Jed got the wagon back on the road. "Let me know if you gals need a break, and I'll stop for ya." Jed leaned forward, focusing on the road ahead.

Dee stared at Jed's back. His broad shoulders pulled against his shirt. His physique was … Before a blush formed, she focused on Edna. "May I ask why you aren't a doctor now?"

"My husband allowed me to practice medicine as his equal. But society frowns on women doctors. When John left for the war, the community let me treat them in his absence. Then he died of dysentery at the army hospital. Because the real doctor wasn't returning, the town hired a new doctor. With no other recourse, I served in a Union hospital and sometimes on the field after the battles. Although my skills were equal to those of the male doctors, I was relegated to nurse's status. Then I answered Dr. Murdoch's advertisement for a nurse."

"Surely, there are places needing doctors now. Jed said Last Chance doesn't have one." A door would open for her new friend. She'd gotten right in the fray of things and not given up.

"It's why I agreed to come along. Besides, the doctor is sweet on Emma Long. This way, he can ask her to assist in the office while I am away. If she works out well, he'll probably court her. Then I'll be out of a job."

"Why hasn't he courted *you*?" While a man might not court a woman based solely on her medical skills, Edna's golden hair and sweet disposition added to her list of qualifications. She seemed the perfect choice.

"There are two reasons Dr. Murdoch has no interest in me. I am ten years his senior and a better doctor." She laughed and leaned forward. "Brother Holt, don't you dare tell Dr. Murdoch what I said."

"No, ma'am, your secret's safe with me." Jed chuckled.

The sun shone bright overhead when they stopped for lunch. Jed chose a place with water and grazing for the horses and a shade tree where they could enjoy their picnic. The ladies began laying out the repast on a blanket, while Jed got the horses staked in the grass.

He glanced toward Dee. Her graceful steps as she carried a jar of lemonade from the wagon held his attention. She'd filled out with all the wholesome meals. Her favorite lavender dress complimented her form. As he approached, her laughter made his heart sing. Her face glowed with happiness. Nothing was more beautiful. .

Jed sat on the edge of the blanket opposite Dee. "Mighty fine vittles, ladies." He took a fried chicken leg and placed it on his plate, along with some pickles, an apple, and strawberries.

"Edna brought the chicken. Genny packed ingredients to prepare supper." Dee smiled, then popped a berry in her mouth. Oh, those lips looked so inviting. He turned toward his plate and searched his mind for something to clear the thought. Psalm 1 came to mind. *The steps of a good man are ordered by the Lord, and he delighteth in his way.*

Edna and Dee chatted like magpies about recipes, sewing, and other womanly pursuits. The more he gazed on Dee, the more his mind pulled Scripture to the forefront for meditation. When he recalled the line *my love, my fair one* from the Song of Solomon, he leapt up with heat rising to his ears.

"Is everything all right?" Dee's hand went to her throat as she stared at him wide-eyed.

"Fine. Everything's fine. No worries, ladies. I need to stretch my legs afore we climb back in the wagon." He included Edna with a sweep of his gaze, tipping his hat. "I'll take the horses to the river for a long drink."

He patted the mares and led them to the river. "This ain't as easy as I figured," he remarked to Prissy. She didn't seem to understand his thoughts like Sally. Yet nuzzling the mare helped relax his confused thoughts. He pulled the other horse toward Prissy and led them to the river's edge, keeping an eye out for any danger while they drank.

All right, I got to take advantage of this situation without showing my hand. I gotta be a gentleman but … watch for signs she might favor me, I guess.

Jed sighed as he hitched up the horses again. The women joined him and loaded the basket into the wagon. "Come on, ladies, we're burnin' daylight."

The two women climbed onto the back bench unassisted. "We're ready." Dee leaned toward Edna. Jed released the brake and the horses moved out. The whispered exchange of the women niggled him. Edna giggled and Dee joined in. No way was he going to ask what they was laughing about. Maybe it was him.

Jed let out a long sigh.

Jed whistled to his horses to pick up the pace as they neared the Fenwick Ranch. The large house, surrounded by a variety of whitewashed outbuildings, came into view. Ranch hands meandered about doing various chores. Edna had taken over teaching Dee the skills needed for camping, and the two had risen with the sun, anxious to continue their journey. Despite being a city girl, Dee took everything in stride. He'd have liked her to be a little helpless so he could rescue her. Now that they were at the ranch, every minute of his time would be full of meeting the people's needs.

Sid Fenwick, a tall, well-built rancher, sauntered up as the two women climbed down from the wagon. "Reverend Holt, a pleasure to welcome you back to the Fenwick Oaks Ranch. And who are these lovely ladies?"

"Sid, this is Doc Murdoch's nurse, Edna Dune, and Dee James. She's agreed to play the piano for our service."

"It's a pleasure to meet you, Miss James and Miss Dune."

"It's Mrs. James. I'm a widow." Dee's face pinked with the explanation.

"And I'm Dr. Dune." Edna shook his hand. "I've been assisting Dr. Murdoch until I find a suitable place to set up a practice."

"Welcome, Doc. We got a passel of patients for you this week. I hope you don't mind starting right away. One of my men done broke his arm."

"Let me get my bag, and I'll be right along." Edna's eyes shone even though her words were matter-of-fact.

A tiny blonde woman heavy with child approached. "Welcome, ladies, I'm Josie Fenwick. I'm so happy you've come. The men will get your things, and I'll show you to your room.

"Dr. Dune here is goin' to take a look at Clay." Sid took his wife's hand. "Are ya all right?"

"Now a doctor is here, I'm elated." She gave Dee a sweet smile. "While the doctor looks at Clay, we can get acquainted."

Jed was left standing next to the wagon like a fifth man in a four-square dance. He shrugged the feeling away and joined the others in emptying the wagon. Putting on his parson's smile, he greeted the men while his mind traveled to the dark-haired beauty who'd disappeared into the house. Well, he'd better get his mind on godly matters, or his preachin' would sound like gibberish.

Chapter 20

Dee sat at the upright piano in the corner of the huge parlor of the Fenwick home, and Josie stood nearby, wringing her hands. "I'm afraid it's terribly out of tune."

"Let me be the judge of that." Dee moved her seat so she was the proper distance from the keys. Excitement coursed through her at the prospect of producing a melody. She tested out the sound with a couple of chords. "It is, but I'd not call it terrible. What would you like me to play?"

"Do you know 'A Mighty Fortress is our God'?"

"Yes." She flipped through the hymnal, and Josie stepped up to hold it open for her.

The hymn flowed from her fingers like a soothing balm. She sang and Josie's alto joined her. When they finished the hymn, they moved on to others.

A male voice spoke from the doorway. "I thought I heard angels singing."

Dee's necked warmed at Jed's compliment. She schooled her face, not wanting to let her feelings show. "Thank you, Brother Holt." She kept her tone neutral.

"Is the doctor available now?" Josie rubbed her belly.

"Yes, ma'am, she and Sid are headed this way." Jed hung his hat on a peg and placed his Bible on the side table next to the piano. "He sent me ahead to ask about coffee."

"Yes and cake." Josie waddled into the kitchen, leaving Dee alone with Jed.

"Did you enjoy playing?" He drew closer.

"I'm rusty, but yes." Rising, Dee closed the hymnal, then hastened to place it on the table next to Jed's Bible. "I'll go help Mrs. Fenwick." She strode toward the kitchen.

Jed stared at the two books on the table—Dee's hymnal next to his Bible. Why didn't she leave it on the piano? Was it a sign? Of course not. What grown man got such silly notions? He'd do better to take note of the way she'd scurried away from him like a frightened hare. No, not frightened. He frowned, turning his hat in his hands. Nervous.

A few minutes later, Dee came from the kitchen with a platter of refreshments. Josie followed, carrying a tray of dishes.

"Let me help you." Jed started toward Dee but instead took Mrs. Fenwick's tray as she struggled to carry it in her condition. It was the right thing to do.

"Thank you kindly, Reverend Holt." Josie smiled at him as he placed it on the table.

"Dee, would you show Reverend Holt his room?" Josie gave them both a strange smile, then began setting the table.

"Follow me. Josie showed me our rooms when we first arrived." Dee led him up the hall to the room the Fenwicks always gave him. No mystery there. He could've admitted he knew the way, but what fun was that?

"Thank you, Dee. Where is your room?"

"Across the hall." Dee opened the door to her room to reveal pink floral wallpaper. "It's lovely." She shut the door and smiled his way. "I'm sure you'll be most comfortable in a more masculine room."

Jed chuckled. "I suppose simple with no frills might be considered masculine." *Sparse* was a better description. "Shall we join the others?" He started to offer his arm, but Dee walked ahead of him.

They found their seats at the dining table, Dee's profile expressionless. Jed pulled out her chair. Edna and the Fenwicks were already seated. Jed took the empty chair next to Dee.

They enjoyed the delicious applesauce cake.

"This is wonderful." Dee seemed to savor her next bite. "If you would be so kind as to give me the recipe, I'd be appreciative."

"I got the recipe from a neighbor back in Ohio. I had to figure out what ingredient she left out. You know you can't give your best secrets away, or everyone else's will be as good as yours." Josie smirked, then sipped her coffee.

"I find that tradition frustrating." Dee pursed her lips. "If I paid you for the recipe, could I persuade you to not leave out an ingredient?"

Josie's brow raised. Had Dee insulted their hostess?

Edna spoke up. "Did you know Dee is a wonderful baker? She is hoping to open a shop. Your applesauce cake would be an excellent addition."

"Dee, I applaud you." Josie clapped twice and smiled. "I will gift you with the recipe if you will bake something special for tomorrow night's dinner. Our foreman, Sam, is marryin' his Hannah, and we always have a celebratory meal when one of our own marries."

"I'd be honored." Dee's smile lit up the room.

Jed basked in her joy. Baking seemed to feed her soul, but a troubling question lingered. *Lord, how am I going to win her heart if she's in town and I'm on the ranch?*

Chapter 21

"You may kiss the bride." Jed closed his Bible as the couple exchanged more than a peck on the lips. The cowhands let out a whoop. Once the kiss ended, everyone crowded around to wish the couple well. The men slapped Sam on the back and kissed the bride's cheek.

Jed stepped away, his chest tight. He'd performed over a dozen weddings since coming to Kansas. This was the first time he experienced envy.

Dee walked past him with a tray of finger sandwiches. *God, is she the one?* She held herself erect and nodded when men spoke to her. Kinda like her first day working on the ranch.

"Need any help?" Jed approached her from behind, her lavender scent enticing.

"Ahh." Dee jumped, then struggled to keep the tray from toppling as she caught her breath. She spun to face him. "I assume scaring me amuses you." Her frown made him take a step back. She placed the tray on the table.

"No ma'am, it don't. Honest." Jed held up his palm as if taking an oath. "I swear."

"Next time, don't stand so close." She crossed her arms and glared. "The refreshments are ready. Your services are not needed."

Jed nodded. Humiliated, he walked away and found a place to stand near the door from where he could watch as men approached

Dee with a smile, and each was dismissed. A few followed her, trying to strike up a conversation. She ignored them. *I reckon too many men trying to make her acquaintance irritates her.* Good to see it wasn't only him.

Mrs. Fenwick stood before the bounteous table. "Everyone." She clapped like a school marm to get the guests' attention. When the room was quiet, she continued. "I've asked Reverend Holt to say a blessing. Then the newlyweds will start the food line. Once you've filled your plate, take a spot at the tables. Mrs. James and I will fill your cups once you are seated."

Jed stepped next to Mrs. Fenwick. "Let's bow our heads." The room stilled. Jed glanced Dee's way. She stood beside a table with three coffeepots, her head bowed. "Heavenly Father, we thank you for this ..." He continued with the rote prayer while his mind turned over ways to make Dee comfortable. "In Jesus' name. Amen."

The line expanded behind Sam and Hannah. Jed held back, preferring to be at the end instead of in the middle of the hungry lot, even if he got less food. It reminded him too much of his time in the prison camp. Crammed into tight lines to receive gruel and bug-infested bread.

While the guests settled at their places, he observed Dee. Once the coffee was served, Jed filled his plate and waited for her to do the same. "Kinda crowded in here. Wanna sit on the porch?"

Dee nodded. She found a tray to carry their plates along with coffee and utensils. Outside, he sat on the top step, leaving space for the tray between them.

"This was a wonderful idea. It is so hot and stuffy in the house." Dee offered a smile.

Jed placed his plate on his lap, diverting his gaze from her beautiful face and his one-sided attraction. "I hope this ain't been too much for ya."

Dee stirred her mashed potatoes with her fork, then glanced his way. "I owe you an apology. My tone was rude earlier. I'm sorry."

"Apology accepted." Jed smiled, then continued to eat—the

flavors extra good because Dee wasn't mad at him anymore.

"It's just …" Dee paused, her eyes focusing to the left, a clear indication she was struggling.

"No need to explain," Jed said between bites.

"Stop." Dee scowled.

"Stop what?" Jed set his fork on his half-empty plate and gave her his full attention.

"I know you think you're sparing me pain. Sometimes I don't want to talk." A bird soared overhead. "But sometimes talking helps me fly like that bird."

"All right. I'm listenin'." Jed continued eating, nodding for her to proceed.

"Thank you." Dee cleared her throat. "This trip *has* been a challenge for me. The men here aren't like those at Single Cross."

"I hope no one bothered ya." Heat rushed through him. So much for being the unbiased listener.

"No, they were just a bit too forward and rowdy for my taste." Dee's smile soothed his irritation. "Sadly, I could tell they were using their best manners." She ran her hands up her arms.

Jed longed to hold her, comfort her. Instead, he kept eating the now-tasteless food. "Did they scare ya?" What a stupid question. He gulped his coffee while mentally chastising himself.

"No … maybe … maybe a little. I kept thinking of Lemont and his horrid friends. But then I pictured my parents and friends at one of our holiday gatherings, and I served those strangers with the same care." Dee placed her plate on the tray, her food barely touched, and stood. "Shall we walk?"

Putting aside his own meal, Jed extended his elbow, and Dee placed her hand on his arm without hesitation. Her touch relaxed by measure the farther they walked from the house.

"Thank you for comin' with me." Jed held her gaze. "Your playing and singing added so much to the service. Several people said it felt like a real church."

"How kind of them. But I'm very rusty, and the piano needed

tuning. Then you asked me to lead the singing. I made so many mistakes." She stared at her feet.

"I didn't notice."

"Oh, I did. But thankfully, no one mentioned them." Dee paused before the gate. "It'll be dark soon."

Jed stood next to her, staring at the sky exploding in a riot of color. He rested his hands on the gate. She placed one of hers on his. Heart lurching, he turned his palm over and grasped her long, soft fingers. Her face was inches from his. A breeze brushed a tendril of her hair across his cheek. If she turned his way, he could steal a kiss.

"Jed, I feel safe with you." Dee continued to watch the sky while his heart took flight with the confession. "Thank you for being so kind to me. Your whole family has helped me feel human again." She released his hand without looking his way, and a sweet sigh escaped her lips. "I'm brave when I'm with you." She faced him. The green in her eyes matched the grass when the sunset kissed it. The moment passed, and she fixed her gaze heavenward again.

Words escaped him as he stared at her lovely profile, the sinking sun highlighting her black hair with orange. He wanted to say he'd keep her safe always, but he didn't have the right. For now, he'd do what he could to mend her fearful heart.

"Let's head back." Dee sighed and smiled his way.

Jed offered his elbow, wishing they could have stayed there forever. She walked closer to him—like a woman who was enjoying his company. Contentment flowed over Jed as the late summer sun cast long shadows. When they reached the house, Edna waited for them on the porch.

She looked like the cat who'd gotten the mouse. "I've exciting news."

Dee retrieved the tray from the step. "Tell us."

"I'm staying in Last Chance. They've asked me to be their doctor." Edna's face glowed.

Dee handed Jed the tray and gave her friend a hug. "I am so happy for you."

"Last night in the tent, you told me to embrace who I am and speak it boldly." Edna put her arm around Dee's waist, and the two women went inside, leaving Jed to carry the tray.

I feel safe with you, circled in his thoughts. Safe was a good start. *How do I get Dee to think of me as more'n safe? Want to marry me?* The thought didn't surprise him. Marrying Dee was what he wanted. Not because she could sing and play piano, nor because she gave wise counsel to her friend, or kept a spotless house and loved children—all the things that made a good wife. He wanted to marry Dee because she made him feel whole. She'd sang to him when the thunderstorm had stolen his confidence. No judgment. She'd held his hand and confided in him. Surely, it was just a matter of time before she loved him … before she needed him … before she stopped being afraid of getting close. But it could possibly take a mighty long time.

Chapter 22

Dee rose from the piano after the second day's service and moved to the back of the group of worshippers gathered in the Fenwicks' home. Attendees who sat with rapt attention, waiting for Jed to speak, filled the makeshift benches and chairs. The anticipation was palpable. It reminded her of a D. L. Moody meeting she'd attended before leaving Baltimore. These people wanted to hear Jed preach.

He stood near the piano. "Let us pray." His strong baritone voice filled the room. "Heavenly Father, we come to You today grateful. Grateful for Your many blessings and for this opportunity to hear what You've gotta say to us. Help me share Your message. In Jesus' name. Amen."

Jed stroked his short beard and smiled at the group before opening his Bible. "A certain man went out to sow …"

His voice soothed Dee's wounded soul. As she had when listening to Mr. Moody, she felt God's presence as Jed explained the parable. No one moved. The silence in the room created a holy assembly. Was she the seed which fell on shallow ground, and when the hard times came, she withered? That's how she'd felt while imprisoned in her marriage to Lemont, wilted and dried up. Not once did she pray for his salvation. Not once did she cry out to God for courage or wisdom. Instead, she'd begged for deliverance, and when it didn't come, she'd allowed herself to grovel in self-pity, and her faith had dwindled to barely a spark. Shame had claimed her.

God forgive me. I let him die.

Tears filled her eyes as the memory of Lemont's screams echoed in her mind. Maybe she could have saved him. She could have gone back inside and tried. Perishing with him would have … what? Made her a martyr? At least she could have run to the well and attempted to douse the fire. Instead she'd run, screaming, to the barn. *God forgive me.*

"I'm ending this sermon with a simple question." Jed paused and looked around the room. Dee stared at the floor and crossed her arms, not wanting to make eye contact. "Which seed are ya? If you're blooming, then thank God for His faithfulness to ya. If you've let hard times steal what God gave ya, here is your time to repent." He spread his arms out wide. A cowboy and two women came forward.

Dee wanted to go, but her legs were wooden. She'd come to play music and lead singing. What would people think if she went forward? Dee dashed the tears from her face and stepped into the kitchen as the time of prayer continued. She dipped a cloth in the water pitcher and dabbed her eyes.

"Now Mrs. James will come and lead us in a closing hymn." Jed's announcement sent her scurrying to the piano.

Dee took a breath, pasting on a smile as her heart pounded. She fumbled through "How Firm a Foundation," letting Jed lead out, not daring to sing with guilt choking her soul.

Once the service was over, tables replaced benches, and they served the final meal.

"I'll be mighty glad to get home," Jed remarked as he sat beside her with his overfull plate.

"You might need a nap after you eat all that." Dee hoped to keep him off the subject of his sermon.

"If I feel tired, I'll let you drive the wagon while I nap." Jed chuckled.

"I can rise to the occasion. Papa let me drive the wagon when I went with him on errands." Dee took a bite of Josie's potato salad and relaxed with this safer conversation.

"What else don't I know about you?" Jed smiled her way.

His gaze seemed to zero in on her need. She shifted her weight on the bench, and the heavy content of her dress pocket knocked against her leg.

"I have a pistol in my pocket." Dee kept her voice light. "I keep it under my pillow."

"Is it to keep me in line on the way home?" Jed whispered, leaning much too close.

"Of course." Dee sipped her coffee, then lowered her lashes and grinned, whispering back. "I must protect my reputation since Edna has decided to stay."

Jed straightened as his face paled. "If you feel uncomfortable, I can leave you here until Miss—I mean, Dr.—Dune returns to Coopersville for her things."

The genuine offer was tempting. "That won't be necessary." Dee's face heated, and she resisted fanning it. "You're a man of the cloth." *Far above me in every way.* "What is the world coming to if you can't trust a preacher?"

"Yesterday, you said you felt safe with me."

Why had she been so bold? She'd keep reminding herself he was a minister. It was only a day. They had separate tents and … she couldn't abandon Genny. Or the pay she received for housekeeping.

"You've come a long way, Dee, from the day I found you holed up in your barn."

Mr. Fenwick, seated on the other side of Jed, pulled him into a conversation about horses, leaving Dee to ponder the changes in her life.

It was true. When Jed had found her in the barn, she was terrified and wary of men. Time at the Holts' had helped her find some of what she'd lost. Dee watched Jed interact with those seated at their table. His relaxed countenance radiated peace, and a bit of it settled in her heart. What a change from her first fearful encounter with him.

Once the meal was over, the people gathered around their wagon to offer a prayer for safe travels. No one remarked about the inappropriateness of their traveling alone. *They must think highly of the preacher.* Jed assisted her into the wagon. His callused hand wrapped around her own, sending tingles into her middle. She pulled free as soon as she settled on the bench. Attraction only led to heartache. She smiled at Josie, and Edna waved farewell as Jed took the reins and whistled to his horses.

Silence lengthened between them, increasingly uncomfortable. Jed almost turned the wagon around, saying they'd stay until Dr. Dune was ready to collect her things. But then she spoke.

"I've been curious about something."

A knot formed in Jed's throat. Was she going to ask about his feelings for her? Dee pointed to the horses. "Why train horses with a whistle?"

Jed's shoulders relaxed. "Lonnie claims it'll save your life." He almost laughed at her confused look. "A whistle carries a distance. If you fall from your horse or need a quick getaway, then a whistle gets your mount to ya faster."

"What if you can't whistle?"

"Well, I reckon it won't do much good then. We Holts are expert whistlers." Jed enjoyed the twinkle in her eye. "Another thing, we use different whistles to give the horse directions. A short note is *get up*. Two short notes is …" He demonstrated, and the horses sped up. "And one long one …" The horses slowed to a stop. A short note, and the horses started again.

"Amazing." Dee clapped. "I imagine no one can steal your horses."

"That's another reason." Jed nodded her way. "The whistle has to be identical."

"What if I whistle now?" Dee's two notes mimicked his and sent the horses into a gallop. Her eyes widened and she screeched.

Jed pulled on the reins and whistled once. They stopped so quick the wagon lurched. Jed's head snapped and he yelped. "What a blame foolish thing to do. I thought you had better sense." He scowled at

Dee, but the sight of her clutching her chest brought immediate repentance. "You all right?"

"Yes." Her face reddened as she straightened in her seat and added a few extra inches between them. "And I agree. It was foolish."

"I apologize for name callin'." Jed cleared his throat. "I got caught off guard." He offered a smile. "You were trying out your whistlin' skills, is all."

Dee shook her head and let out a breath. "It was still foolish."

Doggone it. Now he'd gone and made her feel bad again. He hadn't missed her weeping during his sermon. It had taken every vestige of concentration to continue when he wanted to race to her side and comfort her.

"Tell me something." Dee's voice quavered as the wagon hit a rut.

"Sorry." Jed fixed his eyes on the road lest the rough terrain pitch them out of the wagon because of his distraction.

The bench rocked as she repositioned herself farther away from him. "Would it be hard to train Soldier to obey whistles?"

"He's already responding to the chow whistle." Jed laughed at the memory of the big horse racing his thoroughbreds to the barn.

"The *what* whistle?" Dee turned his way. Funny, how so many common words for him weren't used in Baltimore.

"The one that signals we got food for 'em."

"Then you can teach an old horse new things." Dee laughed. Keeping her smiling wasn't so hard after all.

"Not always. Soldier refuses to come for any other reason, no matter whether I whistle or call to him." Jed found the big brute stubborn and uncooperative most times.

"Lemont was cruel to the horse. Soldier stepped on his foot once and got a beating for his trouble. I don't understand why he didn't rebel and kick Lemont senseless." There was a bitter edge to her words.

"Well, Soldier has bitten a few men and kicked the dickens out of his stable door when he first arrived."

"Oh my." She blushed and looked at her hands in her lap.

"Once he got used to things, he calmed." Jed kept his focus forward so as not to add to her embarrassment. She had nothing to do with Soldier's disposition. "We figured out, no one approaches him from the left."

"Lemont always flicked his bullwhip at him on that side." Dee shuddered and diverted her gaze to the passing scenery.

"We figured as much. He's got deep scars on his flank." As much as that pained him, Jed wished even more that he could have stopped Lemont before Dee's scars ran deep. "Like you, he's adjusted nicely and seems to be trusting us all more."

"Hmm, I've never been compared to a horse." The breeze loosened a tendril of hair from her tight bun at the back of her neck. "But you are right. I'm more comfortable now, being away from the place I hated."

"You know, the land is yours now." Jed wished he'd left the subject alone when a flash of horror filled her face before she turned away.

"I don't want it. I never want to step foot on Lemont's land again. Ever!" She gripped the side of the bench with white knuckles.

"You don't hafta." At his reassurance, her frame relaxed. "But it might bring you healing if you did." Then Jed added—lest his logical response cause her more pain—"You can sell it."

"Would anyone want land where a body is buried? Where a man burned down his own home?"

"Shoot, a grave don't bother most folks. Some homesteaders around here left graves of loved ones along the trail on their way here." Jed gave her hand a gentle squeeze. She turned his way. Her moss-green eyes glistened with unshed tears. "I'm sorry to upset ya, but people most likely would build their home on a different spot." What an idiot. Why couldn't he just hold her hand and enjoy the moment?

When a crow flapped overhead, cawing, Dee disengaged from his grip. "If I were a bird, I'd fly far away. Oh, how I wish I'd never gotten the foolish notion to come to Kansas. What must my parents think of me now?"

It hurt to hear she hated the place he'd come to love. Another barrier rose between them. "I imagine your parents don't think any less of you."

"I wrote and told them the whole truth, and I haven't heard from them since." Tears wet her face, accompanied by sudden, deep sobs.

Jed whistled for the horses to stop. He reached over and pulled her to him. She clung, wetting his shirt with her tears. Her nearness stirred a longing to hold her forever. Once the crying abated, she scrambled back to her side, embarrassment washing over her face. "That was very unseemly of me. Please forgive me."

"I didn't mind." Jed gave what he hoped was a reassuring smile. "Do you feel better?"

Dee pulled a handkerchief from her sleeve and dabbed her face. A smile formed as she pushed the cloth back into its hiding place. "I do, actually, very much."

"Genny says women need themselves a good cry from time to time."

"She is right, you know." She sighed and attempted to press wrinkles from her dress.

"My shirt front is available anytime you need one of those good cries." Jed winked and a rosy color covered her cheeks. Her reaction pleased him more than he dared admit.

Dee shifted the conversation to his family, and Jed regaled her with a few stories of his childhood—a safe topic. She listened with a strange smile about her lips.

"Is it something I said?" Jed asked as he pulled the horses to a stop near a creek where they would camp for the night. "You've been smiling like a possum eatin' persimmons."

She laughed. "I imagined you and your brother as mischievous young boys, and I wondered if Peter and Robert will take after you."

"Probably." Jed chuckled as he dismounted the wagon and came to her side. She allowed him to place his hands on her waist. She leaned on his shoulders as he lowered her to the ground. Her height brought her head to his shoulder. She looked at him once her feet were securely on the ground. For a moment, the temptation to kiss her nearly overpowered him. He stepped away. Kissing her on the way home would only confirm that her anxiety over traveling alone with him was well-founded.

Also, she had a pistol in her pocket. The thought brought a smile.

"Why are you smiling?" She blushed and hurried to the back of the wagon, pulling supplies out as if her life depended on it. He chuckled. She scowled, and they said no more.

Jed set up the tents after tending the horses. He headed to the creek to fill their bucket with water and carried it back to the campsite, where he stopped short at the sight of the crackling campfire Dee had started by herself. "You're a regular pioneer woman, Mrs. James." Being more formal helped keep his heart in check.

"Papa and I would go fishing occasionally. He taught me how to start a campfire." She added water to the coffeepot. "We city girls aren't utterly helpless."

"Good to know." Jed set her bag inside her tent and went to roll out his bedding in his own. He laid on his bedroll to stretch the kinks from his back. Riding horseback was never as uncomfortable on the poor excuse for a road as riding in the wagon.

"Jed." An angelic voice rousted him from sleep. "Jed, dinner's ready." He grinned at the worried expression on her face as she gazed at him through the tent opening.

He stirred and stretched, inhaling the tempting scents of fresh-brewed coffee and biscuits. "I reckon I needed a nap."

"You're not coming down with something, are you?" Dee touched his forehead.

"Nah, just tuckered a mite." The kind of fever he had couldn't be detected with her soft fingers.

A howl sent shivers through Dee as she finished the dishes. For the last half hour, she'd been putting on a brave face. After all, he'd called her a pioneer woman. Her chest constricted, and she struggled for breath with the next howl. Was it a wolf?

The last of the sun's light sank in the west. The brilliant colors provided no distraction from her terror. A third howl made her screech.

Jed dropped the tin plate he was drying and placed his hand on her shoulder. "Ain't nothing but a coyote."

His calm demeanor offered some comfort, but two more howls and an answering one sent her somewhere she'd never thought she'd flee—into his arms. She buried her face in his shirt. "They're vicious creatures. They'll attack us."

"Lemont tell you that lie?" Jed held her close, his breath tickling her cheek. "They're too small to bother ya. Most are afraid of man. They hunt small animals and grab unsuspecting chickens."

"Truly?" Dee lifted her head from his shoulder. "You're not saying it to make me feel better?"

"Truly." Jed stroked her cheek. "Now wolves and cougars are another story."

"What a horrible thing to say. I'll not sleep a wink for fear a wolf or cougar will enter my tent." Dee moved away from Jed. The scent of campfire, trail dust, and masculinity had cast its spell on her. Then he chuckled, breaking the spell. She slapped his shoulder.

"I'm sorry. It's the truth … but campfires keep them away." He placed the tin plate he'd dropped back in the box with the rest of the dishes. "If there's coffee left, I'd like another cup."

He hauled the rest of the provisions to the wagon while she poured two more cups and washed out the coffeepot. By the time he'd returned from the wagon, she'd settled herself on a log near the fire. The angles of Jed's face reminded her of a sculpture she'd seen in a museum. This living man was far more attractive than the marble one.

Jed sat on the ground next to her, leaning against the log. "Can I ask you somethin' been on my mind since we left the Fenwicks'?"

Dee wanted to say no. "I suppose."

"Were those tears at the end of the service a reaction to God speaking to your heart, or were you upset about something?"

What answer could she give that would satisfy him but spare her the real explanation? Nothing came to mind. As her shoulders sagged under the weight of her shame, she caught a glint of compassion in his eyes.

Jed shifted his gaze to the campfire. "Can you tell me about your life back east?"

He'd sensed her discomfort and changed the subject rather than push her to share before she was ready. Relief swept through her. At some point, she *would* tell him, but not today.

"I was born in Baltimore after my parents arrived from Britain. Both have always been house servants. Mr. Hollingsworth liked to say he stole them from two dukes by offering my parents passage to America and a better salary. They met and married on the trip over, and I was their Christmas gift a year later. I'm an only child. My parents were in their forties when they married. Papa said it was like Abraham and Sarah."

"God must have great things for ya, then." Jed glanced her way, then back at the campfire.

"I doubt it." Dee set her empty coffee cup on the log beside her. "Most of my childhood, I was the competition which inspired Juliet Hollingsworth to excel. I was taught by her tutor so she wouldn't be a lonely pupil. When I got better marks, she determined to beat me. A servant rising above her mistress wouldn't do. That's why I received musical training from one of the best instructors. Once Juliet had her debutant ball, introducing her to society, our friendship shifted to servant and mistress. Then there were no more music, art, or language lessons. I was promoted to chambermaid so she could regale me with her male conquests and I could fix her unruly hair."

"Well, ain't that just like rich people?" Jed frowned.

His support was both comforting and attractive.

"What possessed you to become a mail-order bride?" Jed averted his eyes. "You don't need to answer. It was out of line."

Dee hesitated a moment. He deserved an explanation after all he'd done for her. She repeated what she'd told Genny when she'd first arrived.

"He wanted a mistress?" Jed threw a twig at the fire with such force it missed the flames and landed on the other side.

"It's something accepted in his circle. Marry for money but have a mistress."

"No wonder you come here." His sympathy surprised her. The darkness masked his expression.

Dee sighed and continued her confession. "Which led to a bigger mistake, despite my good intentions. My parents were willing to find different positions to protect me. I didn't want to be a burden to them. I thought coming here would offer them refuge."

Jed's hand covered hers, strengthening her to continue.

"I've been sending them funds the last few months. I worry they won't come once I've established my bakery." Declaring she'd open one scared her. Failure had dogged her throughout adulthood. Would this venture be any different?

"Were you thinkin' of them at the service this mornin'?"

She stood up. "I believe I'll retire for the evening." Her own shame outvoted the desire to tell him the truth. What wife abandons her husband in his time of need?

"Before you go, I've been meaning to ask if you'll accompany me to the Fenwicks the next time they come up on my schedule. It'll be a few months."

Dee enjoyed playing and meeting people who had no knowledge of her past. But these trips with Jed could not happen again. His presence was too tempting.

"My priority is to Genny. I am her housekeeper."

"I could ask her." Jed rose and stepped toward the fire, stoking it. "I'm sure …"

"Don't you dare." Dee glared and crossed her arms. "You'll not guilt her into letting me go when she needs me."

"If it's what ya want." The firelight captured the hurt in his eyes.

"And I would never intentionally guilt anyone." Jed turned away and threw more sticks in the campfire.

"I need to make my own decisions. When and *if* I decide to join you again, I will ask Genny myself."

"Of course."

His tight reply indicated the need for better explanation. Dee calmed her voice before continuing. "As a servant, I was instructed what to do. As a slave, my choices were taken away." Jed's eyes softened, and she raised her hand before he responded. "My next priority is to attract customers for my future bakery so I can bring my parents here. I don't have time to waste." She rose from the log. "It's time I think for myself again. I don't need or want your help."

It was a lie, but answering this handsome rancher's pastoral questions on a starlit night would magnify the temptation to fall back into his arms. Definitely the wrong place to confess her sin. Dee's heart pounded as she walked the few feet to her tent and opened the flap.

"Good night, Brother Holt." She didn't turn to face him, their hug forgotten as her sin taunted her.

"Good night, Mrs. James."

Lying on her pallet, she wrestled with her thoughts. *Father, help me be a good daughter. Maybe then you'll forgive my heartless act as a wife.*

Chapter 23

Dee hung the last of the diapers on the line. Every day, the cotton rectangles needed laundering, and they seemed to haunt her dreams. She chuckled as she stretched her back. The azure sky with only a few puffy clouds made her sigh. If only she could capture this in a jar to serve on a gloomy day. Perfection—not too hot, a gentle breeze, and oh, so peaceful. Peace had eluded her since the fire.

Hold that thought. The nanny goat grazed beside the clothesline. How had she gotten out of the fence?

"Once I take this basket inside, I'll take you back to your pen." The goat moved closer to her. "Do you need milking again?" It wasn't time. "You're an odd one today."

Dee turned to collect the empty basket. It went flying as she toppled to the ground, landing face-first in the dirt. The goat stood there, chewing her cud, a placid look on its face.

Dee hissed at her attacker. "I suppose my backside was a fine target for you." She rose, dusted off her skirt, and attempted to grab the goat's collar. The nanny moved out of reach. "How did you get out of your pen?"

"Maa, maa." The nanny goat stood its ground and refused to move.

So much for a perfect, peaceful day. She tugged the collar to no avail.

"Move," Dee yelled, but the beast remained stationary.

"Need somethin'?" Jed came out of the stables and strode toward her. Had he seen her being waylaid?

She let go of the goat's collar and crossed her arms. "Can you help me get her back to her pen?"

"I just fixed the last hole she made. There was no need to put her back until I did." Jed wiped sweat from his brow with his arm. "She's an ornery cuss. I saw her use your backside for target practice." He chuckled.

"Stop laughing." Dee tried not to laugh herself. Instead, she stomped her foot. "I could have been injured."

"But you ain't." Jed grinned. "I know I shouldn't laugh at your misfortune, but it was just too …" Another chuckle exploded from his lips. "Funny."

Dee giggled and shook her head. "Wait until you're the target. Then it won't be so funny."

"Nah, I'd laugh at myself. And I'm sure anyone on the ranch would too." Jed pulled a bit of grass out of her hair. The action sent a pleasant shiver through her. She took a step back. Jed cleared his throat and stepped away as well.

"How do you plan on getting Miss Stubborn back to her cage?" Dee turned from his oh- so-enchanting sapphire eyes and focused on the goat.

He whistled, and the stupid goat followed him. "Works every time."

Dee shook her head in disbelief as the nanny trailed him back to her pen.

"Make sure she can't escape." Dee rubbed her backside, then retrieved the basket. Whistling brought the dog and the horses and now a goat. Could he whistle a bird out of the sky? The picture of various birds resting on his arm brought a sigh. She needed to quit thinking overmuch about the man.

A rider came up the lane. Sheba barked and raced toward the horse. Jed and Lonnie met the visitor in the yard. His horse was as tall as Soldier, and the man's expensive suit set him apart from the ranchers. When he dismounted, he stood a head taller than the Holt men.

Dee scurried into the house. She found her friend in the bedroom folding clothes. "Genny, there's a stranger outside."

"Are the men with him?" Genny peeked out the window. "Gonzalez is taking his horse to the corral. We best prepare food."

"We're going to feed him? Why not send him on his way?" Dee's hand twitched. Why did he set her on edge? His size, for one.

"If you'd prefer to retire to your cabin, it's fine." Genny hurried to the kitchen and began warming the stew left from lunch, Dee following. "I'm sure it's only a horse trader or cattle buyer."

Dee stiffened her back and reached for a fresh loaf of bread and sliced it. "Should I make coffee?"

"I already did. Lonnie usually comes looking for some about now." Genny peeked out the kitchen window. "My, my, what a handsome man."

"Genny Holt, you're a married woman." Dee scowled as she placed a plate on the table.

"I may be married to the finest man in Kansas, but I still can't help noticing a particularly good-looking one." She giggled, then pulled a pie from the pie cupboard. "Good thing I did the baking today. It can't hold a candle to yours, but it will do."

"Maybe he won't come in." Her voice squeaked. She'd come so far battling her fears … and along came a king-size version.

Before she could make her escape, the stranger entered with the Holt brothers, a quizzical look on their faces.

Lonnie placed a protective arm around Genny. "This is my lovely wife, Genny Holt."

The man removed his hat and nodded.

Jed placed a hand on Dee's shoulder. What was this about?

"Nice to make your acquaintance. I'm Lemont James."

Blackness assailed Dee's vision.

Jed caught Dee and slowly lowered her to the floor. Genny held smelling salts to her nose. The salts revived her, and she pushed the sachet away.

"You okay?" Jed stroked her cheek as her color returned. This was exactly the reaction he'd feared. When the stranger had introduced himself, Jed had been tempted to send him packing. But Dee needed to know the truth.

"I'm fine." She extracted herself from his embrace and stood. He rose with her, staying close in case she swooned again. The newcomer stood near the door.

"You all right?" Lonnie asked while Jed held a kitchen chair for her.

She pushed hair out of her face and cleared her throat. "I'm fine. Too long in the sun, I suppose." She took a cleansing breath and turned to the stranger. He, too, wore an anxious expression. "What did you say your name was?"

"Lemont James." He sat across from her. Too close. Genny on her right. Lonnie sat next to the stranger. Jed took the chair to Dee's left and looked between her and the stranger. Her eyes held fear like those of a rabbit caught in a snare.

"I know who you are." The man smiled her way.

"Genny, please serve Mr. James some vittles." Lonnie rose and poured coffee.

Genny set a bowl of stew and fresh bread and butter before him.

"Thank you, ma'am." He shoveled the stew, stopping only to sip coffee. When he paused to butter his bread, Jed spoke.

"The Lemont James I suspect you're looking for died in a house fire a few months back."

"Mr. Clemens at the mercantile said the same. I came to see his widow."

Dee stared at the table, and Jed stroked her quivering hand with his thumb. She placed her other hand on his and held tight. Her leg shook beside him.

"I can take you to his grave," he offered. Whatever it took to put more distance between Dee and the stranger.

The man ate in silence, the air thick with anxiety as they waited for him to speak. Once he finished the stew, he smiled at Genny. "Delicious. Haven't had a home-cooked meal in a while." Mr. James turned to Jed. "Glad the worthless cur is gone. His real name was Ernie Smott. The man stole from me and left me for dead."

Dee gasped and released Jed's hand. He wanted to retrieve it, but instead, placed his arm around the back of her chair.

"We were partners in a silver mine. I financed it, and he had the expertise. He set the explosives, and I handled the paperwork. Our mine appeared to have run dry. We were planning on splitting the profits, then going our separate ways. Greedy sot lured me into the mine shaft with a claim he'd found a new vein. While I inspected the wall, he set off charges. I was trapped for a week. When my men finally dug me out, he'd emptied our bank account and left town."

The real Lemont rose and paced the room twice. "The image of a drunken, worthless slob will forever be connected with my good name." He focused his next words on Dee. "It took me a month to recover from my injuries. I'd hired a Pinkerton to find him. He hit on the idea to search for my name and found a land deed filed in the area."

Lonnie looked Dee's way, and Jed squeezed her shoulder.

"At last we meet, Miss McLain." Longing gleamed in Mr. James' eyes as he stared at Dee. Jed's fingers fisted, and he glared at the interloper.

Dee looked at Genny, who gave a slight nod.

"If you'll excuse me." She bolted from the room and out the door.

Dee locked her cabin door, then sprawled on her bed. He was the real Lemont James. Was that mountain of a man her true husband? Of course not. But his name was on the marriage license, not Ernie-something. But Ernie said the vows.

The old familiar fear rose from her middle. Nausea churned the food in her stomach. She went out the back door and retched. After wiping her mouth with her handkerchief, she returned inside and bathed her face in cool water.

A gentle knock drew her from her bed. "Dee, let me in."

She ran to the door and unbolted the lock. Jed stood before her, hat in hand.

"Come in."

He stepped inside and closed the door. "I know it ain't proper for me to be here, but …"

"Thank you for caring." Dee indicated a chair at her table.

"I know this be a real shock."

Jed sat at the table, and Dee took the other chair. The girls' colored pencils and paper were strewn in the space between them, reminding her that once the children woke from their nap, she needed to appear normal. She stacked the papers and stared at the colored pencils for a heartbeat before she organized them in their box and closed the lid. Jed remained silent, waiting for her to speak. Once her pulse slowed, she asked the question foremost in her mind.

"Does this mean I must marry him?" What a foolish thought. But was her marriage to her late husband even legal? Dizziness overcame her. She took a breath and looked at Jed.

"Do you have the bride contract you signed?"

"No, it burned in the fire. Perhaps Mr. James has a copy. Lemont … Ernest … whatever his name was … didn't have a copy. Another warning sign I ignored." Dee wiped tears from her eyes. "I'm such a dolt."

"No, you're a trusting soul who assumed Ernie was your intended. Best we get a lawyer to sort it all out."

She clutched the pencil box, feeling like a theater-goer watching her life play out before her. If only it was as easy to put back together as filling a pencil box. Detachment might be the best recourse. "A lawyer? I can't afford a lawyer."

"I'll—"

"No, you won't." Dee rose from her place and put the pencil box on the shelf above the table. "I'll use some of the money I'm putting aside for my bakery. It's best to clear this up so I can move forward with my new future." She checked her face in the mirror and turned to Jed. "Shall we go see what Mr. James expects?"

They walked to the main house together.

Jed opened the door, and Dee's anxious look mirrored his own mood. He placed his hand on the small of her back and whispered, "I'll be right behind ya."

Mr. James rose when she entered. She ducked her head. "Sorry to cause you any worry."

"No need to apologize. You've done nothing wrong."

Dee took a seat in the rocker, away from the table. Mr. James took the other empty chair near the fireplace. Jed grabbed a kitchen chair and straddled it. Lonnie and Genny also sat in chairs near the rocker.

"May I ask when he died?" Mr. James spun his hat in his hands.

"Three months ago, tomorrow." She focused on her shoes.

Jed rubbed his chin and leaned forward, waiting for the man to say something to Dee that warranted a fist.

"I'm sorry for your loss." His sincere tone belied the company he'd kept. Was it an act to gain her sympathies? A knot formed in Jed's stomach.

"No need for hollow sentiment. You will understand when I say it was no loss." Dee clipped her words and turned her head away from him. Jed hoped his presence gave her strength.

"I'm sorry I caused you such pain by writing you. If I'd known the future, I'd have never proposed."

This revelation was interrupted by little voices from the bedroom. Genny left to tend the children. The distraction seemed to help Dee gain composure.

"So you're the author of the letters. Now I understand why Lemont—I mean, Ernie—burned them." She shook her head, her hand resting below her throat. How often had she done the same when Jed had approached her unannounced? Was she frightened?

Jed studied her profile. Her tight jaw and stiff back told him she was holding things together the best she could.

"Man didn't like to lose, ever. His violent outbursts kept most of the miners out of his way. I'm more than sorry for what you've endured." Mr. James' sorrowful eyes flashed anger. "Like you, I'm glad the scoundrel is dead. Partnering with him was among the biggest mistakes of my life."

Dee nodded but said nothing.

"Miss McLain, I've been dreaming of meeting you since I received your first letter, and had I been at the stage to meet you, I'd have done right by you."

Was Mr. James intending on marrying her? This wasn't the time nor the man. Jed slapped himself mentally for the jealousy running through him. He'd no more right to Dee's heart than this stranger.

She frowned at Mr. James. "Well, you didn't meet me. The nightmare is over, and I don't care to reminisce." She rose from her chair. "If you'll excuse me, I have chores to attend to."

"Wait, if you please." He rose and stood too close to Dee for Jed's liking. "May I call on you tomorrow? I have a few more questions I'd like to discuss in private."

Dee blanched.

Jed stepped beside her. "This was quite a shock. Give her time. If she cares to discuss the situation further, I'll let you know." He maintained eye contact.

"For now, I'll be at the boarding house in town." Mr. James tipped his hat. "Ladies, gents, thank you for your hospitality."

"I'll fetch your horse." Lonnie opened the door and followed him out.

Dee burst into tears, and before Jed could react, Genny was by her side, pulling her into a motherly hug. "Things will get sorted. You'll see. God will work it out."

Dee pulled away and wiped her eyes with her sleeve. "I need to work this out myself." When she turned to Jed, her eyes were hard. "Can you take me to the lawyer tomorrow?"

"If it's what you want."

Her eyes sparked. Fear and anger had returned with a vengeance. Then she moved away and sat in the rocker, staring at the fireplace. A baby's cry took Genny's attention, but Dee didn't move. The rocker creaked as she remained anchored in place.

Oh Lord, what are You goin' to do about this? Jed hoped it was to send Mr. James packing so things could return to the way they were. Were his suspicions concerning the stranger a caution or plain jealousy? She wouldn't marry up with a stranger again, would she? The idea of shooing Mr. James away with his loaded rifle when the man came again raised its ugly head.

He didn't like the feelings the situation conjured. Time for a long ride. He'd go to the law office in town to make her an appointment for tomorrow.

Chapter 24

Dee tried to hide her disappointment as she took her place on the wagon bench with Genny and Lonnie. The children were in the wagon bed. A trip she'd planned with Jed had turned into a family outing. Sally had gone into labor a few hours ago, and Jed refused to leave his prize mare. Why couldn't Sally have waited until tomorrow? The please-forgive-me expression on Jed's face had been so sweet. *What a horrible, selfish person I am. Jed needs to tend Sally. After all, I insisted on seeing the lawyer by myself.* But it was Jed's calm demeanor she craved at this moment.

She twisted her bonnet ribbon between her fingers. The action kept her from shaking her leg. The Holt girls chattering in the wagon bed sounded like a murder of crows. She glanced back to check on the babies nestled in a box of straw between Jilly and Molly.

"Momma said I getta mind them." Jilly pushed her sister away.

"Na-huh." Molly rose only to fall backward with the wagon's motion. Her wailing woke Birdie from her nap, and she joined in.

"Molly, you hush your fussing right now." Genny's scowl quieted both girls. "If I've told you once, I've told you a thousand times, don't stand up in the wagon."

"Yes, Momma." Molly's voice was contrite.

"Jilly, you are both in charge of minding your brothers." Genny faced forward. "Land a Goshen, those two try one's patience."

Lonnie chuckled. "You're the one who wanted to bring 'em."

"Polly loves the children to visit. She'll be surprised to see how the babies have grown." Genny sighed. "I haven't even seen their sweet babe."

Dee clung to the side of the wagon bench. "I appreciate you all coming along." She hoped saying it would make it so. Having Genny along or even Lonnie was fine. But all the young ones too? She'd hoped for a reprieve for the morning. Time alone was rare now. The girls visited her cabin almost every night to color or ask her to read to them. Although she enjoyed it, too much of a good thing made it sour.

Once they reached town, Lonnie pulled the wagon in front of the mercantile. "Dee, give me a minute to help settle the boys, and I'll come with ya."

"No need." Dee smiled his way. "I believe I can manage."

"If'n you're sure." Lonnie helped Birdie down, then reached for Peter. "I'm happy to accompany you."

"Thank you, but no." Dee strode toward the law office before she lost her nerve. How much should she tell him? Hopefully, the lawyer had the answers she needed.

She froze in the doorway. Mr. James sat in the waiting room. "Miss McLain, what a happy happenstance to meet you here." The pleasure reflected in his eyes made her uncomfortable.

"I had no idea …" Dee stared at the giant man in the small chair. "May I inquire why you are here?"

"I suppose the same as you." Mr. James offered a genuine smile, which caused butterflies to flitter in her stomach. Lines and phrases from his letter filtered through her mind before she gathered her composure.

"You are inquiring if the contract we signed stating our intention to marry is still valid?" She dared not look him in the face, or she'd say something she'd regret.

"Oh, I thought you were here to make sure the land was yours." He removed his Stetson from the adjacent chair and offered it to her.

"The land?" Dee hadn't given it a second thought even after Jed mentioned it.

Mr. James studied her closely.

She avoided his eyes and chose a seat across the room. "Why on earth would I want his land?"

"You're serious?" His amazed look drew attention to a scar under his left eye.

"I never want to step foot on it, ever again. His land has no fond memories for me." Dee placed her reticule in her lap and faced forward.

"Would you consider selling it to me?"

Before Dee could answer, the lawyer came from his office. "I see you are both on time. Come on through." He held the door. When Dee hesitated, he nodded her way. "Please come in."

Dee judged Mr. Winters to be ten years her senior. The bit of premature gray at his temples made him look older, but not wiser if he took his clients in a group. Mr. James waited for her to sit in one of the bentwood chairs in front of the oak desk before he took the other.

"Mr. Winters, I thought I'd have a private meeting with you." Irritation laced Mr. James' statement.

"As did I." Dee glared at the lawyer. How dare he embarrass her this way?

"I'm sorry. Forgive my confusion. Having the same name and seeking legal counsel at the same time …" Mr. Winters dabbed his brow with a handkerchief, then straightened a stack of papers on the corner of his desk.

"No, sir, we are not here together." Mr. James' clipped response required only a nod of agreement from Dee.

"Then what is it you want?" The two sat stone silent. The lawyer steepled his hands and focused on her. "Mrs. James, you go first."

"I want to know if my matrimonial contract is still valid."

"And you, Mr. James?"

"I want to see if the homestead land is legally mine or Miss McLain's." He nodded toward her, his arms across his broad chest.

"Do either of you have any documents for me?" Mr. Winters

looked between them.

Dee's mouth went dry. "No, mine burned in the fire."

"I have a copy." Mr. James opened his saddlebag and pulled out a sheet of paper. "I also have a copy of the deed from the land office." He handed both to the lawyer.

"Very good. Mr. James, if you'll step out to the waiting room, I'll see you next."

The real Lemont tipped his hat toward Dee and gave a slight smile before exiting. Warmth rose up her collar against her will. She gripped the side of her chair, wrestling her emotions to a calm. What if the document was still legal? She tried to keep her foot from shaking as the lawyer read the paper. "It's pretty straightforward to me, Mrs. James. What exactly would you like to know?"

"I had no idea what Mr. James looked like. When the man claiming to be him met me at the train station, I had no reason to doubt." By the time Dee had finished her tale, the lawyer was wiping his glasses with a rag and making *tsk*ing noises.

"I am so sorry to hear you were deceived." He leaned forward. "Fortunately for you, he misrepresented himself. He wasn't a proxy representing the real Mr. James either. So you were not legally married to the false Mr. James." Dee fought a swoon at the revelation. "However, there is still a legally binding marriage contract. A simple conversation with the real Mr. James should settle everything." Mr. Winters went to the door and held it open. "Mr. James. Please step in."

His presence dominated the room. No way would she marry this giant. She focused on the lawyer.

Mr. Winters continued. "Because the matrimonial agreement was between you and Miss McLain …" He looked over his glasses at Dee. "I assume that's you."

Her tongue stuck to the roof of her mouth; she managed a nod.

"Because you are the real Mr. James"—he pointed to the man sitting next to her—"this contract is still valid." He smiled broadly at both of them. "So you may go to the church and fulfill the contract."

"I will do no such thing, Mr. Winters." Dee squeaked out the words through a wall of panic.

"Excuse me, but I assumed you wanted to—no, needed to be looked after or you wouldn't have signed the contract." Mr. Winters stared at her as if she had the plague. "But if it's your wish to nullify the contract, it can be done by paying back the monies given to you for transportation." He glanced toward Mr. James. "That is, of course, if you agree."

Mr. James remained silent for what felt an eternity. "I tell you what. Why not give me a few acres of your land to cover it?"

"I'd gladly give you all the land. I assume it was purchased with the money stolen from you."

"It's highly unusual. Are you sure?" Mr. Winters waited for her response.

Dee nodded.

"Is it acceptable to you, Mr. James?" The lawyer leaned forward as if waiting for a verdict to be pronounced.

"I think it's more than fair. It feels wrong to leave you destitute, Miss McLain."

"I am far from destitute." Anger tinged her response. "I have a job and am saving my money to start a bakery."

"Still, it feels wrong to take advantage." He fiddled with the brim of his hat, then looked her over like Jed did his horses. She gulped and faced him. Their eyes met, and her feet tingled with the urge to flee. "Delilah, may I call you by your Christian name?"

"I suppose." She'd said it and couldn't take it back. He'd been calling her by her Christian name in their last few correspondences.

"I had honorable intentions toward you when I sent those letters. I wrote a few more after I was rescued from the mine, but you never responded—which led me to believe you were no longer interested in our arrangement." He grew silent and stared at the floor. "Under the circumstances, I can't hold you to the contract." Sadness shadowed his face. "Ernie has sullied my name in every way possible. I release you from the contract."

A weight fell off Dee's shoulders. "Lemont, will you please take the land?"

"If you recall from my letters, I prefer Monty, and yes, I'm happy to take the land. But I insist on paying you something."

"No, please don't. The payment would be another reminder of the past I wish to forget."

"I see." He turned to the lawyer. "Can you draw up the papers turning over the ranch to me in exchange for Miss McLain's release from our contract?"

"Of course." Mr. Winters took up his pen. "Come back in an hour. You can sign the papers, and I'll have copies for you both."

Monty held the door open for her. She looked up at him. "Thank you, I feel freer than I have since the fire."

He gave a slight nod and followed her out the door. "I'm headed to the restaurant to have lunch. Would you join me?"

She turned toward him, finding that his eyes were kind. "All right." Why had she agreed? Was it pity for the poor man whose hopes and dreams were crushed by the same villain who had stolen hers?

They walked to the Corner Café. She might pity Monty, but this could be a mistake. They maneuvered through the crowded restaurant to a table in a far corner. He pulled out her chair.

"I'm glad you joined me. It's the least I can do after you generously gave me your land." He offered a smile, then sat across from her. "I thought perhaps you might ask Mr. Holt to join us. I saw the wagon pull in front of the mercantile when I arrived. They're very protective of you."

"They are caring. But I make my own decisions." She placed her reticule on an empty chair.

"I figured Jed—I think he's the one—would have joined us."

"He didn't come to town. And Lonnie and his family are making a social call."

He nodded and cleared his throat. "I hear the special is lamb chops."

"A nice change from beef and chicken. And ordering the special always brings quick service."

The waitress took their orders, and the food was before them in minutes, which was a mercy since Mr. James had begun talking about his plans for the property. She refused to invest in anything that pulled her back to the past.

She tasted her food. "This is wonderful." Then she diverted the conversation with the next thing to pop into her mind. "I plan on opening a bakery by next year. I have regular customers from the mercantile."

"I admire a woman with vision. I look forward to sampling your baked goods."

He sounded exactly like his letters. Educated and endearing. If not for the deception, she might have agreed to marry this man—one more suited to her. Sadness and fear wrestled in her middle. No man would want her now.

"I believe Helen, the owner, serves my pies for dessert." Now she'd added pride to her many faults.

Monty raised his finger to get the waitress' attention. "Do you happen to have any of Mrs. James' pies today?"

"Yes, sir, apple and peach. They're the best I've ever tasted." She directed a flirtatious smile at Mr. James.

"I'll take a slice of each, and for the lady …" Monty turned to her.

"Apple is fine." It pleased her he wanted to sample both.

The pies came, and Monty took his time savoring every bite, while Dee barely tasted hers.

"These pies are better than my own mother's, and better than the finest restaurants in Denver serve."

"You're from Denver?" The question stopped his flattery.

"It's where I recovered from the mine accident." He scraped the plate clean. "You know, the fool actually did me a favor. When we cleared away the rubble, we found gold in the wall of rock. I'm a wealthy man, Delilah."

The way he spoke her name, as if it was the most precious thing, jarred her.

"All I need is a wife."

Her face flamed. "This has been lovely, thank you. But we should head to the law office."

He nodded to the waitress, who brought the check. He paid and followed Dee out the door.

"May I ask you one last question?" Monty's husky voice inches from her ear was unnerving. "If I didn't live on the land, would you allow me to court you?"

She stopped at the law office door and turned to him. *As long as you are Lemont James, the memory of what that imposter did to me will stay forefront in my mind.* "I'm sure you're a fine man. And I know several single women at church who might suit you."

"Thank you for your honesty." Monty opened the door, closing the subject of a future together. Their business took only a few minutes, and they parted company, much to her relief.

Dee joined Genny and her family at the wagon. Genny chattered about her visit with Polly. She half listened, still thinking about Monty's hopeful face.

"What happened with the lawyer?" Genny asked.

"Here is the document that sets me free from everything." She removed it from her handbag and showed it to Genny.

As Genny read it out loud to Lonnie, Dee wondered what her future might have been had the real Lemont met her at the stagecoach station. What was wrong with her? Was she attracted to the man or to what might have been?

"You gave him your property for your release from the contract?" Lonnie scowled her way. "What was the blame lawyer thinking?"

Dee held up her hand. "It was my idea. The land is legally his because my late husband used Mr. James' money to buy it. I want nothing to do with that land. Nothing!" Anger enveloped her for a moment. "I am free, which is all I wanted."

"Didn't mean to rile ya." Lonnie whistled to the horse to trot.

Genny gave her a sideways embrace. "You did the right thing. I see a bright future ahead for you."

She returned her friend's hug. "Thank you. I hope you're right." At this moment, she longed for her mother. She squeezed Genny a little harder before letting her go.

Dee grabbed the side of the bench as the horses picked up their pace. Holding tight to the present was the best choice for now. Whatever the future held, she hoped she'd be brave enough to embrace it.

Chapter 25

Jed watched the brown colt take his first wobbly steps as he washed his arms in a bucket of water. The size of Sally's offspring left no doubt that Soldier was the sire. Later he'd move his mare and her new colt to a clean stall, but for now, they needed to get better acquainted.

I shoulda gone with Dee. Guilt hovered close. *But Sally needed me. Yet … I coulda had Carter see to her.* But Carter lacked his skill with birthings. Sally was his horse, and Dee was his friend. Whatever choice he made, he'd worry over the other.

All morning, his mind had gone over every scenario Dee might encounter in town. What if the lawyer wasn't worth his salt and gave her bad advice? Would she be confused? Frightened? Had she let Lonnie go in with her?

He shook his head to dislodge his worry, but Dee's beautiful face with the sad eyes refused to be banished. Jed leaned on the stall wall and watched the colt nurse.

"Well, little one, I got no idea what you'll turn out to be." Sally nuzzled her newborn. "But your momma loves you, and that's all that matters." Jed made a mental note to suggest Dee have the plow horse gelded. The thought of talking to her about the indelicate matter warmed his ears. Soldier had disrupted his plans for Drake to cover Sally. Dee had disrupted his life in unexpected ways. But there had been progress. Soldier was learning to trust men, and it seemed

Dee trusted him.

Wagon wheels and the chatter of little girls drew Jed to the barn door. Lonnie helped the women out of the wagon before reaching for his daughters. Jed strolled toward them.

Dee looked lovely in the green dress, her expression relaxed. A good sign. He approached her from behind. "How'd it go?"

"Jed Holt, you do enjoy giving me a fright." She caught her breath and glared his way.

"No, but you sure look pretty when you're scared." Jed watched for the beautiful smile that sent his heart racing. But it didn't come. Instead, another frown. "Is everything all right?"

"Yes, of course." Dee crossed her arms. "I am free of the contract and the land."

"You sold it, then?" Why wasn't she more excited? Should he put his arm around her? Probably not.

Dee focused on her feet. "No. I gave it to Mr. James." Then she searched his face.

Jed smiled and put his hands on his hips rather than her shoulders. "Makes sense. If your late husband stole from Mr. James, it's only right he gets the land."

"You understand?" Relief filled her countenance.

"Making restitution is a biblical principle. You done the right thing, and I'm proud of you."

She smiled, then sighed as she pulled a paper from her handbag and passed it to him. "Lonnie thinks I was foolish."

Jed read over the paper. In writing, it appeared she'd paid for her freedom, but her decision had taken deeper principles into account. Lonnie was never good at choosing his words. Dee needed affirmation, not judgment. "Looks like the best way the lawyer could word things to make it all legal. It coulda turned out different. What if Mr. James wanted you arrested for stealing his land?"

"I hadn't thought … but I see your point." She put the paper back in her bag. "Has the foal been born?"

He smiled and removed his hat to wipe the sweat from his brow with his bandana before answering her question. "Yep, you want to see?" Jed led her to the stable. Dee didn't know what Soldier had been up to since they arrived. The new colt oughta excite her. At least, he hoped so.

"Isn't he lovely?" She cooed over the colt. "What will you name him?"

"Since the sire was Soldier, why don't you name him?"

Her expression fell. "I'm sorry. I know you wanted a thoroughbred."

"Nothing to worry about. Sally will have more foals." Jed stood shoulder to shoulder with Dee. "A name?"

She stared at the colt for several moments. "Celtic Fire."

"Interesting. Why Celtic Fire?"

"My father told me my grandfather had a horse with the name. And if he ever had money to buy a horse, that's what he'd name it."

"He's half your horse. I'm gifting you my half of the colt, then you can give him to your father."

Dee stared at the colt with wide eyes, then planted a feather-light kiss on Jed's cheek. She withdrew quickly. "Thank you so much." A blush covered her face as she continued to admire the newborn. Was the kiss merely a response in her moment of joy—or more?

"He has Soldier's brown coat but Sally's black mane. He's beautiful. When will Sally let me touch Celtic Fire?" Dee asked without turning his way. Was she embarrassed over the kiss?

What was the question? His mind was turning to mush. *Oh yeah* …

"It'll be awhile. If you come to the stable every day and bring her treats, she'll warm to you. For now, leave her to tend her colt."

Having Dee by his side, happy and carefree, pleased him. Everything about the woman pleased him. *Lord, either take away these feelings or move in her heart to favor me.* The companionable silence gave him hope. She hadn't fled his presence in a while.

"Baby horsey." Birdie's excited declaration filtered into the stable. Lonnie and the rest of the family came to admire the colt, ending his private moment with Dee.

"So pretty. I want to pet him." Jilly stepped forward and Molly and Birdie followed. Lonnie scooped up Birdie, and Genny grabbed the twins' hands.

"You girls know better." Lonnie scowled. "Sally will bite you if'n you get too friendly right away."

"I promise, when Sally is ready for you to visit, I'll let you know." Genny nodded toward the stable door. She shooed the older girls away and took Birdie from Lonnie. "I'll start dinner before the boys wake up."

Lonnie stared at the colt. "Tarnation, you was right. What are we goin' do with this mixed breed?"

"Nothing. He belongs to Dee, and she named him Celtic Fire." Jed exchanged a smile with her.

"That be fine with me." Lonnie scratched his chin. "If it be all right with you, Dee, I'd like to geld Soldier. So that'a way we don't have any more foals of questionable heritage."

Dee's face reddened, and she glared at Lonnie. "Maybe I want more colts like Celtic Fire." She sighed and shook her head. "I'm sorry, how rude of me. This is your ranch. You've been so gracious to take me in. I'd be remiss to be so selfish. As long as Soldier's fed and cared for, I don't imagine he'll miss any secret rendezvous with any of your mares."

She'd taken the suggestion better than Jed expected. His brother's usual bluntness could be off-putting. "If you want more foals …"

"Not really." Dee shook her head. "I know nothing about horse husbandry. I'm a city girl." She smiled at them. "It's fine."

This city girl had adapted to ranch life. Now, with a foal to tend to, she might like it better here. He added that to his mental list of reasons she might consider marrying him. And the fact that she'd kissed him, showing no fear, went to the top.

"I got chores before supper." Lonnie left them alone.

"Would you care for a walk after dinner?" Jed placed his hand on her shoulder. She moved away rather than jerked from his touch. The only times she'd been in his arms, she was wetting his shirt with her tears. And she only took his hand when she was scared.

"That would be nice." She left without a backward glance.

After dinner, Jed helped Dee with her shawl. They strolled past the barn toward the open field. The sound of crickets and katydids swelled in volume as she breathed deeply of the fresh summer air. "It won't be long until autumn."

The sunset touched her raven hair, highlighting the red undertones. Jed admired her silhouette.

"Autumn is my favorite season." Dee stooped to pluck a wildflower and held it to her nose for a moment.

"Are you happy, Dee?"

"I think I am. Today went better than expected, but …"

"What?"

"Never mind." Sadness shadowed her smile.

"Now I'm curious. You can't start a sentence, then change yer mind."

"Mr. James had hopes I'd marry him."

Jed clenched his teeth. "Did he propose?"

"In a veiled way. He said he was going to build a large house, and he needed a wife. Then asked if he could court me."

"What did you say?" Fire burned in his chest.

"I said there were several single women in town, and surely, one would suit him." Dee crossed her arms. The sun sank over the horizon, putting them in shadows. "Monty's a kind man, but I couldn't tell him that even his name made me tremble."

Jed's jealousy melted, replaced with a desire to erase those memories for her. "It's good you broke your ties with the land. Now you can relax and step into a new future." He stopped and took her hands. "Maybe even marriage."

She stared at their clasped hands, then pulled away. "I have no plans to ever marry."

Was there a catch in her voice? *I'm dumb as a post.* She'd already turned down one man mere hours ago. They stood silent for several minutes as the moon rose.

"You are a great friend, the best I could ask for." She turned toward the house.

Jed trudged along behind her. The prospect of Monty James stealing her from him had made the foolish words pour out. Now he'd ruined any chance of a proper proposal when the time was right. Shoot! There'd never be a right time.

They reached her cabin in silence, and she nodded his way. "Thank you for the walk." She gave him a half-hearted smile and closed the door.

He threw his hat on the ground, then picked it up, dusted it off, and went to find some chores to do.

Dee plopped in the rocker and pushed it into motion. Two men had expressed interest in her today. Monty gave her a glimpse of what might have been. So sad. Then Jed. What was he thinking? *I'm ruined for any man, especially a fine Christian like him.*

Lemont's angry face appeared in her mind. *Ain't much of a lover, woman. A big disappointment. Wives is supposed to enjoy their husband's attention. A frigid woman makes a man's eyes wander.*

She shook the vision away. If doing her duty to please a husband was enjoyable, she didn't know how. Marriage required it, and she could never endure the marriage bed again.

Dee changed into her nightgown and closed her eyes. Each toss and turn brought more memories. Her mind refused to settle until the wee hours of the morning. A rooster greeting the sun brought a groan as she rose from her bed.

"Dee, are you up?" Genny called.

"Come in."

She carried a breakfast tray. "My, you must have had a rough night. Your eyes have dark rings."

Dee ignored the remark. "This looks wonderful. You needn't

have brought me a tray." The smell of fresh-brewed coffee and bacon made her salivate.

"I don't mind." Genny sized her up. "If you feel like a day off, take it."

"Of course not." Dee sat at the table and nibbled the thick bacon. "Yesterday was a big day, and my mind reviewed it all night."

"I imagine it did." Genny looked around the room as if she were searching for her next words. "I'll leave you to eat. Bring the tray to the house. I'll wash the diapers if you'll do my baking."

"You don't have to persuade me." Dee smiled as her friend shut the door.

Baking always helped her make sense of the world. She finished her meal and planned what she might concoct for the mercantile. The bakery was the new beginning she'd focus on. Independence and freedom to do as she pleased. Her heart lightened like bread rising, dissolving the hard lump of despair residing in her middle.

Chapter 26

Two weeks later

Jed shoved the letters for Dee into his vest pocket before loading the supplies. He hefted boxes into the wagon bed. Lonnie was off somewhere speaking to prospective wranglers for the upcoming cattle drive. *I bet he doesn't make it back until I load this wagon.*

Mr. Clemens carried a large bag of beans on his shoulder. "Where do you want this?"

"Wait." Jed climbed into the wagon and took the bag from Clemens. "Thanks."

"I believe that's the last of your order." He waved and went inside.

Jed hopped down and reached for a hundred-pound bag of flour next to a few more crates he needed to load.

"Do you have a few minutes?" Monty James, dressed in work clothes rather than his fancy suit, grabbed a crate and hauled it to the Holt wagon.

"Thanks." Jed placed the flour beside it. "What's on your mind?"

"I need advice." Monty added another crate to the wagon. "I ordered wood for a new house. I'm living in a tent. Don't care to build a soddie. Could you recommend any local carpenters?"

"My neighbors, the Barlows, are the best in the area. They can get your house up in no time. Tell them I sent ya." Jed placed a few smaller parcels under the wagon seat. "You plan on ranching or farming?" He'd hoped the man was planning on leaving. His presence had stolen Dee's peace.

"I haven't decided. I know mining. But I'm open to new things." Monty took off his hat and wiped the headband with a handkerchief. "My priority is a house before winter."

"In my opinion, the land around here is more suited for cattle. But horses is a good option too." Jed's personal feelings toward the man were colored by Dee's reaction. Not a great way to be neighborly.

"I hear your brother is the best horseman around." Monty's compliment pleased Jed.

"Yep. Do you need horses? We got a few we're looking to sell." Jed pulled out the rope to secure his load to the wagon.

"I'll stop by." Monty helped Jed tie down the load. "I'm looking for experienced cowboys to help on my place. Got any recommendations?"

"Most of the good men have steady work. We're hiring some extras to help with the cattle drive. They'll be looking for work when the drive is over. Lonnie could recommend a few."

"Appreciate it." Monty looked toward the street for a moment, then straightened his back and made eye contact. "Is Delilah being courted by anyone?"

"No." *Yes* was on his tongue, but lying always made things worse.

"I've been pining for her since I received my first letter from her two years ago." Monty's expression held a challenge.

Jed's jaw tightened, and he ruminated for a moment on what to say to discourage him. "I'll be honest with you. She's got plans for the future that don't include any husband." He tried to sound matter-of-fact.

"I see the lay of the land. You got feelings for her too." Monty's stare seemed to bore into Jed's heart and find the truth. "Well, may the best man win."

"Miss McLain told me she refused you. Don't come around upsetting her." Jed stepped closer. "I assure you, if she was interested in any man around here, including me, she'd be a willing participant in courting. She ain't, so please don't torment her."

"I have no intention of tormenting. Merely wooing her gently to my side." Monty tipped his hat. "Thanks for the carpenter recommendation."

Too bad he hadn't suggested the Meriweathers—they were slower than molasses in winter.

Monty maneuvered his own full wagon past the livery and onto the road out of town.

"What ya lookin' at?" Lonnie had approached without Jed's notice.

"Nothing. Kinda like the help you gave me loading this wagon." Jed ground out the words.

"What's eatin' ya?" Lonnie glared at him, then climbed into the driver's seat.

Jed took his place on the bench. They were a few miles from town before he had calmed enough to speak of their new neighbor.

"So … Monty James is a determined man." Lonnie shook his head, then pointed at him. "Good thing you'll be stayin' behind to protect her."

"I figure it'll be a while before he has time to come courtin'. Be too busy buildin' a house." At least Jed hoped so.

"No worries, she's smitten with ya. He can't turn her head." Lonnie slapped him on the back.

"What makes you think so?"

"No one else can make her laugh."

"Friends laugh. She only wants friendship." Jed refused to look toward his twin. A smirk probably rested on his face and would need slapping, not a good idea while Lonnie was driving the team. "Can we talk about something else?"

"Genny told me, Dee hopes to have enough set by to rent a building in town by next summer."

So much for a subject change. Dee was still front and center, and Lonnie's information didn't help his mood. "Genny's still going to need help. Maybe even more when the boys start walking and getting into mischief."

"Dee is indeed a big help to Genny, and I like her baking."

"Me too." And her sweet smile and gentle ways. Then there were her raven hair, gorgeous green eyes, and a stubborn streak to match his brother's.

Monty's declaration invaded his thoughts and soured his stomach.

Dee folded the last of the diapers and carried them to the bedroom, careful not to awaken an exhausted Genny. Birdie had a stuffy head that had kept her from sleeping the past two nights. Genny had walked the floor with her. Thankfully, the girls had agreed to nap when the boys were put down.

Dee tiptoed back to the kitchen and sat at the table. She pulled from her apron pocket the three letters Jed had given her. The mantel clock chimed two as she opened the first one, addressed in an unfamiliar hand. Inside the envelope was the letter she'd written her parents last week, unopened. The second held another unopened letter. Why had her parents returned the letters without reading them? Were they ashamed of her? She glanced inside the envelopes to see if she'd missed a note. Empty. The third envelope had clearly been addressed by her mother. Dee hesitated. Did she want to read it? She slid the letter from the envelope and took a deep breath. It was better to read it now than wonder about it until later.

Dearest Daughter,
It grieved us to hear of your misfortune, but praising our Lord He brought you to a better place. Mr. Hollingsworth died from a stroke, requiring his son to return home early from his honeymoon. Young Hollingsworth asked after you and was angry you'd left. We did not mention you were widowed for fear he might seek you out. Once his father's affairs were settled, he insisted we were too old and should retire. His mother's kindness saved us from being dismissed penniless.

What a horrible man. Her poor parents. A tear settled on Dee's cheek as she continued to read.

For now, we are staying at a boarding house, and by the time you receive this letter, we will be on our way to you. When we reach Omaha, we will telegraph you. We will then board the train to Abilene. Papa says we should take the stage from there. I wondered if you might prefer to meet us. We'll send a telegram when we reach Abilene and await your response. We miss you so very much and look forward to being reunited.
Love,
Mother

Dee reread the letter three times before she put it back in the envelope. What was she to do? The postmark was two weeks old. Based on her own travel, they were already in Abilene. Their timing couldn't be worse. Where would they stay? She'd go into town and secure a room at the boardinghouse. Perhaps there was a telegram already waiting for her.

Jed and Lonnie interrupted her fretting. She jumped up. "I'm sorry. I haven't even started cooking."

"We're only here for coffee." Jed smiled her way.

"Genny is napping. Give me a few minutes to make a fresh pot."

Dee took the pot out the back door and dumped the stale coffee in the garden. She stood for several minutes watching the coffee disappear into the dry ground. Parched like her soul. Her grand plan to help her parents had failed, and now they'd see what a failure she was when they had no place to stay. Marching back into the house, she prepared the coffee.

Jed interrupted her anxious thoughts. "Did you get bad news from home?"

The letters lay strewn on the table. Scooping them up and ignoring his question was futile. They would learn the content, eventually. "After a fashion, I suppose."

Before she could explain, Jilly and Molly came running from their room and climbed into Lonnie's lap.

"How's my sweet breaths of sunshine?" Lonnie kissed the tops of their heads. "I got a surprise for you."

"What, Pa?" the girls said in unison.

"Miss Tabby had kittens."

The girls scrambled from his lap and ran to the barn.

"I reckon you best take some of those barn cats over to the neighbors. Be sure to keep the males. Otherwise, we're goin' be a cat ranch instead of cattle ranch." Jed chuckled and Lonnie nodded agreement.

"Yep, I was asking around town if anyone wanted good mousers. I'll get one of the men to haul 'em into town and leave them at the mercantile. Mrs. Clemens said she'd make sure they got good homes."

How she wished she had a good home in town for her parents. Dee poured their coffee, and the men waited. She dreaded the conversation before she'd sorted things out for herself. Wordlessly, she handed the letter to Jed and then placed a plate of cookies on the table, hoping to soften the blow. Jed passed it to Lonnie.

"Looks like we'll be havin' company." Lonnie's response didn't surprise her.

"No, I'll go into town and rent a room at the boarding house." Dee didn't want to inconvenience this sweet family further.

"Why are you renting a room? Did one of you men upset her?" Genny came from the bedroom with Birdie on her hip.

Lonnie filled her in while Dee poured more coffee.

"That's wonderful. We'll make room. Don't you dare leave them in town." Genny smiled as she wiped Birdie's runny nose with a handkerchief.

"I can't take advantage of your generous natures. You've no room, and my cabin is tiny." Dee fought back tears of frustration. "I think I should rent a room for myself too. I could ride a horse back and forth."

"You don't ride." Jed was right, and it irritated her.

"Then hitch Soldier to a wagon, and I'll drive myself."

"He's a handful, and you might get hurt." The man was—oh!—so frustrating.

She grabbed a basket and strode to the door. "I'll go pick some squash."

Dee had placed the last squash in her basket when Jed stood beside her. "You don't need to figure everything out this minute. And we're here to help." He assisted her to stand. "You know I'd do anything for ya." His tender look made her want to lean into him. Instead, she put the basket between them.

"I'm not ready for them to come. My bakery is only a dream. They're old and tired, and now they'll need jobs to support themselves." Tears coursed down her cheeks. Jed took the basket from her and placed it on the ground, then pulled her into his arms. She jerked away and wiped her eyes with her sleeve. "Please, don't make me feel more helpless than I do." She hurried to her cabin, leaving the basket where it lay.

Chapter 27

Dee went through her chores by rote as her mind wrestled to form a plan. She could get a job in town. No, that wouldn't be fair to Genny. But if she stayed, her parents would need to work. But they couldn't, they mustn't …

"I think three times sweeping the room surely has it clean." Genny chuckled from the rocker where she sat nursing Peter.

Dee's desire to discuss her dilemma with Jed fought with her need to figure it out herself. She'd avoided him after her rude behavior yesterday. His embrace had been a welcomed comfort. Yet the closeness scared her, not to mention depending on others to solve her problems.

This afternoon, she'd take the wagon into town and secure a room for her parents. After they'd had a few days to rest, they could discuss the future. At least it was half a plan.

The sound of men's voices outside drew her to the window. She pushed the curtain aside. Monty James dismounted and handed the reins to Gonzalez while Lonnie and Jed stood near.

"What does he want?" Dee scowled and pushed the curtain back in place.

"Who?"

"Monty James." Dee glanced toward the back door, gauging the wisdom of making a quick escape.

"Maybe he's come to buy horses. Jed said he was interested in ranching." Genny burped the baby and laid him on a blanket on the floor next to Robert. Birdie sat nearby, playing with her doll. "I need to check on the girls in the barn. It will give me a chance to overhear the men." She scurried out the door.

Dee took the rocker while Birdie jabbered a song to her doll. She still had a sniffle, so her mother had confined her to the house.

"Up, p'ease." Birdie climbed on her lap and Dee rocked. She hugged her close. The scent of mustard plaster still lingered on the child. Birdie laid her head on Dee's shoulder. She closed her eyes and enjoyed the feel of the small child's closeness. Cuddling Birdie settled her anxiety for a moment. She hummed to the sweet girl.

The door opened, interrupting her peace. Genny entered first, followed by Jed and Lonnie, then Monty.

"Miss McLain." Monty offered a bright smile. "Don't you look the copy of the Madonna?"

Dee frowned. "I don't feel worthy of such a holy comparison." He was up to something, and she wasn't having any of it. "What brings you here today?"

"This." Monty removed a telegram from his vest pocket. "A representative from the telegraph office brought it. I believe it was meant for you."

"Why on earth?" Dee held out her hand, not wanting to disturb Birdie.

He gave it to her. "The telegraph operator saw the name *James* and delivered it to me by mistake."

Before she could read it, he added, "I'm sure you're happy your parents will be arriving on the next stage."

"How dare you read—" Her raised voice brought Birdie's head off her shoulder, and she stared at Dee, concern in her eyes. "It's fine, Birdie." She guided the child's head back onto her shoulder and resumed rocking.

"Until I read the telegram, I had no idea it was for you. My apologies." Monty's contrition embarrassed her. Why was it so easy to jump to the wrong conclusions because of his name?

"Forgive me. I'm not accustomed to others discussing my telegram before I've seen it." She read through it. Her parents had arrived in Omaha and boarded the train to Abilene this morning. They would wait for her response before they continued their journey. If they took the stage, they'd arrive in Cooperville Friday. "I need to reply." She stood and passed Birdie to Genny.

"I'm happy to take you to town." Monty offered a smile that could melt a snowcapped mountain.

She refused to be caught in his gaze and turned to see the scowl on Jed's face. Dee chewed her lip as she glanced at the telegram again, then shoved it in her dress pocket. "You didn't bring a wagon. Mr. James. I don't ride." For once, Dee was glad she couldn't do something.

Jed stepped ahead of Monty "Whenever you're ready, I'll hitch up the wagon and take you to town."

"Perfect." Dee nodded toward Jed, then faced Monty. "That settles it."

"I'll be on my way, but perhaps our paths will cross again." He tipped his hat and left.

She went to the window. Monty mounted, then turned toward the house and waved. She jumped away from the window as the sound of hooves told of his exit.

"You okay?" Jed stood beside her.

"Perhaps I should go by McLain rather than James, so there's no more confusion." She walked to the table and sat. "Is it permissible to return to one's maiden name?"

"I reckon you can do whatever you want." Jed joined her at the table.

"Next time you're in town, have the lawyer help you change your name." Genny set Birdie down to resume her play.

"An excellent idea. I'll go this afternoon to send the telegram to my parents, then I'll see if the lawyer has time to see me." Two more expenses taking money from her bakery enterprise and her chancc for independence.

"Jed, you don't need to drive me to town. I can handle a wagon. You've better things to do." Dee still wasn't confident driving the wagon alone, but she'd not impose on his good nature.

"What I gotta do can wait. You needn't go to town alone. Monty James might head there to meet ya."

What was that tone? Jealousy? No, in her experience jealous men sounded angry.

She didn't need coddling right now. "That's ridiculous. Where d'you get the notion?"

"I have it on good authority he's planning on wooing ya."

"He told you that?"

Jed leaned toward her. "Yep. I told him not to torment you." Then he crossed his arms and scowled.

"I can deal with Monty." At least she hoped she could. "If you really wish to drive me to town, I'd appreciate the company." Why did she let her thoughts slip out her lips? A simple *thank you* would have sufficed. No help for it now. She removed her apron. "I need to change and compose my telegram before we leave."

Jed's grin made the blue in his eyes brighter. Peace radiated through her, chasing the niggling dread away. His presence always calmed her. Now if only her heart would agree with her mind, and she could allow herself to trust him.

"I'll go hitch the wagon." He nodded her way, winked, then disappeared out the door.

Dee blushed, then noticed her friend holding Birdie. Lonnie sat at the table with Jilly and Molly. "Oh, Genny, how thoughtless. I should have consulted you first. If you'd rather …"

Genny took her hand. "Go. Sending a telegram is more important. Take all the time you need to get your name changed. I'll keep supper warm for you both."

"Are you sure?" Dee directed her question to Lonnie.

"No time like the present." Lonnie toasted her with his coffee cup.

Dee didn't have time to speculate what their expressions meant.

She scurried to the cabin to get ready. Her thoughts went to her parents, Jed, Monty, and what she should say in her telegram, all before she reached her cabin door. She was no longer the naïve optimist. When her parents saw her present situation, they could be disappointed. She was in service. No different from Baltimore. Her dreams of a sweet future remained that—a dream.

Jed took the time to wash up and change his shirt before pulling the wagon in front of the house. Dee was waiting, decked out in her lavender dress and a new black bonnet. The rim was smaller, letting him admire her face. She climbed aboard before he could assist her.

She focused on the road ahead, her right hand gripping the side of the seat, her left hand holding tight to her reticule.

"Did you get your note written?" Jed looked her way.

"Yes. I decided to tell them I'd meet them in Abilene." Dee's eyes pled for his approval. "What do you think? Is that the best answer?" She glanced away again. "I don't know the way. I was only there long enough to marry and board the stagecoach to Cooperville."

"You can't go by yourself to Abilene. It ain't a fit place for a woman. Let them take the stage. Why work yourself up over meeting them early? One more week won't make any difference since ya didn't know they were coming in the first place." If she hadn't asked, he wouldn't have said his piece.

Dee nodded. "You're very sensible. Thank you. That's what I'll tell them." Her shoulders relaxed and relief filled her features.

He smiled, pleased she'd taken his advice. "Always happy to help." Jed kept the horses at a slow plod, savoring this alone time with Dee. There was no way Monty James was staking a claim until he could.

"I am so relieved. One less worry. I'll rent a second room in town to be closer to my parents." Dee sighed and set her face to watch the road again.

She couldn't leave. Dee was a part of them now. Family. He wiped his brow with his sleeve, dislodging his hat. He adjusted it. Things would be out of place if she left. The smell of rosewater wafted over him as the wind blew tendrils of hair loose from her bonnet. *Please don't go.*

Focusing on the road, he pulled the reins to the left, directing the team toward town. "You got a place on the Single Cross." He couldn't look at her for fear the same stubborn glint would be in her eyes.

"My parents need their privacy. My cabin is too small. I can always ride to the ranch and help Genny during the day, then head home before it gets dark."

"If you learn to ride a horse, but a woman alone isn't a good idea."

"But I need to be near them." Her green eyes flashed as her voice rose. "I can't abandon them in a strange town."

Jed didn't want to rile her further. Letting out a slow breath, calm took over his agitation. "Let's not fret about it now. You still gotta send the telegram and wait for their answer." The best course of action needed to be presented gradual-like. She was a distracted filly, not wanting to be led into the stable.

As Jed escorted Dee to the telegraph office, David Barlow crossed the street. Once the telegram was sent, Jed walked Dee to the law office and then hunted for the carpenter. He found him coming out of the gunsmith's. "Got a minute?" Jed walked with him to his wagon. "I need you and your brother over at the ranch tomorrow."

"We're rounding up the last of our strays tomorrow."

"I need two rooms added to Dee's cabin before Friday. Her parents are coming. I'll make it worth your trouble."

The man rubbed his chin. "I don't know." The silence between them was thicker than a soddie's wall. "I tell ya what, if you can loan us a few of your men, we can come the day after."

"The rooms will be ready by Friday?"

"Move-in ready."

The men shook on it.

Jed waited on a bench outside the law office for Dee to finish her business. He hoped his arrangement wouldn't make her mad. The door opened, and he rose from the bench and smiled.

"You look pleased with yourself." Dee smiled, then they strode toward the telegraph office again.

"Yep, I'm adding to your cabin so your folks can stay with you. The work starts day after tomorrow."

She stopped and stared at him. "I should be angry with you. If you recall, I said I wanted to bring my parents here on my own terms." Dee crossed her arms and glared. "However, they are coming on *their* terms, which changes everything." She sighed and shook her head. "It will be better having my parents with me. Thank you so much."

Man, he'd do anything to see her face beaming. "What did the lawyer say?"

"I could call myself anything I wanted. Otherwise, it'd cost me fifty dollars to go to court and have it changed back legally." She shook her head. "Fifty dollars is money I am not prepared to spend right now."

"Miss McLain." Jed tipped his hat and offered his arm.

Dee smiled. "Thank you, kind sir." She took his arm. Her long fingers gripped his bicep, sending a tingle clear to his toes.

They stepped inside the telegraph office.

The telegraph operator greeted her with a smile. "Ma'am, there is no reply yet, but that's not unusual. It might be several hours before your party retrieves your answer. I'm happy to deliver it to you."

"Be sure to take it to the Holt ranch." Jed didn't want another misunderstanding.

The telegraph began tapping.

"Wait, it's from Abilene." The operator tapped a reply, then the message came through and he copied it down. "Perfect timing. Your party must have been waiting." He smiled and handed the missive to her.

"Thank you so much." She read it and smiled at Jed. "It's confirmed. I'll meet their stage on Friday."

"How'd it go?" Genny pulled two plates from the oven. Lonnie joined them at the table while Dee filled them in.

"What do you think?"

"About going by McLain?" Lonnie shrugged. "What you call yerself is yer own business."

"I agree, but I was referring to my parents living here. Adding to my cabin is a big inconvenience, and …"

"Sounds like Jed has made the arrangements for the building. It won't disturb us at all." Genny took the pot and warmed everyone's coffee.

"Well, I did agree to send a few of the crew to help the Barlows gather the last of the strays tomorrow in exchange for them coming this week." Jed gave his brother a sheepish look, and Dee cringed.

"If it's a bother …" Dee hated the quaver in her voice.

"As long as you be one of the crew, I'm fine with the arrangement." Lonnie nodded Jed's way.

"I can do that. I'll take Carter."

"Take Benny too. He needs to work on his wrangling skills before the drive."

"I'll tell them now so we can get an early start in the mornin'." Jed rose, grabbed his hat from the peg, then turned and gave her his dimpled smile.

The door shut, and she turned to Lonnie. "I'm sorry."

"Don't be. It's what family does." He rose. "I got a few chores to finish."

After Lonnie disappeared out the door, Dee asked, "Genny, is he just being polite?"

"Ha. You've lived here long enough to know *polite* isn't a word I'd choose to describe Lonnie." She took Dee's hand. "You're family. I grew up an only child. I envy my children their siblings. You feel like the sister I always wanted."

Dee wiped her eyes with her sleeve. "Me too." She sniffled.

A warm, lingering hug confirmed their feelings. Genny filled a hollow place in her heart. And the men's kindness was helping her scars to heal. Once her parents arrived, her loneliness should vanish. Would Mother be fine living here? Or rather live in town? Jed's words, *Let's not fret about it now,* comforted her. She'd take things one day at a time and pray her parents would be comfortable on the Single Cross.

Chapter 28

Dee paced in front of the stage depot. "It's late."

"Don't worry. It'll be here." Jed sat on the bench in front of the building, Sheba at his feet.

"What if something happened?" Dee stopped and stared at him. "The stage could have broken down, or worse, been robbed and the passengers shot."

"You remind me of Lonnie, always borrowing worry from his imagination." Jed chuckled.

"I'm sorry you think my worry is trivial." She glared at him for reading her so well. Her mother had always been a worrier too. She'd explore all the terrible things that could happen and come up with a solution. If nothing went wrong, she was almost giddy. Dee was never giddy, only relieved.

After pacing some more, Dee stared up the road. This time, she could see the stagecoach approach from a distance. Dust followed in its wake as it neared. Wheels rattled and a loud, "Whoa, boys," could be heard as the matching team of four brown horses slowed. It pulled to a stop in front of them. The driver climbed off and opened the door while his partner unstrapped a large trunk from the roof. They pulled it down together, then began heaving the smaller bags to the ground.

Dee gave a cry of joy as her parents disembarked the stage and turned smiling faces on her. She dodged the last carpetbag being tossed down and ran to her parents. Their hugs were a balm to her soul. "I'm delighted you're here."

"We're so relieved to arrive in one piece." Her mother patted her hair, a bit grayer under the familiar black bonnet. "Henry, collect our things."

"Wait." Dee signaled for Jed. "This is Jed Holt. He and his brother own the Single Cross. Jed, these are my parents, Henry and Anna McLain."

"Pleased to meet ya." Jed tipped his hat to her mother and shook her father's hand.

"We're happy to make your acquaintance." Her father gave him his appraising look, then smiled. Relief rushed over Dee at her father's approval. Why? They weren't courting. Yet she wanted her parents to like her adopted family. That was it, of course.

"Let me help you with your luggage. My wagon is over yonder." Jed grabbed four bags, stuffing two under his arms as he led the way to the wagon. Her father, a head shorter than Jed, carried one of their smaller trunks on his shoulder and a carpetbag in the other hand. Papa was stronger than she remembered.

After those were secured in the wagon, each man took a handle on the large trunk and settled it in the wagon bed. She'd forgotten the mystery trunk that had sat in the corner of her parents' tiny room. Her mother kept it locked and never mentioned its content.

Jed had brought the family wagon with the additional bench. Dee sat with her mother in the back while her father took the front seat next to Jed.

"Mr. Holt, I want to thank ye and yours for taking care of me darlin' Delilah in her time of need." Her father glanced back at her and smiled. "She wrote your coming to her aid be an answer to prayer."

"Call me Jed. She was an answer to Genny's prayer for help with her brood."

"Genny is his sister-in-law. She has five of the most delightful children."

Mother adored children and looked forward to grandchildren. Sadness cloaked Dee, knowing it would never be. She put those emotions in the big trunk resting in her heart, weighing against the joy that tried to live there.

"Thank the dear Lord, we've arrived at last." Her mother hugged her. "Our trip felt as long as when we crossed the Atlantic years ago. Maybe it's me old bones not fancyin' travel like in me youth." Fatigue made her mother's proper English flounder. She'd worked hard to sound more refined because Mrs. Hollingsworth hated their Irish accents.

"I didna realize how vast America is." Her father appeared to savor the view. "We arrived in Baltimore and never left the city. This has been a grand adventure."

He'd always dreamed of traveling west. At least she'd given him that.

They arrived at the ranch midafternoon. Jilly and Molly, with Birdie not far behind, ran to greet their guests. Soon they were hugging her parents as if they'd been waiting for their arrival all their lives. Genny and Lonnie held the boys.

"My, my, so many twins." Mother chuckled. "Even you two." She smiled at Lonnie and Jed.

"This is my brother, Lonnie, and his wife, Genny. And the girls are Jilly, Molly, and Birdie." Jed picked up Birdie, and she cuddled close and stared at Dee's parents with a sweet smile. Jed would make a fine father someday. Dee brushed the thought away.

Lonnie stepped forward and shook her parents' hands. He indicated the babies he and his wife held. "This is Peter, and Genny has Robert."

"Strapping lads." Her father and mother reached for the babies, and the Holts obliged.

"We love children." Mother kissed Robert's head. "We only had one, but she is precious to us." The admiration in her eyes sent a thrill through Dee. "Delilah, my dear"—she handed Robert back to Genny—"could you show us to our room so we can freshen up?"

The crew had already taken all the luggage to her expanded cabin. Genny's reminder her growing family would someday fill her cabin, too, had taken away Dee's last objection. The homes were built so close, with little effort they could be connected.

Inside Dee's cabin, her bed and dresser had been moved to the left bedroom, and the furniture she had purchased from the carpenter had been added to the right one for her parents. A stove and two rockers graced the main room. A bookshelf full of volumes rested on the back wall, and the new curtains she'd made hung at the windows.

"I see you have a sewing machine." Mother stroked the cabinet.

"It's Genny's. But we do our sewing in here."

"Did you make the curtains?" Mother inspected them. Dee nodded, a knot in her throat. "Excellent job. She's a good teacher."

"I made my dress too." Dee waited for her mother to critique her work.

"The color suits you. Now, if you'll show us our room, we'll rest before the evening meal."

Papa kissed her cheek. "It's a joy to be together again. I hope we are not a burden to your employers."

"Of course not. It was their idea for you to stay here. They understand the importance of family." Dee hugged him. "You've finally traveled west."

"Aye, and a grand place it is."

Dee showed them to their room and shut the door. In moments, gentle snores could be heard. She sat in her rocker and enjoyed the peace the sound brought her.

They were finally here. Now she needed to convince them she was capable. Perhaps her parents would disapprove of her bakery notion. One letter returned to her had explained her plans. A knock brought her from her musings.

"Jed." Dee stepped outside and closed the door. His masculine scent of hay and field surrounded her. Sheba sat at his feet. She patted the dog to distract her wayward thoughts. "My parents are napping."

"I forgot to bring this by." Jed pointed to a tin tub resting next to the door. "I figured they might want a bath after their long trip."

"Did you buy this?" Dee touched the metal frame. "You've already done so much."

"The men wanted to contribute, to thank you for sharing your baked goods." Jed's smile brought tears of joy. Since leaving the ashes of the past year, it appeared her tears had been released from the bitter cage she'd banished them to.

Dee dabbed her eyes. "Thank them for me. They are so very thoughtful. One more thing to make my parents more comfortable."

"I imagine they're plumb tuckered. Stagecoaches ain't very comfortable." Jed stared at her, causing her cheeks to warm.

She petted Sheba once more. "Is there something else on your mind?"

"Yes—I mean, no, ma'am." Jed cleared his throat. "I'm glad you have kin with ya. I don't know what I woulda done without Lonnie." With a tip of his hat, he strode away.

They'd lost their family and opened their arms to hers. Another reason to admire Jed Holt.

Sheba's bark interrupted Jed as he moved a bag of feed in the barn. "What's wrong with you, girl?"

The newest hire, Benny, entered, his pants baggy on his thin frame. "Reckon she sensed me coming."

"Sheba!" The dog quieted and came to Jed's side. "I can't figure why she's barkin' at you."

"She probably knows I don't care for dogs." Benny eyed the dog, then rolled up his sleeve. "I got this scar from a mean one when I was a child. Pa had to shoot the mongrel to get him offa me."

The long, jagged scar explained why Benny lacked strength in his right arm and favored his left. "I promise Sheba don't bite. Leastways, she ain't bit anyone on the Single Cross."

"If it's all the same, I'll keep my distance." Benny remained rooted to his place at the stable door.

"You need somethin'?"

"Your brother told me to fetch ya."

Oh, right. Jed had lost track of the time. Lonnie had planned a talk with those going on the cattle drive … and Jed, since he owned half the Single Cross and Lonnie insisted that his presence added solidarity. Benny ran ahead, and Sheba walked with Jed to the bunkhouse.

"'Bout time you showed up." Lonnie nodded his way, then began the meeting. "We got one week afore we head out. As usual, Jed will be stayin' here to keep the ranch runnin' and the womenfolk safe. I need two men to help Jed. The rest are comin' on the cattle drive. It'll take about a month to get the cattle to Abilene if nothin' delays us. May take about as long to get 'em sold. You won't collect your wages until then. I expect anyone ridin' for the Single Cross to conduct themselves like gentlemen. I will dock any man's pay who causes trouble along the way. And I might leave a man or two stranded in Abilene penniless if they get on my nerves."

His brother was all bluster. There'd only been one incident where a man didn't get paid, which was a mercy considering Lonnie could have had him thrown in jail for stealing. Benny looked at the floor. What was bothering him? The other temporary hires had worked for the Single Cross before.

Lonnie pulled a paper from his shirt pocket. "I got a list of things need doin' before week's end. That'll keep us on schedule to join the other local ranchers on the drive. Carter, Gonzales, and Jensen, see me after. The rest of you, get back to your chores."

"Fellas." Jed stopped them from leaving. "Miss Dee asked me to thank you for your kindness in providing the tub."

The men smiled and nodded as they walked out together.

"You sweet on her, ain't ya?" The foreman slapped Jed on the back. "You and most of the crew."

Jed took the teasing in the spirit it was given. Standing in the middle of the yard, his mind fixated on beautiful green eyes and sweet cherry lips.

Sheba nudged his hand. "Are you smitten with her too?" He chuckled and strode to the stable to groom Sally, a chore that kept him closer to the house in case a certain someone might need help. The dog started toward the chicken coop. Jed whistled, and she came to his side. "Don't even think about chasing Genny's chickens. I got no idea why they are such a temptation for you." Jed could list many reasons Dee tempted his affection.

Now with her folks here, he needed to be on his best behavior. Friendship was what she wanted, and he wouldn't embarrass her in front of kin by acting otherwise. Would Monty James show up and try to charm her parents with his fancy words? Dee wouldn't be persuaded by them to reconsider marryin' the man, would she? The thought galled him. How could he measure up to the likes of Monty James?

Chapter 29

It had been a week since Dee's parents had arrived when her father greeted Jed at the kitchen table dressed in overalls. "Lad, I'm ready to work." Henry McLain signaled for Jed to take the seat next to him.

"Sir, you're a guest."

"I'll not be a lay-about. I may be getting older, but I can put in a full day's work. Me bones are getting stiff from sitting on my laurels. You'd be doing me a favor, giving me something to do."

"Then I'm happy for the help. I'll show you around after breakfast."

Mrs. McLain stirred a pot on the stove. "We don't know how to enjoy leisure. It's good to be cooking again."

Dee smiled at her mother as she made coffee.

"I'm happy to share my kitchen." Genny smiled at her before heading to the bedroom to tend crying babies.

The McLains seemed to fill a void Genny's parents' death had left. Since dinner last night, the women had been making plans to increase the amount of merchandise Dee sent to town. Thanks to the summer kitchen, baking went on every day. The smells kept the crew coming home for every meal without fail.

Lonnie entered with the egg basket.

"Since when do you gather eggs?" Jed shook his head.

"Since Mrs. McLain wants to treat us to eggs benedict, whatever that is." Lonnie accepted a cup of coffee from Dee. "Where's my bride?"

"Changing the babies." Dee started cracking eggs into one of the new bowls.

Jed looked around. "Where are the girls?"

"Feeding the kittens." Lonnie nodded toward the door.

The front door flew open, and the girls raced toward Mrs. McLain. "Grandmother," they shouted in unison. Bits of straw clung to their clothes.

"There's six new kitties in the barn." Jilly beamed as she took her place at the table.

"Miss Black had babies," Molly added, and Birdie jabbered and clapped her hands.

"Wash up." Dee pointed to the washbasin. The girls scurried to comply.

"Once we finish our chores, we shall go visit the new mother." Mrs. McLain helped Birdie wash her hands.

Genny came out with the boys in her arms. "My, I feel so spoiled now you are here, Mother McLain."

Lonnie and Jed played with the babies and listened to the girls' chatter. The women working together reminded Jed of his childhood when his mother and her maid Ava bustled about the kitchen. Mrs. McLain and Dee set food on the table, and soon everyone was gathered around. Genny held Peter while Lonnie nestled Robert on his lap. The two were starting to sit up.

"We need to fetch the highchairs out of the barn loft for the boys." Lonnie pushed Robert's hands away from his plate, then gave him a hard crust of bread to chew.

"It'll be the first chore I do today." Jed scooped eggs onto Molly's plate while she screwed up her lips in disapproval.

"I hate 'em." His niece pushed the scrambled mass to the side of her plate.

"Molly, stop fussing and eat them while they are hot." Genny's look barred any further argument.

Molly huffed, crossed her arms, then sighed. Taking her fork, she made quick work of the eggs.

Jed laughed at how much she reminded him of himself as a child. He'd followed in Lonnie's shadow and worked hard to be obedient. One day, Molly would become her own person. Was he his own person, even now? Every decision he'd made since the war revolved around Lonnie's needs. He caught Dee watching him before she turned to feed Birdie. Was it time he focused on his own needs? He'd been content single, trusting God to bring him a wife. Was Dee that wife, or was he fooling himself and changing the course God had for his life? Same as when he joined the Union army as a chaplain—his solution to not bearing arms. Look how well that had worked out. Night terrors had changed him. Maybe he should have borne the stigma as Lonnie had. His twin had never compromised his pacifist position, not once. Jed admired his brother's bravery.

"Uncle Jed." Molly's tiny voice got his attention. "Can I please have some jam?"

"Sure, honey." Jed spread gooseberry jam on her bread. She smiled sweetly. Before she could take a bite, Dee lifted her eyebrow at Molly.

"Thank you." His niece spoke more to the bread than him.

"You're welcome."

Molly smeared jam on her face with every bite. Dee stepped beside him and poured fresh coffee in his cup. The familiar scent of rosewater surrounded him. "Thank you, ma'am." He looked up as she leaned across him to pour more coffee in her father's cup. The unintentional closeness stirred desire he tamped down. Once she moved, he could breathe again and turned toward Lonnie. "As soon as I finish my coffee, I'll get them chairs, then head to the fence."

"I'll join you, laddie." Henry gulped the last of his coffee and reached for his hat. They went to the barn, and Jed ascended to the loft and dangled the chairs over the side for Henry to grab. On his way down, Jed nearly missed the last rung of the ladder when Henry spoke.

"What are your intentions toward me daughter?"

"Sir?" Did he have a note clipped to his forehead giving his thoughts away?

"I'm not blind, lad. I see the way you look at her."

"We're friends." Jed picked up a chair, schooling his expression before looking Henry's way.

"Are you, now?" He raised his eyebrow.

Why did everyone jump to that conclusion? What look did he have? He thought back to the puppy eyes Lonnie had sent Genny's way while he denied the attraction. He waited a beat before answering, keeping his voice even.

"It's all she wants. I'll honor that." Truth always seemed to be first on his tongue whether he liked it or not. He hadn't said he was attracted to her, had he?

Henry nodded. "I admire a man who knows how to respect a woman. I've seen far too few as a servant in the home of the wealthy." They left the highchairs on the porch. They'd need a good cleaning before they could be used.

"Now, what would you have me do?" Henry asked.

Jed hesitated, not wanting to offend the man by suggesting a job he might not care to do.

"You know, before I was the master gardener, I was a stable boy. Let me muck your stalls and brush them beautiful beasties." The man's eyes twinkled.

"Right this way." Jed led him to the stable.

Henry entered and went right to Sally's stall. "Look at the wee one. He is a beauty. What's his name?"

"Celtic Fire."

The man's eyes brightened as he leaned over the stall door. "Was the name Delilah's choosing?"

"It's her colt. Her plow horse sired him." Jed wanted to say more, but that would spoil the pleasure for Dee.

"He'll be a strong thing." Henry said something in what Jed could only assume was Gaelic. Soldier whinnied from the far stall.

"Well, now, a kindred spirit." Henry strode toward the large horse and conversed in his language. Soldier leaned over and nuzzled Henry.

"I've never seen Soldier warm to anyone, leastways a man. Dee's late husband abused him."

Henry opened the stall gate. He patted the horse and cooed. "Look here." He pointed at the brand on his flank. "It's been altered. 'Twas a Celtic knot." He traced the shape with his finger.

"Explains why he ignores us most of the time."

"He was trained to obey the Gaelic rather than English. That way, no one could steal him. Appears he's suffered for it." The sadness in the older man's voice touched Jed. "I know what it's like to suffer for being different." He turned to Jed. "Would it be all right if I took over the care of this majestic animal?"

"Maybe you can talk him into pulling a wagon or letting your daughter ride him."

"Why does she want to ride the beastie? He's not proper horseflesh for a woman."

"Because he's hers." Jed's words made Henry chuckle.

"That's me girl. We've never owned anything of value, so this horse be special to her." Henry gave Soldier another pat. "I'll start with his stall, and with any luck, I'll be done with the stable by midday meal."

"You can release them into the corral or the near pasture." Jed left him to his work and went to the shed for fencing material.

Wait until Dee heard about Soldier.

Henry's praise of Jed's integrity put a heavy responsibility on him. There was no way he could compete with Monty and maintain the proper distance for friendship he'd told Henry they had. Drat it all. Monty James was the coon in the chicken coop. He had to figure out a way to discourage the man once and for all, lest Mr. McLain decide Monty was a fine match for Dee. Was an arranged marriage something his family favored?

Pain shot through Jed's hand as he grabbed the barbed wire

without work gloves. Blood trickled down his wrist, and his palm throbbed as he examined the bleeding gash. He wrapped it in his bandana, then tied it securely. No way would he risk Dee ferreting out that his preoccupation with her had caused the injury by going to the main house for bandages.

Chapter 30

Dee pulled the last dry sheet off the clothesline to see her mother standing there, her expression unreadable. She gave one end of the sheet to her mother, and together they folded it. Dee took the sheet from her and placed it in the basket.

A gentle hand rested on her arm. "My dear, you've changed. You're not the look-for-the-silver-lining girl you once were."

Dee didn't want to talk about the past, especially her late husband. She'd managed to avoid the subject so far, but it was inevitable.

"I blame myself." Mother hugged her.

"It's not your fault." Dee pulled away, searching her face.

"Your father wanted to accompany you. I told him it wasn't necessary. I feared we'd lose our positions." Moisture formed in her eyes, and her voice choked. "You lost a big piece of yourself, and we lost our positions despite my efforts."

Her mother's sorrow pricked Dee's conscience. "It was my grand plan. My solution to avoid Tobias Hollingsworth's advances."

"It was a good plan, but had your father accompanied you, he'd have judged his mettle, and you'd have been free to make a different choice." She hugged Dee even tighter before continuing. "When we first arrived in America, your father saw an opportunity to travel west. We had some money saved, and he suggested selling my family's silver to help finance the trip. I would have none of it."

"Family silver? Why don't I remember anything about that?"

Dee moved away and picked up the basket.

"I was afraid if you knew, the two of you would persuade me to sell. It's all I have left of my family."

"That's what's in the trunk?" Dee stood stark still, taking in the revelation.

"Yes, among other things." Mother touched her arm again. "Please forgive me. Had I been willing to leave Baltimore years ago, you wouldn't have endured such cruelty."

Dee pressed her handkerchief into her hand. "Mother, are you God?"

"Of course not."

"He is the only one who knew the future." A bitter taste rested on her tongue and moved to her stomach. "And He let me follow my folly." She patted her mother's hand which still rested on her arm, then moved away. "I've no one to blame but myself."

"Someday you'll find a good man. Things will be different."

If only that were true. Dee walked toward the house, leaving her mother standing alone.

"Wait." Mother came running. "Later, can you help me with something?"

"What is it?"

"I haven't emptied my trunk since I packed it to travel the Atlantic. I'd like to show you something."

"Your silver?" Now that she'd confessed she'd hid their wealth, did Dee want to see it?

"Something else. It's a surprise." She smiled as she matched Dee's pace. "I'll ask Papa to join us." She headed toward the stable.

Odd. When had her mother started referring to her father in such an informal way? Dee took the basket inside. The mention of surprises reminded her she hadn't shared hers with her father. She went searching for him in the stable, calling out from the doorway. "Papa."

"Over here, lamb." He held her mother as she wept. "Shh." He cooed to her in Gaelic and kissed her cheek. "I forgive ye, love. God's timing isna always ours. Don't worry your lovely head." He turned to Dee. "It appears the family secret is out."

"Tonight we'll go through the trunk." Mother wiped her eyes with her sleeve.

Papa hugged her close. "If you feel we must."

Dee patted her mother's shoulder. "Momma says she has a surprise. I look forward to it."

"I've missed you calling me momma." Her mother dabbed her eyes with her father's handkerchief. "The first time I forget my own hankie is when I can't stop crying."

"I've a surprise of my own. You've both been so busy settling in that I haven't found the right time to share it." Dee walked to Sally's stall.

"Jed told me Celtic Fire is your colt." Papa pulled a piece of carrot from his pocket for Sally.

"I'm gifting him to you, Papa."

Her mother beamed while her father stared at her. "Why? You've already given us so much." His lower lip quivered a moment before he found his composure.

"You always spoke of Grandfather's horse and that someday you'd like to have a horse named Celtic Fire. When I first laid eyes on him, I knew he was your horse. Please, let me give him to you."

"I'll not say nay. A more unselfish lass there never will be." Papa embraced her and kissed her forehead.

Yet she'd been very selfish not long ago. So self-centered it haunted her dreams. Giving her father the colt didn't feel like an unselfish act. It cost her nothing and gave her joy. The shadow of guilt shrank for a moment, watching her father's delighted face as he stroked the colt.

Jed put the unused part of the barbed wire into the wagon. He'd sent Benny back to the ranch hours ago to get more nails. In the meantime, he'd found an additional box. *Where in tarnation is that kid?* He climbed up on the wagon bench and disengaged the brakes as Benny came running his way. "Where's your horse?"

"He threw me." Benny wiped sweat from his forehead with the back of his sleeve and leaned over, gasping for breath.

Jed locked the wagon brake and jumped down to examine the boy. He checked his head and ran his hand along his limbs. "That don't hurt?"

"No sir." A blush formed on his cheeks. "Pa used to say I must be made of rock 'cause I don't get hurt like other folks."

"We'll take the wagon back to the ranch, then track the horse."

"He's long gone by now." Benny's eyes shifted to the ground.

"What ain't you tellin' me?"

"Nothing. I mean, it's been near three hours since he dumped me. It knocked me out. When I come to, I followed his tracks to the river and lost 'em."

"He'll come back, 'cause he prefers a dry stall full of hay to a wild night of freedom." Jed climbed back aboard, and Benny followed.

"I'm sorry."

"Apparently, you're not the rider you claim to be. The reason my brother hired you was your brag about no horse could throw you off."

"Every cowboy does a bit of braggin'." Benny's ears reddened.

Jed gave a whistle, and the horses trotted for home. He searched the horizon for the gelding. There were two riders south of them. He whistled, and the team came to a halt. He pulled a spyglass out from the toolbox under the seat to get a better look. The riders made a hasty retreat.

"Somethin' wrong?" Benny stared in the same direction.

Jed put the spyglass away. "Two men up on that hill. Neither looked familiar."

"I didn't see 'em." Benny fidgeted with the fringe on his buckskin jacket. "How far can you see with the spyglass?"

He turned to the kid. "Far enough to see their faces." If they were closer, but Benny didn't need to know that. Color washed from the boy's face. Did he know the men, or was he only scared?

Jed whistled, and the team continued home. "Let me know if you see any strangers."

"Yes sir."

"I'll ride over to the James spread and see if he hired any new men." As much as he wished Monty would up and move, he'd much prefer nosy cowpokes to possible rustlers.

By the time they arrived home, the men were heading to chow. Benny leapt from the wagon. "Slow down, kid, you ain't done until we put this wire away."

"Sorry." Benny walked to the shed, and together, they emptied the wagon.

"Now unhitch the wagon and brush the horses. Then you can get some grub."

Benny climbed aboard the wagon and drove it away.

Jed met Henry halfway to the house. "How's your day been?"

"Dandy. I've missed tending horses. 'Tis a grand mornin' I've had. Delilah gifted me Celtic Fire. She's made all me dreams come true, me sweet daughter." The pride in his voice, mixed with love, made Jed lonely for his own father. They washed at the pump outside. Jed secured the bandana on his hand and hid it behind his back. He didn't want to explain his blunder. Henry dried his face. "Now if the Good Lord would grant her a few of hers."

"What dreams would those be?"

"She used to dream of a good marriage, a house full of children, and a home of her own. Looks like you've provided the house and your brother the house full of children to tend. Now the good man is all that's needed. You wouldn't know any, would ya now?" He winked at Jed.

The two went in for supper while warmth wormed up his neck.

"What happened to your hand?" Genny scolded. "Take that filthy bandage off." Before Jed could explain, she dragged him toward her room, Dee and Mrs. McLain trailing with concerned expressions. "Sit on the bed while I get what's needed."

Dee undid the bandage. "How did you hurt it?"

"Started to pick up barbed wire without my work gloves." Jed stared at his wound rather than Dee's face. "It's not too bad."

"Not too bad." She scowled. "Why didn't you come let one of us tend it? It could have gotten infected."

"I heard barbed wire is very deadly." Mrs. McLain's disapproving expression made Jed feel like a naughty schoolboy.

"I'll take care of this." Genny laid out her supplies. "You two make sure everyone is fed."

As they departed, Genny cleansed the wound with soap and water. "I'm out of carbolic acid, but I think I've gotten it clean enough to prevent infection. What were you thinking?" She looked into his face and grinned. "Or who were you thinking of?"

"Hush. I weren't thinking nothing. That's the whole of it. If I'd had a reasonable thought in my head, I'd have put my gloves on." He glared at his sister-in-law. "Stop your matchmaking and finish bandaging my hand. I'm hungry and got more to do before sundown."

Genny chuckled but said no more. Seemed like everyone was matching them up except Dee. Or was she? She was friendlier. But not the kind of friendly he hoped for. Her father's encouraging wink complicated things. Unless Dee was willing to marry, there was no point pursuing her. He was ready to settle down, while she'd closed that corral gate months ago and put a lock on it to boot. Maybe if he could get Dee out of his mind, he could woo one of the single gals from church.

The thought sat like sour milk in his stomach.

Chapter 31

Dee stood before the window in her cabin as the pink rays of the setting sun touched the earth. Jed strode around the outbuilding, checking things. Every night since the men left for the cattle drive, he patrolled before bedtime. His strong profile silhouetted by shadows brought a smile to her face. What a fine man. Regret erased the smile. If only she'd met him before all that was good in her was stolen. Before she committed the unthinkable.

"What a gorgeous sunset." Her mother joined her at the window. "I've not seen one as beautiful since leaving my family home in Ireland." She patted Dee's arm. "I was raised on a farm, you know. My first husband was a footman for the Duke of Winchester."

"You've never told me anything about him. I'd forgotten Papa wasn't your first."

"But he was my best." Momma smiled at Papa, who stood behind them. "Influenza took my first husband and left me penniless. I had a letter addressed to the Duke of Winchester from my late mother. She had been the chambermaid for the duke's grandmother. When His Lordship tasted my fruit tarts, he hired me on the spot. His cook shared her skills with me. I am sure without that connection I'd have starved."

"Then the Good Lord brought her to me." Papa pulled Momma close.

"My, you two act like newlyweds," Dee teased as she lit the oil lamp on the table.

"We had a lot of time to talk during our travels. We were passengers and not servants. 'Twas grand, like the honeymoon we never had." Papa patted Momma's hand.

"I'd neglected your father. You know the strict rules at the Hollingsworth estate. By nightfall, we were too exhausted to even talk. At least I had you, my darling daughter, in the kitchen with me." Mother sat in a rocker. "For once, I feel so positive about our future. No one is giving us instructions. It's freeing."

Papa sat in the other rocker, and Dee took a chair at the table. Her parents rocked, seeming to relax more with every motion. They appeared younger than when they first arrived.

"Living here has spoiled me." Momma sighed.

"But you keep working." Dee had hoped they'd take their ease.

"We choose to work, lassie. That is the difference. We are respected." Papa pulled his pipe from his pocket.

"And I feel so loved by these friends of yours." Momma had changed since meeting the Holts. Dee understood. Genny was so loving and accepting. The children could lift sorrow from any shoulders. And Jed … his handsome face rested in her thoughts.

"Shall we look through the trunk before it gets too dark to see?" Momma picked up the lamp, and they went into her parents' room. Papa lit the oil lamp on the dresser. Momma pulled a key from her bodice and opened the trunk. Lovely silk material, delicately embroidered, rested on the top. Momma removed it along with stacks of linen suitable for a fine lady's dowry.

"These are so beautiful." Dee stroked the silky material, outlining the embroidery with her finger.

"A gift from the staff for our new home." Next, Mother held out a gold cameo necklace. "This was my mother's."

Dee caressed the lovely gold locket. "It's beautiful."

"Look." Momma pressed a tiny latch, and the cover sprang open.

Dee gasped. "It's the two of you." The intricately painted likenesses were unmistakable.

"It wasn't ready before you left. It was intended for you to remember us by."

"I'm glad I didn't have it. It might have burned in the fire." Or been gambled away.

Her father helped her with the clasp. "It looks lovely on you, darlin'."

"Thank you so much." Her heart swelling, she kissed her parents.

Momma turned back to the trunk, and Dee helped remove the silver tea service, plates, and utensils, each piece inlaid with a unique gold design. "These were part of my great-great-great grandmother's dowry. When my mother placed them in my charge, she warned me under no circumstance was I to sell them. She claimed as long as we had the family silver, we maintained our heritage. We are descendants of William the Conqueror. My great-great-great-grandfather lost his estate gambling on horses, and his wife hid the family silver."

Dee cared little about being a descendent from royalty. If her ancestors were anything like the wealthy Americans she'd known—no, thank you.

"There's something more." Papa beamed her way and nodded to Momma. "A gift to you from Mrs. Hollingsworth."

"Now, Delilah, you cannot refuse this gift. Mrs. Hollingsworth insisted you have it." Momma unwrapped a silver necklace inlaid with rubies, with matching earrings. "This is her way of apologizing for her son's actions toward you."

Dee crossed her arms. The miscreant's behavior had led to her current circumstance, and no bribe could make it right.

"She said you may sell them if you wish. I think they would bring more than enough to buy your bakery." Momma's hopeful smile melted her resolve.

Dee unfolded her arms and examined the jewelry. "These are exquisite. We could buy two bakeries here compared to the prices in Baltimore." She fingered the ruby in the center of the necklace. It caught the light of the lamp and glistened. "But where on earth can I sell it out here?" She folded the necklace back in the cloth.

"Maybe we could make inquiries in town." Papa rose from the floor and pulled himself upright with the bedpost.

The men Dee had been accosted by, Lemont's nasty gambling buddies, came to mind. "Trust me when I say it's a terrible idea."

Her mother finished repacking the trunk. "I'll ask Jed in the morning."

"You'll do no such thing." Dee's tone made her mother flinch.

"And why not?" Her father's question lingered over her.

Panic formed in her middle. "Because … for now, I'd rather keep this to ourselves." What was she afraid of? Jed would have sound advice. Then again, he might think she wasn't as innocent as she claimed. Expensive jewelry from a former employer? People assumed the worst. Jed might not understand.

"I'm willing to sell the family silver for your happiness." Her mother assisted Dee to her feet. "I was foolish to live as a pauper when I could have made our lives better. I'm confident my ancestors won't haunt me from the grave. That was long ago, and this is the present. Our fresh start." She squeezed Dee's hand. Her mother's calm demeanor pushed her fears away.

"I don't know of anyone in Cooperville who could buy it," Dee said, still processing the revelation.

"Might'n we trade for a building?" Papa closed the bedroom door behind them as they gathered again in the sitting room. "It's not uncommon to trade one commodity for another."

Dee placed the lamp she carried on the table and turned up the wick. "The next time I'm in town, I'll talk to Polly. She and her husband own the mercantile. We can trust her to keep our confidence."

"Aren't you anxious to open your bakery?" Her father sat in the rocker and lit his pipe.

"I feel an obligation to help Genny as long as she needs me, after her kindness. With Lonnie on the cattle drive, she needs me more than ever."

"You're a loyal friend." Her mother took up her knitting—a baby cap. The click of knitting needles was the only sound as the three sat in companionable quiet.

Dee turned to the book she'd chosen, *Moby Dick.* She read the inscription. *Willy, I hope you enjoy this adventure as much as I did. Happy Birthday, Jed.* It was dated 1855. She stroked the page. Willy was the youngest Holt. Her heart ached for Jed. So much loss, yet he found joy in life. Papa did the same. Maybe that's why she was drawn to Jed. They made the best of what came their way.

She, on the other hand, kept careful watch for the next tragedy. So much like her mother. They could have been free of servitude years ago. Generations of foolish women. That same folly ran in her veins. Why else did she venture west as a mail-order bride and not had the common sense to get to know the black-hearted man before she married him?

Never again. She had her parents, and they had a plan. They'd get the bakery. And she'd guard her heart from a certain rancher who already had a piece of it.

Chapter 32

Jed crested the hill; pausing Sally, he surveyed the James homestead. The sound of hammers filled the air. Monty was building closer to the road instead of the isolated spot of the burned-out homestead. The barn Dee had hidden in was still standing in the distance. How things had changed since he'd first seen her fearful face covered with soot. He nudged Sally toward the construction.

Monty's fine house spoke of his neighbor's determination. A porch wrapped around the dwelling—three times the size of the Single Cross. A house like this surely needed a wife. Would Dee be tempted by what Monty had to offer? Sparkling emerald eyes captured his thoughts until Sheba barked a greeting at Monty. Jed stared down at his rival from his mount. His jaw tightened.

"What brings you way out here, neighbor?" Monty grinned. "Do you bring an invitation from the lovely Miss McLain, perhaps?"

Ignoring the remark, Jed dismounted and shook his hand. "Making good progress on the house."

Monty beamed with pride. "Thanks for the recommendation. The Barlows are diligent craftsmen. My home will be finished soon. The thought of wintering in a tent reminded me too much of the war." He gave a slight shiver. "But I assume you didn't come to look at my house."

"It is a fine house." Jed nodded toward it. "I come to ask if you'd hired anyone in the last couple days."

"I don't need any men until I buy livestock. For now, I'm building a house, digging a well, and negotiating a price to have a better road graded. I used to be a surveyor. I plan to build a more direct route. It will cut an hour off my trip to town."

"We could use a good surveyor. Lots of land disputes over right-a-ways."

"I got coffee on." Monty led the way to his campfire. "Why'd you ask about hired help?"

Jed accepted the tin cup offered and settled on a log near the campfire, Sheba at his feet. "There were two strangers riding on my land yesterday. Thought maybe they was yours."

"I believe I saw those two. Short guy wore a sombrero, the other gent tall and thin."

"That's them." Jed nodded and looked toward the horizon as if the two would reappear. "Not sure what they're up to."

"I'll keep an eye out. I sent a telegram to a few former employees asking if they'd come work for me." Monty poured the remnant of his coffee on the ground and poured a fresh cup.

"They ranch?"

"No, they were my security team at the mine. If not for them, I'd have died when the mine collapsed. We served together in the war, then went our separate ways when I sold out. I'm hopeful at least one will be interested in a job." Monty blew across his coffee cup before taking a tentative sip. "I apologize for the coffee. Never got the knack for making good brew. I sent a letter to my old housekeeper to see if she's interested. Mrs. Crawford lives with her daughter now. Might not want to leave."

"Widow Anderson might keep house for you. She's had a tough time making ends meet since her husband died. They had no children. She sold his tinsmith business and has been inquiring about work."

"How old is she? I don't want a young woman living with me. People talk."

"She's old enough to be your ma." Jed respected a man who considered a woman's reputation.

He'd risked Dee's reputation, returning from Last Chance unchaperoned, because she wanted to get back to Genny sooner rather than later. Would Monty have done the same?

"Can Mrs. Anderson cook and make a decent cup of coffee?" Monty poured sugar in his cup.

"The vittles she brings to the church socials are tasty, and anyone's coffee is better than this." Jed stared at the dark swill.

"I'll speak with her Sunday."

Jed couldn't find fault with a man who attended church by choice. Drat it all, he'd misjudged the man. *God forgive me.* He dumped his coffee and rose. "I best be on my way."

"Wait." Monty walked with him to his horse. "If you have some time next week, I'd like to come by and ask questions about ranching, maybe help you with chores. Understanding the process will make it easier to decide if I want to invest the time and finances to make it work."

"And if it's not to your likin'?" Jed had it in his blood, but people could learn to love it.

"I'm taking soil samples with the prospect of mining." Monty nodded his way. "And now you've given me another option, surveying. I leave no stone unturned when it comes to opportunities."

"Come early Monday, and I'll show you around and answer your questions. Once everyone returns from the cattle drive, we'll be too busy to take a greenhorn under our wing." Jed laughed and mounted his horse.

"Perhaps I will, at that." Monty grinned before adding, "I might introduce myself to Miss McLain's parents."

"I'm sure they'll be glad to make your acquaintance." If he'd opened the door for Monty to worm his way into Dee's heart through her parents, he'd go to the stable and let Soldier kick him. He tipped his hat, then whistled for Sheba.

Sheba raced ahead, and Jed gave his mount free rein. The idea of better, more direct roads sounded good. Better roads could only help ranchers. And if … no … when Dee moved to town, it'd be a shorter trip to see her. If she didn't find a rich yahoo to marry in the meantime. Monty was a catch, all right. He hoped Dee wasn't fishing in that direction.

Henry greeted him at the stable door, holding Soldier's lead. "I saw those gents you mentioned earlier. When I started toward them, they lit out like the devil himself was after 'em."

"Interesting." Jed took his mount inside.

Henry patted Soldier before leading him into his stall. "It's a wee bit hot for the horses to be standing out in the sun. I've brought them in until the sun be lower."

Jed frowned at two unoccupied stalls. "Where's the chestnuts? Did you send them out to the pasture?"

"After you left, them stalls was empty. I assumed ye'd found a buyer for 'em." Henry scratched his head. "Not the case?"

Jed stormed out of the stable. "Brody, Benny, come out here."

No sign of Benny, but Brody stepped from the shed. "Boss?"

"Where were you this morning?" Jed regretted the growl in his voice at their longtime cowhand.

"Been sharpening tools most of the morning." Brody held out a sickle as he limped toward the door.

"Did you notice anyone around the stable? Hear anything?" Jed walked to the shed, where a variety of tools were stacked near the door.

"No sir." Brody hung his head. "You know I lost the hearing in my right ear when that bull gored me and flung me onto that rock." He rubbed his lame leg. "What's happened?"

Brody was grateful Lonnie hired him after the accident left him crippled. No way would he steal from them.

"Two horses are missing. You wouldn't know anything about it, would you?" Jed stepped closer and Brody stood tall.

"No sir. When I run the grinding stone, it's a mite noisy, and I can't hear nothin' else. Which horses?"

"The two chestnuts." Jed whipped off his hat and slapped it against his leg, sending a puff of dust into the air.

"I can track 'em, Mr. Holt. I know every horse by their hoof print." Brody laid the sickle aside and limped toward the stables.

"I'll trust you to do that. Where's Benny?" Jed scanned the outbuildings.

"He had the last watch, so he's sleepin'." Brody headed to the stable. "I'll saddle up and see if I can find them horses."

"Wait, I want to go with you. Tell Henry to saddle up too."

Jed stomped toward the bunkhouse. He kicked the bunk, rousting the boy from sleep. Benny scrambled to his feet. The smell of alcohol permeated his clothes.

"It appears you found somethin' more interesting in the bottom of a bottle instead of keeping watch. We got two horses missing, no thanks to you." Jed growled, sending the boy toward the door. "You know there is no drinking on the Single Cross. Gather your things. I should send you away with no pay." Jed pounded the nearby table, took a breath, then glared at the lad, whose eyes were big as saucers. "Collect your pay from Mrs. Holt, then get out."

Benny started grabbing his things. "I … I … I got bigger plans." He pointed his chin at Jed, then hauled his saddlebag over his shoulder.

The kid walked to the house, then out the gate. What big plans? Mischief, for sure. Jed's anger still churned as he headed to the stable.

Dee entered with a pitcher and cups. A stray hair hung across her brow. She set the items on the workbench and captured the wayward tresses, tucking them behind her ear. "Genny thought you might be parched by now." She began pouring water into cups. "Where is Benny off to?"

Her father came from the far end of the stable. "The lad was drinking on the job." Henry took the cup of water offered. "Thank you, darlin' girl."

"Will you be able to manage with one less man?" Dee's question made Jed wish he'd counted to ten before firing Benny.

"Guess we have to. We're off to track some missing horses. Likely'll take most of the day. Would ya mind fixin' us some vittles to take with us?" Jed smiled her way, and she returned one of her own.

"I'm happy to." She hurried to the house.

Jed saddled a fresh mount. "I hate leaving the women alone while we chase horse thieves."

"Anna knows how to use a rifle, and I know me daughter has a wee gun under her pillow. They'll be fine for the day." Henry finished saddling another mount. "I'll get the food, and we can be on our way."

The thieves had a head start by several hours. If they didn't cover their tracks, there was a chance. If he'd have left Sheba at home, the thieves wouldn't have gotten near the stable. Rather than dwelling on what-ifs, he needed to focus on the now.

Chapter 33

After losing the well-covered trail of the horse thieves the day before, followed by an uneventful night spent patrolling, Jed left Brody to watch the ranch while he escorted the family to church. The pews were filled with womenfolk, children, and the men from town. As the pastor concluded his sermon, Jed narrowed his eyes and rubbed his chin. Stealing horses while most of the ranch crews were on a cattle drive was clever. Was anyone here involved?

"Brother Holt, you asked to address the congregation." Rev. Logan nodded his way.

Jed dropped his hand to the pew back in front of him and stood to address the congregation. "I've had two horses stolen this week." Murmurs erupted throughout the sanctuary. He described the strangers. "I'm looking to hire a few extra men for guard duty, and I'm encouraging y'all to be vigilant."

"Brother Holt, thank you. Now if you all will bow your heads, we will pray for God's intervention." The people stilled as the reverend prayed. Then they filed out. The men gathered under the oak beside the church.

Jeffrey Schultz, the gunsmith's son, approached Jed, his hat in his hands. "I'd like to help."

"How old are you, boy?" He sized up the skinny lad.

Jeffrey stood tall. "I'll be thirteen next month. And you know I can shoot. I won the boy's division for targets last Independence Day."

The boy had a point. "Think you can keep watch without falling asleep?"

"When we come here on the wagon train, I helped my pa keep watch over his tools. If I'd have fallen asleep, Pa woulda tanned my hide."

His father, a short, broad-shouldered man, came to stand behind him. "He'll do right by you, Brother Holt. But you're not to pay him."

"A man is worth his wages." Jed wasn't taking advantage of the kid.

"It's what neighbors do." Mr. Schultz extended his hand. "My boy needs to learn what it means to be a responsible man."

"When you put it like that, it'll be fine." Jed shook both their hands, the boy's smile contagious. He ran to find his friends, and soon three more boys were offering to help.

Jed grinned at their eagerness. "You boys come out to the ranch before sunset, and I'll put you to work."

He joined his family and the McLains in the wagon.

"I got a telegram." Genny thrust the open paper toward Jed from the back bench. "The telegraph operator got it yesterday but waited to give it to me today, knowing we'd be at church."

Jed handed the reins to Henry and read the missive. "Lonnie made it to Abilene safe and sound. That's good. If he's lucky, he'll get the cattle sold sooner rather than later. The earlier a rancher gets his cattle to the rail head, the better the price he gets."

"I'm praying he comes home soon. I hate when he's gone." Genny snatched the telegram back, and from the corner of his eye, Jed saw her hold it to her heart. It would be added to her scrapbook. Glancing back, he cast a smile over his shoulder, as much at Dee as his sister-in-law.

Might there ever be a day when Dee would chronicle their lives together in a scrapbook?

Dee washed off the table while her mother swept the floor. The week had flown by, busy with putting up food from the garden with Genny and her mother. The storage room off the kitchen and the cellar were bursting with produce. Sharing the load had made the task lighter, and seeing her mother so relaxed as she worked was a treat.

"Momma, we're bored." Jilly sighed as Genny carried canned carrots across the kitchen.

"I know, honey. But we need to get this food canned." Genny smiled at her daughter from the storage room door.

"Canning is boring." Molly pushed her lip into a pout.

"I have an idea." Genny swiveled Dee's way. "Dee, could you take Jilly and Molly berry-picking? There are wild blackberries about a mile up the road. The girls could use the outing."

"You could use a nap." Dee laid the wet rag on a peg over the sink and wiped her hands on her apron. "Through the open window, I heard a babe crying last night. I think it was Robert."

Genny took a seat at the kitchen table and rested her head on her arms for a moment. "Bobby is having an awful time teething. I ran out of chamomile tea. I prefer it to the remedy Polly offers in her mercantile. Babies sleep for hours with that elixir, but it contains opium. I'd rather deal with the fussing."

"A bit of whiskey on a rag can sooth his gums and quiet him soon enough," Momma offered as she picked up Birdie, who held her hands out to her.

Genny shook her head. "Mother McLain, alcohol will never touch my children's lips. Not even a tiny drop."

Momma held Birdie as the child ate a cookie. "I understand. A carrot rubbed on the gums is a remedy my sister preferred. It's hard and too large for him to choke on, but it will help soothe the swelling."

"You spoil her." Genny laughed as Dee's mother hugged her youngest daughter close. "I'm so glad my children finally have a grandmother."

Momma smiled and reached over to give Genny's shoulder a hug. A twinge of jealousy went through Dee. So this is how having siblings felt. Dee shook her head at her own foolish response. Genny was a sister to her, and her mother adored the children. A plus for all of them. But what would it be like to watch her mother hold her own children?

"Jilly, Molly, do you have your baskets?" Dee stood on the porch and peeked inside the main cabin as Genny followed the girls from the bedroom. "Momma, are you sure you don't want to come along?"

"No, dear, it's much too hot. Birdie and I are making a new dolly." The joy on her mother's face as she sewed the doll affirmed Dee's budding longing for children of her own to bless her mother. She shook the thought from her mind. The Holt children would continue to fill that void in both their lives.

Genny handed the girls their baskets. "Be good."

"We're ready, Miss Dee." Molly looked up, and her bonnet slid down her back.

"Molly, a lady doesn't let her skin brown in the sun." The child remained still while Dee secured the bonnet. "Jilly, where is your bonnet?"

Jilly gave a sheepish grin and revealed a small cowboy hat she'd hidden behind her back. "I'm wearing this." She plopped it on her head. "When I grow up, I'm gonna be a rancher."

"I'm sure you are." Dee tightened the loose string to secure the hat. "Let's go, shall we? We want to pick a lot of blackberries for your momma."

"She promised to make blackberry jam." Jilly skipped down the path that led into the copse of trees behind the house, while Molly shadowed her sister, hopping awkwardly.

Sleepiness left Dee as they walked. God had answered her prayers because the night watches had produced no horse thieves. The vigilant boys who'd come to help made her feel safer. She'd make blackberry jam-filled crullers for them when she got back home. The berry patch came into view as they rounded a bend, the briars heavy with fruit.

The girls ate more than they gathered, and their faces stained blue from the berry juice. When they filled the last basket, Dee stretched her back and smiled. "It's time to go. Let me carry your baskets, girls. You might spill."

"We can do it." Jilly hefted her basket. Molly did the same. They started walking toward home. She chuckled at their determined stride and bent to gather the other baskets.

A shadow blocked the sun. Dee jumped as a tall man with a long nose and narrow eyes appeared beside her. His companion's face remained covered in the shadow of his sombrero.

Fear temporarily captured her breath, but she found her voice and attempted to sound brave. "Can I help you?"

"You surely can." The tall one's jaw flexed, and he signaled for the other man to step forward. "Me and my partner here …"

"Mrs. James, we been looking for you." The short one spoke, his voice gravelly. His pocked face and wilted mustache made him fearsome. "It took us a few days to figure out where you'd gone off to."

"We hadn't heard about your dear departed until we came upon his grave." The taller one eyed her like a snake ready to strike. A chill traveled through her.

Dee crossed her arms, trying to appear nonplussed. "You've found me. What do you want?" The urge to run to the safety of the Single Cross quickened her heart. But that would draw attention to the girls, oblivious to her plight as they continued toward home.

"We want the money he was holding for us." The taller one grabbed her arm. "You are going to take us to it."

His grip relaxed when she didn't resist. "Gladly, if I had any idea what you were talking about." She made eye contact, refusing to appear afraid. "If you found his grave, you saw the house was ash."

"We know you got it." The man tightened his grip again.

She bit her lip so as not to cry out. "My late husband kept his business to himself and threatened to end my life if I got too nosy. I assure you, I have no knowledge of any money. Don't you think I'd be long gone from Kansas if I did?" She jerked her arm free. "Now if you'll excuse me." Dee took one step.

The shorter one placed a pistol to her head. She shoved down her fear and returned his stare. "Everything in the house burned. Where would I have found this money?" No way were these men going to intimidate her.

Another gun cocked, and Dee looked on in terror as the shorter one aimed it at the girls' retreating forms. Molly had stopped to eat more berries near the bend in the road. Jilly stood scolding her.

"Stop. Don't hurt the girls." *Please God. I can't believe this is happening.*

"Tell us where the money is." The shorter one leaned in. His foul breath sent her stomach into fits.

Her legs grew weak. "Truly, I wouldn't know where. If it didn't burn in the fire, perhaps it is somewhere else on the homestead." Once the girls were around the bend, she continued. "The real Lemont James owns the land now. You could ask him."

"You could bat your pretty eyelashes and get him away from his place so we can dig around." The taller one smirked. "I'll give you a few days to persuade him." He rubbed the edge of his gun on her cheek. "We'll be watching the ranch, and if you try anything, we'll know, and those little girls might just have an accident."

"A bad accident." The short one gave her a cold stare which turned her resolve to jelly.

"All right," she whispered, and they holstered their guns.

"Smart decision." The taller one's eyes roamed her form. Nausea churned in her stomach.

"May I go now?" She stooped and grabbed the last two baskets with shaking hands.

"You know better than to blab your mouth about our conversation." The short one touched his gun.

Dee nodded and walked as calmly as her racing heart would let her toward home. What else didn't she know about her late husband? Her fists turned white as she carried the baskets. If she hadn't come to the Holt ranch, the girls wouldn't be a target for evil men. This was her fault. She should tell Jed. No. Lemont always carried out his threats, and if these men were anything like him, then … cooperating was the only way to protect them. Taking several cleansing breaths, she walked toward the cabin. Dee schooled her face before entering.

Staying quiet while her hands were busy processing berries gave her time to think.

Her chest tightened. She'd already allowed her husband to die. The thought of those she loved dying because of her brought tears. She wiped her eyes with her forearm, then ran it over her forehead so it appeared she was wiping sweat and not tears.

There was no way she'd flirt with Monty and lead him on. A plan formed in her mind. Hopefully, it would give the men ample time to search the old homestead. If they found their money, they'd leave. If not, she'd find a way to put the target on her back and keep the Holt girls safe.

Delilah sat in the bathtub her papa had hauled to her bedroom and filled. If only those men could be as easily washed out of her life as the dirt and sweat of the day. Lemont's past stuck to her like the brambles in her hair. Would she never be free of him?

"Delilah?" Her mother knocked on the bedroom door. "Let me wash your hair for you." Momma slipped inside, closing the door behind her.

Dee leaned forward, raised her arms, and massaged the lather into her hair. "I can manage."

"I used to help you all the time when you were a girl."

A gasp followed the offer. Dee cringed with shame. Her mother had seen the scars on her back and arms.

"My dear child, how did you bear it? Your lovely skin …" She ran her fingers over the old wounds and kissed her daughter's cheek. "You had written he was heavy handed, but this …" With tear-filled eyes, she massaged Dee's scalp, sending a relaxing sensation through her body. Memories from her childhood of special conversations with her mother as she bathed her for bed came rushing back. Dee joined in her mother's tears, her childhood innocence a distant memory. Life was forever shrouded in the ugliness of her foolish decision, and she'd pay the price for a long time.

After her bath, she dressed in her nightgown and robe, and her mother combed her wet hair gently, removing tangles.

"Momma, thank you so much. My hair can become a nest of knots if I don't brush it twice a day. It is so nice to be pampered."

"May I tell your father about the scars?" She put the comb down and kissed her head.

"While I braid my hair, you can speak to him." A knot formed in her throat. Her sweet father would cry once he learned the extent of her abuse. She could confirm details once her mother opened the conversation.

"I'll make some tea. Come to the table when you're ready, and we can talk."

Dee hated revealing the whole, ugly truth to her parents. But their love was already soothing her wounded spirit. She finished her braid and walked barefoot to the table.

Taking a seat, she accepted a cup of tea from her mother. After a sip, she shared an abbreviated version of her married life, leaving the most horrid details out.

Papa planted a kiss on her forehead, his eyes moist. "Oh, sweet Delilah, if I had known your plight, I'd have killed him without a thought."

"Oh, Papa." Dee received her father's embrace, refusing to shed another tear. "I was alone, trapped, unloved … and too ashamed to write and tell you. I was terrified of another beating if my husband found the letter before I could get it mailed. I quit writing because I couldn't lie. It seemed better that way. He was cruel to me in every way, and I can't see myself joining my life to another man, ever."

"If that's how you feel, I'll chase away any man who looks your way." Papa's words held no jest. "I'll protect me darlin' daughter always." He squeezed her hand.

Dee shivered and sighed. "Let's talk about something more pleasant." She wiped her eyes and gave them a smile. "I've been thinking since you showed me the ruby jewelry. Mr. James might buy it, and then we'd have the money we need for our future."

"Are you sure he has the funds? The jewels are very costly."

Momma always presented the practical side. But she was right, they needed to know the jewelry's true value. There was no time to get it appraised beforehand. This was Dee's plan to get Monty away from his property. Discussing business seemed a better choice than flirting. Her presence might keep him away from the house, or it might be a disaster. Monty could head home much sooner, and then what? No, this had to work. The sooner Lemont's partners left, the better. "What do you think of a picnic?" Dee fiddled with her spoon.

"I assume you mean with Mr. James."

"Yes." Dee nodded at her mother. "He might be more inclined to say yes if he's had some of your fine cooking. A picnic is more private and less likely to be overheard."

"A very wise idea. We'll accompany you." Momma's eyes sparkled.

"No, it's best if I go with him alone." No way was she involving her parents. "He might feel less … obligated if it's only me."

"Are you sure, lassie?" Papa's concerned gaze rested on her.

"Yes, I don't think you'll need to protect me from this Mr. James." Dee smiled as her parents sat in silence.

Papa tapped the table, finally relaxing into a grin. "I canna wait to see the house in town you mentioned. I'll plant a grand garden and sell both vegetables and flowers. Every house should have lovely flowers. I've brought seeds and bulbs." In typical Papa fashion, he was looking at the bright side.

Dee's anxiety eased at their excitement. "That sounds wonderful."

"When do you plan to speak with Monty?" Papa asked.

"Before Sunday. I'll ride to his place and invite him on a picnic after church. Then, once he's eaten Mama's delicious chicken turnovers, I'll broach the subject." Dee pushed the guilt of her ruse to the side. "Please don't mention this to anyone. If Monty refuses, our plan will have to wait until we've saved enough or found another buyer for the jewels."

Please God, I need to do this. But don't You see my friends and family need protecting? I can't fail them.

Her prayer seemed to dangle in the air and then land with a thud.

Chapter 34

Dee and her mother brought the fresh blackberry crullers and some assorted tarts from the summer kitchen and served them to the young volunteers. The four boys ate heartily and took home baskets of more sweets and bread.

The would-be thieves had said they'd be watching the Single Cross, waiting for her to do their bidding. Her insides quivered knowing there were four more people whose lives were at risk.

"Tell your parents we really appreciate your help." Dee waved from the porch and scanned the horizon as the boys rode away. She walked back into the house, and her mother took the empty trays to the summer kitchen.

"Do you think they can resist the smell of your fine baking before they get home?" Jed poured himself coffee. "Got any donuts left?"

"I put back a dozen for us." Dee brought them from the girls' room. "Jilly insisted on hiding them, and after watching those boys eat, I'm glad she did."

"Where are my nieces?" Jed smiled her way as she set the donut tray on the table.

"Genny took the girls swimming at the creek while the babies are sleeping. I think she was looking forward to cooling off herself."

"Why didn't you go too?" Jed bit into the donut. Filling dripped onto his chin.

Dee dabbed his beard with a napkin. *What am I doing?* It seemed natural to come to his aid. She rested the napkin on the table. He grinned and continued eating.

"I don't swim." Dee took a step back, then crossed her arms.

"Why?" Jed's face registered surprise.

"My mother felt it inappropriate for women to be seen in public scantily clad."

Mrs. McLain brought in a load of dried diapers. "True, but it's insufferably hot today. I'm tempted to join the girls."

"You can't swim either."

"Yes, I can. My father wanted to be sure none of his children drown. It was the most embarrassing thing. A boy I liked was peeking at us through the bushes. Papa chased him away, but I swore I'd never be seen in my undergarments again."

Dee chuckled, trying to imagine her refined mother swimming in the river in her underthings. "Momma, what I'm learning about you since you've come west is scandalous."

"Don't you dare speak of this to anyone. That goes for you, too, young man." Her mother's cheeks pinked, and she scurried to Genny's bedroom with her basket of diapers.

"I could teach ya." Jed winked at Dee, bringing warmth to her face.

"I've no interest in learning. At least not from a single gentleman." Gathering her courage, she finished the last of her tea. "Would you have time for a talk?"

She planned to tell Jed the details about her married life that she'd never shared. A shiver accompanied the notion. It could cost her their friendship. A knot formed in her chest. But Dee needed him safe. Knowing the particulars of the abuse might send him fleeing.

"Is now good?"

Nodding, Dee removed her apron. "Can we go somewhere private?"

"I know just the place." Jed rose and led her to the barn. "I'll saddle Sally. She hasn't been ridden since she gave birth."

"My father has been teaching me to ride. I'll saddle Soldier."

"I don't think he's your best choice."

Dee started to argue but decided what she had to share would create enough disruption. Jed chose a beautiful red horse. "Rosie is gentle." He saddled her, and they started out. A half an hour passed in silence. Jed let Sally run full out. Rosie raced beside her while Dee held on tight to the reins. She'd never admit she'd not practiced galloping. Jed slowed to a trot as they approached a creek.

"It's lovely."

The creek ran clear, and the foliage and grass seemed greener and more beautiful than any she seen since coming to Kansas. The babbling water and the singing birds in the nearby trees added to the quiet peace of the place. She didn't want to break the mood of her surroundings with a conversation she dreaded. But it had to be done.

"This is where I want to build my cabin." Jed dismounted and helped her off Rosie. His hand on her waist burned into her skin beneath her layers of clothes, igniting strange feelings. Dee stepped away and focused on the flowing creek. "It's far enough away from the ranch to give me solitude, but close enough to help with chores. I hope to bring a wife here someday."

Dee remained silent, and Jed cleared his throat, causing her to turn his way. "What do you wanna talk about?"

"If you have me in mind, I'm not the one. I never intend to marry. Lemont stole everything from me. I was a slave to our marriage contract. And he did with me whatever he desired." She walked closer to the creek. The breeze off the water cooled her face. "Lemont demanded obedience and looked for ways to abuse me. He called me frigid one minute, then accused me of flirting with his friends the next." She paced the bank to keep from crying. Jed drew closer. She focused on the ground. "Either got me a beating. When he wasn't drinking, he was tolerable but still jealous of any man who looked my way." Dee faced Jed. "The wagon became kindling so I couldn't go to town. You know he locked me in the house when strangers came."

Compassion flared in his eyes. "By now, you should know I'd never hurt you." Jed reached for her, but she kept her arms at her sides.

"There's more." A knot grew in her throat. Tears fought to fall, but she wiped her eyes with her sleeve. "He made me wear a scanty dress when he had men there to gamble. He wanted me to be a distraction, to increase his chance of winning. Whether he won or lost, I got a beating for flirting."

Jed remained silent, his jaw and fists flexing.

"Twice, Lemont offered me up as a bet when the stakes were higher than the cash he had." She shivered and wrapped her arms around herself to hold in the quaking.

Jed sucked in air then, released it slowly as his eyes remained on her.

"When he lost …" Dee cleared her throat, determined to finish her confession. "Lemont warned me not to resist. Let his friend have what he'd won, or I'd get the worst beating of my life. The man never touched me—instead, he crept out the window, embarrassed. The next morning, Lemont beat me, anyway. Called me a whore. When I discovered I was with child, he beat me until I miscarried, saying it wasn't his." She wiped a tear from her cheek. "At least he left me alone to heal."

Dee stared at the creek, not wanting to see Jed's expression. Acid rolled in her stomach. "When he returned two weeks later, he expected thanks for sparing me the shame of bearing another man's child." Tears streamed down her face unbidden. She hugged herself more tightly. "I'm a filthy wretch who never wants to marry again. Actually, according to the lawyer, we were not legally married." Lightheadedness circled her for a few seconds while the horses grazed quietly nearby. "You need to find someone pure, worthy of you. It's not me." She continued to watch the water, expecting him to ride away.

Instead, Jed drew near. "If he weren't already dead, I'd …." Anger edged his words.

She wanted him to ride off in anger. That would make this easier. A lone tear trailed her cheek.

"Dee, if I'd have known those days I paid a visit you were being abused, I'd have rescued you. Told the sheriff. You'd have been a free woman, and he'd have gone to jail." Jed pulled off his bandana and offered it to her. "He's gone. You're free. You can have a fresh start."

Dee took the handkerchief but refused to face him. "I intend to enjoy my fresh start—with my parents. We will open that bakery. Stop pursuing me."

Jed turned her to him. His sapphire eyes held love, and she gasped. "Dee, honey, I'm in love with you. Do you truly want me to stop pursing ya?" His breath tickled her face. "I'm a patient man. I'll wait for you to come to me." He pulled her close and wrapped his arms around her, offering a sweet kiss.

Oh, it felt so right, yet frightening. She melted into him, his strong arms drawing her closer, deepening the kiss. *What am I doing?* She pushed away and slapped his face. His look of shock shamed her.

Straightening her spine, she glared. "Don't ever do that again."

The hurt in his eyes tore at her. What kind of man confessed his love after a woman revealed such a horrid past? A wonderful one. Her heart ached with the love she longed to give him.

But she had to walk away. His life was in danger.

Dee mounted her horse and let the mare run full out until they arrived at the ranch. She left the horse in the yard, knowing Jed would be right behind her. She went to her cabin. There was no one home. She locked the door and closed the curtains as tears streamed down her face. Could she ever face him again?

Chapter 35

Jed avoided Dee the rest of the evening, eating dinner in the bunkhouse with Brody. The next morning, he was up early to mend the fence in the farthest pasture. He'd confessed his love, and it made no difference. She'd stay a widow forever rather than take a chance on love.

But he couldn't find it in himself to become bitter. Man, Lemont had hurt her bad. Guilt chased Jed like coon hounds on a hunt. If only he'd seen the abuse.

Jed grabbed his lunch from the back of the wagon and sat on the ground. Sheba lay beside him, waiting for him to toss her scraps.

Jed spoke to the collie. "I know she has feelings for me." She fit so nicely in his arms, and he could still taste her sweet lips. "That slap was more for her benefit." He touched his cheek. "She's afraid. Ain't sure if it's of me, marriage or something else." Jed finished most of his sandwich and gave the rest to Sheba. She gulped it in two bites.

He took a long swig from his canteen, then pulled out an old pan and filled it with water for his collie. "There you go, girl."

After the dog cleaned the pan of every drop, he put it away.

During the many months Dee had lived on the Single Cross, Jed had learned to read her face. The woman was afraid of something. Not just him. The more he thought about it, the more certain he became that her behavior didn't match up. She'd snuggled into him even though everything else spoke of her wanting to put distance between them.

He patted Sheba before putting the tools in the wagon. Then he lifted the dog onto the bench and joined her.

Dee had mentioned her husband's gambling buddies yesterday. His jaw twitched at the memory of the two who'd accosted her in town. Had they returned? No way would he let another man touch her.

He fumed as he whistled to the team. "We're gonna keep watch, Sheba. We gotta protect Dee."

How he wished his brother were home. Talking things over with Lonnie gave him perspective.

Dee kissed Birdie's cheek as the child nestled asleep in her arms. Would Jed's children look like Birdie? She shook the thought away. He'd avoided her since yesterday. Why did she care? Pushing him away was for the best. If her plan worked, she'd be able to move from the Holt ranch very soon. The men would find their money and be on their way. Everyone would be safe. But Jed would never speak to her again.

Dee absentmindedly rocked Birdie. Genny entered from hanging laundry and scooped the child up. An emptiness came over Dee as the feel of the child lingered. She'd made the decision to block Jed from her life. Protecting this kind family fell to her, and if loneliness was her penance, then so be it.

She stared at the cold fireplace. If only the fire had happened during the day instead of the dead of night. Maybe she'd have been braver.

Her heart raced, and her chest constricted as memories of Lemont's screams filled her. The flames licked the walls as she struggled to open the door. Once free, she raced toward the barn, shrieking. The smell of burning flesh made her retch. The corner of the barn became her prison as her body froze in place.

A scream lay trapped in her throat. She gripped the rocker arms to keep from passing out.

"Dee." Genny touched her shoulder. "What's the matter? You're white as a ghost."

She could hear her friend, but the day terror had her in its grip. Flames surrounded her. Lemont's screams drove the fear.

Genny placed a cool cloth on her head. Her voice sounded far away. "Come back to me, my friend." She pulled Dee's left hand from the rocker arm. Then she loosened her right fingers and helped her rise. From somewhere, Dee heard her mother's voice. Then blackness overtook her.

When she awoke, she was lying on Genny's bed, dusk surrounding her. She scrambled from the bed and lit a lamp. Darkness made the terrors worse. A foggy shroud hung over her still, but her mother's voice drew her into the kitchen.

The family and Brody were eating dinner.

Every eye peered at her. Embarrassment stole her voice.

"Miss Dee, did you have a good nap?" Jilly's innocent question brought a smile from somewhere in her fear.

"Yes, I must have needed it." She sat at her place at the table, Jed's concern-filled gaze on her. Oh, how she wished he'd hold her close, his nearness banishing her fear. Instead, she pressed her palms together to stop her hands from trembling. Then she smiled at the family.

Genny began passing the dishes to her. Dee took small portions. She stared at her plate. A strand of hair fell in her face. *I must look a fright.* She pushed the hair behind her ear and began eating. The food had no flavor, but she needed to appear normal.

"I've made a special tea for you." Mother set the cup before her. Dee drained it, the warmth flowing down her throat. Her mother's touch as she squeezed her shoulder brought her more into the present.

"Thank you. It's perfect. May I have more?" Dee found another smile and gave it to her momma. She continued eating, listening to the surrounding chatter.

"Dee." She became aware that Genny addressed her. She focused on her friend. "Carter picked up another telegram in town today. Lonnie should be home tomorrow or the next day."

Dee nodded. "Wonderful news. I'll do the dishes since I slept until dusk."

She finished her meal and gathered up the plates and cups, then poured hot water from the kettle into the wash pan. Jed added cold water from the pump before she could object. "Thank you." She didn't look at him while adding soap flakes. The scent of hay and masculinity sent a wave of calm through her. *Seems he's always rescuing me. No, it can never be.*

Jed stood there, silent.

"What?" She steeled herself from any attempts to change her mind.

"I just wanted to say that whatever's troubling ya, I'm here to listen. There's nothing the good Lord can't handle." He picked up a towel and began drying the dishes.

"I have a lot on my mind, I'll admit. Nothing I need a listening ear for, though." She'd already burdened him enough. "Thank you for your concern." She kept her voice formal.

They did dishes in stony silence. The clink of utensils in the pan echoed in her ears, reminding her the day terror rested on the edge of her emotions. Every little sound was magnified. Not since the fire had she felt like this. Would she ever be free of the memory?

Once they finished the last of the pots, Jed spoke again. "I'll be praying for ya." He laid the towel across a kitchen chair and left.

Her shoulders sagged, and she restrained her desire to sob.

The pleasant smell of cinnamon greeted Dee as she readied herself for bed. Momma had placed a pot of the spice on the stove. She claimed the scent was relaxing. Dee padded to the stove and breathed it in, filling her lungs. She let out a long breath. Fear intruded. Were there other men from her husband's past coming to collect a debt?

She pushed the thought away. When Jed's handsome face came to her mind, she let it linger.

Dee's parents sat in the rockers—two people who undoubtedly shared true love. Momma knitted while Papa read the *Almanac.*

Dee took a seat at the table. "Tell me how you knew Papa was right for you."

Momma patted Papa's hand. "It took a while. I was instantly attracted, but I assumed it was because I was lonely. My first husband had died a year before I sailed to America. I didn't want to dishonor him, but truthfully, I never loved Gregory. Our parents had arranged the marriage when we were children. It's like being a mail-order bride, but your groom isn't a total stranger. We had nothing in common. He spent most of his time trying to become wealthy. I'd buried the family silver in the woods behind our home, fearing he'd sell it. He invested in ridiculous things and growled at me when he lost money. Gregory never laid a hand on me, but neither did he care for me. We had two stillborn babes and three miscarriages before he passed away. He claimed we lost the babes because I was frigid. And I believed him."

"Stuff and nonsense." Papa laid aside the *Almanac*. "Anna caught my eye the moment she tripped over me on the deck of the ship. She never got her sea legs. She spent her days with her head over the side."

"Not the entire time." Momma batted his shoulder playfully. "If I had, we'd never have fallen in love." She turned to Dee. "Your father was so different from my late husband. I was afraid at first. Could this man be real? What was his true heart? Gregory had been polite and attentive until we married, then he left me alone most of our ten years of marriage. Taking a chance on happiness was risky. My past had colored my expectations."

"That's how I feel." Dee took a deep breath. "My husband was a monster, and I fear every man has a monster within."

"Now, darlin' girl, you know it's not true. Every man on the Single Cross is a gentleman, to be sure." Papa rose and patted her head. "I need to check something in the barn."

Dee appreciated her father giving her private time with her mother. She dropped her voice. "Momma, how did you overcome ..."—she stared at the table and whispered—"being frigid?" Dee's face warmed to her ears. "Wifely duties hurt, and I couldn't bear a lifetime of pain."

"Delilah, true love doesn't hurt. A kind man will do all in his power to make you feel comfortable." Her mother's face flamed red as she cleared her throat. "When we married, my body responded to your father because I loved him completely. Our union was tender and passionate." She sipped her tea before adding, "Your father always makes me feel like royalty." Her cheeks stayed red.

Her mother was speaking the truth. She'd seen the way her father doted on her. Maybe it would be true of her someday. Reaching for Momma, Dee squeezed her shoulder. "Thank you for talking about something so private. I needed to hear it."

Jed followed Genny to the door as Sheba barked wildly. Lonnie and the ranch crew filled the yard. Genny ran to her husband and kissed him shamelessly. Lonnie lifted her into his arms and carried her into the house. Jed stepped aside. His brother never tired of holding his wife. A twinge of jealousy pricked him.

Dee stood at the chicken coop door. Was she blushing? He strode toward her. "Dee, do you need help to collect the eggs?"

She frowned at him. "You know I don't."

Jed removed his hat and stepped closer, blocking her escape. "Would you do me the honor of another walk after supper?"

"You know my answer, Jed Holt."

Jed nodded and walked toward the group unloading the remaining supplies from the drive. Joining in the task didn't stop his mind from dwelling on Dee. Why did he keep making himself a target for rebuff?

Lonnie sat on the bench regaling Brody with some stories. Jed perched beside him, half listening. When Brody went back to work, Lonnie gave Jed the once-over.

"It's a good thing you stayed behind. We had two thunderstorms and a bit of hail. The cattle gave us fits. Thank the Good Lord, I got 'em to market and got a good price. Even sold a few of the wilder horses."

"I thought we were keeping 'em." Jed didn't care whether his brother sold the horses. His mind was fixated on Dee, and he needed to distract it. "You said they could learn to work the cattle."

"Well, the money I got for 'em will let me offer a good price for Tyrone Sutton's brood mare. Her bloodlines are—hey, what is she doin'?"

Jed followed his brother's line of sight. Henry held Soldier's lead as Dee climbed on the fence, then onto his back. Shaking his head, Jed excused himself and approached the corral.

Dee cooed Gaelic to the stallion. He nickered in response.

"Don't try any funny business with my precious cargo aboard." Henry rubbed the horse's muzzle.

Seemingly unaware of Jed's presence, Dee laughed and leaned over to whisper in Soldier's ear. He pranced, then moved toward the gate.

"Be careful, girl. He's a handful." Henry walked beside the pair.

Dee kicked the horse's side and Soldier trotted, quickly leaving them far behind. She sat straight in her special-made saddle.

Jed stood next to Henry, willing Dee to return safely. "Why d'you let her ride him? He's a plow horse, for goodness' sakes." His growl made Henry laugh.

"She'll be fine. The horse loves her. He won't cause her harm. He responds to the Gaelic and Dee's sweet voice." Henry watched his daughter. "It's a shame she didn't learn the horse was a true Irishman earlier. I know Soldier would have allowed her to ride him and rescued her from her beast of a husband."

Jed waited to see if she turned around or went to town. Instead, she took the path toward Monty's place. Someone ought to follow her. Jed headed for the barn, Henry a few paces behind him.

"I wouldn't follow the lass if I were you. She'll be madder than a scared skunk if she sees ya." Henry crossed his arms.

Jed saddled Sally, anyway. Before he had a chance to talk himself out of his foolishness, he mounted Sally and took the same trail Dee and Soldier had.

Jed stopped near the tree line. His pulse raced as he and Sally hid in the trees. *Fool schoolboy stunt.*

Dee rode up to Monty, who was sitting in a chair on his porch. Jed moved Sally closer. But if he got close enough to hear the conversation, he might be seen. Monty kissed her hand while she remained on Soldier. Jed wanted to punch the man. Monty seemed right pleased by the smile on his face. Dee nodded, then she turned Soldier toward home and his direction.

Soothing Sally to silence, he waited until Dee passed, then raced to a shortcut and arrived moments before her. But the bigger challenge would be not showing that she'd torn his heart out by choosing Monty.

Chapter 36

"I hope this works. If he is agreeable, we can start making plans for the bakery." Dee tied her new green-feathered bonnet in place. The golden silk frock made her feel sophisticated, even though the design was simple. She hadn't mastered more difficult dress patterns. *Lord, you know I need this to keep everyone safe.*

Momma placed the jewelry in the bottom of the picnic basket. She wrapped two place settings in a cloth and laid them on top. "That should keep it from prying eyes." Then she added her chicken turnovers, apples, cookies, and a jug of water.

Henry hitched a second wagon for his family to ride to church, giving Lonnie more room for his family in the first wagon. Jed and the crew rode their horses. Dee refused to look his way. Surely, he'd spot deception on her face.

At church, she settled between her parents to ensure Jed and Monty sat elsewhere. Jed took a spot in the front row with the pastor.

Monty stopped near Lonnie. "I'd like to introduce my good friends and security, Mark and Ned Kirk." The two men shook Lonnie's and Henry's hand and tipped their hats to the ladies.

"It's a pleasure to make your acquaintance." Mark winked, and Dee pretended not to notice. The brothers were both broad-shouldered but shorter than Monty with light-brown hair. The three men took the pew in front of her. Drat.

"Shall we pray?" The pastor croaked out the invitation. "With the loss of my voice, I've asked for the elders' help." His last word came out in a whisper.

Mr. Schulz stood and led the opening prayer. Another of the church elders gave the announcements before the song leader began the first hymn.

When the hymn before the sermon concluded, Jed strolled to the podium. Dee sat straighter. No one had mentioned he'd be preaching. Hopefully, he wouldn't speak on *thou shall not lie*.

Jed opened his Bible. "Let us pray. Father, you know I am unprepared today. I ask Ya to put Your words in my mouth. In Jesus' name."

The congregation said *amen* in unison, as was their custom, and Jed scanned the room—everywhere but at Dee. "Today I'd like to read …"

Jilly whispered, "Momma, I need to go." She squirmed in her seat.

Dee leaned across her mother and caught Genny's attention. "I'll take her." She rose and led Jilly to the side door closest to the outhouse. Staring at Jed through his sermon was too much to bear.

"I'll wait out here," she said as Jilly opened the privy door. "You take your time."

The girl nodded and went inside.

A shadow blocked out the sun.

"I saw you talk to Mr. James the other day." The gravelly voice was unmistakable. A shiver went through her. The man pulled her several paces from the outhouse. "Did you invite him out?" The shorter of her persecutors had replaced his sombrero with a floppy-brimmed Stetson that shaded his eyes.

"Yes, today after church." She whispered, hoping Jilly couldn't hear.

"Keep him away for most of the day. Gus is digging." Lemont had never mentioned that name.

She found her backbone and spoke in a calm voice. "Monty has two new employees. They came to church with him." Maybe now these thieves would leave.

He swore under his breath, then placed his pistol on her temple. "You best keep your end of the deal."

She stared into eyes mirroring Lemont's before he hurt her.

"I will." She managed to keep her voice steady even though her knees wobbled.

He holstered his gun. The little breakfast she'd eaten wanted to come up. She glanced toward the outhouse, and when she looked back, the man was gone. The sound of hooves galloping away faded. She took a deep breath, willing her stomach to calm. "Jilly, are you all right in there?"

"Yes, ma'am. I'll be right out." Jilly opened the door, holding her nose. "It smells in there. Momma puts flowers in our privy."

"And it certainly helps." Dee checked to be sure Jilly's dress hadn't gotten caught in her undergarments. "Take my hand and walk quietly. We'll go in the front door and sit in the back. It's impolite to disturb the sermon."

They slipped into the back pew, where an elderly man sat snoring. When Jilly reached toward the man, Dee shook her head. "Leave him be."

The noise muted Jed's words. Dee watched his animated gestures and the way he paced in front of the pulpit. He certainly gave the appearance of a preacher. But the perspective from the back of the room showed three more men sleeping, including Carter. Gonzalez elbowed him, waking him with a start. A brown-eyed boy, not more than three, smiled and waved at them. Jilly waved back. Dee pulled her hand down.

She and Jilly rose for the closing hymn as Mrs. Schultz took her place again at the piano. The music woke the man next to them. He sang enthusiastically, as if he'd been engaged with the service the whole time. Jed said a closing prayer and escorted the elderly pastor to the back of the room to greet the congregation as they filed past.

Dee waited until Genny came near her seat. Jilly took her mother's hand, and Monty offered his arm. Dee hesitated, then placed her hand lightly on his arm. Storm clouds formed in Jed's blue eyes. She pulled her arm free as heat filled her neck.

"Fine sermon. Jed, I had no idea you could preach." Monty shook Jed's hand.

When Jed glanced at Dee, she found herself explaining. "I took Jilly to the privy, so I missed most of it, and then we sat—"

"Near Mr. Jensen, yes. His snoring carries to the front at times." Jed's gaze caused her heart to race. "It wasn't much of a sermon, being as I was asked to speak a few minutes before church started. See you at home later?"

"Much later. We're going on a picnic." Dee couldn't lie, but she couldn't tell him why either. Jed's look of disappointment crushed her heart.

Monty tipped his hat and offered her his arm again. She took it, her face warm. The Kirk brothers followed them out.

Monty escorted her to her wagon, where she retrieved the picnic basket. He carried it to his wagon, then he helped her in. As he walked to the other side, she glanced toward the church. Jed stared her way, his expression set. Shame filled her. Why did she look? Her action made her appear a hypocrite.

The Kirk brothers came alongside the wagon on their mounts.

"I want you to ride at a distance but keep watch." Monty released the wagon brake and headed out of town.

"If I had known they were joining us, I'd have brought more food."

"They're not. The men have their own food. They'll be standing guard while we eat, then meet me at the house later." Monty turned her way. "Where would you like to picnic?"

"I know a quiet place on the Holt land near a creek. It's beautiful."

"Will Jed mind?" Monty's inference was clear.

"Genny and Lonnie won't."

Hopefully, Jed would never know that she'd shared his special spot with Monty. It was secluded and took some time to get there. Their lives depended on keeping Monty away from his land most of the day. The distance meant less time she had to entertain him during their picnic. And if he refused her business proposal, the day would end sooner. "Can I ask why you have bodyguards?"

"After almost dying in a mine, I feel safer with men around me I can trust. I've spotted those strangers a time or two since Jed mentioned them—the ones he thinks are stealing horses. If they want horses, I don't have but mine and now the Kirks'. I'm suspicious they have other intentions, so I have the Kirks on regular patrol."

Dee almost blurted out what she knew, but that would only bring trouble for everyone.

They chatted about the weather and the potential opportunities Monty saw for his new land and the town. "The Widow Anderson has agreed to be my housekeeper. I hear she's a good cook, and if her coffee is half as good as yours, I'll be happy."

"So kind of you to offer her work. Polly—Mrs. Clemens—says she's had a difficult time since her husband died two years ago."

Monty smiled her way. "Where's this spot you speak of?"

She pointed. "Up ahead, beyond those trees, but the path through the woods is too narrow for a wagon."

Monty turned the vehicle to skirt the copse of trees, then parked near the water, which sparkled in the midday sunshine. "It's a beautiful spot. This creek runs through my land too. But this is the prettiest section I've seen." He helped her down, then handed her the basket and collected a blanket from the wagon. "Where shall we picnic?"

"Under that tree." Dee took the blanket from Monty and spread it out. Then she opened the basket and set out their meal. "My mother makes the best chicken pies. She makes them into turnovers for picnics. Our former employers had a large estate and were often having outdoor parties in the summer. This was Mrs. Hollingsworth's favorite."

As Monty sampled the fare with appreciation, Dee chattered on about the parties for several minutes. Finally, she said, "I'm sorry to monopolize the conversation. Tell me something I don't know from your letters." She did her best to eat while Monty spoke of his various successful businesses.

"The one thing lacking in my life is a wife. I've waited too long to start a family." Monty gave her a knowing look and reached for her hand.

Making it unavailable, she grabbed another turnover. "First, let me say, I have no designs on marriage. My reason for asking you to join me today was a business proposal."

Monty wasn't as easy to read as Jed. His furrowed brow could mean disappointment or anger. Dee shivered, then pressed on. "Since my parents are here, I want to move forward with opening a bakery in town. I also want to buy a home for us." She dabbed her lips with her napkin. "Mrs. Clemens sells my baked goods at the mercantile, and there's never any left for the next day. I'm confident my bakery will succeed. My mother has recipes we have yet to make because they are too fragile to transport from the ranch to town in a wagon."

"So you want me to loan you the money?" Monty's voice was flat.

"No." She pulled out the cloth bundle. "I want to ask you to buy this." Dee unwrapped the ruby necklace and earrings.

Monty examined them closely, holding the necklace up to the light. "I can see these are extremely valuable. Where did you come by them?" He eyed her with suspicion as he wrapped it back in the cloth.

"A gift." She crossed her arms and kept her tone even. "Truly. They're not stolen, if that's what you think."

"Why work as a housekeeper if you have these?" Monty's brows went up again.

"My mother brought them." Dee didn't want to reveal that part of her past. "My parents received the jewelry from our former employer, Mrs. Hollingsworth."

"I see." Monty nodded. "What did her husband think of her passing on this expensive piece?"

"This was given to her by her first betrothed. He died in an accident. When she became engaged to Mr. Hollingsworth, he insisted she never wear it again. He forbade her from giving it to their daughter. Then, after he had a stroke and died, her son inherited and fired my parents."

Monty stared at the creek, tapping his finger on his knee. "Would you mind if I asked your mother to confirm your story? After all, you were married to my former partner."

Dee wanted to slap him. How dare he? She unbuttoned her sleeve and pulled it to her shoulder. "This is what happened to anyone who touched his possessions." Monty blanched at the sight of the ugly, jagged scar that crossed her upper arm. She rolled her sleeve down and re-buttoned the cuff. "You may ask either of my parents. They will be involved in setting up the bakery, and they encouraged me to sell the jewelry."

"My sincerest apology. You must understand why—"

"Yes, I do. The cad was a crook." Dee put her cloth bundle back in the basket with shaking hands. What more could she say to convince him? "Until I overheard Jed tell his brother of your former mining interests, I had no idea who would have the funds to give me a fair price."

"Why didn't you ask the bank for a loan against it?"

"My father doesn't trust banks, but apparently, he trusts you." The sarcasm in her voice surprised her. She needed to be charming—lives depended on it.

Monty laughed and took her hand. "Miss McLain, I apologize for accusing you."

They turned as horses crashed through the trees. Three riders came toward them. The Kirks held a gun on Jed. He glared at her. "Will you tell these fools this is my land?"

Jed fumed, not only that these men didn't believe him, but that they'd gotten the drop on him. He'd come across the couple by accident, as he'd gone riding to clear his head of Dee's lovely face. When Monty had given her an expensive necklace—an engagement gift?—a rock had formed in his gut.

"Brother Holt, were you spying on us?" Dee leapt to her feet, anger written across her face, her voice unsteady.

"No ma'am. This is my land and my thinkin' spot. If you recall, I told ya that." He didn't care that his tone was harsh. She deserved it. Delilah seemed a suitable name. She'd lied to him. Well, failed to mention where they would be picnicking.

"Gentlemen, release Mr. Holt. I am aware we are on his land." Monty turned to him. "I apologize. Miss McLain led me to believe it was all right."

"It's fine." Jed patted Sally to give himself a moment to calm down. "She could have informed me of her plans, and I'd have not come in this direction."

"Momma knew where I was going." Dee began putting the food back in the basket. As if that settled it.

"Sorry, boss. Those other hombres were near the old homestead, and they lit out on seeing us. Then we ran into Mr. Holt and thought he might be with them." Mark nodded toward Jed.

Dee's face pinked clear to her hairline. Why?

"What were they doing on my land?" Monty folded up the blanket.

"Digging holes near that burned-out house." Ned put his rifle back in its leather scabbard, and Mark followed suit.

"Miss McLain, bring your parents by the house—say, seven tomorrow evening—and we'll discuss things then." Dee refused to look Jed's way as Monty assisted her into the wagon. "Jed, want to see what the strangers were up to?"

"Once you drop off Miss McLain, I'll fetch my brother, and we can all have a look." Jed and Monty's men rode beside the wagon.

Once Monty set the brake at the Single Cross, Dee scurried off the bench seat and grabbed the basket from the wagon bed. "Thank you, Monty. I'll see you tomorrow night."

She rushed to her own cabin without a backward glance. Jilly and Molly stopped their attempt at skipping rope and followed her.

Lonnie abandoned his whittling on the bench near the barn and greeted Monty with a handshake.

Monty nodded toward the Kirks. "My men said they caught those two interlopers digging on my land. Want to come see what they were up to?"

Lonnie hollered at the cowhand near the stable door. "Hey, Carter, saddle me a horse."

"Got one still saddled. I'll bring it right out."

As Lonnie mounted, he turned to Monty. "How was your picnic?"

Jed glared at him, regretting that he'd mentioned it over lunch. His brother winked in response.

"Not what I expected." Monty said nothing further.

Other than courtin', Jed couldn't imagine another reason to have a picnic.

"What were them men up to?" Lonnie asked as they rode to Monty's place.

"We found holes dug all over the old homestead." Mark offered the information as they crossed onto the property. "I recall ol' Ernie Smott always doing something suspicious."

"You both knew Dee's late husband?" Lonnie looked between the men.

"Unfortunately." Ned nodded. "Ill-tempered cur."

"That's what Dee said." Jed recalled the details she'd shared. Maybe he'd misjudged her meeting with Monty. But what else could it be?

They rode to the old homestead. At least twenty holes peppered the landscape near the house.

Monty got down from the wagon. "The diggers obviously knew Smott. He hid his money rather than put it in a bank. I saw him bury it once, but it was his business, not mine." He squatted to examine some tracks, then rose and walked to the next hole. "Maybe I should have made it my business."

"Don't seem like they found what they was lookin' fer." Lonnie placed his hands on his hips. "Good thing you seen these holes in the light of day. You mighta injured yerself or your horses coming around here in the dark."

Jed assessed hoof prints to the left of the burned-out house. "Do you think your work crew knew them?"

"How big was the crew?" Lonnie joined Jed at another hole.

"Twenty. I offered the Barlows triple pay if they got the house done before the end of the month. They telegraphed their cousins, and they brought their crews too. Quality work and quick." Monty scratched his chin. "They were all related, and I'm sure they didn't know my old partner."

Ned grunted and offered a new insight. "I'll bet the horse stealing may have been a side job for the crooks while they waited for your crew to clear out."

Lonnie squatted, tracing his finger in the dirt. "Every horse has a unique print. This mark has a deeper hole from a loose nail, and that one has an *X* in the middle from his special shoe. Yep, these are the stole horses." He flexed his jaw, making the *C* brand on his face look even fiercer.

"Fetch some shovels. Let's fill these holes before someone gets hurt." Monty's men went to do his bidding. "Might ride into town tomorrow to see the sheriff. Maybe he has wanted posters of people I'll recognize." He stared up at the sky and sighed. "I blame myself for this."

"Smott taking your name don't make this your fault." Jed kicked loose dirt into the hole.

"Had I used my real name, things would have been different."

"Lemont ain't your name?" Lonnie's jaw flexed again.

"I'm Lee Montgomery Summerfield. I took my mother's maiden name, James, and combined my first and middle name. I wanted to prove myself apart from my father."

"Why does Summerfield sound familiar?" Jed took a shovel from Mark.

"Because …"—Monty shoveled dirt into a hole—"Summerfield Mining is the biggest coal mining venture in Pennsylvania and West

Virginia. My uncle had no children, and when he died, he left his wealth to me. I didn't even know he was dead until I mustered out after the war. My father wanted me to partner with him, but we'd had a falling out years earlier, so I refused."

"I understand a man's need to prove himself." Jed finished filling the first hole and went to the next.

"Had I kept Summerfield, Ernie using my name would have caused trouble. My father would have sent a detective to check on me." Monty tossed dirt into a hole harder than necessary, then patted it flat with his shovel.

"What's our next move, boss?" Ned tamped down a fresh-filled hole with his boot.

"Keep watch, and I'll go to the sheriff in the morning."

Lonnie trailed Jed toward home as the sun set, his expression reflective. "We should talk to Dee tonight. She might know something."

"What could she possibly know? If you trust me, believe me when I say she don't know anything."

They glared at each other.

Lonnie looked away first. "I trust you to tell me if she mentioned anythin' that might endanger my family."

Were they in danger? *God, I hope not. Protect all of us.*

They rode home in silence, relief settling over Jed when Lonnie dropped the idea of questioning Dee. Was she lying about not knowing her late husband's business? After seeing her with Monty, he didn't know what to believe.

Chapter 38

Jed stopped whitewashing the shed to watch Lonnie work with a new pony. He led him around the corral on a short lead. Dee hadn't come to breakfast, and her parents only said she had a headache. He'd debated checking on her, then thought better of it. *Don't need her mad at my good intentions.* It'd be inappropriate if she was truly being courted by Monty. That big ole necklace sure hinted that was the case.

He finished whitewashing the front wall of the shed as a rider came into the yard. Mark Kirk dismounted. Lonnie escorted him to the barn, and Jed followed, closing the door.

"What d'you know?" Lonnie took a wanted poster Mark held out.

"Boss said this one gambled with Smott."

A hatless man appeared on the page. His description matched the shorter of the two horse thieves. "'Roland Bartlett, alias Mexican Bart. Wanted for armed robbery in Omaha, Abilene, Houston, and Dallas.'" Lonnie clicked his tongue. "Why's he nosing around Monty's place?"

Mark passed him two more posters.

"'Gus Harmon, wanted for murdering a Wells Fargo guard while robbing a stagecoach.' Says here he's wanted for robbing trains too." Lonnie stared at the last poster, then handed it to Jed.

The face on the page was unmistakably Lemont, but his alias list started with Donald Richards and included several others. Smott musta been a new one. "How come no one arrested him the year he lived among us? He's wanted for murder and bank robbery in the same places as the other fellas." Jed resisted the temptation to tear the poster to shreds.

"The sheriff got the poster after Lemont died." Mark took back the papers. "Boss wants you all to come out after dinner to discuss the situation." He dug in his vest pocket. "He gave me this note for Miss McLain."

"I'll see she gets it." Jed reached for it.

"Nope, I'll deliver it myself. When the boss tells me to do something, I see it to the end." Mark and Jed held each other's stares.

Lonnie cleared his throat. "Miss McLain said she has a headache. I imagine she's in her cabin with her parents. My brother'll take ya to her."

Jed grunted before leading the way. He knocked and Dee's mother answered. "Mr. Kirk has a message for Dee from Monty."

He figured she'd block the door and insist on taking the letter herself. Instead, she stepped aside. Dee sat in the rocking chair in her blue house dress with her hair flowing to her waist. Mark grinned and stepped forward. Jed considered tripping the fool.

"I heard you were suffering from a headache. I hope you're feeling better." Mark held out the letter.

"I'm much better, thank you." As she took the note without returning his smile, Jed smothered a smirk.

"Mr. Summerfield sends his regards."

"Who?" Dee examined the envelope with a slight frown.

Jed spoke up. "That's Monty's real name. James was his mother's maiden name. Long story." He tried not to stare at her raven curls. He envisioned the silky locks between his fingers. Had she chosen him over Monty, he might have had the privilege.

"Thank you for delivering the note." Dee slipped it in her pocket. "Do I need to respond?"

"No need. I imagine when this blows over, he'll send another message." Mark tipped his hat.

"When what blows over?" Dee's face paled.

Mark looked to Jed. "I'm not the one to answer that." Monty must have instructed him to deliver the posters and the letter and nothing more.

Dee stared at Jed, waiting. "Well?"

"I can't tell ya. Not right now, anyway." Jed avoided her eyes as he followed Mark out.

Dee waited until her parents took a nap following their afternoon tea to open the note. She washed up the tea service, changed into her work dress, then sat in the chair nearest the window for the best light.

My dear Miss McLain,
It is with deep regret I must cancel our meeting tonight. Something has come up that needs my immediate attention. Once it is taken care of, we will reschedule.
Sincerely,
Monty

Now what? Did Monty suspect something? A shiver accompanied her to the door. She peeked out and looked both ways, shut it, then checked the windows. After locking the doors, she closed herself in her room and paced.

"Whatever Monty is attending to involves Jed and probably Lonnie." Muscles tightened in her neck, intensifying her headache. Maybe Jilly had overheard the conversation from the outhouse. The child mentioned things at the strangest times.

Glass shattered behind her, and she screamed. A paper-wrapped rock landed at her feet. Bending, Dee extracted the note with trembling fingers, but before she could unfold it, Papa darted into her room, and someone pounded on the front door.

"You all right?" Jed shouted through the wood.

"What happened?" Papa gaped at the broken window.

Jed followed her mother into her bedroom. Teary-eyed, Dee gave him the rock. He embraced her and stroked her hair as she wept, his presence comforting, his shoulder a welcome respite. Wait. Why did she gravitate to him when she needed to keep her distance? When her parents were right here? She pulled away and wiped her face with her hankie.

Papa removed broken glass from the window. "Did you see who threw it?"

"No." She peered out to discover that most of the Holts' crew had gathered on the other side. Heat warmed her neck.

"You all right, ma'am?" Carter examined the broken window, concern on his face. Had he thrown the rock? How ridiculous.

"I'm fine."

Her father and Jed joined the others in searching the area. Arms around each other, Dee and her mother watched through the broken window. The men stared at the ground and carried on an animated conversation. Finally, Papa returned to the cabin with Jed.

"Well?" Her mother raised her eyebrows at her father.

Papa hugged Dee and Momma close, but Jed answered. "We found hoof prints. It looks like one of our stolen horses." He scowled. "If the men don't find the culprit before dark, I'll get the sheriff in the morning."

"Is that necessary?" Another rock formed in Dee's stomach. Why would anyone torment her by throwing a rock through her window? "Perhaps it was some boys making mischief."

Jed remained silent, his jaw flexing.

Papa moved toward the door. "Best I get some wood and cover the window."

"I believe there's an extra pane of glass in the shed." Jed squeezed Dee's hand and left with her father.

"My, my." Momma toed a sliver of glass with her slipper. "I'll fetch the broom. The sooner we move to town, the better."

Dee helped clean up the mess. "I suppose I should put my hair up and go help Genny. Best to be out of Papa's way while he repairs the window."

"Let me fix your hair." Momma picked up the brush from the dresser. "Sit, child." Dee complied. "You're shaking."

Her mother's ministrations helped calm her. They finished just as Papa appeared at the door.

Momma rose with a smile. "We're done here."

Her father rested the glass on her dresser and stepped close to embrace Dee. "I'll not let anything happen to my precious girl." He kissed her forehead, then went to work.

Dee stood and brushed off her skirt, turning to her mother. "Let's go see what Genny needs. I've wasted most of the day."

"A headache demands rest. Perhaps you should take to your bed after your fright?"

"No." Dee softened her sharp tone. "Once the window is repaired, I'll feel better. Until then, working will get my mind off things." She slid her hand in her pocket, wishing for time to read the scrap of paper. Only those vile men would be so bold as to throw a rock through her window. Maybe they'd decided to move on with this one last reminder to keep her quiet. Living with Lemont had taught her patience. She'd wait until she had time alone to read it. But she could tell her parents about her earlier missive. "By the way, Monty sent a note canceling our meeting with a promise to reschedule."

"All in good time." Papa nodded as the women headed toward the main house.

"Why would anyone throw a rock through your window?" Momma stopped a few feet from Genny's door. "I know you're keeping something from me."

"That's not true." Dee didn't dare look her in the eyes.

"I know you too well." She sighed. "You're a grown woman and can keep your own counsel, but when you are ready to tell me, I'm here to listen."

Fear was a terrible counselor. It had her in its grip once again. "I know." She kissed Momma's cheek.

In the Holt kitchen, the babies were crying, the girls were fussing, and Genny looked ready to cry herself. "I didn't want to disturb you. I've been doing pretty well when you're off doing other things—well, until today."

"Don't worry, we're here now." Momma took Robert and Dee went to the girls.

The normal chaos of a houseful of children was music to Dee's ears, something productive to focus on. Putting the cabin in order kept her too busy to read the note, but by dinner, her patience had dissolved and the unread paper beckoned to her.

Dee put Robert in his highchair next to her spot as the family gathered around the table. "I'll be back. Start without me."

Everyone stared at her.

"The privy." Her face warmed at the admission.

Once she'd closed the door to the outhouse, she unfolded the paper.

It could have been a bullet. Meet me at the other side of the grove at eight tonight if you know what's good for you.

She refolded the note and slipped it back in her pocket. Returning to the cabin and taking her seat at the table, she ate in silence. The children's chatter filled the kitchen. No one wanted to alarm them, but Jed kept glancing her way. She offered a smile and focused on whichever child was speaking, as if they were sharing the wisdom of the world.

"You feeling better?" Jed's caring look made her drop her gaze.

"Yes. Thank you for asking."

When the girls finished their meals, Genny took them to their room to occupy them with a project out from underfoot.

"I canna understand why someone would throw a rock through Delilah's window." Papa shook his head, then slurped the last of his coffee, the scowl on his face uncharacteristic of him. "Those mischief-makers have me dander up. I'd like to go to that meeting tonight with Monty."

"That be fine." Lonnie pushed his plate to the center of the table.

"We tracked the horse to the river, then lost the trail. Wiley hombre, that's for sure."

Jed shifted in his chair. "Don't know what's afoot, but doubling the guard tonight should keep them away."

Them. So Jed suspects Gus and his friend. Dee nibbled at her now-cold food.

When the men went back to work, she cleared the table, and Momma started the dishes.

A few minutes later, Genny returned to the kitchen. "Dee, I want to lend you something." She reached in the cupboard drawer and produced a small Colt revolver. "Lonnie bought this for me the day after we married. We'd had trouble with some unsavory characters, and he didn't want me defenseless in his absence. I've only used it once—shot a coyote in the chicken coop."

"I have a derringer under my pillow." Handing her mother a couple of plates, Dee stared at the gun.

"The derringer is only good at very close range, and you only get two shots. And after the rock through your window, you need to be prepared for any future encounters." Genny's words made her tremble.

Dee slipped the gun in her dress pocket rather than argue.

Chapter 39

After the evening meal, Jed had cleaned all the rifles. Not since the war had he been so diligent in the care of his weapons. This threat battled with his pacifist nature. *Please God. Keep everyone safe.* He couldn't bring himself to ask the Lord to stay his hand from using his gun when his family was at risk. Dee was at risk.

As the sun rested on the horizon, Jed sat on the front porch steps. He'd finished whittling the horse for Dee. It was a lame excuse to spend time with her. Fidgeting with the toy, he tried to formulate the question he needed to ask.

"I suppose you're blocking my path for a reason?" Dee's frown didn't bode well.

Jed rose. "I finished Soldier."

Standing on the lower step, they were face to face. Her green eyes danced as she examined the toy.

"I love it. Thank you." She put it in her dress pocket.

"Can I have a little of your time?"

"I suppose." She wrapped her arms around herself as they walked.

The path toward the lone tree in the side yard was too short. The dusk brought a dampness to the air. Dee pulled her shawl closer. The evening shadows played about her lovely face, highlighting her cheekbones and slender neck. He forced his hands in his pockets. Once they reached the tree, she turned.

"What is it you need?"

Jed couldn't decide if her tone was anxious or irritated. "I have one question—are you and Monty courting?"

"No. I believe I told you that before." Her hands now rested on her hips.

"I saw Monty give you an expensive necklace." Jed stared into her flashing eyes.

A rosy hue covered her face. "What you saw was *me* give him the necklace."

Jed's jaw tightened. "Why would you give him a necklace?"

She looked away. "I asked him to buy it. I plan to use the money to buy the empty building at the edge of town for my bakery. There's a nearby house with a few acres my father can turn into vegetable and flower gardens. He plans to sell the produce and the flowers."

"Why didn't you ask me? I'd have helped." He sounded like Jilly when she didn't get her way. "Why the secrecy?"

"If he didn't buy the jewelry, it would be—embarrassing."

Something smelled like cow pies in July. "Do your folks know about this?"

"My mother gave me the jewelry. The necklace has matching earrings. She even fixed the picnic lunch when I met with Monty." Dee's eyebrow arched "You don't believe me?" Her glare pinned him with shame.

"It's not that, it's—"

"I'm sorry if I've offended you by not asking you for help." Her face softened with her voice. "But you've already done so much for my family—for me. I can't impose on you again. My parents didn't come here to continue as servants."

"They're not servants. They're guests—no, family." Jed watched her face for a smile. None came. Instead, her brows crested together as they always did when she was deep in thought.

"I promised my parents we'd have a place of our own. They came sooner than expected because of circumstances beyond their control. We need to be independent. Our family has been household staff for generations. They are excited to start a new life free of servitude."

Jed had been ignoring the inevitable. The McLains filled a void for Genny and the children. Shoot, they'd brought back a bit of his own parents to him. "I'm sorry if we made them feel like servants."

"My parents are not idle people and are happy to help. And they love your family. But we want—no, need—to fulfill our dream. When you mentioned Monty was a man of wealth, I hoped he'd have the funds to buy the jewelry. Momma wanted me to sell it. And before you ask, it was a gift to me from Mrs. Hollingsworth."

"I see." Jed rubbed his neck, trying to sort things out in his mind.

"You don't." Dee crossed her arms. "Fine. Think what you will. My parents didn't steal it."

His hesitation had cost him her trust. The thought of her leaving had robbed his good judgment.

Before she could walk back to the house, Jed grabbed her arm. "Wait. I never said that. It's … I don't know your parents well enough to not wonder." He was digging a deeper hole. "I mean to say, I'd feel a mite better if you'd at least told me your plan. I could have gone with you."

Dee sighed. "You've declared your feelings, which would have made things awkward with Monty." A whisper of a smile formed on her lips. "And jealousy doesn't become you, Brother Holt." He pulled her closer. Dee jerked away and took two steps back. "And don't ever try to kiss me again." Anger flashed in her eyes before she bolted for home.

Jealous was a label he didn't care to wear.

Dee waited for Carter to move away as he patrolled the area behind her home. The deepening shadows of night darkened the area behind her cabin. She crawled out of the bedroom window and hurried toward the trees.

She stood near the tree line, her hand on the revolver in her pocket. *Thud!* Something fell from the tree behind her.

As she started to turn, something cold and hard contacted the back of her head, and a voice she recognized spoke. "Ma'am, you stay still now."

"Benny!" Dee gasped.

"I gotta tie your hands, so don't get no notions." Jed's former employee secured her wrists with rope, then led her to where two horses waited. "Put your foot in the stirrup, and I'll boost you up."

"Benny, why are you involved in all this?" she asked as he settled her in the saddle.

"I owe my uncle." Benny tied her hands to the pommel. "Sorry about the ropes, but Uncle Gus said I had to." His apologetic tone gave her hope of an ally. Maybe if she could keep him talking, she could learn something useful.

"Owe him?"

"When Pa got sick, Uncle Gus gave Ma money on account she was his sister. Then Ma died, and he come around and said I owed him for all the help he'd given my family." Shame in his voice, Benny kept his eyes on the knot he was securing. Then he mounted his own horse and gathered the reins of hers, and they set out.

Dee tried to memorize the path they were taking, but the waning moon gave little light.

Jed rode in silence beside his brother and Henry to the meeting with Monty. He still mourned the way he'd shoved his boot too far down his throat. Now Dee would never give him another chance.

"Henry, can I ask you something?" He turned in his saddle to take in Henry astride Soldier. "Actually, I got two questions. The first, why are you ridin' that plow horse when we got a stable full of good saddle horses?"

"Laddie, you dunna know the history of this fine horse flesh. Soldier's bloodline goes back to the war horses of the Crusades. A knight rode a horse like yours most times. But when he went into battle, he rode this strong beast's ancestors." Henry patted Soldier. "They were covered in armor, and their very size intimidated the enemy. They're fast, strong, and were trained for battle. If there be a battle afoot, I want this brave horse under me." Henry said something in Gaelic. The horse pranced like a thoroughbred, light on his feet. "What was your second question?"

"Did you know what your daughter was doing when she went on that picnic with Monty?"

"Of course." He chuckled. "I can imagine what you assumed." Hopefully, the dim light of dusk would cover the embarrassment warming Jed's face. "Our plan was to come for dinner tonight and discuss the business arrangements. Monty wanted the jewelry appraised so he could offer us a fair price. And I agreed mentioning it to you boys prematurely wasn't wise."

"What necklace is this?" Lonnie slowed his horse to join the conversation.

"A silver and ruby necklace with matching earbobs. It's quite valuable, and I thought Mrs. Hollingsworth a wee bit loony gifting it to us. I made her sign a paper verifying the gift in case anyone questioned it. I brought it along to give to Monty tonight."

Now that Jed had more details, it all made sense. "But why the picnic?"

"Why does a woman do anything?" Henry shrugged. "Dee wanted to butter him up before asking. While we men get right to the point, don't ya know?"

Relief pushed the irritation away. Dee wasn't rejecting him for Monty. Something else stood in the way. He intended to find out.

Dee and Benny arrived at a cabin beyond Monty's property. A light shone through the front window on the path to the door. Benny helped her down, then pulled her forward by a lead on the wrist ropes. He opened the front door and ushered her in.

Dee was greeted with the barrel of a gun and the smirking face of the tall outlaw. She jumped back and bumped into the short one. Benny looked away as she struggled to get loose of the man.

"Good job, nephew." The tall one nodded to Benny, then grinned at Dee. "Ol' Uncle Gus has big plans for the kid. He's got talent. The boy can heave a rock quite a distance. And the sweet thing was, if he got caught, the Holts would think he was just being vengeful because they fired him." Gus snickered, then pointed to a chair. She sat.

"I've done everything you've asked, even told you Monty had two bodyguards." Dee's voice stayed calm, although her insides twisted in a knot and acid rose to her throat.

"That complicates things, so we need to find the money tonight. Benny's been watching and listening. His pa was a mountain man before my sister civilized him. Taught the kid to creep about like a heathen. Now I get to finish Benny's training." The boy grimaced when Gus grabbed his shoulder. "He's my blood."

"She ain't gonna run, Uncle Gus. She come peaceful-like." Benny's defense renewed her hope for escape.

"I don't plan on shooting her. She's insurance." He looked Dee over and licked his lips. "I see why Smott pretended to marry you. A fine-looking woman could make any man real comfortable."

A wave of nausea came over Dee. Of course, the lawyer had said as much. Calling the license invalid didn't sound as torrid. She prayed she wouldn't vomit in front of these men. The room swam, but she fought the faint until her head cleared.

This was not the time to swoon. The weight of Genny's gun in her pocket served as a reminder she wasn't defenseless. Thankfully, Benny hadn't been sharp enough to pat her down. She glared at the man. "What do you need me to do?"

"You're findin' the money for us." Gus nodded to his partner. "Bart, after tonight, we'll be rich men."

"I said I don't know where it is." Were these men insane?

"Well, you either think mighty hard, or you won't be thinking ever again." He raised the gun to her face.

An internal shudder sent her pulse soaring, and goosebumps peppered her skin. His angry eyes telegraphed his intent to follow through with his threat. She gulped for breath, and her mouth became a desert.

"Untie my hands first." Then they would be free to use her weapon.

God, I know I'm not worthy of Your answered prayer. Please help me. What is left of the house to hide anything?

"Don't play me, woman," Gus growled as Benny untied her.

She rubbed her wrists. *The fireplace.*

"I recall Lemont came home one night and told me to go feed the horse. When I returned, there was a loose brick on the chimney. Perhaps he put money there."

"'Bout time you loosened your tongue. Let's go." Gus pointed the gun toward the door.

"What?" Heat rose through her.

"You're going with us." Bart jerked her up from the chair. "Benny, go on ahead and scout it out."

Jed and the others arrived at the newly finished house as the mantel clock in the parlor chimed eight. Monty shook their hands. "Punctuality is a virtue I respect. Come have a seat. There's coffee."

"Your house is impressive." Jed surveyed the parlor as they passed through it to the back of the house. The smell of new construction still hung in the air. A large, round table sat in the middle of the dining room, with the kitchen door behind him. A stone fireplace filled the wall to his left, and a long hallway opened to his right. A giant chandelier of elk horns hung from the ceiling over the table.

"Thank you." Monty poured everyone coffee. "Mrs. Anderson made a fresh pot before she retired for the evening."

"That's good to know." Jed winked before tasting his brew.

Monty laughed and offered them some cookies. "Compliments of Miss McLain by way of the mercantile."

"That reminds me." Henry pulled a folded paper from his pocket. "This will verify the jewelry was gifted to my daughter."

Monty set it aside, casting a glance at Jed and Lonnie. "I assume you two know my business arrangement with Miss McLain."

"Yes." Lonnie cleared his throat. "That be your business. We best be getting to the point of ours."

Guilt pricked Jed's conscience. Lonnie was right—it wasn't his business. The McLains had every right to do as they pleased. Generally, Jed preferred not to meddle in other people's affairs. But he couldn't stop barging into Dee's.

Mark and Ned came in and sat at the table, reaching for the coffeepot.

"Everything is quiet outside, boss." Mark snagged a cookie.

"We believe those men think Smott was hiding money on my land." Monty leaned forward. "My plan is to stake out the homestead. Tomorrow night, the sheriff and his deputies will join us. In the dark, the thieves are less likely to notice us lying in wait."

"If they're desperate enough, they'll be back," Ned added. "These are dangerous men. They've killed before. Nothing says they won't do it again."

Mark brushed crumbs from his vest. "The house is gone. We looked around and found nothin' when we caught 'em diggin'."

Jed clenched his cup tight. Dealing with murderers scared up memories of soldiers sent to burn crops, poison wells, and steal livestock to demoralize the enemy. Those men killed civilians for sport. Bile rose in his throat.

"Ernie liked secret hiding places." Monty blew over his coffee to cool it. "At our mining office in Colorado, I stumbled upon a secret drawer in his desk when I was searching for an invoice. There were thousands of dollars in it. I accused him of embezzling from the company. He said he didn't trust banks."

Jed sat straighter as the tale unfolded. "*Had* he embezzled?"

"No, every dime was accounted for. But if he had one hiding place, he had others."

"This whole thing gets more and more bizarre." Henry shook his head.

"So you think there's something left of his hiding places after the fire?" Jed finished his coffee and refused the refill Ned offered.

"I think so. Or more importantly, the thieves do. And when they return, we'll catch them."

The moon was high in the sky when Dee and the men left the hideout. Benny galloped ahead. Gus pulled her up in front of him on his horse, and they rode close to the homestead, then waited. A bird call signaled the all clear. They left the horse in the woods.

Gus hurried her along until they stood in the burned-out interior of her old home. Memories of abuse surrounded her. The house fire crept into her subconscious. But this time, instead of trembling, clarity came. Lemont's crazed expression. He was living out his nightmare. Coming after her with the lighted kindling, attempting to set her on fire. She'd had no choice but to run. She couldn't have rescued him while he was lost in the past, reliving some dark chapter from the war. The revelation settled in her heart, releasing the immense guilt hiding there.

"Which brick?" Gus pointed at the fireplace.

Dee scanned the chimney in the dying light. "This one."

He released her arm and stepped forward.

Gus dug around the brick with a knife. It moved freely, causing the two bricks below to fall out. "Lookee here, Bart. There's a hidey hole." He tugged free three bags stamped with *Bank of Omaha*, checked the contents, and grinned. "Look at all this cash." He pulled out a few banded stacks of greenbacks.

Bart pushed him aside and reached into the hole. "Let's check the other side for a secret chamber. Smott was a genius at hiding money."

The men found another loose brick and pulled out four Bank of Dallas bags.

Dee's heart pounded. Had they robbed the bank before she came as a mail-order bride or while she lived in the house? Didn't matter now. All she wanted was to wash her hands of the whole thing. "Can I go now?"

"We still gotta find the Wells Fargo cache." Bart drew near. "Wouldn't happen to remember where it is?" He ran his finger over her jaw. "My way to persuade you is more fun than Gus' fist." He touched the button on the front of her dress.

Ire rose in her. Dee fumbled for the gun in her pocket. The man grabbed her arm before she could get off a shot, and they wrestled for control. He wrenched her arm up. Pain circled her wrist. The gun went off. She threw it toward the shadows, where it hit the ground with a thud.

Gus swore under his breath. "Stupid woman. That gunshot will draw attention." He slapped her hard, but she stood her ground and glared. If she died tonight, she'd do it without cowering. "Boys, grab those bags. We'll take what we got and get outta town."

"Fine by me." Bart scoffed. "You're the one who robbed Wells Fargo."

Gus hauled Dee up on the horse with him. His foul breath whispered near her ear. "Now you're part of the gang."

Dee shivered. If no one had heard the shot, she needed to find a way of escape.

When they arrived back at their hideout, Benny doubled back to see if they were followed. At the table, Bart pulled money from one of the bags and started counting.

Throwing belongings into a knapsack, Gus glared at him. "Put it away. We need to pack up, pronto. And you …" His eyes lit on Dee. Gus' glare softened. "I refuse to kill a good-lookin' woman, so I reckon you're now our cook."

If rescue didn't come, death would be better. Fear whispered that she'd never be free.

Benny rushed in, breathless "We gotta go. I watched from the trees. There's six mounted men nosing around the homestead."

Gus' face twisted, and he swore. "Benny, you take the lady with you. You're lighter, and it will be easier on your horse."

Dee took her place behind Benny and held on as they galloped away. At the first opportunity, she'd escape or die trying. This time, she'd not shrink back and accept her captivity.

Chapter 40

Jed and the others had been preparing to take their leave from Monty's when a single gunshot split the air. The men ran to their horses and headed to the homestead site. Hoofbeats pounded in the distance. Paper money along with bricks littered the ground.

"Looks like the men found what they were looking for." Henry dismounted with the others.

Monty paced across the floorboards of the burned-out structure. "We need—" The floor beneath him cracked and gave way, and he fell through the weakened flooring.

"You all right, boss?" Mark and Ned grabbed Monty's arms and helped him out.

Monty dusted off his pant leg. "I'm fine."

"Lookee there." Lonnie squatted, pointing into the hole. Jed joined him. "There's a treasure chest in here."

Jed and Lonnie ripped away more flooring to enlarge the space. Mark and Ned jumped in and hoisted out a heavy metal box.

Monty lit a match and shined it on the name plate. "Wells Fargo." He gave a frustrated sigh. "I'd intended to dismantle the rest of the cabin before I started building. If I had, the crooks would be long gone or captured by the sheriff." He blew out his match, took Ned's side arm, and shot the lock off.

Opening the lid, they found stacks of paper money and bags of gold and silver coins.

"That no-account Ernie was might busy." Ned took his sidearm from Monty.

"There's more here than Wells Fargo payroll." Monty gestured to his men. "Take it to the house and lock it in my safe."

"Do you think they'll come back with dynamite and try to blow up your safe?" Henry scanned the sliver of light on the horizon.

"Smott's ability with explosives is why I made him my mining partner, but these men aren't Smott. I doubt they'll chance coming back after that gunshot got our attention. They'll probably hightail it out of the area. We need to notify the sheriff."

Dee's father redirected his focus to the ground. "And we need to find that gun."

"Here it is." Jed spied a Colt revolver between two discarded bricks and lunged to scoop it up. "The initials *GH* are carved in the hilt." He handed the gun to his brother.

Lonnie clutched the weapon to his chest. "How did they get Genny's gun? God, don't let nothin' happen to her."

Jed had to take long strides to keep up with Lonnie as he raced to his horse, Henry not far behind. Lonnie galloped away, Jed and Henry matching his pace.

By the time Jed dismounted and entered the main cabin back at their ranch, Lonnie was holding Genny close. "We found your gun. I thought …"

"Oh no." Genny pulled away and looked at Jed, fear in her eyes. "Where's Dee?"

"Dee had your gun?" Cold horror washed over Jed along with the revelation.

Genny's hand fluttered to her chest. "I gave her my gun in case she was accosted."

Henry turned pale in the lamplight. "What's happened to my girl?"

"She went to bed early complaining of a headache." Dee's mother dashed out toward their cabin, Henry and Jed on her heels.

Dee's room was empty. The bed hadn't been slept in. Jed's fingers curled around a scrap of paper on the dresser, and he read aloud, "'It could have been a bullet. Meet me at the other side of the grove at eight tonight if you know what's good for you.'" He turned wide eyes on Dee's parents. "Someone threatened her. Did you know?"

"Of course not." Henry tugged the open window closed. "Foolish child must have snuck out her bedroom window to avoid the men on guard duty."

Mrs. McLain wrung her hands. "I told her she could come to us with anything. Why didn't she listen?"

Jed crumpled the note, his jaw tight. "Those outlaws musta took her to find the money. We heard a gunshot." A tremor of panic trailed through him. "She might be wounded. I'm going after her."

"Not without me." Henry went for his rifle. "They've got me precious child."

Jed headed toward the stable. He grabbed a rifle from the door. Lonnie greeted Monty and the Kirk brothers as they arrived. Ned led a pack horse behind his mount.

"It's already dark." Monty let out a frustrated sigh. "But maybe we'll catch up to them."

Jed didn't wait while Henry filled the others in on the note. Instead, he exchanged his mount for Sally. Speed was needed. "Sheba." The collie came and sat before him. Jed squatted and stroked her head. "You're going to help us find Dee." She followed as he led Sally into the yard.

Lonnie came from the bunkhouse with Carter at his side. "Carter's going for the sheriff, and half the men are going to watch Monty's place. The others are guarding our family." He mounted Drake, then bent down to give Genny a kiss as she ran up to bid him a safe return.

Mrs. McLain went to the dog, hugging her back. "Find my daughter."

Sheba pawed her arm.

"She's not a hunting dog, but she can sense horses before we do." Jed slid his rifle in its scabbard, then checked his handgun. "We've lost valuable time. No telling how far they are ahead of us." What if the only woman he ever loved was dead beside the road? The sky darkened more with each passing moment.

"My men brought provisions." Monty mounted his horse. "We can grab some rest when it's too dark, then push on at dawn."

"I'll follow your lead, gentlemen. But if I get anywhere near those thieves who have my daughter, I'll shoot them where they stand." Henry's stone-cold words got a nod from the others.

Jed didn't want to kill anyone, but he wouldn't let Dee die by hesitating. Life wouldn't be worth living if he did.

♡

After hours of riding, the outlaws stopped in an open area off the secondary path they'd taken.

"It's too dark to ride on. Them that's following can't see neither. They'll wait 'til morning." Gus pulled his saddlebag from his horse.

Benny helped Dee dismount. "I'm mighty sorry, ma'am." His whisper was full of regret. "Truly, I didn't wanna do this."

Gus rummaged through his pack as he scanned the area. "We'll not risk a fire. In this dark, it'd be a lighthouse to guide anyone to us."

"What about wild animals?" Benny's fear reminded Dee he wasn't even a man yet.

Bart slapped the kid's hat off and snorted. "Still wet behind the ears."

Benny retrieved his hat and stared for a moment.

"Tie her up so she can't escape." Gus threw a rope to Benny. He did as he was told, taking care not to hurt her.

An owl screeched as it flew past them, tearing a scream from Dee.

Gus clamped his filthy hand over her mouth. "Sounds carry mighty well in the night." He growled in her ear as he removed his bandana and secured it in her mouth.

Benny escorted her to a tree, then placed a ragged blanket on her shoulders. "Uncle Gus told me to stay close. He's taking first watch, so don't try nothin'. You know he'll hurt you for sure if you do." The youth rolled up in his blanket a few feet away.

Dee curled her stockinged feet under her. When they'd stopped briefly to water the horses, she'd left her shoes at the edge of the road. Then, when they'd turned off the main road, she'd dropped her toy horse from her pocket.

Dampness seeped through her stockings from walking from the horses to the tree. Mosquitoes buzzed around her head and stung her exposed skin. She had no idea where she was. Closing her eyes might not be the best option, but fatigue tomorrow would be worse. She'd learned to sleep lightly while married to a monster. Daylight would give her a chance to find a way to escape—and maybe those searching for her would find her clues.

At first light, Jed whistled for Sheba, which woke the others. They rose without a word, mounted up, and resumed their search. The dawn stayed gray as the sun rose.

"The sky bears watchin'." Lonnie pointed at the dark clouds rolling in to cover the morning sky.

Jed's heart pounded. He couldn't turn back or curl up in a ball of panic. *God, deliver me*. The vision of Dee's soot-covered face, full of fear, reminded him to be brave. This woman he loved had endured so much and come out on the other side. He'd not let a little rain stop him.

Lonnie stared at him. Jed nodded. The gesture told his twin he wasn't backing down.

"Look." Mark jumped off his horse and retrieved something from some tall grass near the side of the road. "A shoe."

Jed leapt down from Sally. "Here's another. It's covered in dew. She dropped it last night." His hope soared for the first time since they'd left the Single Cross. "We're on the right trail."

Horse hooves sounded behind them. The sheriff and his deputies approached.

"We wondered how far you got last night." The tall, lean man with gray at his temples leaned on his pommel and tipped his hat in their direction. "We tracked hoof prints to the Hathaway homestead. They're back east visiting their daughter. The empty house was a perfect hideout. We found the place a mess, and an empty bank bag." He looked them over. "Appears you made slow progress last night with no moonlight to guide ya."

"We just found Dee's shoes, so I say we keep on this road for now." Jed spurred Sally on, then slowed, not wanting to miss any clues.

It ain't right, Lord. She's been through so much. She needs good in her life, even if it's not with me.

A couple hours later, one of the young deputies whistled to halt them. "There, over in the grass. What's that?"

Jed rode alongside, then swung down to palm the wooden item. Relief blazed through him. "It's the carving I made her of Soldier." *Thank you, Lord, for another clue.*

"Which way now?" Lonnie extended his legs in the stirrups. "Don't look like that toy is giving us any direction."

"I disagree." Henry pointed to trampled grass heading into some trees. He turned Soldier toward the path, and the others followed in a line. Jed took the drag position, wishing the trail was wider so he could race ahead.

Dee held tight to her captor as they picked up their pace. Benny's horse was last in line. He'd been dropping money he retrieved from his saddlebag. She did have an ally.

The sunrise was masked in clouds. The storm had to wait, or Jed would never come to her. Was he searching? Surely by now, everyone knew she was gone. Had they found Genny's gun? Were they following the trail she and Benny were leaving?

God, please help me escape, or bring Jed to rescue me. Papa must be searching, but she was certain Jed led the charge. Why hadn't she opened her heart to the man who made her feel safe and cherished?

Jed and the others slowed their mounts to a walk as the unfamiliar trail wound through the woods. At a fork, Lonnie spotted a small bundle of greenbacks, and they followed the left branch. Before long, they entered a clearing where the pressed-down grass gave evidence of a night camp.

The sheriff drew back on his reins. "Let me look around a bit before we go on."

Jed resisted the urge to yell they were wasting time. Along with the others, he dismounted and explored the campsite. Sheba sniffed about an opening in the trees where the narrowed path appeared to continue, a trail of greenbacks strewn along the way.

"This way," Jed called as he dashed for Sally, Sheba woofing at his heels. "Someone marked the direction they went." Someone probably not Dee. The possibility that one of the outlaws might be helping her made his hope mount.

Everyone mounted up and headed out. Jed glanced at the growing thunderclouds. *Lord, give me bravery.*

They hadn't gone far when the cloud released it burden. The downpour soaked them in a moment and reduced their visibility to almost nothing. Greenbacks soon floated past them as the rainwater created a path to lower ground. Sheba raced ahead, and the men followed, trusting her instincts.

Panic rose in Jed with the first crack of lightning. He gripped the saddle horn and let Sally carry him forward.

The thunderstorm increased in intensity. "We need to find shelter," Monty hollered over the wind.

"A little farther," Jed pleaded.

Lonnie nodded, his bandana tied over his hat to keep the wind from blowing it away. He fought his prancing stallion. The horses' anxiety made things worse. Getting thrown from a spooked horse in a thunderstorm could end a man.

Another crack of lightning was followed by a horse screaming in the distance. They were closer to their quarry than they'd thought!

When they rounded the next bend, Jed spotted a ramshackle structure squatting beneath the trees. He turned in the stirrups to warn the others. "A shack up ahead."

They slowed and approached with caution. Sheba crept to the porch and looked back, waiting for Jed's instructions. He signaled, not chancing a whistle. Instead, a whinny came from a large lean-to near the shack, and Sheba bounded in that direction. The men steered their mounts back into the woods and led them on foot to the rear of the lean-to.

Inside, one of the Single Cross' stolen horses nickered a greeting.

Lonnie examined the animal's front leg. "This one has gone lame. That may be the reason they stopped here. Figured the storm'd slow us."

The men stroked their horses to soothe them while they waited out the storm and watched the shack. Jed touched his sidearm, then jerked his hand away. Calm. He fisted his hands before extending his fingers, letting out a slow breath.

Monty peeked through the slats of the lean-to. "I see movement. Someone's near the window."

Jed joined him, taking a turn looking out. "It's Benny." Why hadn't he taken the boy to the sheriff instead of firing him? "Dumb kid is in a whole mess of trouble. When I get my hands on him, he'll rue the day he was born." His usual compassion for others lay hidden behind his need to save Dee.

"Settle." Placing a hand on Jed's shoulder, Lonnie used the same term and tone that calmed a nervous horse. "Keep a watch. We need to be sure Dee is still with 'em."

"Why wouldn't she be?" Jed glared at his brother, anticipating his reply but refusing to consider it.

"She's lost her usefulness. They might have—"

"Don't." Jed held up his hand. "She's alive." He could feel it in his soul. When his little brothers had died in the war, he'd sensed a deep loss before he ever got the letter from Lonnie. Today that feeling didn't hang over him.

He peeked out again. "There." A bit of a blue dress behind Benny. Relief welled up. *Thank you, God.*

"If you want hot food, then I'll need a fire." Dee kept her voice meek, although she wanted to scream. This was not the time to appear fearless.

Her ally came to her aid. "No one will notice smoke coming from the chimney in this storm. 'Sides, we're soaked to the bone." Benny wrung out his shirttail. "Catching a fever could lead to pneumonia or something worse."

"Fine. A small one. Only long enough for a hot meal and to dry us some." Gus glanced toward Bart, who stared out the back window, watching the trail.

"Suits me. Don't look like they'll get here anytime soon. The path is filling with water."

"I heard tell, Mr. Jed Holt is a'feared of thunder and lightning since he come back from the war." Benny's smug tone belied the apologetic look he gave Dee.

"Ain't that interesting?" Gus threw logs he'd found near the fireplace in the grate.

Water poured through a hole near the far wall. Benny found an old pot and filled it with rainwater.

"Here you go, ma'am." Benny passed her the pot. "I have fixin's for a stew in my saddlebag."

The pot had spider legs and sat neatly on the small fire Benny prepared, which soon provided a false cheer to the shack's interior. There was only one chair and a wobbly table. The smell of sweat and mildew permeated everything.

Benny chopped up the vegetables and jerky and threw them in the boiling water.

Once the ingredients were in the pot, Dee stayed near the fire and stirred the stew, the heat drying her clothes. She batted back tears. Not trusting those who cared about her to help her had put her in this dismal situation.

"They've started a fire, so they got no clue how close we are." The sheriff continued stroking his horse. It was still fidgety with the storm raging outside the crowded shelter.

"I got a plan." Lonnie rose from his place on the floor. "We find something to block their chimney. Someone can stand on Soldier's back and crawl up on the roof to stuff it inside."

"You know the beastie won't let anyone but Dee or me on him. I'll ride bareback to eliminate the noise of the gear." Henry stripped Soldier of his saddle and even his bridle. "I'll use me knees and hold onto his mane."

One of the deputies scoffed. "You think that'll work?"

Henry gave him the evil eye. "He trusts me, and I'll tell him we're saving Delilah."

"You think he understands?" Ned shook his head.

"More than you know." Henry pulled a rolled blanket from his saddle. "I'll stuff the blanket in the chimney,"—he pulled a loose board from the lean-to—"then secure it with this."

A streak of lightning lit the sky. Jed shook and Sheba nudged him. He petted her and took a deep breath. "We secure the back door, then they gotta come out the front."

"Jed, you sneak up there and hold the door closed." Mark peered through the slats at the lean-to. "I'll cover you."

"Me and my men will wait near the front corners of the house for them to run out." The sheriff's damp boots squeaked when he rose from the floor, and his horse nickered. Everyone froze, but the storm carried the horse's protest away in the wind.

"A position near those trees to the south will give us a direct sight of the front door." Monty chewed his lower lip, appearing to weigh his options. "While Mark covers Jed, Ned and I will work our way over there."

Lonnie pulled cartridges from his pocket and loaded his rifle. "Then Mark and I will hide near the fence row to watch the back door and my brother."

Plan in place, they started to move. "Wait." Lonnie looked at Jed. "I think a prayer is in order."

Jed nodded, but no words came. Panic caused his heart to race. If he didn't do this soon, he'd be curled up on the floor, and Dee might die.

Lonnie led the prayer. "Father, give us the courage of King David and the wisdom of Solomon as we put our plan in action. Let no life be taken."

Jed took another deep breath. The words of the prayer rested in his heart. His hands stilled. The storm shrank to a small place in his mind. Each man nodded and got in position.

Low to the ground, Jed crept toward the back door. He grabbed the doorknob and braced himself as Henry came rolling off the roof. The thunder drowned out the older man's cry.

In moments, voices and coughing rose in the shack.

"Stupid woman don't know how to tend a fire. Benny, open the back door."

"It's stuck." Benny's attempt was met with resistance as Jed used all his might to hold the knob still.

Smoke bellowed out the cracks in the walls, but the men still didn't budge.

"Hurry." Gus coughed. "Put the fire out."

Benny motioned for Dee to move toward the back door, then signaled with his eyes for her to back up. She leaned against the door. He darted to the fireplace and added a log. More smoke filled the room.

"What are you doing? Are you touched in the head?" Bart punched Benny, drawing a scream of protest from Dee. He whirled to throw the remainder of the stew on the blaze, then he kicked the dampened logs away from the fireplace. He held his arm over his mouth as a cough overtook him. Reaching the front door, he flung it open.

"Throw your guns down and surrender!"

At the authoritative declaration from outside, the door opened behind Dee. She squealed as someone grabbed her around the waist and whisked her away while gunfire erupted. Jed!

She wrapped her arms around his neck and clung to him as he carried her to the safety of a lean-to. He held her close. Relief flooded her as he stroked her hair.

"You came for me." She caressed his jaw, and tears trickled down her face. "I feared the storm would keep you away."

"Nothing was keeping me from coming for you." He planted a kiss on her forehead and set her on the floor. "Don't move. I'll be back."

Dee jumped as a spray of bullets peppered the main shack. Those inside returned fire. Then silence.

"Don't shoot." Benny came out with his hands up. "Uncle Gus is bleeding bad."

"Shut up," Gus screamed from somewhere in the house. "They won't take me alive."

A few more bullets were exchanged as Benny ran toward the lean-to. He fell to the ground, blood flowing from his leg. Had his uncle shot him?

"Over here," Dee called to him.

The boy struggled to rise, then Soldier grabbed his collar and hauled him to the lean-to. Henry dismounted and pulled Benny inside.

"When did you teach him that?" Dee hugged her father.

"I didn't." Henry shook his head. "I guess he decided the boy was a friend. Strangest thing I ever seen."

"Why are you covered in mud?"

"I fell off the roof."

"Papa, are you hurt?" She touched his shoulder and searched her mud-caked father for injuries.

"Seeing you makes me right as rain." Henry took off his belt and made a tourniquet for Benny's leg. "Soldier ran to my aid before the shooting started. I climbed aboard, and the next thing I know, we're dragging this scallywag across the yard before the next round of gunfire."

Dee peeked through a slat. The sheriff and his deputies had the other two men, Gus bleeding from a shoulder wound. Bart appeared unscathed. Jed, her father—none of her rescuers were hurt. She sent up a prayer of thanksgiving.

A deputy found them in the lean-to and bandaged Benny's wound while the sheriff waited. Dee approached him. "Sheriff, don't put Benny in a cell with the others. He's a good boy. His uncle forced him to help."

"I'll take your word on it." The sheriff tipped his hat.

Benny's gaze bespoke his gratefulness for her generous intervention.

As everyone began to mount up, the deputy put the boy on one of the stolen mounts. "We'll return your horses once we have these men locked up."

Lonnie grabbed the reins of the lame horse. "I'll be taking this one now. You'll have to make do with what you have. This one needs tending."

True to the Holt brothers, always looking out for the wounded. Dee smothered a smile and went in search of her rescuer.

Jed helped her mount Sally, then swung up behind her. She turned her face to his and kissed him before she had a chance to evaluate the right or wrong of it. He returned her ardor, and feelings she'd never experienced spread from his lips and filled every inch of her.

"Now that you kissed me in front of God and everybody, does it mean you love me, or was that just a thank you for rescuing you?" Jed pulled away from her and waited.

"Did it feel like a thank-you-for-rescuing-me kiss?" She smirked and whispered in his ear, "You've managed to worm your way past my defenses, and I'm willing to take a chance now. I love you, Jed Holt."

Dee and Jed rode toward the grave marker at the burned-out home site. He helped her down from Soldier.

"When I was here last, I remembered something. The house fire came back to me clearly. My life was in peril. I could never have saved him." She reached for Jed's hand. "Up until I realized that, my guilt about not saving Lemont … *Ernie* … tormented me."

He tugged her close with his free arm. "I wish you'd told me sooner."

"I couldn't. But now, the guilt is gone. The fear of making you or Lonnie angry with every move I made has left. I am free to move toward a brighter future." Her smile matched her declaration. "Stay here a minute."

She walked toward the grave, knowing he would be praying for her.

Monty had replaced the makeshift cross with a new one. *Ernest Smott* was all it said. No *rest in peace*, not even a date.

A breeze passed over Dee, cooling the warmth circling her neck. "Lemont … I know that's not your real name, but that's who you were to me." Her lips trembled. "Whether the dead can hear me or not, I'm here just the same. I forgive you for every vile word you spoke against me, every beating, and all the horrid things you expected from me." Tears streamed down her face. "I know you can't hurt me anymore. Today I lay to rest this past year. I have so many wonderful friends who remind me every day that I have worth. Today I choose to believe them instead of your lies."

Peace washed over her like a gentle waterfall, cleansing the bitterness and doubt that still rested in the hidden parts of her heart. She walked toward Jed. He pulled her to him and planted a kiss full of promise on her lips. How she loved this wonderful man. He'd not given up until he'd rescued her heart.

Author's Note

This a work of fiction, but the heart of the characters' struggles ring true today. Although this is a romance at the core, every person brings to a relationship expectations and struggles from their past. In *Rescuing Her Heart*, I tried to address some of those more intense things. PTSD was as real in the mid-1800s as it is today. Domestic abuse was often ignored. There were no organizations to help battered women. And soldiers had nowhere to go to deal with the memories that haunted them. Often they had neighbors, family, friends, and the church community to come alongside and help them as best they could. I hope, if any part of Delilah's or Jed's struggle resonates with you, that you will seek professional help. And find an inroad to forgiveness for yourself and those from your past.

I love connecting with readers on social media.

Website: www.cindyervinhuff.com

Facebook: https://www.facebook.com/author.huff11

Twitter: @CindyHuff11/Huff

Instagram: @CindyErvinHuff

If you enjoyed *Rescuing Her Heart,* it would be so helpful if you could post a quick review on Amazon, Goodreads, or any bookseller site you enjoy.

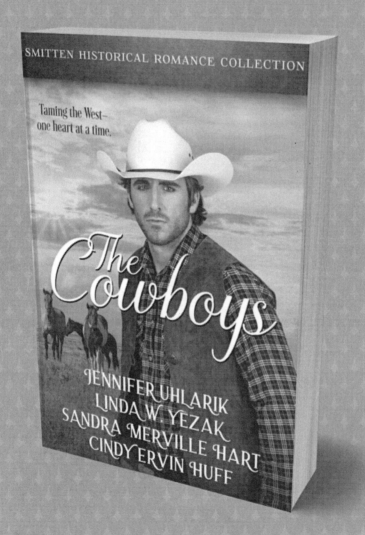